11199

NANCY BILYEAU, a former magazine editor, has written seven historical novels. After working at newsstand magazines ranging from *Rolling Stone* to *Good Housekeeping*, she pursued her love of historical fiction by plunging into writing. In 2012, Nancy published her debut novel, *The Crown*, which was selected as a 'Page-Turner You'll Tear Through' by *Oprah* magazine. She followed it with Tudor thrillers *The Chalice* and *The Tapestry* before writing *The Blue*, an 18th century-set novel revolving around the porcelain and art world, and its sequel, *The Fugitive Colours*. In 2020, Nancy published *Dreamland*, set in early 20th century New York City. Her latest novel, *The Orchid Hour*, continues her novels set in the Big Apple. Born in Chicago and raised in Michigan, Nancy has lived in New York, and reveled in learning its history, since the 1990s.

PRAISE FOR NANCY BILYEAU'S *THE ORCHID HOUR*:

'A beautifully layered and utterly seductive tale' – Emilya Naymark

PRAISE FOR NANCY BILYEAU'S *THE BLUE*:

'Nancy Bilyeau's passion for history infuses her books' – Alison Weir

'Fascinating' – Ian Rankin

PRAISE FOR NANCY BILYEAU'S *DREAMLAND*:

'Achingly believable' – *Publishers Weekly*

'Fast paced, engrossing' – *Library Journal*

By the same author…

Genevieve Planché
The Blue
The Fugitive Colours

Joanna Stafford
The Crown
The Chalice
The Tapestry

Novels
Dreamland

Novellas
The Ghost of Madison Avenue

THE ORCHID HOUR

Nancy Bilyeau

LUME BOOKS

LUME BOOKS

Published in 2023 by Lume Books

Copyright © Nancy Bilyeau 2023

ISBN 978-1-83901-518-2

Typeset using Atomik ePublisher from Easypress Technologies

www.lumebooks.co.uk

CHAPTER ONE

ZIA, 1963

The first time a newspaper reporter said getting my side of the story out into the world would be good for me, I said goodbye – politely – and set the telephone down before laughing. You'd think that after forty years, the reporters would have figured out this wasn't the most persuasive way to get what they wanted.

But no.

"Hello, Mrs. De Luca?" said the voice on the other end of the telephone. The man sounded surprised to be talking to me. "I'm speaking to Mrs. Audenzia De Luca?"

"That's right," I said, surprised myself to get a telephone call from a stranger in possession of my full name and not pleased at the sound of his barely suppressed excitement. He sounded like a hunter who couldn't believe his good fortune when a twelve-point buck ventured within range.

Talking fast and pushing for friendly, the man said, "I'm really glad to have reached you. I'm a journalist writing a story for the Sunday edition on the revelations of Joseph Valachi at the Senate hearings on organized crime, and I'd like to—"

My fingers tightened on the powder-blue telephone receiver. "I'm

1

sorry, but that doesn't have anything to do with me," I said, nice and calm.

"We now know Valachi was part of what's called the Genovese crime family. And before it was named after Vito Genovese, it was Luciano, the Luciano crime family. That's *your* family."

"I'm not part of a family named Luciano," I said.

That's when his voice shed its friendliness, "Yeah, sure. Maybe that's not *technically* your name. But you're Zia De Luca, the hostess of The Orchid Hour, the club that Charles Luciano owned, and you had a front-row seat to all the—"

Once again, I interrupted him and, to my relief, held a grip on my calm. "I was never the hostess of The Orchid Hour."

I could almost hear the gears of his brain clicking as the man tried to find the right button to push. "Uh-huh. Mrs. De Luca, look, I don't want to embarrass you. I want to help you get your side of the story out. With the Valachi hearings, a lot of people are discovering the truth about the crime families of New York. You were there at the start. You wouldn't want any mistakes to get into print. This interview will benefit you."

"No," I said. "It wouldn't benefit me. I'm hanging up now. Goodbye."

I put the phone down, and when I let go of the receiver, my hand trembled.

I peered around my apartment as if I expected the reporter to materialize in the middle of my living room, dirtying up the beige wall-to-wall carpet. No, I was alone. In New York City, it's hard to find a quiet room. My apartment was no exception. I lived on the seventh floor of the building, facing Second Avenue. I stood still and worked to quiet my nerves while listening to the familiar noises drifting up from the street. The traffic hummed: cars, buses, trucks, and taxis. A snatch of music on the radio. People were talking. Laughing.

Ring.

Ring.

Ring.

This reporter was going to keep trying to get his interview. I'd have to change my telephone number. Another unlisted number. And I must act before they could use their tricks to connect the phone number to the street address.

I wouldn't be able to reach anybody at the telephone company at night, though. And I was too unsettled to stay here. How could I fix dinner, read a book, or watch television with a reporter on my trail? It would be impossible to concentrate on *The Ed Sullivan Show*. I had to get out of here.

Supper at my favorite Upper East Side spot, the Lexington Avenue Diner, made sense. They had a Salisbury steak patty with grapefruit sections on the dinner menu that I was partial to. Or I could see a movie. Alfred Hitchcock's *The Birds* was still playing at the local cinema. I'd never run screaming from a seagull myself. It might take my mind off my problems to see that.

But I did not seek out the company of a Salisbury steak patty or a flock of homicidal birds. I was too mad for either one.

I didn't need an obnoxious reporter to tell me about the Valachi hearings. That *ratto di fogna* – I think "convicted hoodlum" is how the TV news put it – broke the most important rule in front of the entire world last year. "We call it Cosa Nostra," Valachi said to the senators, lawyers, and reporters in Washington, D.C. That dumb soldier said the words! Leave it to Vito Genovese to keep this guy around.

I walked several long blocks east, headed to a spot I knew overlooking the East River.

When I reached my favorite park bench, it was just about twilight. I liked sitting here in the evening. No one knew I did this. My son Michael would have a fit if he could see me. "The city's so unsafe!" he frets. Whenever he says that, I have to fight to keep from laughing. No one needs to tell me that New York City isn't safe.

A long rusty barge chugged by in the East River. Even though there was nothing interesting about it, I turned on the bench to watch the barge head south.

And with that, a memory enveloped me.

I was sitting on another bench, looking at the river. Only it was sixty blocks south of here. A hot day. The kind of day I could feel the sweat trickling down my back under my dress. Back in Palermo, I was famous in my family for not being bothered by the heat. Even when everyone else wilted in the *Mezzogiorno*, enduring a climate more like Africa than Europe, I'd be fresh and frisky.

But here, in New York, I was six months pregnant, and that slowed me down. Miracle of miracles, Giovanni and I found a place to sit down, dappled with shade, the heavy heat lightened by an occasional river breeze.

Giovanni was my favorite brother, and Armando, my husband, was his best friend. We three were together a lot. That Saturday was one of the rare days we had off, and we could relax. They both worked at Armando's father's store, De Luca's Cheese. I helped too or kept house alongside my patient mother-in-law.

That afternoon, we watched an excellent stickball game off Avenue B, and afterward, my husband announced he would find me a place to sit and rest with Giovanni while he searched for lemon ices. It *must* be lemon, as everyone knew that was my favorite flavor. We were pretty far east, outside the unacknowledged but real borders of Little Italy, so that search could take a while.

"Zia, what language is that?" asked Giovanni. He pointed at a long rusty barge slicing through the harbor with peevish vigor.

I squinted at the writing on its dark side, but the barge had eased away before I could fully make it out. "Maybe Portuguese," I guessed. "Up from South America."

He nodded. "South America, yeah, that's gotta be it." Giovanni believed whatever I said. Since we were children, he paid me my due without a grudge for being the one who excelled in school.

"Whatcha talking about?" asked Armando, looming over us.

"Sweetheart, you found 'em!" I cried, for he held lemon ices in both hands. My husband, beaming with triumph, insisted we eat quickly because it was already turning to slush. As I devoured my ice, I noticed Armando's long nose had got a little sunburned during his quest. I'd smooth lotion over his whole face tonight, maybe layer it with cucumber slices if he'd let me.

After I finished my lemon ice, he helped me to my feet, and we turned away from the river.

The three of us headed back to Mulberry Street, where I lived in a flat with Armando and his parents above the store. Giovanni lived with our parents and among fellow Sicilians on Elizabeth Street, which ran parallel to Mulberry. Our family came to New York City in 1906 and, after a miserable two years in the Lower East Side tenements, moved to Little Italy. It may seem bizarre to people today, the confident second or third-generation Italian–Americans, but we did live on streets depending on what part of Italy we came from. I caused a fuss when I married into a Neapolitan family.

By now, it was more than halfway between noon and sundown, which meant the taller buildings cast sidewalks into the shade. We crisscrossed here and there to try to dodge the sun while covering the distance. My brother and my husband walked nice and slow, one on each side, protecting my precious self.

We were only one block away from our neighborhood, from Little Italy, when I heard the words. A man and woman came toward us on the same stretch of narrow sidewalk. They were twenty years older. The woman wore a huge pink straw hat with fake roses pinned to the brim. Below that brim, a pair of sharp eyes moved between us. Armando, tall and gangly, had light brown hair, and my hair was dark red. But there was no mistaking Giovanni's origins. He was a true Lucania man – olive skin, thick black hair, and wide-set brown eyes.

"Look at that – those dirty Italians breed so young," the woman hissed to her companion.

Armando and Giovanni didn't hear her. They were debating a point in the stickball game. But I heard. It was such a vicious blow that I could feel it all these years later, sitting alone in the dark. I could feel it in my throat, my heart, and the belly carrying a child that afternoon, the innocent child that called forth the woman's hatred. And I could not only hear her words. I could still see the stiff, red, fake roses jammed to the brim of her hideous pink hat.

The lights were coming on across the city in 1963. One of the reasons I liked this bench was that it put my back to Manhattan. No skyscrapers rose on the other side of the river. People in their Upper East Side penthouses don't get a dazzling view. They get plain, practical Queens, now, mostly in darkness.

I did spot a few lights glowing much closer in buildings sitting on the spit of land between Manhattan and Queens: Roosevelt Island.

People were living there now. I'm not sure I'd want to, not with its history: a prison, a cluster of workhouses, a smallpox hospital, and a barbaric lunatic asylum just for women. Many of the littler islands of New York City have grim stories attached to them. Not like Sicily, where an exciting ancient legend goes with every island, every cliff, and wave. Circe beckons, or a cyclops stomps. A young woman entranced by a beautiful flower gets pulled from the sunshine into the underworld.

A cold wind, edged with the sour stench of the East River, made me shiver. I shoved my hands deeper into my coat pockets. And with that, I could hear my cousin Sal's voice, ripe with amusement, "What do you expect, Zia? They all wanna know the truth about what the life was like."

And what *was* it like?

Nothing like the newspapers said, that's for sure. I knew where the reporter who called today might have got some of his ideas about me. It was from five years ago, in the middle of a story in my least favorite newspaper, the *New York Daily News*: "*The notorious gangland family included Audenzia De Luca, hostess of the nightclub The Orchid Hour.*"

I was never, ever the hostess. That wasn't my job. There was only one host.

I can still see David da Costa in my mind, wearing his perfectly tailored black tuxedo jacket, white waistcoat, and white bowtie. He would glide toward guests who'd just stepped inside and say, "Welcome to The Orchid Hour, please do let me know if you need anything." How dazzled they were by him, men and women, famous actors and writers and politicians alike. I couldn't figure out how much he calculated his effect on people, if he was aware that he left them speechless and wide-eyed.

But what put *me* in The Orchid Hour with David da Costa? I thought it was righteous rage. I've had many years since to wonder if that was the entire truth.

Newcomers have rarely understood that New York was a glittering metropolis, but it was hard, like the diamonds studding the cane of a Wall Street banker. Every person from a faraway place finds difficulties here, and my family was no exception. Yet it was more than that. The city breathed cruelty everywhere, from the tops of its skyscrapers to the tar-lined concrete sidewalks. And that presented tests. How can anyone triumph in New York without becoming cruel themselves?

"*It can't get any darker than midnight.*"

There must be a thousand Sicilian proverbs, but this one became my favorite, this one I clung to.

Even though I came to believe the proverb was wrong.

CHAPTER TWO

ZIA

The story I must tell doesn't begin in 1963 on the Upper East Side of Manhattan. Nor does it start a half-century before that, when I was expecting a baby, married to a young husband who'd spend so long finding me a lemon ice. With all my heart, I wish that I could linger there.

But no, this story begins in the spring of 1923.

The first thing to know is my husband was killed in the Great War the same week as my brother. They signed up to fight together, just as they did so many things. And they came close to dying together.

While I was in the depths of my grief, I lost my parents to the Spanish Flu. I caught it the same time they did. I knew nothing for five days, chilled and roasted by a fever sent by the devil, until it broke and left me so weak I could barely raise my head an inch from the pillow. They didn't dare tell me about Mama and Papa for another week for fear it would finish me.

I survived, but for what? Who did I have left?

My son.

Michael was my reason for opening my eyes in the morning. And not just for me. My father-in-law and mother-in-law kept going

9

because of their grandson. I was still part of a family, living above the De Luca cheese shop, by then known as the best cheese shop in Little Italy. I helped in the shop when I wasn't working my regular job at the public library. But I was a different person than before the war and the pandemic. How could I not be? We had all changed. Or at least, the people I'd known for a long time had.

I'd sometimes wonder, after meeting someone new, what that person had been like in the "before" time. Were they once kinder? Less bitter? Perhaps hope had once leaped in their heart, or the worst possibility hadn't been the first thought that came to mind in each situation.

The person who made me wonder that most particularly was Edie Dodwell, who worked alongside me at the Seward Park branch of the New York Public Library. It was one of the city's many Carnegie libraries, but ours alone had a special focus on immigrants. I was hired to do regular librarian tasks and work as needed with the Italian patrons. As for Edie, she was a proper librarian with a degree from college, and she rarely let me forget it. She'd read many works of fiction. But her thoughts didn't dwell on the greatness of literature or the finest qualities of mankind. Courage, sacrifice, devotion? Those weren't the qualities that she was alert to. She liked weakness. People's flaws were what made her smile.

That day, I was standing beside Edie at the First Floor Librarians' Station, which was no more than a counter behind a curved wooden barrier three feet high. Edie said softly, "Well, look who's a bit early. The king of the Flat Tire Club."

I glanced up from the cards I was filing to take in Edie's profile. She always combed her bob hairstyle to extend precisely to the bottom of her earlobe. I was tempted to ignore her, if not for the knowledge that an ignored Edie would make it her business to come up with more snide utterances to get a rise out of me. It seemed like she had a new one every week: "What a cake eater," or, "She thinks she's a high pillow."

I followed her gaze, which was aimed across the library toward the long wooden table nearest the door to the park exit.

What's important to know is that somebody filled each and every chair between the spot where Edie and I stood and that long table. It was the middle of the afternoon in the middle of the week, the busiest time for the Adult Reading Floor. And while most of our patrons did their best to follow the rules and keep quiet, that didn't mean they kept still. Newspaper pages fluttered, and people passed books back and forth. A few tried to sneak a bite of food from bags held on their laps.

I wasn't sure who Edie had in mind with her crack about the king of the flat tires – which I supposed meant being a dullard – until my gaze found a certain man sitting slumped forward in his chair, looking down.

Yes, it must be Mr. Watkins.

It was true that in the six months or so since becoming a regular, Mr. Watkins, who studied the poems of Walt Whitman and Henry David Thoreau, rarely appeared until an hour before the library's close. How incredible that Edie noticed him now, in the afternoon crush, for he was a man easy to miss. About fifty years of age, Mr. Watkins always wore a plain black suit. He had a long face and a carefully trimmed mustache. Whenever the man spoke – which wasn't too often – he was rigorously polite. I appreciated that quality. Few who came to the Seward Park branch had manners like his. The others weren't nasty by nature so much as they didn't know better. Mr. Watkins did.

He stared down at the table in front of him, caught up in his poetry reading, I assumed, but as someone blocking the way shifted, I realized that the table before him was clear of a book or a newspaper, even a pamphlet. He'd been staring at nothing. That was a *bit* odd, but nothing compared to what happened next. He sat straight and turned his gaze toward the librarian station, squinting as if to bring Edie and me into focus.

Edie chuckled – and if I didn't like the look of her smile, I *really* didn't care for the sound of her laughter – and said, "I think he's sweet on you, Zia."

Even for Edie, this was going too far.

"Nonsense," I said, tapping the top of my card stack for emphasis. Still snickering, she said, "He'd be quite a catch for you."

I could have offered some mild remark – not a rebuke but sufficient to shut her up – and carried on with my work at the librarians' station. I had plenty to do. The filing system I designed gave us a more reliable way to track the books that patrons checked out, but to reach peak efficiency, we had to stay on top of it.

However, something about the way he sat slumped in his chair, staring, made me wonder about Mr. Watkins. I'd seen this one other time. A few weeks ago, the library arranged for a reading of the new poem *The Waste Land* on the library roof. The idea was that the poem began with "*April is the cruelest month…*" so we would schedule the event during April. Everyone loved the roof. But it turned out to be very cold that day. Few patrons turned up. The ones who did, clutched their coats tightly or fidgeted in their chairs. Only Mr. Watkins made it through the reading without movement or complaint, his coat not even buttoned at the top. There was such a haunted look in his eyes as if he were trapped in the deadly trenches of Europe and not sitting at a library on the Lower East Side.

My fingers curled around the index cards. Mr. Watkins sought refuge in the library, as so many people did, whether they were immigrants or not. He didn't deserve ridicule.

"He might have a question for the library," I announced and left the station to head for him, moving quickly so that I didn't have to hear Edie's next crack.

As I drew closer, Mr. Watkins kept his gaze fixed on me. The man had something on his mind.

"Is everything all right, Mr. Watkins?" I asked when I reached his spot at the table.

He stood up, took off his hat, and said, "I have a question to ask of you, Mrs. De Luca."

Staring up at him, for he was a good foot taller, I noted his bloodshot eyes, puffy lids, and grayish skin. *No sleep last night?*

Keeping my voice light and pleasant, I said, "Well, that's what we are all here for, to answer questions."

Mr. Watkins frowned, "But it's not a question for anyone employed by the library. It's a matter for you alone, Mrs. De Luca."

"Well, let's have it," I said.

He blinked twice. I wished I hadn't put it that way. I prided myself on my courtesy within these walls. But Mr. Watkins stood up straighter to deliver his question. Once again, I had an inkling that he dealt with serious matters in his other life, the one outside the library. He was accustomed to questioning people.

"I've been informed you speak Italian, Mrs. De Luca, but is that the same as speaking Sicilian?"

It wasn't what I expected, but considering my position at the Seward Park Library, the question was reasonable. "No, Mr. Watkins," I said. "They are separate languages."

The peculiar hope that had been dancing in his eyes flickered out, and he looked more exhausted than ever.

"But I speak and write both Italian and Sicilian, if that's of any use to you," I continued. "And French and Spanish as well. I understand Latin, and I can write it, but to be honest, I don't speak it very well."

"Splendid, oh, that's splendid," he said. "Mrs. De Luca, you have no idea how welcome this news is."

He said that in a louder voice than I'd ever heard him use before, louder than anyone should use in the library. Heads turned. I could feel their curious eyes, their ears perking up. People don't usually celebrate good news in the middle of the Adult Reading Room. Mr. Watkins, however, seemed oblivious to drawing attention. And he had more to say.

"I'm interested in a translation," he said. "I've received information about a play written by a Sicilian playwright named Luigi Pirandello. I don't know whether the play is written in Sicilian or Italian, but the point is, I don't understand either language, and I'm not sure if it's been translated yet into English."

"I'd be happy to look into it for you this week." I spoke just above a whisper to induce him to speak more softly.

He took a step closer, lowering his voice, to my relief, and said, "I've already made inquiries, and I believe it's too soon to expect an English translation. The play was performed for the first time in Milan last year. What I was wondering is, if I could secure a copy, would you translate it for me?"

I felt confused once more. I thought poetry was his chief interest. "Are you in the theatre, Mr. Watkins?"

"No, heavens, no." His mustache twitched as if the idea were absurd.

14

Out of the corner of my eye, I spotted Nathan Rosenberg – another regular, a pale young man with a long black beard – turning around in his chair to listen. Pretty soon, I could start charging tickets.

"My interest is in the play itself," Mr. Watkins said, his voice rising again. "I want to read the script. There's a character in it, an idea that he has, a situation that I must—" He broke off, and now, it was no longer his mustache that twitched but his lips. He was mouthing words but was not able to come out with them.

Mr. Watkins' behavior had the effect on me that unexpected outbursts often do. I folded my arms tightly and took a step back, saying nothing. My mother used to call it "Zia's tortoise shell."

Mr. Watkins said, "You know what it means to be with a madman?"

"What?"

Mr. Watkins gave a little shudder. "Forgive me, Mrs. De Luca. It's a line of dialogue. From the play. I am interested in having it translated."

"Oh, I see." I'd never done a complete translation before.

"I'd pay you to do it, Mrs. De Luca. You could name your fee."

"Pardon me?" said a female voice to my left.

It was Edie, of course. Her lips curved in that false smile. With her fair hair and blue eyes, you might say she had an angel's face except for the little extra roll of flesh under her chin.

"There's a meeting of the first-floor librarians with Mrs. Tuckle," she informed me. "It starts in five minutes."

"But there was no meeting scheduled today."

"It's something urgent," she said, excited. "Doors have been slamming, and I heard Dolores from the Children's Floor was crying in the stacks."

With that, she turned to go. I assured Mr. Watkins I would talk to him later and followed her to the main stairs. She wore pleated

15

dresses that gathered at the side, tied in a big bow, like a present no one wanted to open. Today, her hem twitched against her calves as she hurried up the steps.

Aside from monthly staff meetings in her third-floor office, I didn't see much of Mrs. Sylvia Tuckle, library director. What I did know of her, I respected. She was in her forties, with a mother's broad bosom and a fondness for sensible shoes and spectacles, but this woman was like a ship's captain, making decisions rapidly and sticking by them, as when she hired me two years earlier. Mother Benedicta, the principal of my old school, recommended me when asked. After glancing at a file and asking a few questions, Mrs. Tuckle had said, "You'll do perfectly, Mrs. De Luca."

This afternoon, when I stepped into the director's office, I felt more ill at ease than the day of my interview. We'd never had an unscheduled meeting before. Although Edie often exaggerated, if someone was weeping, that was a bad omen.

There was something else that was strange – the light. Mrs. Tuckle's office had tall windows overlooking Seward Park. But instead of the warm gold of late afternoon filling the room, the skies outside were dark gray, full of imminent rain, and it cast a gloom over everyone's faces. I wondered why she didn't turn on her square desk lamp.

We settled into two chairs opposite the mahogany desk where Mrs. Tuckle sat, her wrists resting on the papers across it. "Edie, Zia, thank you for coming on such short notice," she said.

I nodded and smiled. And deep in my lap, I tore at a cuticle in my left thumb. I knew two things to be wrong, and it had nothing to do with the rain coming. Mrs. Tuckle had greeted me by name but not looked me in the eye. Unusual for her. And then there was Rachel. The fourth person in the room, the head adult librarian, Rachel

Rodman, didn't desire to take a seat. She stood on the other side of the room, staring out the window, her shoulders tensed under her dress, shaking her head. Rachel had been at the library for five years, hired for her languages – Russian, Hebrew, and Yiddish – and valued for her abilities. It would take a real crisis to upset Rachel Rodman.

"Well, ladies, I fear I've asked to see you to share some unfortunate news," said Mrs. Tuckle. "It looks like one of you will have to be let go."

CHAPTER THREE

ZIA

Edie and I couldn't be more different, but we reacted similarly to Mrs. Tuckle's announcement. We sat frozen in our chairs.

It was Rachel who broke the silence. "Reprehensible," she declared from her perch at the window, drawing out each syllable. Tall and slim, with a long, oval face, Rachel's dark eyes blazed. If Edie made me think of a sleek partridge, Rachel resembled a proud hawk, deadly should she decide to swoop.

"Rachel, restrain yourself from such comments," said Mrs. Tuckle sharply. "This is not happening because someone here at the library performed their duties poorly. It's because of economics."

"Oh, no doubt!" cried Rachel. Everyone knew about her political leanings. Aside from the fact that Rachel walked around with *The Forward* tucked under her arm, she liked to jokingly lament that Leon Trotsky was a regular at the library in 1917 before rushing back to Russia to lead the revolution – "I missed Trotsky by one year!"

Mrs. Tuckle said, "To properly understand these circumstances, one must grasp the special nature of the Carnegie libraries."

I composed my face into one of polite interest, but I stopped listening. I'd already heard about the generosity of Andrew Carnegie

18

so many times, as well as the kindness of patron John Jacob Astor and the artistic genius of Stanford White, who designed the library. In Sicily, the wealthy give money to the hungry or the orphaned discreetly. They hope that by making these donations, they'll win God's forgiveness for their sins. In New York City, those who help the poor demand attention for their charity, even putting their names in big letters on the walls of buildings they pay for. What they expect of God, I've no idea whatsoever.

Throughout Mrs. Tuckle's speech, Edie shifted in her chair and glanced in my direction twice. It wasn't hard to guess her thoughts. Edie was wondering who among us would lose their job.

I didn't need to wonder.

My heart thumped slowly and painfully. I liked my job. Part of it was the building itself – a brick box that somehow managed to convey elegance just blocks from the tenement slums. It gave me a jolt of happiness to walk around the corner each morning and see the sun casting its golden circle on those pale brick walls. I liked the inside of the library even more than the outside. It was so clean here, especially first thing in the morning. That ammonia smell wafting off the freshly scrubbed staircase? Heaven. Perhaps no one can truly understand this affection for a beautiful, orderly building unless they've been forced to spend time in cramped and filthy ones, as I have.

Moreover, the work meant a lot. Being around books all day was a pleasure. I felt I was making a difference in someone's life when I helped a person not born in America with their reading. English was such a difficult language to learn. I made it my business, discreetly and tactfully, to correct the pronunciation of those who weren't saying English words properly. I helped anyone open to being helped, but there wasn't much doubt that I was most valuable to my fellow Italians.

A native English speaker would be the best teacher, but few could afford that. I could tell within ten seconds if I was talking to someone from Sicily, Naples, or Calabria and assisted them accordingly with dropped consonants and extra vowels.

And then there was my salary. My father-in-law insisted that I keep some of it for myself. He always said I should have money for dresses or any personal things. I cared little for dresses. I was saving the money for my son. I didn't want the De Lucas to pay for everything. He was my boy, and I knew the time would come when he'd need things.

While I was feeling sorry over losing this job, Mrs. Tuckle and Rachel Rodman were hurtling toward a full-fledged argument. Rachel had begun pacing the floor, waving her arms.

"You do know that this April was the best month in the history of the New York stock exchange?" she fumed. "And we are expected to believe that there's a shortfall serious enough to force the firings of public librarians?"

"Oh, Rachel, there's not that direct a pipeline between Wall Street and City Hall," said Mrs. Tuckle.

"No, because we can't have the workers benefiting from capitalist profits, can we?"

"Enough. This meeting isn't one of your socialist coffees," Mrs. Tuckle snapped. She turned toward Edie and me and said, "The decision will be made within the next several weeks. I've been asked for my recommendation on how to cope with the directive, but also, there will be people coming in next week from the central library. They'll be evaluating the library and how it operates. I just wanted you to be aware."

Edie spoke for the first time, saying, "It's a good thing they weren't here this afternoon to see Zia with Mr. Watkins."

Mrs. Tuckle's eyes widened. Rachel, who'd returned to her perch at the window, said, "Edie, what are you talking about?"

Edie just shrugged and smiled.

I should have been aflame with rage, but all I could do was shake my head. "Mr. Watkins had a request, that's all," I said.

"Mr. Watkins, who's Mr. Watkins?" asked Mrs. Tuckle.

After shooting Edie a glare, Rachel said, "He's an older man who comes to read in the late afternoons. Always wears black. He looks like an undertaker. Hardly the lothario of the Seward Park branch."

Edie giggled as if she'd never heard anything so amusing in her life, "I know! I said he was king of the flat tires. Imagine my surprise when I heard him trying to offer Zia money."

A silence of at least five seconds was broken by the rumbling of thunder. The afternoon sky had turned a purplish gray with a tint of sickly yellow. The room looked like a poorly maintained aquarium, and we were the trapped fish.

Rachel said, prompting me, "Zia?"

I cleared my throat and said, "It was for the English translation of a play. Mr. Watkins is interested in a Sicilian playwright. I think the name is Pirandello."

"Everyone knows he's harmless," said Edie brightly. "It's only because the main branch has set strict rules on fraternizing with the patrons. Someone else might have overheard and not understood."

I felt Mrs. Tuckle's scrutiny. It was fleeting, but it was the first time she had looked right at me. She said, "It's time we brought this meeting to a close. Jennifer must be frantic holding down the fort on the first floor."

The three of us shuffled out. Before we reached the staircase, Rachel told Edie to go on ahead. If it were me asking, Edie wouldn't have done it. She stuck out her lower lip in an exaggerated pout but did what Rachel told her to do.

Rachel dragged me to the end of the corridor. Though we got along quite well at the library, I couldn't remember the last time Rachel had sought me out for a private conversation.

"If only the workers of the city would unite and rise up against the ruling class," she muttered, still furious.

"Is the ruling class running the public library?" I asked. "I thought they'd be too busy counting their gold bars to count the number of people working on the first floor."

I didn't intend to mock her, but I wasn't in the mood for politics. I'm sure that the "ruling class" caused misery, but Rachel's idea for change didn't seem workable. Weren't her precious Trotsky and Lenin botching it in Russia? There were advertisements everywhere to please give to the international relief fund to stop famine. More than five million Russians had starved to death in the last two years.

Right now, I couldn't help but be concerned with my own life. It looked like I was losing my job, and I wanted to be alone to think about what this would mean, not just to me but to my son and the rest of the family.

"Zia, you shouldn't let Edie treat you like that without fighting back," she said sternly.

"She was being ridiculous," I said. "I explained what happened with Mr. Watkins."

"She was trying to make you look bad at a juncture when Mrs. Tuckle has to fire one of us."

The concern pulsing in Rachel's big brown eyes moved me.

"Edie's foolishness doesn't concern me, and it shouldn't you," I said. "No matter what she does, I'll be the one to go. Most immigrant adult readers who come to the first floor are Russian Jews, so you are essential. There aren't as many Italians. Fewer now than two years ago when Mrs. Tuckle hired me. And Edie is the one who went to college. I don't see it going any other way."

As Rachel took that in, the rain that had threatened for much of the afternoon finally unleashed itself, rattling the window at the end of the corridor.

"Perhaps you're right," she said reluctantly. "But I do hate to see someone I respect being bullied."

"Who's being bullied?"

"You, Zia. She's a bully to you."

I laughed, "That? Do you think that was bullying? Hardly."

Rachel, however, did not laugh, "I wonder about what you've been through in your life, Zia, I honestly do."

This wasn't a subject I wished to continue. "I'm aware that Edie doesn't like me," I said. "I haven't given her cause that I know of."

"The way you've chosen to live is cause enough, I fear."

Behind us, the rain lashed the window even harder. A gust of wind forced its way inside through a crack at the top, making the blinds shudder. I was twisting with discomfort myself.

"Zia, you're twenty-six years old, correct?"

I nodded reluctantly.

"Mrs. Tuckle told me your age when she hired you. She told me Edie's age too. So I know that you were born in the same year. Edie lives with her parents in Murray Hill. She's aware parties are going on everywhere, but she does not get a single invitation. Edie cuts her hair and shortens her hems, and nothing's happening. She's getting desperate. She's praying that there's still a chance. But here you are, wearing your long, straight wool skirts, your hair tied up in a bun, never a trace of lipstick, and you're indifferent. For you, youth is past, and you couldn't care less. See? You're a reproach to her."

Part of me was offended by her bluntness. Part of me was intrigued by her insightfulness. But there was one thing Rachel had said that cried out for correction.

"What I wear and how I conduct myself aren't 'choices'," I said. "There isn't any other way for me."

"No?" Rachel's eyebrow shot up. "Well, I won't debate it. I hope that you'll make a case for yourself to Mrs. Tuckle. You don't know all the factors that enter into something like this. The worst thing would be to lose your job here without fighting back."

How little Rachel understood. Because that scenario was not the worst thing. The worst would be to plead, to "make a case," as she had put it, and to fail. I could never, ever put myself at risk of that sort of humiliation.

"It's almost time to go, isn't it?" I said. "We should organize umbrellas for this downpour."

Rachel grinned, "That's the nut of it – you're so organized! But I've said my bit. One more piece of advice: While we're being watched, stay out of cozy conversations about crazy playwrights."

"I beg your pardon?"

"Luigi Pirandello! They say he's gone mad. The audiences storm the stage. Or maybe I read that they threw rocks."

"Over the play that he wrote?" I asked, incredulous.

"Yes, but that was in Italy. People don't get that worked up about theatre in New York. I can't imagine anyone storming the Ziegfeld Follies! Well, goodnight, Zia."

Soon, I had more urgent matters to deal with than the mental states of Sicilian playwrights. It wasn't a confrontation with Edie or a request from Mr. Watkins – I didn't see either one of them on my way out. No, my problem was I'd left my umbrella at home. So much for my organizational brilliance. De Luca's Cheese Shop was on Mulberry Street, which was a fifteen-minute walk minimum. No streetcar or subway offered a route that could help.

The smart bet was to wait it out here. Furious spring rains wore themselves out fast. But I very much wanted to leave the public library. I felt as if it were a building that would soon expel me for good. It seemed essential to expel myself first.

And would it kill me to get a little wet? I was wearing a hat and a light coat.

I admit, when I stepped outside, the slap of chilly rain made me consider a retreat. But I pushed forward, head down.

"Mrs. De Luca? Mrs. De Luca?"

I peered up. Dusk mixed with rain made it hard to figure out who had called my name. Other people streamed out the library door, and many were on the sidewalks.

One figure, a tall man wearing black, detached himself from the crowd and approached me, extending an umbrella as big as a small tent.

"May I offer you a ride in my car, Mrs. De Luca?" asked Mr. Watkins.

CHAPTER FOUR

LOUIS

"I don't wanna have to tell you again, keep your voice down, Yael," said Louis Buchalter.

"Sorry, Lou!"

Yael Shapiro clapped her hands over her mouth, but she wriggled in her car seat. She bounced up and down. Her frizzy black hair threatened to escape from one of her pigtails. If someone stopped to give this couple a hard look, he feared everything could fall apart.

Louis had asked Yael to come along after what happened to him on the job the previous two days. He'd followed The Target carefully, not that he went many places. Home and work, that was it. A deep-red-brick townhouse on Washington Square, then City Hall. End of the day, he went back to Washington Square, and he never went out at night. At midnight, Louis would head home to Brooklyn. And at six in the morning, he was back, waiting for The Target to come through that ivy-mantled door.

But in between, Louis tossed and turned in his narrow bed. He worried that a man alone in a car, driving slowly, idling, or parked for a long time in nice neighborhoods like those drew suspicion. Twice, a cop rolled by his position, nice and slow, and Louis swore that he got the once-over.

Having a young lady beside him in the front seat might take the heat off. Too bad he didn't know any young ladies. That was why he'd swung by Midnight Rose's – the store opens all day and night in Brownsville – and paid Rose to borrow Yael, the counter girl, for the day. He always got a kick out of Yael. She might make for decent company on a job like this.

But here was the thing. Louis didn't realize how thrilled she would be to be chosen. Yael was like a crazy puppy let out of her cage, "It's a great car, Lou. You wanna let me drive? I can do it. I'm a real good driver!" There was no way that would happen. Louis fretted she would ruin the upholstery if she didn't calm down. It was his car – The Fixer had given him the money for the Model-T because he said if there was any trouble, it had to be in Louis' name – but somehow, the vehicle didn't feel permanent. If he messed up, The Fixer could claim the car. Any scratches would be bad.

He tugged on his tie. He hated wearing one, but again, The Fixer had insisted. He told him that if Louis wanted a shot at a job like this – big money and a car, along with a chance to move up – he had to wear a suit and tie.

He scrutinized the people on the sidewalk across from his spot, parked on East Broadway. Even with the rain coming down, he could see The Target wasn't among them. He was still inside that public library. His big Bentley car and driver were out here, waiting. Louis found a place behind him and across the street. It was tricky though because there were two exits: one into the park, behind a row of trees, and one onto East Broadway.

27

"I'll do better, Lou, I swear," Yael said. She made a big show of folding her hands in her lap, sitting up straight, and pressing her lips together.

"Now you're talkin'," Lou said. "Cuz you're not talkin'."

After one more visual sweep of the street, he turned back toward Yael.

A big smile stretched across her face. But even in the fading light, Louis could see her skin was paper thin. She wasn't yet eighteen years old, but the girl had wrinkles. Her hands were like the talons of a bird.

She works the counter in a candy store, she shouldn't look like such a starvation case!

But Louis knew the truth. A tiny girl with pasty skin, eyes as big as mixing bowls, sharp knees, and sharper elbows, she hadn't ended up this way because of a couple of skipped dinners. Yael had never had enough to eat.

Louis recognized it in her because it had happened to him. Maybe not as bad as Yael, but after his father died when he was fourteen years old, leaving eleven children behind, Louis went around hungry a lot. He robbed that first pushcart for food for his belly, not money for his pocket.

"You couldn't ask Gurrah to go along with you on a job like this, right, Lou?"

"No chance," Louis chuckled.

Gurrah Shapiro, his on-and-off partner, was pure Brooklyn. He could never wear a suit and tie and blend in outside the brownstones of Washington Square or the leafy mansion that was New York's City Hall. Gurrah was just an inch taller than Louis, maybe five foot five, but he weighed close to two hundred pounds, most of it muscle. He had ears that stuck out, a broken nose, and lips like rubber tires. If Manhattan cops got one look at Gurrah, there'd be questions.

"Caution, caution, that's the key to this assignment," The Fixer had said. "Report to me all of his movements but do nothing that draws attention to yourself. I must know everywhere he goes, for how long, and who he sees. That's all I want from you… for now."

Louis frowned. So far, the only person he'd seen The Target associate with was his driver. The man was a little younger than his boss but walked with much more vigor, and he wore a real uniform: a burgundy jacket with wide lapels and a matching cap. This all struck Louis as strange. The Target looked shabby by comparison. What man would want his driver to be decked out better than him?

The Fixer said Louis couldn't set foot inside any of the buildings. His job was to follow in the car and watch. This stop at the library was something different at least. Plus, Louis was less worried about the cops here, parked on East Broadway. The building looked fancy, but the neighborhood was borderline at best. He wondered why The Target spent time in this library branch.

Yael said, "Gurrah's ugly, but nothing like Pretty Amberg. You know the story about the circus, right, Lou?"

"No," Louis grunted, half listening. More people were walking on the sidewalks, on both sides of the street. They had their umbrellas up. Louis had never had a regular job, but he knew that this was when many people left the office. It didn't seem likely a tired old man like The Target could get past him to reach his Bentley automobile and driver, but you never know.

"A scout from Ringling Brothers saw Amberg, and they followed him for six blocks then pulled him aside to ask if he'd come work for the circus. They were gonna pay him a lot. Because he's so hideous, they wanted to bill him as 'The Missing Link.' He wasn't mad. He said it was a compliment."

Louis threw back his head and laughed. Now, he was glad he'd pulled Yael into this. "You hear all the good stories at Midnight Rose's, don't you? Tell me, who are the fellas talkin' about the most these days?"

"That's easy. Albert Anastasia."

"Really?"

"Yeah, they like to talk about how Anastasia killed a guy with his bare hands on the docks because the other guy didn't give him respect."

Five years later, everyone's still talking about how Anastasia beat that longshoreman to death. Louis shook his head. How could he compete with that? So many tough guys like Louis and Gurrah were trying to push their way up. They'd tried to make their mark on the docks. But even at his foulest, Gurrah wasn't as dangerous as Anastasia. And Louis? It used to be that his slim, compact body and deceptively innocent face were assets. He could break into buildings and cars more easily than most guys. But that was small-time stuff, and he kept getting pinched. A year ago, he was in prison.

Louis tightened his grip on the steering wheel. This was his chance. Maybe someday, the regulars at Rose's would talk about Louis Buchalter.

"His name's really Umberto Anastasia," Louis said. "You know that, right? Dunno why he switched to Albert. Never heard of an Italian who doesn't want to be Italian no more."

Yael said knowledgeably, "Everyone changes their names once they get serious about the life. You gonna do it too? You gotta nickname you can use?"

Louis didn't answer. He had a nickname in his family coined by his mother. "Lepke" meant Little Louis in Yiddish.

"You know, Yael, Anastasia got arrested and went through a big trial, they almost fried his Italian behind because he left a lot of witnesses.

A lot. So, yeah, he's tough, he likes to hurt people, but is he smart? No witnesses, no indictment – remember that."

"No witnesses, no indictment." She nodded gravely, "I won't forget, Lou."

She fell silent for a while, the only sound being the drum of rain on the car roof, when suddenly, she leaped forward, grabbing the dashboard, "Lou, he got into the back of his car!"

Louis peered across the street. Yes, the driver was starting up the car. And yes, squinting through the rain, Louis could see the outline of a man's head in the back seat.

"Damn it, how'd I miss that? You got good eyes, Yael."

Louis turned the ignition. Time to start following again. As soon as The Target's car pulled out, Louis did as well. The Bentley turned left and left again.

"What's he doin'? Goin' round the block?" Louis muttered.

The Bentley slowed to find a spot and double-parked just short of the park walkway leading to the library's front door. Louis, with difficulty, found a spot where he could keep watch over the Bentley. The minutes crawled by.

"Maybe he forgot something?" suggested Yael.

"Then why don't he go inside? No, I think he's waiting."

"What could he be waiting for?"

The driver sprung out of the Bentley, hurried around, and pulled the door for The Target. As his employer unfolded from the back seat, the driver opened an umbrella and offered it to him. Taking the umbrella, The Target made his way to the park entrance, not the East Broadway one.

Louis rolled down the window to get a better look at the library entrance. A slight figure stood a few feet from The Target, a woman without an umbrella, just a damp hat on her head. She was sure to get drenched. The two of them were talking to each other. Louis could tell this wasn't their first meeting. The Target took a step closer to her and held out his umbrella humbly. He knew her.

"He's not waiting for a what, he's waiting for her," said Louis with a smile.

Finally, he had something to report.

CHAPTER FIVE

ZIA

"Just give Teddy the street address, and we'll be there in no time, Mrs. De Luca."

I wasn't sure which seemed the most unreal, that Mr. Watkins owned this luxurious automobile and employed a driver named Teddy who wore a uniform fit for the Waldorf Astoria or that this Adult Reading Room regular was perfectly at ease. His back seemed to melt into the plush upholstery. He had one leg crossed, his arm resting lightly on the car door. It was as if he were a different human being than the one who perched so stiffly on our library chairs.

"De Luca's Cheese, 132 Mulberry Street," I said, and the car eased forward like a purring lion.

"After a full day of work at the library, you put in time at this shop?" asked Mr. Watkins, concerned.

"Oh, I don't work a full shift. I go over the books, or I help with the special orders. They've got the customers covered in front."

"It must be pleasant to work alongside the members of your own family." The way Mr. Watkins said it, I knew he'd never worked with his relatives in a shop or anywhere else.

33

"They're the family of my late husband," I said. "The De Lucas, I mean."

"Ah. Yes. Your husband was killed in the war, I understand."

I nodded. If he understood it, it wasn't from words that came from my mouth. It made me a little uncomfortable to know that he'd asked someone a personal question about me. I'd ignored Edie's jibe about breaking the "no fraternizing" rule because I wanted to get out of the rain, and I was positive that Mr. Watkins had no designs on me. In front of the library, he said he wanted to discuss the play translation with me while we rode in his car. But he wasn't bringing that up now.

The car stopped at an intersection. Outside, on Mr. Watkins' side, an electric streetlight pulsed, throwing a harsh, blinking white halo around his head. He'd fallen into silence, staring into the back of Teddy's cap.

He said nothing for a few more seconds, the wipers on the windshield swishing back and forth. And then, his voice just above a whisper, Mr. Watkins said, "*He who was living is now dead. We who were living are now dying… with a little patience.*"

A chill ran through my body as I tensed, folding my arms across my chest. "Pardon me?" I asked.

A flicker of a gaze must have alerted him to my discomfort, "Forgive me, Mrs. De Luca, that is one of my favorite lines from *The Waste Land.*"

I relaxed but only a trifle. It still seemed a strange thing to say.

"I didn't mean to startle you. T. S. Eliot's poem speaks very directly to me, and I think about it quite often. You know that the young men of New York State served in greater numbers than any other in America, don't you?"

"No. No, I didn't know that."

"Four hundred thousand young men left New York. Over thirteen thousand died over there." He paused. "My son, Edward, was killed in the war, just as your husband was." Again, he hesitated and then said, his voice thickening, "Edward died at the Battle of Belleau Wood."

"Oh, I am so sorry, Mr. Watkins. Please accept my condolences for your loss."

"Thank you."

"You have other children?"

"No, I don't. My wife passed away when Edward was a child."

This explained so much. Five years after the war ended, Mr. Watkins was still in full mourning. He didn't have a wife to comfort him or another child to pin his future on. He was completely alone.

Full of pity, I reached out to pat his arm. Under the material of his jacket sleeve, I felt him tremble as if seized by a spasm.

Just at that moment, the car jerked to a stop. Caught in the headlights was a string of young people, laughing and jostling one another. They had chosen this spot to cross the street, halfway down the block, rather than the crosswalk. Not an umbrella among them – it was as if the rain didn't exist. A parade of fur coats, top hats, and silk dresses sauntered by. A man at the front handed a silver flask back over his shoulder, another man lurched forward to grab it, but a blonde girl wearing fur jumped up to get it first. The group convulsed into laughter, "*Mona! Mona! Mona!*" they chanted.

As soon as the last reveler scampered past, Teddy steered the car forward. I heard a scrap of muttering from Mr. Watkins. To my surprise, he was bent over in his seat, his fists clenched.

"Mr. Watkins? Are you unwell?"

He shook his head, inhaled deeply, and I realized that it was anger, not an illness, that had seized him. "What did you think of that spectacle we just witnessed, Mrs. De Luca?"

"The young people?" I asked uncertainly. "I don't know. Nothing. They should obey the traffic laws, I suppose."

"*Traffic* laws? I wouldn't say that was the most significant law they were breaking. But they're far from alone, yes, far from alone. I know that. It's the entire city. What a complete and utter travesty." He unclenched his fist. "Eight million soldiers dead. No one cares. No one cares about anything. There could be a reckoning – there will be a reckoning. It's in my hands."

Now he'd lost me again. Was he upset about the group drinking alcohol? Prohibition was passed into law three years ago, but a lot of people ignored it in New York. They found ways to drink in private homes, parties, or speakeasy bars.

Instead of asking Mr. Watkins what he meant, I needed to prepare to say goodbye. Our car had turned onto Mulberry Street. We'd reached Little Italy just as the rain stopped. People spilled out of the markets on the buildings' ground floors, carrying bags. Children darted here and there. Men shared a smoke in doorways. On the higher floors, mothers stuck their heads out the windows, shouting for their children to come home or sharing news with a neighbor. Their mothers' eyes missed nothing. And with that, I realized the danger. To be seen leaving a car, the door held open by a chauffeur, and worse, a man – not an Italian – sitting inside, could be noticed. It was best that the car did not stop in front of De Luca's.

I leaned forward and said, "You can stop the car here, sir."

"But we haven't arrived at your address yet, Madame," said Teddy. "It is on the next block, correct?"

"I must escort you to the door," insisted Mr. Watkins. "You shouldn't walk the streets of New York City alone."

I covered my mouth to suppress a hoot of laughter, "How else do you think I get around? I'm in my own neighborhood now. I couldn't be safer."

"We haven't discussed the Pirandello translation, Mrs. De Luca."

Teddy was slowing the car, not stopping it, I noticed. He only took orders from his boss.

"We can discuss the play at the library, I'm there every weekday, Mr. Watkins," I said. *Well, for now, anyway*, I thought. "Now, stop the car if you please."

"Teddy," said Mr. Watkins softly, and the driver brought the car to a stop. He sprang out to come around the door to open it for me.

Mr. Watkins leaned over and said, "I hope I haven't upset you."

"Not at all," I said firmly.

The door swung open, but as I turned, I felt something tug on my arm. I glanced back. It was Mr. Watkins reaching out to me as I had to him minutes before. "You are the only person who can understand," he said.

There was a questioning look on his tired face. I was half in, half out of the car, and could only manage to say, "Thank you, good night, thank you." A horn honked loudly – we were holding up traffic – and I moved to the sidewalk, swiftly swallowed up by the crowd. No one appeared interested in my appearance. I feared someone looking down from a second or third-story flat might take notice and start the chain of gossip. I controlled the urge to peer up to see if anyone watched me. It was best to act as if a large automobile always dropped me off in the neighborhood.

As I hurried along Mulberry Street, I thought how impossible it would have been to explain to Mr. Watkins that though I might be living in a large city in North America in the twentieth century, I was bound by *ordine della famiglia*, the unforgiving, centuries-old code of the villages of southern Italy.

I did wonder what he'd meant by, "*You are the only person who can understand.*" Was he talking about the translation? Or was it something else?

As soon as I stepped inside De Luca's Cheese, I was drawn into the business of the shop. It wasn't a large space, but we were ambitious in what we sold – only the finest quality. We made use of every inch of space. I breathed in the earthy, creamy, faintly sour odors of the many kinds of cheese on display, balanced by sweeter odors of the fresh peppers and sausages and salami we sold as well.

I glimpsed my father-in-law, Luigi De Luca, behind the main counter but way off to the side, talking to our most important cheese supplier, Lorenzo Silvia. The customers who lined up to pay for their cheese – or meat or vegetables – handed their money to Roberto Pellegrino or his son, Paolo. Roberto's wife, Ileana, wrapped up the purchases. The Pellegrinos were the family of my mother-in-law and had worked in the shop since I could remember.

I eased my way past the eager shoppers to reach Papa. After my own father died, he had gently suggested I call him that if I wished.

"Just let us know if you need help with that problem," Papa, a tall man with stooped shoulders, was saying to the much shorter and swarthier Lorenzo Silvia.

"Nah, I've got three more nephews, young fellas who are ready for anythin'. And they'll be packin'! The next fucker who tries to—"

Papa cleared his throat, sending a meaningful look in my direction, for I was a few inches away. "Sorry for my language, Zia," Mr. Silvia said.

"Oh, don't give it another thought," I said. Bad language didn't bother me much. And even if it did, I wouldn't give Mr. Silvia a hard time. His mozzarella was so famously delicious – creamy rich with a mineral undertone – that some people suspected he had found a way to breed water buffalos in America.

"Papa, I'll be downstairs," I said. "Good to see you, Mr. Silvia."

"It's always a pleasure to see the De Lucas," said the man, relieved that I had taken no offense. Cupping his mouth with both hands, he called, "Even enjoy seein' you, Roberto, but you're dead wrong about that fascist!"

"I'm tellin' you, Mussolini's the only man who can make Italy strong," Roberto Pellegrino shouted back across the store, clutching a triangle of Parmesan.

"Tellin' me? You're tellin' everyone!"

Everyone in the store burst into laughter. It was true that Roberto never shut up about Benito Mussolini, who, with his club-wielding "blackshirts," had marched on Rome last year. Roberto read every Italian-language newspaper he could get his hands on. Mussolini, now prime minister, was promising the dawn of a new era for poor, war-battered Italy. I quietly sided with Mr. Silvia. I never believed in any politician's promises on either side of the Atlantic.

Downstairs, I took out the books and started going through them at the card table. Running my finger down rows of numbers helped crowd out my worries. Especially tonight when receipts looked good. If it weren't for our major purchase two years ago, the giant icebox humming and vibrating behind me, we'd be rolling in money. We were still paying the debt on it, but thanks to the icebox – the biggest and most modern one in all of Little Italy – we'd secured the choicest cheeses from Mr. Silvia in New Jersey and the other top-notch suppliers owning farms circling New York City.

I recognized Papa's heavy, measured steps as he came down.

"Everything okay, Zia?"

This was the opening to tell him what had happened. The library has to let someone go. It looks like it will be me. But the words didn't come. Among all the emotions churning inside me, the uppermost was humiliation. I couldn't help feeling like a failure.

I forced a smile, "Of course. What could be wrong?"

"I thought upstairs you looked... well, never mind."

Eager to change the subject, I said, "What was Mr. Silvia's trouble?"

"Bootleggers. They stopped his truck carrying the mozzarella and didn't believe the Silvia drivers when they said there wasn't any booze stashed inside. These crooks were lying in wait, planning to rob trucks bringing booze to the city. It seems they were so mad that they took some of the cheese and ruined the rest."

"What a disgrace," boomed Roberto, coming down the steps, followed by his wife. It must be closing time. Roberto had a bald head and a large belly. Food was his second-favorite topic after politics.

"In Rome, Mussolini is cracking down on crime – he's going after the street hoods just as much as the crummy socialists," he said. "But not here. No, the police, the politicians, they're too weak. Or dirty."

"Enough of that, Roberto," said his wife, Ileana, but lightly, with an indulgent smile. "Let's talk about Zia's birthday party on Sunday."

"That's right!" said Roberto, clapping his hands. "I've got everything for the lasagna de carnivale. The pork ribs, the ricotta, the veal, the eggs, the tomatoes, the caciocavallo. I ground the pasta sheets myself, just like we were in Naples. I'm going to show that Sicilian family of yours how to make a real lasagna!"

I laughed and held up a hand, "No need to go to such trouble. My birthday, I'd rather not even think about it, you know?"

"That's nonsense, we want to have a nice party for you, Zia," said Papa. "You deserve it."

Turning in my chair to Roberto and Ileana, I said, "Your one day off, you want to spend it with me – and food?"

"What else?" he said.

They stood in a little half-circle above me, smiling. They weren't my blood family, but they cared about me. When Armando chose me, they accepted me within their ranks for life. I thought about Mr. Watkins, riding alone in his grand car on the dark city streets, whispering morbid lines of poetry. I was lucky.

A throat clearing at the top of the stairs broke the mood. The Pellegrinos' son, Paolo, bent down and said, "Nettuno is here."

Everyone's faces fell.

Papa said, "Tell him just a minute."

He shuffled to the locked strongbox in the corner, knelt, and took out a small cloth bag, already filled.

"We can't spare it, Papa," I said.

"No choice, Zia." He turned to take us all in, his eyes resting the longest on Roberto. "Everyone stay down here," he said in his sternest voice, rarely used.

A moment later, he was upstairs. The door closed behind him.

I could no longer sit at the card table. I paced the small cellar as the Pellegrino family huddled in miserable silence. Nettuno was here for his payoff, his "tribute," just after closing time. Yes, this was part of every businessman's life in Little Italy. The Society of the Black Hand.

When I was newly married to Armando, I was in the store one night with Papa, just the two of us closing up. Nettuno, a black-haired man I'd never seen before, banged rudely on the door, and to my surprise, Papa let him in. But he protested in the doorway, saying something to Nettuno I couldn't make out, and within seconds, Papa was flying back across the store.

Nettuno pinned Papa against the counter. With his left hand, he twisted Papa's arm. With his right, he held a knife to his throat. He murmured something to my father-in-law, a string of obscenities, as he rode up higher against him, twisting his arm higher, harder, like he was an animal mounting another by force. Papa made a sound of pain deep in his throat.

And what did I do during this sickening attack? I stood in the corner, disbelieving. Nettuno, spotting me, sneered, and said I was good for only one thing, and the thing was so obscene, so outside of my understanding of what men and women could do, that I nearly vomited.

After he'd paid Nettuno and locked the door, Papa pressed a handkerchief to his throat to see if there was blood. Amazingly, there wasn't.

"You can't tell Armando about this, not ever," he said. "Swear to me. Swear on the Virgin."

"I can't hide it from him," I cried. "Armando should know – something should be done."

"Nothing can be done," said my father-in-law. "And if you tell him, you could end up losing your husband."

So, I never told Armando. Since the day that Nettuno hurt Papa and said the thing to me, I cursed him. They were said to be powerful curses, true Sicilian ones. I even cast the Evil Eye on him, and yet seven years later, here he was, still robbing us.

Nothing could feel worse than this helplessness. I winced to think that I'd told Mr. Watkins I "couldn't be safer" in my neighborhood. What a painful joke. We all cowered before the Black Hand, criminals who preyed on their fellow Italians.

I broke off my pacing and rushed up the stairs, ignoring the Pellegrinos' alarmed warnings.

Papa's eyes widened in shock when I burst through the door, but my attention was fixed on the black-haired man with his back to me.

Slowly, Nettuno turned around. Now, it was my turn to be shocked. He'd aged more than seven years. His face was lined and slick with sweat, though the night air was cold. His eyes were bloodshot. Even from ten feet away, I could smell him. He was foul.

Nettuno's dark red lips twisted into a smile as if he knew what I was thinking. He patted his pocket tauntingly and left De Luca's. He might not swagger as he had years ago, but he left with our hard-earned money just the same. "Protection," the Black Hand called it. These payments were supposed to ensure that they would come to protect the store from any danger. But they were the only danger.

"Why did you come up here, Zia?" asked Papa, more baffled than angry. "What did that accomplish? You're such an intelligent person. I can't believe you'd do this – put yourself in a bad situation."

What could I say? Learning that I could lose my job, coupled with Edie giving me a tough time and Mr. Watkins acting strange, put me in a reckless mood.

"I had to do it," I said, looking away.

"But I told you to stay downstairs."

Something snapped inside.

"You told me to never tell Armando what he did to you, and I obeyed because I didn't want to lose him like you said I would, but I lost him anyway," I cried. "I had to look Nettuno in the face. I had to let him know I'm not afraid anymore. And I'm not, Papa. I know he might still have his knife. I don't care. It's better to be dead than to be a slave to scum like Nettuno."

"No, Zia," said Papa. "It's not better to be dead. Life is what you want. It's always better to be alive."

CHAPTER SIX

FRANK

"I'm here to see Mrs. Hudgins," Frank told the nurse on duty on the fourth floor. The fellow in the lobby had recognized him immediately, but this uniformed woman with tidy brown braids was new to him.

"Your timing is perfect," she said. "We gave our ladies their bath and shampoo this morning, and they should be all nice and ready for Sunday visits."

Frank, holding his bundle of slender flowering forsythia branches, turned away so she wouldn't see him frown. He'd heard that line before from the other nurse, and he hated it. It made him think, "God, if this is what she looks like now, what does she look like *before* they fix her up?"

The nurse with the braids waited until three other family members had assembled. Frank had noticed that, for whatever reason, the hospital liked to take them into the Special Ward in fours. He recognized two of the three from past visits. A heavyset man in his forties, who'd shown up the last five Sundays without fail, peered over at Frank and then shuffled a few inches closer. He seemed to be on the verge of saying something. Frank had an open face, weather-beaten – from his fondness for long walks – and a down-to-earth way about him that made other people feel they recognized him from somewhere. He reminded folks of an old friend from school, or the owner of a neighborhood store. People told Frank things they wouldn't necessarily tell anyone else. And at times, afterward, they wished they hadn't.

The nurse took out a large keychain and said, even more brightly, "Here we go."

Inside the ward, the smell hit Frank like the tallest wave at Jones Beach. No matter how much he girded himself, that odor made his stomach turn over. He told himself that it came from the cleaning fluids staff used, not the bodies of the patients in the ward. As hospitals go, it was by far the best one he'd ever set foot in. The staff tried hard to make it less grim than other such facilities. It didn't even have "hospital" in the name. Highland Retreat sounded like a place someone would want to go to.

Frank's wife, Berenice, was in the last bed on the left, closest to the big window overlooking the Hudson River. She was sitting up, wearing a light blue robe, one of three he'd purchased for her stay here. Frank always liked her in that shade.

"Hello, sweetheart," he said when he reached the foot of the bed. No response. During some visits, she showed recognition. Three weeks ago, she'd murmured, "Frank."

It seemed that today would not be one of the good days. Berenice looked down at her blanket, her gaze rigidly fixed, the hallmark of *encephalitis lethargica*, or, as everyone called it, "the sleeping sickness." Her body was that of a human statue, her thoughts completely unknown – *if* she had thoughts at all while in this trance. The two years of suffering had taken their toll. Her face was gaunt. Her blonde hair, once lustrous, hung to her shoulders in ashen strands. But the most worrying aspect for Frank was the light sheen of sweat on her skin, especially since she'd supposedly just been bathed. He'd asked a few times if the perspiration was a sign of fever, but the nurses said no. Another mysterious aspect of this disease.

Frank sat in the folding chair drawn up to her bed, determined to push forward.

"Spring is in full swing, Berenice. Your favorite season. You always said, when winter was at its worst, 'We need to hang on until the first forsythia blooms.' Well…" He lifted his bundle of yellow blooms, and a rush of almond-like scent filled his nostrils. Is that what forsythia always smelled like? He had no idea. Frank held out the brilliant branches to her, close enough so she could smell them herself.

"If you're wondering where this came from, because, yeah, there isn't any forsythia growing outside our building, I noticed it on the grounds last time I was here. A whole bunch of yellow flowers. So today, I made a little stop with my pocketknife. What are they going to do?" He half-smiled, "Arrest me?"

Berenice's eyelashes fluttered.

He leaned closer, his heart quickening, dropping the bundle of forsythia into her lap, "Berenice? Can you talk to me?"

Nothing. Silence. From another part of the room came the thunderous crash of something hitting the floor, followed by, "Oh, no. Oh, dear." Probably a spasm. One feature of the disease was sudden thrashing – tics of movement accompanied by teeth-baring, and facial contortions.

Frank thought he detected another eyelash movement, not because of a blink but from some effort Berenice was making.

"It's Frank," he whispered. "I'm here."

46

The nurse's voice sounded at his elbow like a bullhorn, "And how is our visit going, Mr. Hudgins?"

Frank drew back, reaching for the forsythia bundle on her blanket. "Fine, fine," he said.

"Mr. Schmidt is hoping you can stop by his office before you go."

Frank nodded shortly. He didn't appreciate this prompting. What did they fear? He would sneak out the side door?

After an hour with Berenice, searching for any little sign of hope and not finding it, Frank made his way to the office of Samuel Schmidt, the director of Highland Retreat.

Taking an offered chair, he reflected that the smooth-cheeked, portly Mr. Schmidt resembled a bank manager, which made a certain amount of sense.

"*Encephalitis lethargica* is an exceptionally difficult disease, Mr. Hudgins," the director said solemnly, folding his plump hands on his spotless desk.

"Because the doctors don't know what causes it, how to treat it, or how long it will last?" Frank asked.

"Just so," said Mr. Schmidt, but he shifted uneasily in his chair.

Frank reminded himself that he was in no position to cause problems. Choking down his frustration, he said, in his most sincere voice, "I realize everyone here is doing the best they can." He pulled an envelope from his jacket and said, "I thought I'd bring the check in person this time."

"Thank you," said the director, reaching for the envelope. "While I appreciate your safeguarding it, it's stipulated in the contract for your wife's care that the fee is due on the first of every month. You've missed the date twice already this year."

Frank nodded, "The postal service is unreliable. That's why I thought it best to do it this way to make sure it didn't get delayed or go astray."

The director looked at Frank for a moment, "We have three other patients with *encephalitis lethargica* here. I'm pleased to tell you there's a public facility in the Bronx – Beth Abraham Hospital, with significantly more patients with the disease. At least a dozen of them. And you'd be closer to Mrs. Hudgins. If you'd like to speak to the physician in charge, I could arrange it."

"No," Frank said sharply. "I don't want to move my wife down to the city."

"I'm afraid I don't follow. You live in Brooklyn, don't you? Isn't that Mrs. Hudgins' home?"

"Berenice is from upstate. We met up here. She always loved the Hudson Valley. She never took to the city, not really. She only lived there because I—"

It was the change of expression in the director's face that stopped Frank's torrent – the dawn of understanding, mingled with pity.

"You'll get your check on the first of the month going forward," Frank said, rising from his chair. "If you'll excuse me, Mr. Schmidt, I have to hit the road."

Once he'd left the hospital, Frank didn't go to his car, though. Why had he unburdened himself like that to a hospital director worried about getting fees on time? Frank needed to sort himself out for the trip down. Maybe a short walk would help.

The beauty of the hospital's grounds was a mixed blessing. Frank's initial thought had been that once Berenice started her recovery, she could draw strength from picturesque strolls on the path carved into the meadow that rolled all the way to the Hudson River. Other patients were managing it, arm in arm with loved ones visiting this Sunday afternoon. But Berenice was never well enough to leave the fourth floor.

He took a little comfort in her being able to see the river from her bed should she wish it. The wide Hudson flowed straight past the hospital and the town of Highland before hooking west near Kingston. The fourth floor was high enough to allow Berenice a real view, topping the grove of ancient, towering oak trees interspersed with young pines that bordered the hospital and blocked the sightlines of the lower floors.

Frank could smell those bracing pines now, along with fresh grass and sweet lilac. His wife was right, of course, about the air. It "felt" different here. He used to scoff whenever she said that – *We're just eighty miles from the city* – because they had to live in New York. That's where his job was. He didn't like to acknowledge the obvious advantages of living upstate.

He could remember everything about the first day. He'd been with his oldest friend, Johnny, and two other fellows for the weekend at a cabin outside Kingston. It was Johnny's bachelor weekend before getting married, and they'd been drinking heavily at night, puking in the morning. Frank woke up Sunday morning having had enough, and that morning, he went for a long walk alone, coming across a row of old stone houses. One of them had a tavern serving food and coffee, and he'd walked in.

There she was, an apron around her waist, her blonde hair piled up on her head, taking an order, and the minute he saw her, he knew he wanted to marry her.

At Highland Retreat, benches had been placed every few yards along the pathway. The older man from the foursome on the fourth floor sat on one alone. He beckoned to Frank as if he'd been waiting for him to keep an appointment they'd set.

Frank sat on the bench next to him. This wouldn't be pleasant, but it felt inevitable.

"Your wife?" the man asked.

Frank nodded.

"I'm here for my daughter. Fourteen years old. Fourteen." The man rubbed his shiny forehead. "Allison wanted to be an artist, you know. She got permission from the Rhinebeck Library to borrow a book on this woman artist. Mary Surratt. I never heard of her, but she's a hero to Allison. She was so excited, lugging that big book into her room. It was half her size." His eyes filled, "A week later, the spasms started, and the nightmares and sweats, and then she turned into this... this ghost. Her hands are like claws now. An artist? Jesus. Jesus."

At the listing of the symptoms, the same ones that had tormented his helpless wife, Frank winced.

The man groped frantically for something in his pocket. His shoulders slumped in relief after he found it. "Here you go," he said, taking a drink from his flask and then holding it out to Frank. "It's good gin."

"No, thanks," said Frank.

"Sorry, sorry. I didn't mean to offend you. You're a man of faith?"

"Not exactly," said Frank. "I'm a cop."

CHAPTER SEVEN

ZIA

It could never be a short trip to my brother Massimo's house in the Bronx that Sunday, but there was so much tension inside the automobile that the minutes crawled by.

I kept reminding myself that the Pellegrinos were kind to give us a ride. We didn't own a car. And it meant that Paolo had to take his two siblings by subway because everyone couldn't fit into their family auto. Roberto and Ileana rode in front, with me, Papa, Mama, and Michael in the back. By the time we crossed 42nd Street, my legs ached from Michael sitting on my lap. And we still had a ways to go.

I'd half expected the Pellegrinos to back out of the party after our angry words in the shop. It had happened after Nettuno left and Papa and I returned downstairs.

Roberto had said, "I have to ask you something, Zia. Your brother Massimo invited the Lucanias who live on East Tenth Street? They are your cousins, right?"

"Yes, my father was first cousin to Antonio Lucania. He and his wife, Rosalia, will come, I expect. Some of their kids may be there. Massimo usually invites them. Why?"

To my astonishment, Roberto, who never hesitated to speak his mind, looked at the floor, biting his lip. Finally, he said, "Is their son, Salvatore Lucania, going to be there Sunday?"

You'd have thought that the encounter with Nettuno would have left me drained of fury. But I felt anger rising inside.

"I doubt it," I said through gritted teeth. "We don't see him that often. But what if he were? Why would that be a problem?"

"Zia, I'm not saying anything about the whole family. It's just when it comes to Salvatore, well…" He turned toward his wife. In the harsh light cast by the electric lamp, Ileana looked as white as a corpse, unable to speak, so her husband kept going, "Constanza Bartolomeo was Ileana's best friend in school. She has nightmares to this day. She just can't be anywhere near the Black Hand. Nettuno is bad enough, but—"

"Sweet Jesus, you're… you're bringing up Constanza Bartolomeo," I stammered. Of all the Black Hand's heinous crimes, this was the worst – kidnapping a seven-year-old girl to pressure her businessman father to pay up and then murdering her even after he did. "Sal is *not* with the Black Hand. He got into some trouble when he was a kid, yeah, but my cousin is a gambler, nothing else. You can't put him in the same category as the criminals who kidnapped Constanza or that creature Nettuno. He doesn't hurt people."

Exchanging a glance with Papa over my shoulder, Roberto muttered, "Whatever you say, Zia."

"I know why you bring up Sal," I said, my cheeks hot. I felt Papa's hand, loving but cautionary, on my shoulder. I managed to swallow my words.

None of the Pellegrinos brought up my cousin Sal again. Not at the shop in the following two days, and not in their automobile this afternoon. They were elaborately polite. And, as promised, Roberto had slaved over the lasagna. Its smell filled the car. I cracked the window open because the rich sausages, cheese, and pork made me woozy.

The thing was, ten lasagnas couldn't ease my hurt feelings. After all these years, my husband's family still regarded my family with suspicion because we were Sicilian. Never mind that the Neapolitans have their gangster class, the Camorra, as do the Calabrians, with the 'Ndrangheta. No, in the hearts of all Italians, the Sicilians are never to be trusted because of the scourge of our island – the Mafia.

Mama took note when I opened the car window. She nodded but without her usual warmth. She was upset with me too, and it had nothing to do with the Mafia.

Two days ago, she asked me to speak to Michael about helping Father Thomas at church. When Armando was eight years old, he'd started wearing a special robe to assist at services along with two other boys. Mama had already spoken to Father Thomas about Michael doing the same. The difficulty? Michael said he didn't want to, not just once but every time his grandmother brought it up.

"Not you too, Mother," Michael howled, burying his face in his pillow when I did my bit. "I don't wanna do it. I just don't wanna!"

While helping Mama with the dishes later, I told her I'd had no more success than she had with persuading Michael.

"I don't understand it," she said. She was a tiny woman, close to my height, with a quiet manner. Right now, though, she was drying a dinner plate with such determination that it squeaked under her cloth. The church meant a great deal to her. She went to mass at least once a day.

"I think he'll come around," I said. "Until he does, we can take pride in how well he's doing in school. He won a prize in mathematics."

My mother-in-law's hand froze on the plate, "Mathematics? Mathematics? Michael must commit himself to God. This is the path. Armando never struggled against it, ever. I think, Zia, if *you* truly, honestly believed, Michael would too."

I insisted that Michael's spiritual life was important to me. Mama said nothing more about it then or the next day, but I could tell she was upset.

After we passed the other, smaller Little Italy in East Harlem, the Pellegrinos' auto hit a bump on First Avenue. It made Michael jump up in my lap and come down hard. "Ouch!" I yelped, and then tried to cover it up with a laugh. Papa was the only one who said something. "Coming home, you can sit on my lap, Michael. You're getting too big for your mother."

I shot him a grateful glance, and he smiled back. Even though he was the only one in the car I'd done wrong by – I regretted what I'd said to him about Nettuno – Papa didn't seem angry. Like Armando, he never held a grudge.

After a few more minutes, the car slowed to a sputter. Ahead was the Willis Avenue bridge connecting northeast Manhattan to the southern Bronx. Traffic had slowed, lining up for the bridge. We weren't the only ones who, on a spring Sunday, were keen to escape flat, soot-stained Manhattan for the forests, hills, and meadows of the Bronx.

Michael peered out the window as we rumbled across the Harlem River.

"In less than one minute, we're going to be on the mainland of America," Michael announced. "You know the Bronx is the only borough of the city that's not on an island."

"But what about Queens – or Brooklyn?" challenged Roberto from the front seat.

"They're both on Long Island, Uncle Roberto. Everyone thinks Long Island is too big to be one, but it's still an island, even though it's a peninsula."

"Okay, I give up, kid," he chuckled as he steered the car off the bridge and onto Morris Avenue.

My son eased over on my lap to get the best view of the river. As I watched the steel garters of the bridge flash over his eager young face, it hit me with the strength of a blow. Michael must go to college. No one in our families had gone past high school, but my son was going to be the one. I'd find the money.

Could there be a worse time to lose a job?

Massimo and his wife, Bianca, lived just a short drive inside the Bronx in the community of Morrisania. My brother worked at one of the steelworks in the borough, and you couldn't blame him for wanting to live nearby and raise his children in a house with a tree out front and a yard out back.

There was just one problem – Italians weren't too welcome in Morrisania. Sure enough, after Roberto found a place to park on the street and we piled out of the car, we could not miss the hostile stare of an older woman across the way, standing on her stoop.

I focused on the happy shouts of all the children playing out back. Michael grinned and started to scramble in the direction of the cousins. "Say hello to your Uncle Massimo, then you can go play," I said, pointing my son toward the front door.

A chorus of hellos and happy birthdays greeted us as we stepped into the living room. I was surprised to see so many relatives. There were lots of Lucanias. Not my cousin Salvatore, I noted after a quick check of the room. But two other children of Antonio and Rosalia were there. The older couple looked a little frailer than the last time

I'd seen them, at Christmas, but they hugged me with vigor. Our two families had come over on the same boat from Sicily. There was so much we endured together.

"You look tired," was the greeting I got from Massimo after he stooped to hug me and I kissed his freshly shaved cheek.

"So do you," I replied. Massimo may have been nearly six feet tall – tall for a Sicilian – with arms like hard rippling sausages, thanks to years at construction yards and steelworks, but I spotted wrinkles etching his brown eyes and even a patch of gray hair. And he was not yet thirty-five.

Our exchange drew chuckles from the others. My oldest brother and I had a stormy history. Giovanni and I had been playmates. From the day I could walk, Massimo bossed me around, though he would call it looking after me. As soon as possible, I made it my business to evade or defy him.

"That library treating you okay?" he demanded.

"They are," I said quickly.

"They better," he grunted. "Well, today, you'll rest up. And you'll eat."

We two, the last survivors of our family, had a clear, though unspoken, understanding. The Rules of the Family, *ordine della famiglia,* dictated that my older brother was in charge of my life after the deaths of my husband and father. As head of the family, he could have insisted that my son and I live with him. The fact that we'd drive each other crazy under one roof was secondary. But he knew that if I took Michael and came to him, it would devastate the De Lucas. So he'd held back.

After kissing each of my other relatives in Massimo's living room and accepting the gifts pressed into my hand, I made my way to the kitchen. There, of course, was Massimo's wife, Bianca, aproned and leaning over the stove, stirring the sauce in a tall pot. The smell was intense – not just the tomatoes, onion, and garlic, but oh, those *herbs*. I'd always been in awe of her. Massimo was my mother's pride and joy. Mama cooked his favorite dishes at the drop of a hat and laundered his shirts nearly every day. Everything must be perfect for her oldest son. Somehow, Bianca never put a foot wrong.

"You look so pretty today, Zia," said Bianca. "I'd swear you were turning twenty-one. Such a girlish figure."

"That's funny. Your husband just said I looked tired."

She laughed, pushing a strand of black hair behind her ear. "Oh, that's Massimo," she said as if he were a sweet puppy.

Before long, all the women were in the kitchen, helping Bianca or heating their own dishes. That's when I heard about the plan for later. After our early dinner, set to start at three o'clock, Massimo, using a connection, was taking anyone interested to see the brand-new Yankee Stadium just a mile away. Babe Ruth and the rest of the team, who'd begun playing in the Bronx just last month, were out of town today, so Massimo could get us inside.

When it came time to eat dinner, we crowded tightly around two long tables pushed together in the living room and covered with Bianca's best dark cream tablecloth, bordered in knotted lace. The kids had their own table, but it was half in the living room and half in the kitchen because there was only so much space. Massimo didn't want the children shoved away into the kitchen, the door shut between us. He loved his kids, my son, his cousins' children, each youngster here. To children, he showed a whole other side, patient and gentle. He'd come home from the steelworks at night, near shattered with exhaustion, yet play his kids' favorite card games for hours.

For dinner, Bianca served her signature special Sicilian dish – Beef Braciole with prosciutto and raisins. Roberto, in particular, praised it to the skies, though I'm sure he considered his lasagna superior. All the dishes were quite rich, especially when paired with heady wine. I didn't know where my brother got a bunch of bottles of red at this point. To prepare for Prohibition, people stashed away as many wine and liquor bottles as they could, but most of the booze ran out after a year, two at the most. These bottles had crispy new labels and not a speck of dust. It must be another of Massimo's connections.

I ate slowly and sipped the wine with care. Conversation had taken over the table. Once everyone's health was disposed of, family gatherings turned into passionate debates over Italian affairs ranging across twenty centuries. Was Julius Caesar wrong to cross the Rubicon with his army? Was the Borgia pope poisoned by a Medici rival? Did Garibaldi's dream of a unified Italy turn into a nightmare? To us, these questions were alive. Still, Roberto found a way to wrench the conversation to the present and, specifically, Mussolini's new government.

Antonio Lucania, my father's cousin, raised an eyebrow at Roberto's support for the new prime minister. "Two years ago, Italy nearly followed the USSR and became Communist, right? The factory workers went on strike, and the peasants claimed the land. And Mussolini, he was a socialist for years, a journalist, right? And now, he's a fascist, closing newspapers and sending his militia out to break open heads. And the whole time, he's making promises of glory for Italy?"

"Promises you can trust," vowed Roberto.

"The conquerors come with their promises, and the people always end up with nothing," said Antonio, shaking his head. "That's the story of Sicily anyway."

As the men plunged into a debate, his wife, Rosalia, leaned across the table with a smile. I braced myself for her inevitable question – *Do you ever think about getting married again?* It was tedious enough when I had to fend her off, but it was worse than tedious for my in-laws. Such a possibility terrified the De Lucas, and I didn't want to have to calm my mother-in-law down later.

But instead, she asked another question, one that ordinarily, I would have welcomed. "You still have the job at the library, right, Zia? And it's going well?"

"Oh, yes," I said.

"Everyone is very proud of you," said Rosalia. "I hope you know that."

I forced a smile – and made a point of pushing a meatball across my plate to break her fond gaze. What on earth was I going to tell people after I got fired?

It was then that I realized Massimo was drinking too much wine. His voice had grown louder and his comments more belligerent. One of our cousins mentioned someone that Massimo knew, and he said, "That potato eater? He's just another Mick on the make. Watch your goddamn wallet."

I heard giggles erupting at the children's table. And I spotted Roberto Pellegrino exchanging a look with his sister, my mother-in-law.

Not in front of the Neapolitanos, Massimo, I fumed silently.

It got worse.

Massimo pointed down the table at Antonio and Rosalia and demanded, "Why do you still live in that building after all these years? You must really love the Hebes to stick with East Tenth Street. Jesus, I couldn't wait to get out of that Jew neighborhood."

"That's enough of that, Massimo," I said.

My brother tilted back in his chair, eyeing me. "Yeah, you gotta have a swarm of Jews in that library, Zia. You're telling me none of them ever gives you a hard time?"

A man's voice said from the back corner, "Nobody gives Zia a hard time more than once."

Every single person turned toward that voice.

It was my cousin, Salvatore Lucania.

CHAPTER EIGHT

ZIA

Sal stood in the corner, between the hanging olive-green drapes and a painting of fierce-browed Saint Agatha, bringer of miracles. I hadn't heard Sal come in and had no idea how long he'd been listening.

But I could feel a smile spreading across my face.

"Hey, Sal," I said. "Didn't know you were coming."

"Hey, *cucina*," he said, holding up his right hand and rippling his fingers as if playing the piano, a smile deepening the corners of his mouth.

"Welcome," said Massimo, rising to greet Sal as host. But after one step, he stopped, rubbing his lower back and shaking his head, probably trying to clear the wine sloppiness. Sal solved the problem by moving across the room to meet Massimo more than halfway. Standing face to face, shaking hands, they were the same height, and while both black-haired and brown-eyed, how unalike the cousins were. It wasn't just that Sal was younger. He looked different in some indefinable way. Sleeker, I finally decided. His black hair gleamed, and his white shirt peeking out from behind his jacket glowed. He wore some crazy blue tie with swirls on it.

I knew, without even looking, that Ileana and Roberto must be upset that Sal had indeed shown up. But it was Antonio, Sal's father, who spoke.

"Why did you give them our address?" he called out. "They came two weeks ago."

"No, please, don't start," his wife pleaded. He waved her off.

"Who's that, Papa?" asked Sal, perfectly calm. "Who came?"

"You know who. The police! Precinct headquarters said you gave our address as yours, and you haven't lived with your mother and me for years."

At the word *police*, a ripple of unease made its way around the table. No one in this room – no one in their right mind – wanted anything to do with the New York City police. They specialized in giving Italians a tough time.

Sal merely shrugged, "Ah, that's nothing. The cops wanted to ask me about someone, a man I don't even know. Don't give it another thought."

"Don't give it another thought?" his father shouted. "They come in with their badges, and they look down on us. They scared your mother half to death."

Rosalia could no longer contain herself and shouted, nearly as loud as her husband, "They don't scare me so bad. You're just saying that! Let Sal sit down. He just walked in the door."

His face beet red, Antonio roared, "I wish he'd just walk *out* the door."

Rosalia, overcome with emotion, took out her handkerchief and wiped her eyes.

Through it all, to my amazement, Sal didn't react. They might as well have been yelling over lost laundry. But when his mother started crying, he said to Massimo, "I think I'll just leave my gift for Audenzia and go."

My brother smiled uncomfortably, "Yeah, okay. Probably best, Salvatore."

Even then, my father's cousin Antonio wouldn't let it go. He growled, "That's not his name no more. Haven't you heard? He goes by Charles Lucania now."

No one spoke up for Sal, not even his brother and sister. Out of the corner of my eye, I spotted Roberto and his wife whispering to each other.

I pushed back my chair and said, "I'll walk you to your car, Sal."

"*Zia.*"

It was a woman's voice, the tone reproachful. I wasn't sure who spoke.

I closed the door behind us after we emerged onto the street. There was at least an hour of daylight left.

"I just wanted to get a closer look at this," I announced, tugging his tie. "What kind of design have we got here – swirls? *Swirls?* You've come to this?"

"It's a new style, which you would know if style meant anything to you," he said, laughing. Whenever he laughed, my cousin's looks changed. Sal had skin pitted from a smallpox attack when he was a child, his eyes were set wide apart, and his bottom teeth were crooked. Somehow, he managed to carry himself like a good-looking guy regardless. But when he laughed like this, it wasn't swagger. It was real. You could call him handsome.

On the sidewalk, looking back at Massimo's house, I said, "And here I thought your father was calming down in his old age."

"Nah, even if he's on his deathbed, he's still gonna be yelling at me," Sal said. He shrugged, and I reflected on all the screaming lectures, slaps, shoves, and outright beatings that his father had doled out over the years. Some I witnessed, some I just heard about. I felt a stab of guilt that my birthday party was the cause of Sal's colliding with his father.

"Okay, so where's your car?" I asked, scanning the line of vehicles on the block for his Model-T, a battered black one with yellow tire walls.

He pointed way down the street, beyond my line of sight, and we set out in that direction. "You know, another thing is, everybody was drinking a lot of wine before you showed up," I suggested. "Maybe they're not so used to it."

"Yeah, and that Amarone is a top vintage."

"How would you know? Oh." I stopped walking. "The wine came from you."

"Yeah, Massimo got in touch."

This wasn't the best news. I couldn't restrain myself from saying, "Sal, listen, you're not a bootlegger, right? I heard a bad story from Mr. Silvia at the shop. In South Jersey, some bootleggers held up his truck full of mozzarella thinking it was booze coming up from Atlantic City. It got rough."

"Me? Shake down a cheese truck? I don't think so. No, Zia, I just made a call about the Amarone. I know some people."

"Really?" I pulled on my cousin's arm to make him stop to face me. "Tell me what's going on. Are you sure you're just a gambler these days? No rough stuff?"

"No rough stuff." My worldly twenty-six-year-old cousin looked me straight in the eye as he said it, and beneath the clothes and the heavy hair pomade and the smooth moves, I saw his eight-year-old self. That boy had never lied to me, just like I had never lied to him.

"In fact, I got a sweet business deal to celebrate, Zia. We could have raised a glass to it in Massimo's house. I got a nightclub opening soon. It's gonna be special – gonna be famous. You'll be hearing its name soon – The Orchid Hour."

At that moment, a young woman, her hair covered with a blue polka-dot scarf, pushed a stroller past us, the baby asleep. She didn't notice me. Her attention was fixed on Sal, who was making quite a splash on the sidewalk, no question.

The pause in conversation gave me time to try to absorb this new development of Sal's.

"It's named 'orchid' – as in the flower?" I asked, wondering if this was a codeword for a drink or a dance or something.

"As in the flower."

Now I was onto much bigger questions. I wasn't sure what a night-club was, though I had a shrewd idea what would go on – dancing and drinking alcohol. The second was illegal. It seemed a risky proposition.

"This is *your* business, Sal? You like to have a good time, sure, but what do you know about running a club?"

"I'm not running it. We got someone perfect for that job. He's got a lot of ideas. I put some money in. I'm an investor."

I wanted to congratulate him, to be happy for him, but something about this didn't sit right. How could a young fellow with no real job besides being a gambler, and no education, have pulled together enough money to invest in a fancy club?

"I dunno, Sal."

"Zia, what do you want from me?" he said, his jaw tense. "I'm not gonna work a regular job. Look at your father-in-law. He's got the weight of the world on his shoulders trying to keep a cheese shop going on Mulberry Street. And how about your brother? Christ, he's so beaten down from twenty years of hard labor, he looks like an old man. Killing himself to get a cheap house in the Bronx. And the people who run this city, you think they'd have it any other way? Italians are crumbs to them. I'm not gonna be a crumb."

I'd never heard a speech like this from my cousin's lips. I had no idea that he observed so carefully and cared so much. I felt as if Sal was on the verge of telling me something else, something that would explain all.

But with that, his intensity dissolved. The confessional door had slammed shut for the day. Sal cocked his head, thrusting his hands in his pockets, and said, "It's your birthday, Zia. Enough about me. How are you? How is the library?"

"It's fine. Everything is fine."

He frowned and took a step closer, "Nope. Try again. What happened?"

"Nothing."

"You can't fool me, Zia. Talk."

I inhaled deeply, "Okay, it looks like I'm going to be fired." As briefly as possible, I explained what had happened at the library.

"That's a tough break," Sal said quietly. "I'm real sorry."

"Thanks," I shrugged. "Hey, I should get back to the party. They're going to go to the new Yankee Stadium soon for a look-around."

"You're kidding."

"Nope. My brother knows the groundskeeper or something. What, you didn't think this turnout today was on account of me, did you? Now, where's my birthday present? You claim to have one."

Sal pulled a small box out of his jacket pocket. I took a step back, blinking at the gift wrapping – a radiant light blue that lit up this dusky Bronx street like a tiny meteor.

"Haven't you ever seen a Tiffany's box before?" Sal chuckled.

"No, I haven't."

I opened the box with great care, my fingers caressing the cream-colored ribbon, soft as silk. Inside, I found a silver bracelet with an object nestled underneath. I lifted the bracelet to see what it was, and the object leaped up. A delicate chain linked them. It was a charm bracelet.

The charm was of a sailboat, the ruffle of a breeze carved into its tiny sail.

"I'll never forget," he said simply.

"Me, neither."

"If you ever need anything, *cucina*, all you gotta do is ask. You got it."

He broke our solemn mood with a glance over my shoulder and a chuckle, "Uh-oh. Looks like Vito's waited long enough. I told him I'd only be able to stay a little while."

A shiny maroon automobile eased toward us. I could make out a dark-haired man at the wheel.

"You got a ride here?" I asked, confused.

"That's my car, Zia. You haven't seen me since I bought it."

"If it's your car, why is this fellow driving it?" I asked. And how could this Vito be okay with sitting outside Massimo's house? I wondered.

Sal didn't answer, he just waved the car toward us. The young man, younger than Sal, popped his head out the window and said, in an Italian accent, "I don't wanna rush you, but we got tickets, 'member? Bell goes off in under two hours."

To answer my questioning look, Sal said, "Ringside seats to the fight tonight. Tickets cost a bundle. Vito Genovese likes boxing as much as I do. Ok, gotta go."

Sal pulled me in for a hug while Vito watched. It made me uncomfortable. He had a hard face for someone so young.

"Happy birthday, Zia," said my cousin. "And don't forget, you ever need anything and—"

"Come *on*, Charlie," said Vito.

My cousin turned to look at Vito. I couldn't see the expression on Sal's face. But in a split second, Vito's smirk died. He turned to face forward, his hands gripping the large steering wheel.

Sal made his way around, slipped into the front seat, and the two of them zoomed off. The car went fast – faster than anyone ought to drive on a street where kids played – before Vito turned left, and they disappeared.

CHAPTER NINE

ZIA

The day that events were set in motion, events that no one could stop, I spent an hour hiding in the library. I'd found an ideal spot for a private lunch break, a stool at the end of the Non-Fiction/Science stacks. There I devoured a book about orchids and the human madness they inspire.

I read: "*In the year 1917, the* cypripedium calceolus, *the Lady Slipper Orchid, was declared to be extinct because the wealthy collectors of Great Britain had financed so many orchid hunts in their competition to possess the most beautiful of this variety of orchid that none could be found in any part of the world. The Lady Slipper Orchid had been stripped from the Earth.*"

I'd always been intrigued by the obsessions of wealthy collectors. It wasn't that I wanted to chase after diamond pendants, breed thoroughbred racehorses, or hunt for a hidden Egyptian tomb. But these pursuits were alien to the grim toil for food and shelter that much of the world was consumed by, including my own family when I was a child. Rather than contemplate human suffering, I liked to imagine what it would be like to care for nothing but digging up the tomb of King Tutankhamun. Or, now, collecting the most exquisite orchids on the planet.

I'd spotted this book, *History of the Orchid, the Royal Family of Plants, With Thirty Illustrations*, on the pile of library returns. Orchids had been on my mind ever since my cousin Salvatore told me of his nightclub venture. Why would anyone name it after this flower? I entered the book as a return, but instead of reshelving it, I read it over two lunch breaks while nibbling sandwiches.

Seeing Sal on Sunday left me with questions, and I was not the only one. When I returned to Massimo's house, no one brought my cousin up to me, with a single exception – my son. I hadn't thought about that when I followed Salvatore out the door. Now that he was eight years old, Michael was curious about people's words and deeds.

"I asked Grandpapa why you are the only one who likes cousin Salvatore, and he said it's because you don't give up on people you care about even after other people do," he said.

"He said that?" I hadn't thought of myself that way.

"Well, first, he said you are loyal, and I asked what that meant, even though I already had a pretty good idea."

I laughed, but the following question from Michael wasn't too amusing.

"Why do you think Sal gets into so much trouble? Uncle Roberto said it's because Sal isn't smart."

"He's wrong about that," I said, trying to tamp my rising temper. "Sal is one of the most intelligent people I know." My son looked confused now. And I was in a quandary. I did not want Michael to think that what Sal was doing – whatever he was doing – was okay with me. But I couldn't condemn him, especially not after what Roberto Pellegrino had said.

"Honey, it was different when we first came to this country. My parents had started us learning English before we left Palermo. Sal's parents didn't do that. He had to go to a different school and didn't know more than a few words of English when he started. His teacher was cruel to him. The other children were too."

His eyes bulging, Michael said, "Was anyone ever cruel to you, Mother?"

Swallowing hard, I lied, "No, no one."

Michael was too young to hear the truth. It was hard for us all. When we first came to New York, Massimo was responsible for protecting Giovanni and me from attacks on our way to and from school. He did his best, but the torment was constant. I remembered what it felt like to be mocked, tripped, and kicked in the small of the back, to have my hair yanked out so hard my scalp bled. I learned to hold up my arms to protect my head in case there was a shower of pebbles – or worse. When we rounded a particular corner, a mother would stick her head out the window and scream to her sons, "Get the dagos!" Life got less dangerous when we moved out of the slums and into a flat in Little Italy. But I could never forget. Even now, I have dreams of running in terror from my pursuers, their hateful laughter ricocheting along the dark alley.

I know that, for his part, Sal got into some serious fights when he was not much older than my son is today. One of the rules of the street was to keep enemies from attacking you the next time they see you by making this encounter so bad, so filled with vicious blows, that they'll look for someone else to hurt. Sal did what he must to appear strong.

But his triumphant street brawls were the first step to becoming "Salvatore from 14th Street" – his nickname by the age of twelve. City officials sent him to a Truancy Program school when he was fourteen. My father, who always saw the best in people, urged his cousin

Antonio not to turn his back on Sal, even after an arrest for illegal wagering. After my father died, Antonio hardened against his son. There were more arrests, although he never went to prison. I hoped Sal would "straighten out," as my father always insisted he would. Yet, here he was, riding around in a fancy car and talking about opening a nightclub named The Orchid Hour. This new stage worried me.

And after reading the orchid book on my lunch breaks, I was no closer to understanding the flower's possible significance to my cousin. What could it have to do with a nightclub?

The book had done one thing – it did me the excellent service of taking my mind off my problems. First, I had no idea that the orchid was the oldest flowering plant on Earth. How could a plant survive millions of years? While they may appear fragile, orchids show a defiant resilience. In some places, they grow from the branches and trunks of trees and in the crevices of boulders, without visible access to water or soil. Orchids were kept by Confucius and mentioned in the writing of a student of Aristotle.

What kept me most interested was not the writing of ancient philosophers but the more recent misadventures in the world of *orchidelerium*. That was the name for the orchid craze that took over Victorian England. Rothschild's bid against dukes for the most precious orchid, preferably a variety of Lady's Slipper. People were willing to throw ten thousand pounds at the purchase of a single plant. With so much money at stake, orchid hunters traveled the globe to find the rarest and most beautiful plants for their clients, journeying to remote mountains and thick jungles.

I couldn't believe what these men willingly endured. Shipwrecks and animal maiming, diseases, and thievery – they were common. Orchid hunters burned down jungles after securing their prizes so no rivals could get the same rare flower. Rivals murdered one another.

The orchid craze hadn't been going for too long in America, but it existed here too. The plants were conveyed from South America, Mexico, and the East Indies. I read how certain wealthy Americans hired small armies to run private greenhouses so that they could show off their orchid collections. Debutantes from rich families longed to wear orchid corsages. The problem was that people who grew flowers for corsages and other displays had to invest so much money in importing orchids – they couldn't sprout from seeds – that the growers had to hope that the high prices to be charged and the unusual long life of the orchid made it worthwhile in the end.

"Oh, here you are," said Rachel Rodman, standing over me. "I've been looking everywhere."

Closing my book, I said, "I'm sorry, is my break finished?"

"No, no. That's not it. I'm not sure why you are here, eating your lunch on a stool instead of in the staff room."

I shrugged. "I am in the middle of an interesting book. I wanted to concentrate."

Ever since our meeting in Mrs. Tuckle's office last week, I'd had the distinct feeling that I was being talked about. The other people in the library were overly friendly, even Edie. When I walked into a room, voices grew hushed. Mrs. Tuckle still wouldn't meet my gaze. If authorities from the central office observed us, I didn't spot them. Neither did I see Mr. Watkins, which surprised me after his emotional request last week. Had he decided he no longer wished to have the Pirandello play translated? But he sometimes disappeared for a few days at a time, only to show up in the late afternoon at a reading table once more.

Right now, I was more concerned about Rachel. She shook her head, her palm covering her right eye.

"Zia, I'm sorry," she said in a low voice.

"So, it's decided? I'll be the one fired?"

The oddest sensation came over me. I felt lighter, like I'd shed a heavy overcoat. What a strain the week had been.

"I want you to know that I tried – I pointed out how excellent you are at your work. How organized you are. No one listens to me."

Rachel's anguish touched me. But I also wondered if she suffered from coming face to face with evidence of her own powerlessness. Rachel's hero was Trotsky, whose life motto was, "*Be an implacable enemy of the capitalist state.*" And here, she couldn't even save the job of one little woman!

Rachel said tentatively, "You should be able to find another position. Perhaps as a secretary?"

I covered my mouth to stifle the laughter.

"Why is that funny?" Rachel asked, honestly confused.

"I doubt any businessman would trust me to type his letters. You've heard of those two Italian gentlemen, Nicola Sacco and Bartolomeo Vanzetti?"

Her eyes widened at the names of the Italian anarchists sentenced to die in the electric chair – their trial had dominated newspapers' front pages for months.

"Oh, Zia, what do those two have to do with you?"

"Businessmen, policemen, the Protestant clergymen, what do they all have in common? They hate the 'Mediterranean,' which is the nicest name they have for us," I explained. "We're aliens, Rachel, whether we got off the boat five years ago or were born here. Despised. Not many Americans will hire an Italian man to do anything but manual labor or wait on tables, hem trousers, trim hair. And an Italian *woman?* Oh, please."

Rachel sighed. "One day, I'll take you out to coffee to explain just what these righteous New Yorkers think of Jews. But for now, I suppose lunch is over."

I nodded and gathered my luncheon bag and book, preparing to return to the main desk.

Rachel said, "Maybe you'll get back in time to break up the chat between Edie and Mr. Watkins."

"What?"

"I saw them talking right before looking for you. I must admit, Mr. Watkins didn't look too happy with whatever she said."

This conversation felt wrong. I hurried back to the main desk, wondering why Mr. Watkins, who never came this early in the day, would show up now and talk to Edie.

From across the Adult Reading Room, I spotted Mr. Watkins heading for the door. He'd be on the street in ten seconds. Why was he already leaving?

I reached the front desk, where Edie went through a stack of returned books. She looked up and smiled. It was horrible, more of a triumphant smirk, her eyes narrowed above her full cheeks.

"Did you have a nice lunch, Zia?" she asked, a trill of laughter underlying her words.

I got to the door as fast as a person could without breaking into a trot.

"Mr. Watkins!" I shouted at his disappearing back, no longer walking but running. In seconds, he'd be swallowed by the crowd on the sidewalk.

He turned around, staring at me in surprise, and then made his way back.

"Do you want – to talk about the Pirandello – translation?" I asked, out of breath.

"That's why I came to the library today," Mr. Watkins said. "However, I was just told…" He frowned, biting his lip. Although not as exhausted-looking as the last time I was with him, Mr. Watkins seemed nervous.

"Forget whatever she told you," I said firmly. "Do you want the translation? What's the title?"

"Henry the Fourth," he answered.

"But that's Shakespeare, Mr. Watkins."

"No, no, it's written by Luigi Pirandello. The play is about a man who falls from a horse and wakes up believing himself to be the Holy Roman Emperor and insists on everyone treating him that way. It's about the nature of reality, how we all make our reality."

"I see," I said, although this was near gibberish to me.

He said, "In the play, there's a line of dialogue, '*Woe to him who doesn't know how to wear his mask, be he king or pope.*' I need to read the rest."

The crowded, noisy sidewalk wasn't the place to discuss the nature of reality.

"We can go over the translation details inside," I said, pointing at the library.

With a glance at his pocket watch, Mr. Watkins said, "No, I must get to the car. There's a series of meetings, and then, tomorrow, I leave for Washington, D.C. for an important appointment. Why don't I meet you with the car at the end of the day, and Teddy will drive you to your family's shop as before. What time?"

I told him six o'clock and returned to the front desk, but the whole time, I was thinking, "Slate of meetings? A Washington, D.C. appointment?" Tonight, in Mr. Watkins' automobile, I planned to find out his line of work. I'd had the idea he was retired or a man of leisure. That wasn't the case. At this point, curiosity about the man consumed me.

At the desk, I steeled myself to work alongside Edie. She asked why I'd gone outside, and I ignored the question, going on as if she hadn't opened her mouth. I did not speak to her for the rest of the afternoon, not even when she said I was wanted in Mrs. Tuckle's office. I nodded and made my way upstairs.

"Zia, I have unfortunate news," said Mrs. Tuckle, finally making eye contact.

I had never been fired before, so I've no basis for comparison, but it did seem to me that she managed that part of it well. She was direct yet compassionate. She conveyed how sorry she was without, of course, saying that she or anyone else had done anything wrong.

In response, I said I understood and I appreciated the time I'd spent working at the library.

"You have the temperament and the skills that any employer would wish for," she said. But then, for the first time, Mrs. Tuckle looked troubled.

"Your married name is De Luca, correct?" When I nodded, she said, "What's your maiden name?"

"Lucania."

"Oh. Hmmm. That's a shame."

I tensed in my chair. "Why is that?"

"You don't look Italian, Zia. Certain assumptions about the races are unfortunate and unfair, but we must accept the new science. I attended a lecture on the field of eugenics last month at the Museum of Natural History. Do you know anything about the scientific data they are collecting?"

Dreading what was coming next, I said, "I know that Charles Darwin's cousin coined it, using the Greek word *eugenes*, meaning 'good in birth'."

"Well, if you know that much, Zia, you must also be aware that these scientists – researchers and academic leaders from Princeton and Harvard – have drawn conclusions about certain races and their capabilities. You don't have the coloring or facial structure of the Italian race. This gives you an advantage."

I could not speak.

"Zia, it is pointless to dispute science. Calvin Coolidge, the vice-president of the United States, wrote that '*Biological laws tell us that certain divergent people will not mix or blend.*' He wrote that for *Good Housekeeping* magazine!"

I would prefer that this woman, someone I'd respected for over two years, had called me a "stupid dago" than quoted "biological laws."

I said, "Mrs. Tuckle, you said tomorrow would be my last day. I would like *this* to be my last day."

"Why? Zia, I'm sorry, but you must be practical. This is what eugenics teaches us."

I rose to my feet. "I've taken up enough of your time today. I'll collect my things."

The worst moment for me was the length of the hallway between Mrs. Tuckle's office and the third-floor washroom. I covered that with wobbly knees and quivering lips. I dampened a hand towel inside the lavatory and pressed it to my face. I must not leave the library in tears. I refused to give Edie that satisfaction.

Once calmer, it took only a few moments to collect my personal belongings, for I hadn't kept much at the library. I could feel curious eyes on me as I slipped notebooks, pencils, a couple of magazines, and an extra sweater into a large bag. However, no staff member said anything. Rachel was occupied elsewhere, thank goodness. She was the only one who could cause me trouble. I might not have been able to hold my emotions in check with her. I certainly had no intention of telling Mr. Watkins about being fired, not tonight. His translation assignment could prove a helpful distraction.

I rallied myself to walk across the Adult Reading Room for the last time. At least I'd never have to hear the voice of Edie again. But that wasn't enough to hold back the sadness that washed over me.

I decided to walk out the main door, the one leading to East Broadway. As I drew closer, I inhaled deeply. Just a few steps more.

I heard a loud bang outside, not on East Broadway but in the park, outside the other entrance. I pushed my way through the door.

It was early dusk outside. The streetlamps had yet to be lit. I could see a small group of people huddled in a circle just inside the park, ten feet from the curb, between East Broadway and the side of the library. There was something long and dark at their feet.

"Did you see it?" asked one of the men at the curb.

"No."

"Me neither."

Like someone sleepwalking, I made my way toward the form stretched out. It was a person wearing a long black coat, blood pooling beneath his back, his eyes shut and his mouth open. It was Mr. Watkins.

CHAPTER TEN

FRANK

Lieutenant Frank Hudgins had worked enough crimes to know that assumptions often change from what cops believe at the beginning of a murder investigation. As facts are established, everything shifts. A seeming crime of passion turns into a murder for gain. A mysterious death is revealed to be a sad suicide.

Rarely did everything change as drastically as with the police department's investigation of the murder of New York Deputy Mayor Miles G. Watkins.

Frank was at his desk at Police Headquarters at 240 Centre Street when the telephones started ringing. All of them. The phones were put in last year, and when they jangled at the same time, it caused a noise to make your ears bleed. After the phones were answered, doors opened and slammed, indicating that something big had happened. Someone whistled loudly and said, "Damn."

Within ten minutes, everyone on the floor knew Watkins had been shot dead on a street nine blocks from City Hall. At first, it sounded like a possible political assassination. Frank was more than old enough to remember a crazy anarchist shooting President McKinley in Buffalo. Frank had never heard of Miles G. Watkins, but that didn't mean anything. He could be significant.

Captain John Aloysius Devlin, Frank's oldest friend and superior, seemed to think so. He charged across the precinct floor. His mouth twisted into a grimace, his light blue eyes darted back and forth. He barrelled into the police chief's office, the door slamming shut, and remained there fifteen minutes.

Frank waited to find out if he'd be needed in the investigation. "This'll be a case for the feds, we won't get a piece," said Larry Barringer, the oldest of the homicide investigators and someone who was usually right about matters concerning jurisdiction.

The door opened, and John Devlin emerged with the others, but he said nothing to Frank, just rolled his eyes a fraction as he passed his friend's desk.

There was a time when, even if he didn't get assigned to a big murder, Frank would have hung around the precinct for a while to soak up the excitement, but tonight, he was home by eight. He made a sandwich and finished his letter to his sister-in-law on Berenice's condition. Frank had a telephone in his home, but his in-laws upstate didn't. He tried to keep them informed in letters, not that there was any news.

The following morning, bright and early, nothing was as Frank expected at 240 Centre Street. The floor was quiet. No sign of any feds. Yet when he peered into John Devlin's office, he saw the police captain sitting at his desk in his suspenders and undershirt, his chin darkened with blonde stubble. He'd spent the night there for sure.

"Turns out this Watkins was a nobody in a fancy office," Devlin said, waving him in. "He didn't have much to do. The state Republican party made the mayor park him in City Hall as some kind of favor swap."

"A Republican in City Hall?" That surprised Frank. For as long as he could remember, all the mayors had been Democrats – the party had a stranglehold on New York City.

"We got a Republican in the White House now, remember? And they show up in Albany. Sometimes, Tammany Hall needs a favor from high places. Point is, they gave Watkins three areas to be in charge of, to be a kind of liaison with the federal government, but he didn't go to meetings, didn't file hardly any reports. Didn't even show up at City Hall half the time. From what I hear, he was a real sad sack. His kid was killed in France, and he never got over it. It seems like people felt sorry for him when they thought about him at all. He was sidelined."

"So why would anyone shoot him?"

Devlin came around to take his uniform coat off the hook on the wall. The morning light streaming in the window revealed that his old friend had had a bit of a rough night. His eyes were bloodshot, and his round face looked puffy and chalk-white despite the faint freckles across his nose.

"I'm thinking a botched holdup or just some maniac looking for kicks," said the police captain, putting on his coat. "Either way, it makes us look like real shit – even a deputy mayor isn't safe on New York City's streets. So we gotta make an arrest fast. I need you on this."

"It's a little late to interview eyewitnesses."

"Oh, we got those statements. Nobody saw much. It was getting dark. He was shot from behind. Looks like the shooter was crouched between two parked cars on East Broadway. One woman saw a puff of smoke coming from there. Another witness saw a man run across the street afterward, but he didn't see his face. All he can say is the man was small and moved fast. We got the bullets. The autopsy may tell us more."

"Small. Like a kid?" Frank thought for a minute but shook his head, "Doesn't sound like a kid."

"What we're hearing is Miles Watkins had some kind of connection to the public library. He went there a lot during the day and was shot directly outside its main door, near the curb."

"The library?" Frank laughed a little, "The man might not have been too busy at City Hall, but hell, he was spending all his time at a public library?"

"There could've been a reason. He had these three areas, remember? One of them was immigration. That public library, the Seward branch, is known as the Immigrants' Library."

Frank nodded. It was a tenuous connection, but it was something.

"What I need you to do is interview his fellow deputy mayor and anyone else he saw a lot of at City Hall. I can't send just anyone over there. They'll want to see the lieutenant's stripes. Get a feel for Watkins' recent movements. Find out if he had enemies, though I'm getting the clear message that no, he wasn't the kind of politician to make enemies. He wasn't really a politician at all. He used to be a state's attorney until his kid was killed and he went on extended leave and never returned. But he had stature in the Republican Party, the clubs, and so forth. Larry is talking to them today. I'll need everyone back by four for a briefing. And your usual thorough reports on my desk before you leave."

Devlin met Frank at the door. Now that he was dressed, the captain had somewhere to be. Frank got a whiff of his breath – a mix of whiskey and the spearmint gum he used to cover it up. A rough night indeed.

Frank tapped his arm to pose one more question, "You said that Watkins was in charge of three areas. Immigration was one. What were the others?"

Devlin opened the door and strode into the room. Heads turned. For a second, Frank thought he wasn't going to get an answer.

Over his shoulder, Devlin said, "Prohibition – enforcing the Volstead Act. And the U.S. Coast Guard."

Frank didn't need his automobile to get to City Hall. It took twelve minutes to walk to the sprawling, leafy park that surrounded the century-old building containing the mayor and his staff in the most densely populated city in America. Frank had had reason to step inside City Hall a handful of times. That was enough for him to know that the building's stately beauty – French Renaissance-inspired exterior, grand curved staircase, and mural-plastered rotunda – did not mean the people employed here were organized. He'd be cooling his heels in the lower lobby for a while before anyone came to talk to him about Miles Watkins, and that first person would be insignificant.

Another mistaken assumption.

"What a terrible tragedy," said Deputy Mayor Philip Needsmith, a stout, balding, affable man in his forties whose handshake was nonetheless unpleasant – both moist and overly firm. "The mayor is out of town, or he'd want to speak to you personally. If there's anything you need, anyone you want to speak to, please let me know."

"Thank you. Let's start with you, sir," said Frank. "Fill me in on Miles G. Watkins."

He didn't learn much from the deputy mayor besides that Watkins came from a well-off family. He owned a brownstone off Washington Square and property in Oyster Bay, Long Island. That would need following up, Frank thought. Who was set to inherit? Needsmith also confirmed that Watkins hadn't attended many meetings or spoken up when he did. He seemed withdrawn and melancholic. It was inconceivable that he'd made enemies.

"I have to say that Immigration and Prohibition are both pretty important issues in New York City, so I don't understand why Mr. Watkins wasn't needed," said Frank.

"But that's just it!" cried Needsmith, jabbing the air with his pointer finger. "They're extremely important to the welfare of the city. Quite a few fellows were jostling to take a lead role on both Immigration and Prohibition and even the Coast Guard, his third responsibility at the city, state, and federal levels. Younger fellows than Miles, and much more ambitious. I'm afraid he was sidelined."

The person who Frank interviewed the longest was Watkins' young secretary, Miss Faye Arky. A sharp-chinned woman wearing wide, garish bracelets at odds with her demure navy skirt and blouse, she'd assisted both deputy mayors. Now, it was down to one.

Frank had investigated several dozen murders. Dealing with people who were grieving was part of the job. Faye fit that description. Her eyes were puffy; she clutched a handkerchief.

"I'm sorry, I know this is a difficult time," Frank said.

"It's just that I have work to do. I have to get back to it – I have to," she stammered.

"This won't take too long, Miss Arky, but when a murder's taken place, police must examine the life of the victim to better get to the truth," he said in his most serious tone. "It's vitally important to the investigation."

"But what happened to Mr. Watkins has nothing to do with here, with this office," the secretary insisted. "Some terrible criminal out of nowhere shot him on East Broadway."

Frank said, even more firmly, "Yes, and I'm here to find out why Mr. Watkins was on East Broadway, why he was in the library yesterday, why he went to that particular branch so often."

Finally, she started talking. Frank was able to establish that Faye Arky knew her boss made a habit of going to the Seward branch in the late afternoons, but she had no idea what sent him there in the first place, why he kept going, or which days he went. She maintained appointment books on her desk for both deputy mayors. With great reluctance, she opened her book for Mr. Watkins. Most pages were blank.

"He didn't want me to keep his calendar," said Faye Arky, blinking rapidly, a red patch flaring on each cheek. "It was Mr. Watkins' choice, not mine."

Was this because he was embarrassed to have so little to do? Frank wondered. That was one explanation. But there were others too.

Frank turned the pages until he found the present week. The day that he died, there was nothing on Mr. Watkins' calendar. Nor for the day after.

"I only saw him in the morning," said Faye Arky. "He left just after noon and—" her voice caught, "I never saw him again."

"How about files or notes he kept himself? I'd like to see his desk now."

"Why?" She clutched her handkerchief even more tightly. "He kept next to nothing in his office. For whatever reason – and I'm not privy to the causes for how things work here – Mr. Watkins was sidelined."

Frank studied her for a moment, "Did someone tell you to use that word, to say that Miles Watkins had been sidelined?"

She stepped back, hands aflutter, her bracelets banging loudly against her wrists, "No! Of course not. Why would you say that?"

Frank didn't answer her. After a glance at Watkins' office, which was indeed devoid of anything useful, he decided it was time to leave City Hall.

On the way down the wide curving staircase, he reflected on the importance of instincts. A good policeman had to have them. In the last couple of years, he'd worried he no longer got the hunches that led to breaking cases open. Seeing that his instincts were still alive and kicking was a relief.

Back at 240 Centre Street, Captain John Devlin grabbed Frank as soon as he walked onto the floor. The captain no longer looked exhausted. His eyes were sparkling.

"We've got a new angle on Watkins," he said. "There's a young woman involved. She works at the library."

"That would explain a few things," said Frank, although the picture he'd painted of the victim so far was of a man weighed down with melancholy, not someone with the energy to court a young librarian.

"We've nailed down a timeline," said Devlin. "He was at the library at noon. Stayed for about an hour and left. He went to the federal building for a few hours, then told his driver to go back to the library. He got out of the car to greet this girl at the door. They've done this before – he picks her up outside at closing time. We had to really pull it out of Watkins' driver. For some reason, he held back on her last night."

"And you see a motive for murder here?"

Captain Devlin crowed, "I sure as hell do! She's Italian – born in Sicily. It's got to be a vendetta, right? Jealous boyfriend. We pulled her in for questioning. She's in Room Four. I want you to have a run at her. The women feel more comfortable with you than any of our other guys. Find out if her stepping out with Watkins drove any of the guineas in the neighborhood crazy."

"Got it. But before I question her, what do you mean when you say Watkins was in the federal building yesterday?"

"Someone else will follow up on that. Just concentrate on the girl. Her name is," he glanced at a card in his hand, "Audenzia De Luca. Sounds like a dish, right?"

Frank thought longingly of his lunch that he'd stashed in the desk's top drawer this morning. He was more interested in that dish than in dealing with a hysterical, defensive female named Audenzia De Luca. He shoved a fresh notebook and pencil into his pocket, poured himself a cup of coffee, and headed for Room Four.

In that first second, when he stood in the open doorway, he thought there'd been a mistake, and one of his fellow cops had put his school-girl daughter in the room until he was ready to leave. He saw a slight form, a girl with her head bowed, her dark red hair neatly parted, and her hands folded, fingers interlaced, on the bare table. She wore a black blouse that looked like a uniform from one of the stricter private schools.

When she looked up, he realized this was not a girl but an adult, one somewhere in her twenties.

"Miss De Luca?" Frank said.

"It's Mrs. De Luca," she said, not offended but in the tone of trying to help someone who made an honest mistake.

Thanks, Johnny, for not telling me she was married.

Feeling conscious of the coffee cup in his hand, he said, "Would you like something to drink? Coffee or a glass of water?"

"No, nothing, thank you. I'm hoping that I won't be here too much longer. My family is sure to be worried about me."

"Your family?" Frank set down the coffee and laid the notebook on the table before sitting opposite her. "Do you mean your husband?"

She fixed the full strength of that somber gaze on him. Audenzia De Luca reminded him of someone, though he couldn't think who.

"My husband is deceased," she said.

Damn.

"I'm sorry." He opened the notebook to a blank page, "Was it recent?"

"Not all that recent. My husband died in the war."

He often felt a silent reproach when faced with war widows. *You're alive when the brave soldiers are dead.* Frank was sensitive about not having served during the Great War. He was thirty-one in 1917, older than the age of conscription, but he could have volunteered if he'd wanted to. He hadn't wanted to. He never saw why America entered that war.

Audenzia De Luca didn't ask him if he'd served overseas or anything else. Frank couldn't say there was skepticism or contempt in her expression, but he felt scrutinized. It was as if *he* were the one being questioned.

It was time to take control. Frank focused on the facts. He asked Audenzia the usual background questions, where she had grown up and gone to school, who she lived with now, and how long she'd worked at the library. Police Headquarters stood in Little Italy, and Frank was somewhat familiar with the community. Her story fit the mold of immigrant women in New York City up to a point. Strictly brought up, she had gone directly from her father's home to her husband's. She differed from that mold in her flawless English and getting a job at a Carnegie library. She was intelligent, yes, and that raised the possibility that she was intelligent enough to pull off a deception.

"Do you have a boyfriend, Mrs. De Luca?"

"No." She tilted her head while studying him. "What is the point of such a question?"

"As I'm sure you know, we've brought you here to assist in the investigation into the murder of Mr. Watkins."

She sat up straighter. "I wish I could be of help. By the time I got outside, he had been shot and was on the ground. I didn't see anyone who might have committed the crime. But to be honest, I didn't look around. I had a hard time taking in that it had really happened." She shook her head. The memory pained her, though, Frank noted, she was dry-eyed.

"Mrs. De Luca, I think we're more interested in your personal connection to Mr. Watkins," he said.

She frowned and drew back in her chair. She would have to be a highly proficient liar to fake confusion this well.

"Personal? I didn't even know his first name. I had no idea he held a job with the city's government."

"He was the deputy mayor."

She turned to look out the window, though the half-drawn, dirty-yellow Venetian blinds obscured the view. "I suppose that helps explain some of the problems this city has," she said dryly.

Frank coughed, struggling to cover up his laugh. Would a woman in a romance with a man say such a thing?

Determined to push her, Frank said, "You have accepted all these rides in Mr. Watkins' automobile. It would suggest something a lot closer than library patron and librarian."

She didn't flinch. "Last week, Mr. Watkins offered me a ride to my father-in-law's store because it was raining. He was also interested in finding out if I could translate a play by a Sicilian playwright into English. We were supposed to continue the conversation yesterday, but it didn't happen. So I accepted that one ride from him."

Frank's instincts told him that Audenzia De Luca wasn't interested in Watkins, but that didn't mean he hadn't fancied her. And that could have had consequences. She was attractive enough, while not being by any stretch of the imagination the type of woman who roped in most men these days – the high-spirited, flirtatious, daring flapper. There was nothing bubbly about her. She wasn't modern at all. In fact, Frank had figured out who she resembled. It was that portrait with an ornate frame hanging on a wall of the Metropolitan Museum of Art. Berenice had dragged him to the museum a few times. Audenzia looked like one of those unsmiling princesses found in the Medieval art wing.

"It seems to me he liked you more than the other librarians," Frank said bluntly. "Any idea why?"

After a few seconds, she said, "I think it was because he'd lost his son, and I'd lost my husband. He said I was the only one who could understand." She paused. "He was very disturbed by certain things. He read poetry to cope, I think. He talked about reality, and he quoted a part of the poem *The Waste Land* to me, '*He who was living is now dead. We who were living are now dying… with a little patience.*'"

A chill galloped up Frank's spine, and looking at Audenzia, he knew she had the same reaction. That was a hell of a thing for Miles G. Watkins to say one week before someone shot him in the back.

"You'd agree with the assessment that he was a defeated man?" Frank said.

She bit her lip, "I don't know about that. I think Mr. Watkins was making an effort to do something very recently. He said he had important meetings the afternoon he died, and he was planning that trip to Washington, D.C."

"What?"

"Don't you know about Mr. Watkins' plans?" she asked.

Frank turned to another clean page in his notebook. "I need you to tell me everything he said to you yesterday. Every single word."

Twenty minutes later, Frank was headed for the Briefing Room. Captain John Devlin grabbed him before starting the meeting. "You're going to lead off with what you got out of the De Luca woman."

"Yeah, that interview definitely gave us a lead."

Devlin grinned. "So, she was his squeeze?"

"Nope. She wasn't. That's not the way to go."

Devlin's smile sagged. "Then how could she be good for a lead?"

"Something's not sitting right with me at City Hall. This whole business of his being sidelined – what they told you and what they keep telling me. But what if I tell you he was trying to get off the sidelines the last few weeks?"

"And someone had him shot for it? Because he took an interest in his work? Jesus, Frank, that sounds completely nuts."

"Yeah, I know. But I talked to two different women today, here and in City Hall. One of them was scared. Really scared. And it wasn't Audenzia De Luca."

CHAPTER ELEVEN

ZIA

I've always told my son how important it is to be truthful. So, after I left the police headquarters and walked home to Mulberry Street, I knew I must tell everyone – Michael, my father-in-law, my mother-in-law, and Roberto and Ileana Pellegrino – about Mr. Watkins and what happened to him and what happened to me because of it.

I made sure first that Papa said it was okay with him. Once I had his approval, I asked everyone to come upstairs to our flat after we closed the shop for the night. While Michael ran up and down the stairs all day, just as his father Armando had, I took pains to make sure that my son was out of the shop at closing time. That's when Nettuno came for his payoffs.

I explained that a regular patron of the library, a man who turned out to be the deputy mayor, had asked me if I could translate the Luigi Pirandello play *Henry the Fourth*, but before I'd agreed to do it and we'd worked out the details, he was shot by a stranger in front of the library. That's why the police had brought me to their headquarters to ask me questions.

The family all expressed concern, though their points of view differed. Mama and Ileana were horrified that I'd seen someone I knew dying on the ground. Michael was devoured with curiosity about my going inside the awe-inspiring Police Headquarters – an enormous brick building to be sure – and talking to police officers.

"Did they get tough with you?" Michael asked eagerly.

"Oh, surely they wouldn't," said Mama, but she was taut with anxiety.

"No one was tough," I reassured them. "Some questions were direct, but that's to be expected. They want to find the person who committed this crime. Part of that is getting to understand Mr. Watkins, and I have to say, he wasn't easy to understand."

Papa said, "Did you happen to notice the rank of the police officers you spoke to? Were any of them sergeants? Or detectives?"

"The man I spoke to the longest, Frank Hudgins, is a lieutenant," I said.

"Really?" My father-in-law looked startled.

"Is that bad?" I asked.

"No," he said. But Papa pursed his lips and went quiet for a while.

Roberto couldn't get over a deputy mayor named Miles Watkins being keen to read a translation of Pirandello. "In Rome, at the premiere performance of *Six Characters in Search of an Author*, I heard that the people in the audience went berserk, screaming, 'Madhouse!'"

"I don't know why Mr. Watkins was so drawn to Pirandello's plays," I admitted.

"It's unusual," said Roberto, rubbing his chin. "Americans, they prefer simple stories with everything on the surface, like children's tales. Or the men want to leer at a line of dancing girls. We Italians love plays and novels and pictures that are difficult, ones that we can debate all night. No one is more challenging than Luigi Pirandello. For him, there is one truth and then another truth beneath that one, and then even that truth can be false."

Something about Roberto's words made my pulse quicken. Maybe *that's* why he wanted to read the play, I thought, but before I could complete a mental deduction, my mother-in-law said, "Zia, we should make arrangements for someone to escort you home from the library. I don't want you going in and out of this building by yourself until this criminal's been caught."

The time had come. My embarrassment could no longer prevent me from telling the family the truth.

I said, "An escort won't be necessary. I'm not employed at the library anymore."

My being fired came as a surprise to everyone. I'd been working at the public library for so long. I told them what had led to my dismissal, leaving out only Mrs. Tuckle's hurtful suggestion that I use another name to keep prospective employers from realizing that I'm Italian.

After the surprise came sympathy mingled with reactions that once again revealed their true feelings, in this case about my working at the library. Roberto and Ileana were glad to hear I'd have more time for De Luca's Cheese. To them, the shop was the center of the universe, not just because they worked there but because they passionately believed it was the best of its kind in Little Italy, in New York City, on the entire east coast. My son and mother-in-law were happy for another reason – they expected to see more of me at home. "Could you meet me at school and bring me home?" asked Michael, delighted. I smiled and enfolded him in my arms. But my shoulders stiffened. How could he go to college without my working to put the money aside? We were both being swallowed by the shop, not just now but forever.

My father-in-law spoke up and said he had something in mind for me, a late birthday gift. It was a special delivery just arrived, a record of the opera *Turandot*. We'd listen to it on the phonograph together tonight.

The De Lucas have a profound connection to music. It goes beyond the fact that Naples has been the beating heart of opera for over three hundred years. Armando had told me the family's theory was they could hear music differently than other people because they were refugees from Atlantis and not fully human. He said it with a laugh to let me know that it was a family joke. But there were times I wondered. Armando's voice was so pure, it was unearthly. He was incapable of hitting a false note. As for Papa, he *inhabited* music. He heard instruments no one else could detect and picked out arrangements that he felt certain the composer had created to drive home a sweeping climax or support a subtle shift.

Whenever he listened to opera, my father-in-law would put on a fresh shirt, pour himself a snifter of Cognac, light a thick wax candle, and sit in his upholstered chair in the corner. He drank the Cognac only on these occasions. The ritual took place once I settled Michael for the night. Luigi adored his grandson, but any interruption of the music caused pain.

Buying the phonograph, ordering the opera records, and securing the Cognac were Papa's only indulgences. He never traveled, and he owned no automobile or fine clothes. He shared his deep devotion to music with Armando, and now, I was the one who listened to records with him. I did not do it to try to take my dead husband's place. There was nothing so crude about it. Ever since I was a child, I have liked music while never having the same talent as the De Lucas. When it came to opera, my response wasn't analytical. I wouldn't say it touched my heart. It went deeper than that. Opera seized hold of my soul.

"So, tonight, we pay a call on Puccini's Chinese princess," I said after Papa set out the snifters of Cognac.

"A princess from his imagination," said my father-in-law, smiling. "Which is the best kind."

As opera storylines go, I always liked the princess story but for my own reasons. She was a beauty with a heart of ice. When her father forced her to choose a husband, she produced a riddle of three questions. Each suitor who failed would be sent to the executioner with a stamp of Turandot's foot. She would submit to no man! When I was a teenager, she could have been my heroine. Until I met Armando, I loathed the thought of marriage. The boys' clumsy efforts to get their hands on me filled me with disgust. I would have loved to be a haughty virgin princess, ordering beheadings.

These flimsy or childish or gruesome stories never diminished my experience of listening to opera. The music pushed me high and dashed me low. And it opened me to feelings that were different from the ones of my ordinary life, the mild pleasures and nagging irritations, the underlying resentments and regrets. In the grip of an opera, I found myself out of breath or fighting back tears. I *became* the characters.

"I wanted you to hear *Nessun Dorma* tonight," said Papa.

"It's amazing," I said, still shaken by the ending.

He continued, "The right tenor who can hold the B natural is important, but the message of the aria, that's what I wanted you to hear – '*I will win.*' I know you endured something terrible, seeing your friend dying on the ground." Papa laid his hand on my arm, "And you lost a job that I know made you proud. It made me proud. But you will persevere. I have confidence in you, Zia."

I nodded and gripped his hand. "Thank you, Papa," I whispered.

I woke the following day, determined to fulfill my father-in-law's faith in me. I would find a new direction for my life, but until that happened, I'd be of use at home and the shop.

Midway through the morning, I ended up going on a special errand. De Luca's Cheese Shop had begun doing business with restaurants outside Little Italy. The "appetizer" was taking off as a popular feature, offering a small first course. The cheese appetizers required… cheese, and we had the best. Papa was putting together sample cheese trays and mozzarella ball and fruit dishes for the restaurant suppliers to try. Roberto didn't see why we should go in this direction, but I backed Papa.

It was a bit early in the season, but I planned to scour every stall and store on Mulberry Street, Broome Street, and Grand to find not just the tastiest but the most attractive fresh fruit.

The neighborhood seemed to burst with business today. Not just grocers but bakers, butchers, cobblers, barbers, tailors, newsstands, and cigarmakers. The small stores were on the ground floor, with tenement apartments above. But why, oh, why did Mulberry Street have to resemble a Southern Italian town of 1890? Pushcart vendors made the sidewalk hard to navigate while horses drew carts down the street, finding space alongside the impatient automobiles. Did any other part of the city have this many horses?

I was shaking my head over horse droppings in the street when a familiar face appeared in the doorway of 164 Mulberry.

"Salvatore!" I cried. "I thought you didn't have time to mingle with us peasants." I took a closer look and said, "And you're dressed like a grocer's clerk. Did you decide to go slumming? Is this how you plan to present yourself at The Orchid Hour?"

My cousin, dressed in a blue cotton buttoned shirt and plain trousers, laughed. "You are the one who's not usually on Mulberry in the middle of the day." He frowned, "Wait, does that mean what I think it does?"

"Yes," I said, my throat tightening.

"Did it go badly?" he asked. "Was anyone cruel to you, *cucina*?"

A certain glint in his eyes suggested that if someone had treated me poorly, that person would have a problem.

"I don't think being fired can ever be a pleasant way to spend your time," I said slowly. "No one was cruel, or at least, Mrs. Tuckle didn't believe she was at the time, I'm sure. She did give me 'helpful' advice that… well, I didn't feel helped at all."

I told Salvatore about Mrs. Tuckle's recommendation to change my name and the scientific research she said was making a case for Italian inferiority.

The glint hardened in my cousin's eyes. "I know about this," he said. "Eugenics is dangerous."

It never failed to surprise me how Salvatore, whom I'd never seen open a book, kept so well informed.

"It's insulting, no question. How is it dangerous?"

He said, "Ask yourself, Zia, why they're doing it. What's the purpose? They're drawing up a law to ban Italians, Jews, Asians, and a whole lot of other people from coming to America. And this scientific crap is how they're going to push it through. That's the first step."

"Lord, if that's the first step, what's the second?"

"To start sending people *back*. Lemme tell you, I ain't going back to Italy."

While I tried to take this in, Sal had a question for me.

"I heard about the killing on East Broadway. Were you in the building when the deputy mayor got shot out front?"

99

I nodded, "Not only was I there, I knew him. I was brought into Police Headquarters yesterday to tell them everything I knew about Mr. Watkins."

"Brought in?" Sal squinted at me. "Cops don't do that unless you're a suspect."

"Oh, that's ridiculous," I said. "I didn't do anything wrong, and they know it. Don't give that another thought, Sal. The police won't be needing to talk to me anymore."

"You're sure about that?"

Sal was staring intently over my shoulder, and I turned to see Lieutenant Frank Hudgins bearing down on us. The sight of his blue uniform and cap made the wary crowd skedaddle out of his way. He didn't seem aware of that and smiled politely when he reached me and Sal.

"Hello, I hope you're feeling well today, I just need to follow up with a few more questions, Mrs. De Luca," he said.

Just as in Police Headquarters, I was struck by the contrast in this police officer. The first two men I had spoken to, briefly, were all bluster and boldness. With Lieutenant Hudgins, he moved with confidence, his sentences conveyed forceful authority, but his eyes said something else. They were clouded with a weary sadness. Even when he smiled, it was there, the pain.

"Do I have to go back with you now?" I asked.

"No, that's unnecessary." He looked around, realizing that to conduct official business in a crowd wouldn't be ideal. Only then did his gaze rest on Sal, who remained by my side. I was glad he wasn't wearing the same flashy clothes as in the Bronx. He really could be any laborer in Little Italy.

"This is my cousin, Salvatore," I said. I omitted his last name, remembering how Sal's father had raged about visits from the police.

But to be so informal while making an introduction to Lieutenant Hudgins was not right. Now an awkwardness hung in the air.

"Salvatore Lucania," Sal said, extending his hand to shake. So much for "Charles." I held my breath, waiting for the reaction.

But the name meant nothing to Lieutenant Hudgins. He nodded, let go of the handshake, and lost interest in my cousin.

With a little wave to me, Sal moved on. I was left standing on the sidewalk with a police lieutenant who had questions to ask when I was sure I'd answered them all.

"I do have a shopping errand to perform for my father-in-law," I said, pointing toward Grand Street.

"Isn't there a decent bakery on Grand – that place, Ferrara's?" he said. "I could use a cup of coffee."

"Decent? Yes, I'd say so." I couldn't keep the sarcasm from my voice, but he didn't seem to notice that either. The man was preoccupied.

Ferrara's Bakery and Café was almost thirty years old, opening five years before De Luca's. It was a preeminent bakery of Little Italy and a place where Papa and the owner liked to debate opera over espresso.

Lieutenant Hudgins ordered a large coffee – no sugar – and a cherry cannoli, which was a strange order, but they filled it at Ferrara's without comment. I insisted I wanted nothing. A non-Italian police lieutenant buying me a meal, even a cup of coffee, was sure to cause talk through the neighborhood.

"Have a seat," said Lieutenant Hudgins, heading for a small table.

I didn't want to sit with him while he ate, but neither did I want to explain why this wasn't proper to someone so ignorant of our culture. I took a chair.

He took a large bite of the cannoli before saying, "You didn't mention that you got fired from the library."

"It had nothing to do with Mr. Watkins," I said.

He sipped his coffee, watching me closely, staying quiet.

"Did someone say the two things were connected?" I demanded.

"The 'no fraternizing rule' was mentioned when I talked to your former colleagues this morning."

It wasn't hard to imagine who that helpful library colleague would have been. But before I could explain, he leaned across the table and said, very seriously, "You have to tell me everything Deputy Mayor Watkins said to you about his work, his meetings, and that trip to Washington, D.C."

"But I told you everything. I didn't leave out a syllable." Out of the corner of my eye, I could see one of the Ferraras wiping down a table, probably trying to eavesdrop. Keeping my voice as calm as I could, I asked, "Why do you need me to explain what Mr. Watkins did? Doesn't his office at City Hall have records of his movements?"

"No, it doesn't. His driver confirmed taking him to the federal building on Duane Street in the afternoon, but so far, we don't know who he talked to. And no one else said he intended to take a train to Washington, D.C. You're the only one. His driver insists he didn't know."

A horn blew outside. The espresso machine bubbled in the corner. Two boys who should have been in school shouted with laughter as they hurtled past Ferrara's.

I tried to wrap my thoughts around this news. Why would Mr. Watkins not tell anyone in New York about going to Washington, D.C. except me? Someone must have made the arrangements. This didn't make any sense.

"Lieutenant Hudgins, that is what he told me," I said helplessly.

He gulped down the rest of his coffee and stood up, suddenly in a hurry, "Fine, then I need to speak with your father-in-law and your mother-in-law."

"I'll take you there," I said.

"No, Mrs. De Luca. Just give me the address where they can be found. It's best you're not in the room."

I didn't say anything, I couldn't in front of the Ferraras. Out on the street, just as we were about to go in different directions, he said, so quietly I could barely hear him, "I'm trying to help you."

What he didn't say, but he might as well have, was, *You need help*.

As much as I wanted to rush home, I forced myself to buy some fruit for the shop at three different stands. When I finally walked through the door, I could tell immediately that Lieutenant Hudgins had come, asked his questions, and gone. To my humiliation, his goal was to confirm what I'd told him, to learn what time I came home from the library on the weekdays and whether I went anywhere alone on the weekends. "He seemed like a fair man," Papa said. "He didn't make these questions sound as if you'd been improper."

When I had a moment alone with my mother-in-law, I said, "It's unbearable that you would think for a minute that…" I couldn't finish the sentence.

"Zia, don't," she said, hugging me. "Papa and I know your nature."

My in-laws learned from Lieutenant Hudgins that Mr. Watkins was not only an important man at City Hall but also rich. More and more, the actual person who'd shown up at the library – shy, sad, and rather odd – was replaced in the minds of those who had never met him as a well-heeled man with a big job. The kind of man who would have a mistress. But even if he did and I were that mistress, what did that have to do with his murder?

I had trouble sleeping. As much as my in-laws reassured me that this ordeal was ending, I was consumed with nervous dread.

I woke early and made breakfast for everyone while Mama got Michael ready for school. After forcing down half a slice of bread, I went down to help Papa get the shop ready to open.

I wasn't there five minutes when Roberto Pellegrino charged into the shop, waving the *Daily News*.

"There's a story on the third page," he said breathlessly, "and it's all about Zia!"

CHAPTER TWELVE

LOUIS

When Rose Gold installed three pay phones at the back of her store last year, people in Brownsville couldn't believe her gall. Who would pay five cents to talk on the phone? A guy was lucky to earn twenty-five cents an hour. And then to drop a nickel to talk at the back of a little store in Brooklyn that sold cruddy candy and flat soda?

Rose shrugged off the doubters. "The machines don't take pennies, so I don't take pennies," she said. "The cheapest coin hole they got is shaped for a nickel."

Louis Buchalter didn't like getting taken advantage of any more than the next man, but Rose's phones made sense to him. Maybe one in five people in Brooklyn had their own telephone. And even if you had one installed in your home, would you want to be shouting your business into a receiver if you weren't strictly on the up and up? When Louis got out of Sing Sing last year and moved back to Brooklyn, he heard Rose's pay phones were a good way to get in touch with your bookie or arrange a buddy's bail.

At this moment, though, Louis was not setting up anything shady on the phone. He was patiently listening to his sister from Bridgeport, Connecticut, during their weekly call.

"Why won't you tell me what you're doing for money, Louis?" she pleaded. "Mother is so worried about you, she doesn't sleep."

"Tell Mother not to worry. I'm fine. I'm not getting into any trouble. I go to bed early every night."

With the toe of his shoe, Louis pushed a dirty sandwich wrapper into the booth's corner. Was a trash can and mop too much to ask of Rose?

"But you've said things like this so many times before," insisted his older sister. "And then you get arrested and bring shame on us. One of our brothers is a rabbi, a *rabbi*, in Colorado. Another one a pharmacist. Me, I teach school. And you can't manage a real job? Why?"

A gentle tapping on the pay-phone glass door made Louis glance over his shoulder. It was Yael, giving him a time's-up signal. It didn't seem like he'd been on too long – he didn't see anyone waiting. But in this case, he was fine with saying goodbye.

The second he was out of the booth, Yael jerked her thumb toward the street.

Louis' heart jumped at the sight of the skinny messenger outside, leaning against a pole as he looked up, adjusting the brim of his hat. This was how The Fixer always sent for him. So, he was needed again.

Louis made it out of Rose's as quickly as possible without looking like he was in a hurry. The skinny messenger continued fiddling with his hat as Louis approached. It was as if he were trying to shield his face from the afternoon sun. Only problem, there was no sun. Rose opened the candy store under the elevated train tracks.

"You have an appointment," he said to Louis, still squinting skyward. "At five o'clock. The same place you met before. You'll be there?"

"Sure."

The messenger shot off as soon as Louis agreed, to get out of Brownsville, no doubt. Louis looked up at the spot the guy had been standing under and saw a flapping of gray wings. He'd never noticed that the pigeons gathered up there. Maybe the guy had a terror of pigeon crap.

It was a warm day, and Louis realized he was thirsty. He popped back into Rose's to buy a Coca-Cola for the ride.

"Here's your change," Yael said at the counter. She said nothing else, no wink or knowing smile. Anybody watching them would think he was just another customer at the counter. Louis couldn't help but be impressed.

His car was parked half a block farther up on Saratoga Avenue. Louis heard that when the fellow named Charles S. Brown snapped up this land parcel on auction in the middle of Brooklyn, he expected it to attract the finest New York families. To make them feel as if they were in their element, he had named the streets after resort towns upstate like Saratoga Springs.

And what would Charles S. Brown make of it now? Louis wondered. In the last two decades, the bridges built between Manhattan and Brooklyn had delivered hordes of people desperate to escape the Lower East Side slums. In the end, Brownsville wasn't much better than the tenements they'd fled from. Many landlords tore down dilapidated two-story wooden houses, some without running water, to build tenements, what else? Like Rose's, the stores were cramped and dirty. They stood alongside offices for the Socialist and American Labor Party politicians who all swore they knew how to improve the human condition. Louis' mother was horrified when a clinic opened on Amboy Street that, rumor had it, helped poor women avoid getting pregnant and deal with unwanted babies. Louis privately thought it seemed like a good idea. But it didn't matter what any of the Buchalters thought. Police raided the clinic and shut it down fast.

To get out of Brooklyn, Louis chose the Williamsburg Bridge. His destination was 49th Street and Broadway, and it was a good thing he'd left Rose's right away because the streets were jammed in both boroughs.

As he drove, Louis cheerfully wondered what new business needed to be taken care of. He didn't worry that anything had gone wrong with the murder he had committed three days ago. He knew no one had gotten a look at his face when he shot Watkins, and nobody had chased after his car. Moreover, The Fixer had summoned him the very next morning to tell him that he knew for a fact the police had no description of the shooter, no license plate, and no clues at all.

"I pride myself on having a feel for people, but I must say that in your case, I hit the jackpot," The Fixer had said in that soft voice of his, just above a whisper.

Louis had glowed at the compliment, but he'd had to fight down the impulse to say, "Now you see why you didn't need no Albert Anastasia!"

It'd been touch and go there for a bit whether he'd be the one to do the shooting. After following Watkins for a week and delivering his reports, Louis found his assignment had changed overnight and radically. The Fixer, looking more perturbed than ever before, had sent for him first thing in the morning. The news was Deputy Mayor Miles G. Watkins had to be removed that day or that night – at any point before seven the following morning, a Friday.

"You haven't… done this kind of work before, have you?" asked The Fixer.

Louis shook his head. "But I know my way around a gun. I can do this job, I can do it just the way you want it done."

The Fixer said, frowning, "This isn't one of my areas. There's a man who can be relied on when it comes to it, but he's never seen Watkins before, has no familiarity with his routine. And it doesn't matter anyway because he's in prison."

That *had* to be Anastasia.

The Fixer said, "This is ridiculous – they can't expect me to try out someone new on this sort of thing on short notice." His tone was fretful and resentful. He was the most powerful person Louis knew by far. Who could be in a position to give orders to The Fixer? Or, rather, who were "they?"

"You don't need anyone new – I'm your man," Louis insisted.

With some reluctance, The Fixer told him where to pick up the gun, a revolver, for the job. He'd have to bring it back – the gun wasn't for keeps. It was absolutely crucial that no one sees him do the deed.

"There won't be a witness," said Louis. "You don't have to tell me that."

But The Fixer kept hammering away. Louis could not be identified, he must not be caught. If he were caught and he squealed, that would be curtains for him *and* for those he held dear.

Louis tried to hide how thrilled he felt. This was a job so important, The Fixer himself was threatening his life and his family's lives. *He'd done it. He made it to the big time!*

The last thing the older man had said was, "You can't tell anyone you did this. Louis, I like you, I got plans for you, but I'd not save you from a bullet if you squeal."

Louis didn't tell anyone, not anyone new anyway. He decided this edict didn't apply to Yael because she was already in the know. The day of the murder, he had taken her with him as always. She'd kept the car running on a street around the corner from the library. Yael had a cool head throughout. The kid was swell.

Lindy's sat on the east side of Broadway between 49th Street and 50th Street. Two years ago, it opened as "Lindy's Delicatessen" and was such a hit with the raffish end of the Broadway mob that the owners, Leo and Clara Lindemann, decided to put in tables and hire waiters and make it an actual restaurant. The one thing Lindy's had never been was a cafeteria. Yet you could see all three words etched in the Lindy's front window in different places – *Delicatessen*, *Restaurant*, and *Cafeteria*.

It seemed like everyone in New York knew The Fixer considered Lindy's his unofficial office. He could be found in the back booth most evenings. After that, he made the rounds – looked in on a high-stakes illegal poker game, stopped by a dinner party, hit a couple of speakeasies, and sat in cigar-filled back rooms with one or more of the New Yorkers who were careful never to appear with him in public. Others smoked and drank, it should be emphasized. The Fixer did neither.

"I'm expected," Louis said to Leo Lindemann, who was rubbing his temples at the front cash register. He was a young man with an old man's nervous system, thanks to running a popular business open late hours off Times Square and all which that entailed.

Lindemann showed no sign of recognizing Louis, but he knew who must be expecting him. He pointed at a stool where Louis could wait his turn. It took fifteen minutes for the mustachioed man sitting in the booth opposite The Fixer to finish his business. That was enough time for Louis to inhale the cooking odors from the kitchen and get an eyeful of the dishes sailing out on waiters' trays. Oh, the hot sandwiches at Lindy's were swell. There was the sugar-cured ham, the pastrami, the brisket, and Louis' favorite – the hot primed rib sandwich with mashed potatoes and gravy. If only he could order something to eat. But Louis worried that wouldn't go over.

When it was his turn, he approached The Fixer with his usual humility. The man's two bodyguards tracked his movements as he walked the restaurant length, their jackets stretched tight over their brawny arms and shoulders.

As for The Fixer, he wore his usual herringbone tweed checked jacket with three-button sleeves over a matching waistcoat and a narrow dark tie. He was just shy of forty years of age with meticulously trimmed dark brown hair topping a long, unlined face. His position at the pinnacle of power in New York City didn't seem to have aged him.

"Thank you for returning the borrowed object to our associate," he said as Louis slipped into the seat opposite him. His voice was just above a murmur.

He must be referring to the revolver, Louis thought. He nodded agreeably.

"Did you read the *Daily News* this morning?" asked The Fixer.

Louis shook his head, "I read the *New York World*."

"You should read the *Daily News* too. As many newspapers as you can. Knowledge is everything."

The Fixer handed him the *Daily News* folded back to page three. One of the headlines read, "*Librarian Reveals Watkins' Other Side*."

"Oh, that one," Louis said. He scanned the short article. "She doesn't reveal much."

"No, if you read the article carefully, the reporter didn't talk to her at all. He used other sources. Through these other sources, what's brought out is that Watkins did speak to her about his life. Just how much did he say? Where did he draw the line?"

Having no idea of the answers to these questions, Louis kept silent.

Nancy Bilyeau

Across the restaurant, a table occupied by four young men broke into laughter. They were diving into their food, which Louis had longingly watched go out of the kitchen. It was the famed Lindy's Special Platter – brisket, salami, spiced beef, and smoked tongue, all the meats adorned with pickles and potato salad. To Louis' embarrassment, his stomach grumbled.

The Fixer didn't seem to hear it. He said, "Someone at City Hall or the Police Precinct might have thought it'd be a useful diversion to bring Audenzia De Luca into this. I'm not sure I agree."

The older man pursed his lips, contemplating something. Louis watched, awed. He was witnessing the man's famed brain work a problem through. There was no one, absolutely no one in New York who calculated the odds better than The Fixer.

Laughter rocked the table of four men again.

"Have a look at those fellows, they're all newspaper reporters," said The Fixer. "You could be one of them, don't you think? Your age, the way you dress."

Louis' empty stomach tightened. Was this a slam? Those men weren't dressed too well, with their sleeves rolled up and worn hats. Louis should've put on a tie today. What a mistake.

"Louis, I'd like you to find out what the De Luca woman knows," The Fixer said. "Let me tell you how you're going to do it."

112

I couldn't say which was worse, the people who showed up at the store and asked what was going on or those who pretended they hadn't read the *Daily News* story and came to look me over.

Papa and Roberto told them all, loud and clear, that the story in the newspaper was wrong. I had enjoyed no "special friendship" with the murdered deputy mayor, and no one fired me from the public library because of improper behavior.

Yet here I was at De Luca's Cheese Shop and not at the Seward branch. It begged the question. Mama and Ileana thought I might prefer to stay upstairs during this horrible period. But Papa believed I should carry on as I usually would to convey that I'd done nothing wrong. That was the best way to silence gossip.

From his scrunched eyebrows and deep frown, I knew how much it upset Papa when, after they'd purchased their cheeses, regular customers said, "Oh, I heard about Zia…" My in-laws had a fine reputation in the neighborhood. Perhaps, I thought, there was a little envy and spiteful glee over the De Lucas being embarrassed. We had the new refrigerator in the shop, a telephone and another upstairs, and on top of all that, a record player. It might not seem like the splendor of the wealthy, but it was a lot in Little Italy.

Only one person came forward to defend me and that was from outside the neighborhood. Rachel Rodman put in a call to the store to tell me that she hadn't talked to the *Daily News* reporter and didn't know who had. "But we both know it must have been Edie," she said. "I've already told Mrs. Tuckle that she must do something to correct the errors in that horrible article. You weren't the 'confidante' of Miles Watkins. That article said he told you about his dead son? C'mon. Where did they come up with that?"

My fingers tightened on the telephone receiver. "I don't know," I said.

That, of course, was a lie. I did know. It must have been Lieutenant Frank Hudgins. I told him about Mr. Watkins' son. I'd felt he was a man of good intentions at the police headquarters. At Ferarra's, he'd looked right at me and said, "I'm trying to help you." But now, everything I'd told him was in the *Daily News*.

I hadn't had too high an opinion of the police up to this point. After all, the police headquarters was located in Little Italy, yet they ignored most crimes on our streets. Still, I hadn't hated them with the same strength as others in my neighborhood, who saw the cops as nothing but prejudiced dumb brutes. I'd have known how to deal with Lieutenant Hudgins if he'd acted like a prejudiced dumb brute. But he'd shown me courtesy, and combined with the sadness tugging at his eyes, I'd been fooled.

Thanks to that police lieutenant, my father-in-law had to stay on top of telephone calls from journalists – at least four pestered us – and get rid of the nervy writer who showed up at De Luca's in person for, as he put it, "a follow-up."

I took just two personal telephone calls myself, both upstairs. The first was from Rachel. The second was from the last person I wanted to see that awful article.

"What the hell have you gotten yourself mixed up with, Zia?" demanded my brother, Massimo.

His voice only grew louder as I tried to defend myself. We ended up fighting as only the two of us could. Each knew the vulnerabilities of the other and where to strike.

"If our mother and father were alive, they'd be so ashamed right now," he bellowed.

I slammed the phone down, tears burning my eyes. My loss of control alarmed my mother-in-law, who was frying breaded chicken cutlets a few feet away in the kitchen. So far, she'd been on my side. But she was the most pious matron on Mulberry Street. I couldn't count on her support forever, especially if she lost standing at church.

I pulled myself together, helping with dinner and getting my son ready for bed. I thought I'd put up a good front... mistakenly.

"What's wrong, Mother?" Michael asked as he wriggled his way under the covers.

"Nothing," I reassured him, pulling the blanket up and patting his pillow.

"That's not true," my son said. "You're sad. I can tell when you're sad."

I sat next to him and cupped his precious face in my hands. "I have some problems to solve, but they're my problems, and I don't want you to worry."

"Would it make you happy if I helped at church like Grandma wants me to?"

Now, where did that come from? I wondered.

"Grandma would be happy, which makes me happy," I said carefully. "But Michael, I only want you to do it if you're willing, if this is something you want."

Michael, his hair spread out on the pillow in little ringlets, thought for a moment, "I didn't want to do it for a while because I don't think of God the same way Grandma thinks of God."

"What do you mean?"

"She says God is looking after me and protecting me."

"Yes, that's what God does."

Michael's face crumpled in confusion, "I don't understand. Why doesn't God want me to have a father?"

My heart lurched as if it had left my body. I wasn't ready for this conversation, but ready or not, I'd have to try. "You do have a father, he's not with us here, Michael. He loved you very much. He was a good person, you must always remember that."

"He's in heaven right now?"

"Oh, yes. I know he is."

"Okay."

I kissed my son good night and got into my bed on the other side of the bedroom, the one I once shared with his father. So, now it begins, I thought bleakly. Trying to explain the inexplicable, to heal the wound left when Armando died.

I tried to empty my head of all this turmoil. I had to get sleep to face the challenges of the following day. Who knew what I'd have to deal with? After a few minutes, I could hear Michael's shallow breaths of sleep. I, however, was more alert than ever. Instead of clearing myself of feelings, I lay stiff and tense on the mattress, my arms crossed. I realized what emotion was doing this to me. Anger. But not with Lieutenant Frank Hudgins or Massimo.

I was seething with anger at Armando.

With a baby and a wife, you could have gotten out of enlisting in the army. But my brother was determined to go fight, so you had to go too. Now, I'm left here alone, having to defend myself against humiliating articles in the paper. Even after this dies down, I have to go on bringing up Michael without a father – and be stuck with your parents for the rest of our lives.

Lying in the darkness, I covered my mouth with both hands, even though I hadn't said a word aloud. Thinking those sorts of selfish, nasty things about my late husband and his parents filled me with horror. I prayed, I repeated a poem I learned long ago, I even silently sang the *Turandot* aria to exorcise myself of such anger. Finally, I fell asleep.

The next day, in a spirit of atonement, I was determined to be of the greatest help possible. I insisted on making breakfast for everyone, and after finishing the dishes, I headed to the shop. There was that same uncomfortable feeling of being scrutinized by customers who'd heard the gossip. But I was getting better at pretending not to notice.

I felt a little hope that the worst was behind me. Roberto said he'd stopped at the newsstand at dawn and found no additional newspaper articles about me. I wasn't even mentioned in the short articles saying the police had no leads on the investigation. Watkins' killing seemed to be sliding off the front pages of tabloid newspapers altogether. Roberto brought in the city's more serious newspaper, the *New York Times*, not because it contained an article about Mr. Watkins but for an article about Benito Mussolini and his plan to give the vote to women in Italy.

I picked up that newspaper later in the day to see what stories *were* deemed most important. They all had to do with money. The dominant headline was about Germany's shattered finances. Berlin was "*in crisis,*" I read, but "*Germany lost the war and must foot the bill.*" Here in America, a high official in Washington, D.C. faced charges of taking a huge bribe. There was some struggle between the U.S. Treasury Department and the J.P. Morgan Bank. "*The House of Morgan does not dictate national public policy,*" a government spokesman thundered.

The story that I couldn't help but find intriguing was that of a rum-running boat that had pulled off quite the deception in New Jersey. The boat had flown special red flags designated for vessels carrying dynamite. "Look out, dynamite aboard!" the crew had shouted into the night mist, should someone miss the flags and get too close. In reality, the ship was "*laden with liquor,*" and its disguise enabled the crew to bring the booze right to the dock near Atlantic City. This was given as an example of the many tricks used by brazen bootleggers. "*'Our cutters are preventing only a small part of the illegal alcohol trade,' said Coast Guard Commandant William Reynolds. 'This is entirely unprecedented in the history of our nation.'*"

One of the surprising things I'd learned about Mr. Watkins was that, in his capacity as deputy mayor, he'd been a liaison between the city and the Coast Guard. I wondered if he'd known about their frustrations.

As much as I'd have liked to read more about the dramas of the rum runners, my personal drama reclaimed my attention.

The minute the stranger came strolling into the shop, I knew the story. I exchanged a quick glance with Papa. He knew it too. Our "customer" was about thirty, wore his hat low over one eye, and had a cigarette hanging out of his mouth. He walked around the store, stopping in front of our table displaying Caciocavallo cheese. I kept doing what I was doing – wrapping some cured meats behind the main counter.

"I'm looking for Audenzia De Luca," he said to Papa.

"Mrs. De Luca isn't here."

"Yeah?" I felt his gaze slide over me and hover doubtfully. It helped that I'd had no picture in the paper. I suspected that I did not fit the man's expectation of Mr. Watkins' "confidante."

"When will Mrs. De Luca be back? I think she'll want to talk to me and get her side of the story into the paper."

"I don't have any idea," said Papa. Coming from him, that was a rude response. These people must be getting to him. But the reporter didn't react badly. I suppose he was used to hearing much worse. He handed Papa his business card to give to me and left.

I shook my head at the sight of that card. "How did he put it? I should 'tell my side of the story'?" That made me laugh.

Papa said, "Maybe he'll be the last."

Fearing that that wasn't a sure bet, we agreed I would go downstairs to work on the accounts. Just as always, the numbers took my mind off other things. Our sales were fairly steady, but we showed a dip of late. I hoped that our special-order trays, which we had spent real money on as speculation, would find favor with the restaurants. I didn't want to hear Roberto's sniping if the experiment failed.

When Papa came downstairs, I thought it was time to close and go to the flat.

"Not yet," he said as I started to put away the account books. "Roberto had to go around the corner to Dilapalo's, but Ileana's up in the shop. I just wanted to see how you were doing, have a moment here, just the two of us."

I smiled, "That would be nice."

It might have been his standing under the bare light bulb screwed into the ceiling, but my father-in-law looked tired. And I was responsible for this extra burden.

"Any more journalists in the afternoon?" I asked.

"Two on the phone, two in person."

I groaned, "I'm so sorry, Papa."

The bell tinkled upstairs – the one attached to the front door so that when it opened, everyone knew. Only a few seconds later, a man upstairs said, "Hello? Anyone here?"

Papa sighed, "I guess Ileana went with Roberto after all." He pointed at the card table, "You wait here. Just in case."

He trod upstairs, resentment etched in his movements. For Papa's sake, I hoped it wasn't a reporter. But unfortunately, I heard that question seconds later – "Is Mrs. De Luca here?"

"No, she isn't here and won't be back."

"Yeah? I really gotta speak to her," the man said. He sounded young with a Brooklyn accent, a little rough around the edges. They all seemed rough. It wasn't a gentleman's profession.

"She doesn't have anything to say to you," said my father-in-law. This was the harshest tone I'd ever heard him use.

"She might once she hears our offer. We are willing to pay for Audenzia De Luca's story. It'd be a nice bankroll, believe me. I have the money on me. We could do it tonight."

I winced at the sound of something so distasteful. Only women with bad morals sold their stories to the paper, like gun molls.

As if he could hear my thoughts, the reporter said, "It's not just the floozies who sell their stories. The sob sisters, believe me, they must pay women to get them to talk. It's more common than you think."

Papa said, "I've heard enough. What newspaper do you work for?"

This quarrel upstairs was making me feel sick. I couldn't sit any longer, but I had no intention of showing myself upstairs. That would be the worst thing I could do. I paced around the refrigerator. The young man had a response, but I couldn't quite make out the name, moving around as I was.

"Do you have a boss?" Papa demanded. "What do they call them — editors? Who's your editor?"

Again, I couldn't understand what he said.

"You won't tell me his name?" asked Papa. "Why not?"

Speaking louder, no longer trying to persuade, the reporter said, "You don't have to take it like that. This is a fair offer."

"Get out of my store," said Papa. He marched to the door leading downstairs. "There's nothing honest about you, and I *will* call your newspaper tomorrow."

He came crashing down the stairs, his face red with anger.

"Are you all right?" I asked, feeling a little scared.

He took a deep breath. "I'm fine, I'm fine. I shouldn't have lost my temper, it does no good. I'm sorry, Zia."

"Are you really going to call his editor?"

"No," he said, rubbing his temples. "Best to put this behind us."

The bells on the door jangled again. "I hope that's Roberto and Ileana," Papa muttered. But we heard no voices or steps. Roberto was a talkative man with a firm tread. Ileana would have made some noise herself. Not a floorboard creaked. Someone had walked inside the store and was now standing there.

"I hope that's not him coming back," Papa said.

"The reporter?" I said, aghast.

"Let me make sure. I'll be back in a minute."

Papa straightened his shoulders, took a steadying breath, and mounted the steps. He opened the door normally, not tearing it open in anger. A few seconds later, I heard him say, "May I help you?"

The loud explosive pop sounded like an auto engine backfiring. In the store? Did a car back up into De Luca's? Such an accident seemed impossible, yet that was the explanation in my head as I ran up the stairs.

No automobile in the store. No broken windows.

An acrid smell hung in the air, one I'd never known before.

"Papa? Papa?" I charged toward the door, assuming he was out on the street. There was an accident and someone needed help on Mulberry Street. Luigi De Luca would always help a neighbor in need.

I only got a few feet when I stumbled and fell face-first on the store floor. I'd tripped over something. I sat up and saw Papa, motionless. I had fallen over him.

The first of the waves enveloped me. I saw nothing, heard nothing, and felt nothing until Ileana screamed, a high, piercing howl. Roberto shouted, "My God, no. No!"

Someone was shaking me, "*Are you hurt? Zia, Zia, what happened?*" Hands felt my arms, legs, the back of my head, and other parts of my body.

"She's not wounded, Sergeant," I heard.

The second wave seized me, a stronger one. I was numb to everything and everyone, even the pushing and pulling. From far away, people called my name. I preferred the numbness. It was like a warm hug.

A horrid ammonia smell shot through my brain and jerked me from the numbness.

A man wearing a police uniform – not Lieutenant Hudgins, someone younger – said to me, "Mrs. De Luca, can you hear me?" I was sitting in a chair now, next to the counter. People filled the shop. It was loud and frightening, totally unlike our neat, orderly store. Someone sobbed, but I don't know who.

I nodded.

"The smelling salts worked," a voice said.

"What happened? Were you in the store when this happened? You must tell us who shot your father-in-law."

I opened my mouth, and nothing came out. I tried again. It was a hoarse, faint sound, but it was my voice.

"I was… in the basement. With Papa. We heard the bell. The door. Didn't know who. He went upstairs to see. I heard… explosion."

"When you came upstairs, you saw no one else in the store? No one ran out?"

"No."

The third and strongest wave claimed me. I passed out of the world of police and family and friends. After a long while, I felt like I was being pulled into the ocean. I saw those sorts of high cresting waves from the deck of the ship crossing from Palermo. Sal and I stood in the secret place we had carved out for ourselves, up where steerage passengers weren't supposed to be. We tried to imagine together what was beneath the waves, what kind of creatures.

I realized it wasn't a memory. I was with Sal again, and we were thrilled to look out over the Atlantic. The terrible thing hadn't happened. Maybe it never would. We had a second chance at that, a second chance at everything. This time, when we got to New York City, it wouldn't be so bad.

"Do you see any dolphins, Sal? They said there would be dolphins."

"No, Zia," my cousin said. "Not right now. We might see them later."

"Mother of God, she thinks she's on the boat from Palermo." That wasn't Sal's voice, it was my brother's. I'd never heard him like this. His voice was trembling.

"Shhhhhh," said Sal. "That won't help."

"Why do I have to be quiet?" I asked. "Do you think they can see us? Will we have to go down below?"

"You don't have to be quiet," Sal said, squeezing my hand.

That made me feel better. But what my cousin said next confused me. "It's time to leave this place, Zia. I know it's hard. You gotta do it. Michael needs you."

I shook my head, "I don't have a son yet. There is no Michael. No Armando."

I didn't hear any more from Sal. His voice went away. But strangers bothered me. Someone pulled my eyelids up, which hurt, and shone a bright light in my eyes. Cold metal instruments pressed down on my skin. I even felt strange tapping on my knees.

It was my brother, Massimo, who spoke to me next. He wasn't shaky now. He was firm and direct. He talked to me in Sicilian – he always sounded less fierce in that tongue.

"There's nothing wrong with you, Zia, not physically. You have to come out of this now. Okay? They won't let you stay in this hospital much longer. You should be over the nervous shock by now. The doctors say Beth Israel isn't the place for people with melancholia. You can't take up a bed for that here. If you can't start making sense, they're going to put you in the kind of place… I don't want you there. You don't want to be put there, believe me."

Nothing he said made sense, so I backed away from Massimo in my head. After a while, his wasn't the only voice. Another man said something. Massimo said, "Go ahead and try. Nothing else is working."

I didn't know who the second man was because I kept my eyes closed, but his voice made my breath come faster and my stomach turn over. He'd done something wrong to me. Somehow, I knew that. I didn't want him here.

"Mrs. De Luca, the person who shot your father-in-law is in jail. Victor Nettuno has been arrested. He can't hurt anyone else now."

I opened my eyes. That's when I realized I was lying in a bed, a white curtain pulled around me. It didn't smell too nice. Massimo had said "hospital," and good God, that's where I was, not the ship crossing the Atlantic or any other distant, magical place.

I didn't belong here.

Lieutenant Frank Hudgins stood next to the hospital bed, staring down at me, clutching his police cap.

"What did you say?" I asked.

"Victor Nettuno has been arrested for shooting Luigi De Luca."

"No," I said. "No, that's wrong. You've got it wrong."

CHAPTER FOURTEEN

FRANK

It took Frank a little time to realize that Zia De Luca was angry with him. She seemed distraught and disoriented, which was what he'd been warned about. But it was more than having gone through a crisis. Zia felt hostility toward Frank, and she told him why.

"You told the newspaper everything I said at Police Headquarters even after you said you would help me," she said, glaring from her hospital bed. Her brother, who Frank mistook for that cousin from Mulberry Street at first, had retreated to get the nurse. This gave them time to discuss the murder of her father-in-law.

"I didn't talk to any of the newspapers, Mrs. De Luca," he said, not defensively but gently. She was a frail, tiny figure propped up in bed, wearing a light-blue, frayed hospital gown. Her auburn hair, uncombed, tumbled below her shoulders. She drank a glass of water the nurse had brought, but after putting the glass down on the side table, she scowled at him once more.

"How did they learn what I told you?"

On that question, Frank had no idea. He'd written up his report based on the interview with Audenzia De Luca, two female employees of the Seward branch library, and her father-in-law, Luigi De Luca, who now, strangely, was also deceased. That report had gone to the desk of his superior and friend, Captain John Devlin.

Two days earlier, when Frank saw the *Daily News* article, he was dismayed and hurried to Johnny for answers.

"There's been a leak," said the captain with a grimace. "I hate it as much as you when this happens. I don't know how it happened."

"It's like someone handed the *Daily News* my report," said Frank. "The girl or anyone from the De Luca family could make a stink. What am I supposed to tell them?"

"Any of the De Lucas get in touch with you, send them to me," said Captain Devlin. "That's my job. And listen, don't you go see her or telephone her, got it? This is dicey, a leak in the middle of a murder investigation. Stay away for now."

Frank didn't like it. He also didn't like that the inquiry into the murder of Deputy Mayor Miles G. Watkins was going nowhere. The dead man's secretary, Faye Arky, was adamant that Watkins hadn't told her anything about meetings in the federal building or a train trip to Washington, D.C. He hadn't confided in any friends or extended family. Frank didn't plan to tell Zia this, but the leading theory was that the deputy mayor had invented his "important" meetings and D.C. trip to try to impress her. The flaw was that Watkins' driver did take him to the federal building and wait outside.

Usually, when a shooting took place, the police had a clue. Not with Watkins. It was like the killer had appeared out of nowhere and then vanished. The autopsy had yielded only the expected results. The bullets were the caliber for the kind of revolver popular with criminals, nothing to follow up there either. No police informant had heard a peep on the street from gangster circles. As for financial gain, his property and money were all going to a younger sister living in St. Louis who hadn't talked to Watkins in five years.

The De Luca murder, for all its devastating loss, was easy to solve by comparison. The victim's brother-in-law, Roberto Pellegrino, told police about the Black Hand extortionist harassing De Luca for years. When they picked up Nettuno, he denied the shooting but had a long record of robbery and violent assault – and no alibi for the evening of the Mulberry Street shooting.

Yet now, Zia De Luca was telling him they had the wrong man?

Frank defied the captain's order to stay away from Zia when he heard from the cop investigating the De Luca murder that she had suffered some breakdown and was in Beth Israel Hospital on the Lower East Side. "She won't talk. She's in her own world."

That had jolted Frank into action. He knew what it was like to try to talk to someone unable to respond. The thought of the intelligent, well-mannered Zia De Luca deteriorating into the same state as Berenice was unbearable. He had to help.

To the amazement of Zia's brother, she emerged from her mental stupor when Frank told her about the arrest.

"Nettuno is a despicable creature, but he had no reason to murder Papa," she insisted once they were alone. "He'd just been paid his usual cut within the last two weeks. We didn't refuse. The Black Hand strikes when you try to refuse. Why would he commit murder?"

"Someone like Nettuno, he doesn't need a reason that you or I would understand," Frank said. "He might have been drunk. Or his mind could have been scrambled by narcotics. His record has an arrest for drugs. Your brother-in-law said that Nettuno comes right before closing time. That's when the killer showed up. Your father-in-law might have said something that set him off."

Zia hit the side of the bed in frustration. "He didn't have *time*. Papa opened the door, stepped onto the floor, and I heard the shot. There weren't even ten seconds between the time Papa opened the door and was shot. You're telling me Nettuno walked in the door of our shop, and without even asking about the money he'd come to collect, which wasn't due for at least another week anyway, he immediately took out his gun and fired?"

Frank thought that didn't sound the likeliest scenario. But it wasn't out of the realm of possibility.

She sat up straighter, her eyes widening. "I remember something. Oh, I remember. Listen. Papa said, after he opened the door, 'Can I help you?' He was polite. Which means he didn't know the person who was waiting there or knew him only slightly."

That made something shift for Frank. As much as he didn't want this case to collapse into dust, she was right. It didn't sound like Luigi De Luca knew his killer by sight, which screwed up the Nettuno theory.

"Then there's the journalist who came just before that to try to give me money, and he and Papa argued."

"Whoa!" Frank threw up his hands. "Slow down, slow down, and tell me everything."

After hearing the entire story, Frank said, "Who else knows about this? What did the officer on the scene say?"

"I didn't tell anyone. In the store or here. I gather I've been feeling ill." She looked around as if she were fully taking in the surroundings for the first time. "Lieutenant, I must leave. I can't even think what Mama is going through. And Michael…" Her voice broke. "My son needs me. He loved his grandfather."

She took a deep breath to rally, and said, "I need a comb. I can't look like this going home."

129

Frank was able to beg one from a passing nurse and handed it to her. He watched Zia work the comb through her dark red hair, pulling and yanking with determination.

"I'm sure that your brother should be able to get you discharged from here now that you're more yourself," he said.

Frank had tried to separate his personal life from Zia's crisis, but he heard the wistfulness in his voice. Zia had pulled herself out of it, just as he always hoped and prayed that Berenice would – and never did. Just looking at her working through her hair made him feel strange.

As for how Zia might be feeling, she regarded him with that intense scrutiny. There were depths to her eyes, a far-seeing quality he had never witnessed in another woman. Even now, consigned to a hospital bed, Audenzia De Luca exerted a certain… power.

She said, "Yes, my brother can be very forceful. I should be out of here soon. But I won't be at peace until I know that you will look into this journalist."

"Look into him?"

"He made my father-in-law angrier than I've heard him since, well, forever. They had a fight. You must see that that needs to be looked into?"

Frank shook his head. He refused to humor her. It wouldn't do her any good to run around spouting delusional theories. "Mrs. De Luca, you're saying a newspaper reporter, after being denied an interview with you, came back and shot your father-in-law in the chest? That's just not possible. He'd have to be completely out of his mind."

"He didn't sound crazy, no," she said reluctantly. "But he was as angry as Papa, I'm telling you. He didn't like it when Papa said he would call his editor at the newspaper office to complain."

"You don't even know which newspaper he worked for."

"Lieutenant Hudgins, please call the big newspapers in New York City and find out who this man was. It shouldn't be impossible. I don't think the editor in charge of him would hide what they were doing. It's not illegal to offer to pay for someone's story, is it? They'll tell you, you're the police." Zia pursed her lips, thinking hard. "I didn't see him, but I heard his voice. He sounded young to me. And I think – I think he's from Brooklyn."

Frank realized a weakness in Zia's theory. "You told me before that your father-in-law said, 'Can I help you?' like he didn't recognize the person in the store. But they'd argued minutes before. So that rules out the newspaper reporter."

But she didn't back down. "There's something about that reporter. Something that is really... not right. You need to find out about him."

He sighed. "I couldn't do that, even if I wanted to. I'm not assigned to this case, Mrs. De Luca."

She frowned. "So, why are you here? Why do you even care about me or my family?"

That's a good question, he thought.

"I am on the Miles Watkins investigation, and you are a part of *that* investigation," he said stiffly. "I thought it would be helpful to inform you about the arrest in the death of Mr. De Luca. But the cases are in no way connected."

She said, "They are connected. The two deaths. They are."

"No, they aren't. Mrs. De Luca, you've been through a terrible shock. You're grieving. You aren't seeing this right. You need to go home and be with your family."

She raised a finger and pointed it at him. "You owe me a debt."

"A debt? Look, this isn't Sicily." Frank was sorry the second he said it. He shouldn't be insulting a woman in a hospital bed.

Zia pointed at him with even more force.

"I told you everything at Police Headquarters in trust that you would take care of that information, and I read about it in the *Daily News*. And you have no explanation for how it happened. Just like you have no idea who shot Mr. Watkins, even though it happened in public on a crowded street. Maybe that's good enough for your police force, but it's not good enough for me. Now, I'm asking you to find that reporter. I'm not asking you to fly to the moon. You can do it. It's best if it comes from you. But if you won't, *I* will make the telephone calls. If they don't answer, I'll go in person and wait outside the newspaper offices for someone to come out."

Frank put up both hands in surrender. "Enough, enough – I will call the newspapers. But you must accept whatever it is that I find out. Then my 'debt' is paid."

"Fine," she said. "And remember, I heard his voice. I would recognize it again."

Zia's brother and the nurse appeared at his side. It must be time to prepare her for discharge. But he needed to say one more thing in private. Frank asked them to wait out of earshot for another moment.

"Mrs. De Luca, I will find out what there is to know about the reporter who came to the store, but don't tell anyone else about him until after I've returned with my findings."

"Why?"

He didn't have a good answer. He couldn't talk to her about his gut feeling. She had little enough respect for him as it was. But the truth was, even though he didn't believe this reporter was the murderer of Luigi De Luca, something was going on, and he didn't like it. And Mrs. Audenzia De Luca seemed to be the center of it all.

In any case, it was unlikely the cop assigned to this case would go back to Zia with any questions. They had Nettuno behind bars. It would be with the prosecutor now.

"I won't say anything to the police, but I have to tell my family what I know," Zia said.

"No, especially not them. They're suffering a loss, the arrest is giving them a feeling of justice being done. You shouldn't rip that away without evidence."

"It's no good if the feeling is based on falsehood," she said.

Suddenly, it struck him, the absurdity of the situation – an immigrant woman who was an hour away from transfer to Bellevue giving him orders, arguing with him.

"Mrs. De Luca, just do what I tell you," Frank said brusquely, "for everybody's safety."

CHAPTER FIFTEEN

ZIA

Hundreds of extended family, friends, and neighbors attended the funeral service for my father-in-law at our parish church. Mourners filled each pew, and after there were no more seats, stood in the back. I know that Mama, in her grief, took comfort in the outpouring of love for Luigi De Luca. She had not been alone for a moment since Roberto had the terrible duty of telling her that her husband had been shot. So many people wanted to express sympathy and offer support. Our kitchen overflowed with dishes brought by friends. We had enough lasagna to last through Memorial Day.

The crowd reacted as one when Father Dominic said, "This life was taken by someone unfit to breathe the same air as Luigi De Luca." I heard hisses, strangled moans, and even curses. Everyone knew the priest was referring to Nettuno. Lieutenant Hudgins was right about how Little Italy regarded his arrest. A dozen times, I heard, "Thank God that animal is behind bars."

The lieutenant was also correct about how those closest to my father-in-law regarded Nettuno. They felt more anger than anyone else in the community but also relief and gratitude that justice was swiftly obtained. The Society of the Black Hand was *not* all-powerful.

How would they react if I said I thought that Nettuno was innocent? What would happen if I said the murder seemed connected to an unknown journalist who sought me out in the store shortly before Papa was shot?

The knowledge sank in that if I were proven right, I could end up bearing the blame for my father-in-law's death. It was stiflingly warm in the church with so many people crowded together, but I felt a chill deep in my bones. If only I'd never gotten mixed up in the investigation of Mr. Watkins' death. I wouldn't have landed in the newspaper, and Papa would still be alive.

I'd already taken note that people seemed uncomfortable in my presence. For Mama, there was an uncomplicated, caring concern. But I was still the woman written about in the *Daily News*. Moreover, after Papa was shot, I didn't help anyone cope. Instead, I lost my mind and had to be taken to a hospital. I'd shown such weakness and found it mortifying that everyone knew about it.

"And how are *you*, Zia?" People asked, lowering their voices to deal with the walking invalid.

I told everyone I was fine and thanked them for asking while trying to shift attention away from myself. They all seemed relieved and willing to make the shift.

Mama sat in the front row of the church with Roberto on her right side and Ileana on her left. A lot of other Pellegrinos materialized to prop up the family. They shared my mother-in-law's anguish at not just losing her husband but the fact that, due to the crime, his body could not be laid out at home in the proper way. He should have been cleaned, specially clothed, and placed in a bed with his feet facing the door. That would enable his spirit to leave. Tall candles lit day and night prevented spirits from hiding in the shadows. All mirrors would have been covered. The spirit must enter the next world quickly and with ease. All these customs existed to make that happen.

No, because of police involvement, men took Papa to the morgue and from there to a funeral home. Nonetheless, because he'd been such a good man, everyone was convinced his spirit passed untroubled to the afterlife. There would be no torment.

Sitting in the church, I reflected that Papa didn't have anything like the Pellegrinos, a sprawling clan of New York City. He had come over from Italy, an only child, with his parents. They were the ones who opened the store and poured everything they had into it. Papa had a single child, Armando, who had only one child himself. I sat on the far side of Ileana, my arm around Michael. It occurred to me that of all the people gathered in this church to mourn Papa, my son was the only one who shared his De Luca blood.

Massimo told me he was surprised that Mama had not asked Michael and me to ride with her to the cemetery. But I knew that there was only room for three in the funeral director's car, and Mama was relying completely on her brother and sister-in-law right now. Besides, Michael was getting much-needed support from *my* brother and sister-in-law.

I couldn't help but be grateful for Massimo. My brother had jumped into his car and driven to Little Italy the minute he heard about the shooting. He scooped up Michael and took him to the Bronx before heading to Beth Israel for an all-night vigil in my room. But that didn't mean he was without opinions.

"You'll need to watch the Neapolitanos like a hawk," Massimo whispered as we left the church for his automobile to drive to St. John Cemetery.

"Don't be like that," I said. "Papa was born in Naples, you know. These are his people. There's a picture of the patron saint of Naples, Saint Gennaro, in his coffin. He told everyone he wanted that."

"Who's talking about saints? That cheese store was always supposed to go to Armando, his only child, right? And then, after Armando died, it was set up for Michael. Or was it? Does it belong to the widow? You need to get your hands on the paperwork and the will. Block the Pellegrinos. First thing they might try is to bounce you from the store. They'll say, 'After you being in the hospital and all, you're too fragile to work.'"

I couldn't get my mind around trying to angle for money and stability. I didn't want to accept Massimo's cynical view. But it was true that the Pellegrinos were obsessed with the store. Without Papa, I wasn't sure where Michael and I stood.

This just gave me one more thing to worry about on the long drive to the cemetery. If only Lieutenant Hudgins had shared with me any progress on his investigation. I'd heard not a word from him. He'd said, "I'll come to talk to you end of the day Friday, Monday morning at the latest." Part of me hoped that he'd prove me wrong about who killed my father-in-law. But I knew I was right.

St. John Cemetery was in a place called Middle Village. I assumed the name came from its location: deep in the borough of Queens, east of Manhattan. Middle Village had more farms than you'd see in the rest of New York City, even in other parts of Queens. My son, sad as he was, pointed out the cows drowsily wandering behind fences, and the flustered chickens eyeing our car as it rumbled by. We passed a row of wooden houses followed by a cluster of German restaurants right before turning off the road into the cemetery. During the Great War, the German signs had become English ones, but I noticed that

Gasthaus and other German words had returned, painted in black Gothic letters on those white signs.

The cemetery itself was full of flower-dotted meadows and graceful maple trees. Birds chirped and cooed in the branches. Being a Catholic cemetery, it had a lot of shrines and stone angels rising above the headstones. You'd see not only priests but also monks, friars, and those brown-habit-clad Franciscan Sisters of the Poor shuffling around. It was verdant and very peaceful. I've occasionally thought that St. John had to be a nicer place for some of the Italians buried there than the cramped, noisy, violent neighborhoods where they had spent their lives. I'd read that thirty-five hundred people might live on a single block in Little Italy. In a cruel irony, only death could give them breathing space.

Papa had selected St. John years ago because, being so far from Manhattan, it yielded a crypt he could afford. Neapolitans had firm and specific ideas about burials and tombs, just as they did about dying itself. I know these ideas go back not just hundreds but thousands of years. Papa once told me Naples is built on a massive underground complex of Greek tombs, governed by a mysterious cult of death. And on everyone's horizon rises the raging Mount Vesuvius, forever on the verge of eruption and wiping out entire cities. In Naples, death was always present, above and below.

It seemed like half the people in church made the long trip from Little Italy to Middle Village. They parked their automobiles and waited patiently for the hearse to rumble forward. The pallbearers carried his flower-strewn coffin to the grave beside the crypt, and we followed in a short silent procession. I walked with Michael, right behind Mama and Roberto and Ileana. I avoided looking at the family crypt. I'd visited it many times, as my husband rested there.

Papa had designated places inside it for himself and his wife – and for me, too, to rest beside Armando. Today, for whatever reason, the sight of it filled me with dread approaching a fear that I worried I'd be unable to control.

It would seem logical to carry the coffin into the crypt this afternoon. But that's not how they always did it in Naples, so that's not how we were doing it today. The loved one is buried or placed somewhere in waiting and then, after a specific amount of time, set in the crypt in a separate ceremony. I don't know if Papa had asked for this, along with having the picture of Saint Gennaro put in his coffin, or if these were Mama's wishes. It wasn't my business. I was just grateful I wouldn't have to step inside the crypt with my nerves so shattered.

The priest began to say his words, yet I could not follow them. It was hitting me, as if for the first time, the enormity of losing my father-in-law. I'd lived under his roof since I married Armando in 1914. He always said I was like a daughter to him. While no one could replace my father, the truth was I always got along very well with Luigi De Luca. I looked up to him. His kindness and thoughtfulness meant the world to me. What would I do without his gentle face at the dinner table, in the store, in our corner of the living room listening to opera? When I thought of what he'd said about the aria in *Turandot*, his insight into what troubled me, pain clawed me.

Papa had reached only fifty-two years of age. It wasn't fair. He should have lived long enough to see Michael grow up. I had sworn I would not lose control, but tears streamed down my face, and I couldn't stop them. It wasn't only the grief of losing him, as wrenching as that was. A voice inside kept clamoring – was I responsible? Had

I brought about his death? Thank God for the veil that hid my face. If only I could stop my body from trembling.

Massimo laid his hand on my back. That helped me go still. No one was tougher on me than my brother, but it was as if that was his prerogative alone. He was fierce in protecting me from anyone else's criticism or judgment.

The priest finished. It was time for each of us to lay a red rose on the coffin. My mother-in-law, her head bowed, did so first, with sad dignity. To my enormous relief, I managed to follow her example. No breakdowns. I helped teary-eyed Michael pick out a red rose so he could pay tribute.

Many people lined up to lay down their roses. I noticed a new group of mourners, a cluster of men arriving late. They hovered to the side, down by the cemetery road, talking to one another. The one in the middle was the most important. A dozen others all seemed to turn to him in deference. But in any setting, he would have stood out for his size. He was enormously fat. He wore a black suit as was appropriate for a funeral. He must have had it custom-made to fit over that belly.

It took the man a few minutes to reach the line of people with roses. To my surprise, people began getting out of line and making deferential gestures, even bowing, as if encouraging the large man to move ahead of them.

"I don't believe it," whispered my brother Massimo. "That's Joe the Boss."

I half-turned to look at him inquiringly. "Whose boss?"

"Holy Mother, don't you know who Joe Masseria is?" my brother asked.

"No."

"Last year, he took over the Morello family. They control Little Italy, East Harlem, a chunk of the Bronx."

"What do you mean, 'control'? What businesses does the family control?"

Massimo said, "The gangster kind."

How could he have the gall to attend the funeral of a man everyone believed to have been killed by another gangster? A petty criminal, not a "boss," but they were cut from the same cloth.

The man I now knew to be Joe Masseria beckoned for someone else in his group – a man also dressed in a dark suit, though younger and a lot slimmer – to come forward. With a sickening lurch of my stomach, I recognized him. It was my cousin, Salvatore Lucania. After listening to whatever Masseria said, Sal nodded and turned toward the funeral party.

I took a step back when I realized Sal was heading right for Massimo and me. I didn't want to be singled out by an emissary from a gangster. My brother said crushingly, "Keep your mouth shut, Zia, and let me handle this."

Massimo stepped in front of me and shook hands with Sal.

"What's going on, cousin?"

"Mr. Masseria wants to pay his respects to the widow, Mrs. De Luca, and say a few words to her directly," said Sal, as matter-of-factly as if he were telling us that a plumber wanted to install new pipes in the building.

Massimo swallowed and said, "Let me ask her."

I couldn't hear what my brother said to Mama. She stared at him, not comprehending. Her brother Roberto jumped in and spoke animatedly to Massimo for a couple of minutes. Mama clung to her brother's arm, her face crumpled in confusion, before tapping Roberto's arm to calm him down. Finally, Roberto nodded.

Sal said, "Thank you," and with all eyes on him, he beckoned to Joseph Masseria.

It wasn't a hill Masseria had to climb to reach us, it was a modest rise of ground. But due to his weight, Masseria moved slowly. Or perhaps he just found the grass slippery. At last, he made it to the funeral party. His face shone with sweat. First, he flung a rose on the coffin. Then he turned toward my mother-in-law.

"You have my condolences, Mrs. De Luca," he said in English with a strong Italian accent. "Why this person would do such a terrible thing to a fine man like your husband, I don't know. I don't know. He won't do anything like that again."

"Thank you," Mama said.

Roberto leaned forward to say loudly, "Yes, the murderer is in jail."

Masseria's gaze flicked in Roberto's direction, and he gave a little smile. His plump cheeks rose when he did so, turning his eyes into narrow slits.

"If you need anything, anything at all, you just gotta ask," Masseria said to my mother-in-law. He bowed solemnly, his right hand pressed over his heart. It was a showy, faintly ridiculous gesture. No one could ever drum up the courage to laugh at Joe the Boss, though, and I'm sure he knew it. He turned toward my cousin and said, "Thank you, Charles."

Masseria bowed and shuffled back to where his group waited for him, my cousin maintaining a pace of two steps behind him, which wasn't easy because Sal is tall with a long stride.

Joe the Boss didn't get back into his car right then and leave St. John, as I'd expected. Some of the mourners approached him. He shook hands and chatted with them amicably.

After the last rose was flung and people were beginning to return to their automobiles, I asked my brother what exactly Joe Masseria oversaw.

Massimo said, "Gambling, loan sharking, the rackets, the ladies. Probably bootlegging."

I felt a rush of anger with Sal. He hadn't been straight with me at my birthday party. He hadn't denied he was mixed up with criminals, but he definitely hadn't indicated he was in cahoots with one of the biggest crooks in New York. If Sal's parents had come to the cemetery today, they'd have died of shame.

A funeral was no place for me to have it out with him, though. When Bianca said, "Let's get you back to Mulberry Street," I agreed it was time to go.

I told Mama we would meet at home, and we started toward Massimo's automobile. But I couldn't keep from glancing over at the Masseria group along the way. The fat man was still talking to the mourners. Twenty feet behind him, arms folded, leaning against an automobile, I spotted Sal. I guessed he couldn't leave the cemetery before the "Boss."

With that, it became impossible for me to leave the cemetery without confronting my cousin.

I said to Massimo, "I'll be at the car in a minute – stay with Michael," and hurried to Salvatore's car.

"Zia, what are you doing?" my brother demanded, but he was talking to my back. As I got closer, I saw who should be with Sal but Vito, the hard-eyed young Italian he'd had in tow in the Bronx. They were in close conversation, puffing cigarettes.

I flipped the black veil off my face. Sal was going to know who was telling him off. He caught sight of me as he extinguished a cigarette into the ground with the toe of his black shoe.

"Hello, Zia," my cousin said. "I didn't want to pull you away from the De Lucas here today. I planned to come by to see you tomorrow and make sure you were okay."

"Don't bother," I said.

Sal raised his eyebrows at me, but he didn't seem offended. He asked Vito to excuse him while he talked to me for a minute. Vito shrugged, not in a hurry. He must not be holding onto any boxing tickets today.

Sal gestured for us to talk a few yards away, among the tombstones.

"So, you work for Joe the Boss?" I asked my cousin.

"I know him, and he knows me," Sal said, calmly pulling a thread from his sleeve. "You could say our paths tend to cross. He heard about your father-in-law and wanted to do something – to come out here to the cemetery. He couldn't just show up like a nobody. He was looking for someone who knew Luigi De Luca personally. Someone told him I knew the family. He asked me, as a favor, to intercede."

I said snidely, "I bet it helps you if Joe the Boss owes you one."

"Well, Zia, as a matter of fact, yeah. It could come in handy."

Sal's refusal to show any embarrassment over demonstrating to everyone that he associated with criminals drove me crazy. Taking a wild guess, I said, "This must mean Joe Masseria has a piece of The Orchid Hour too."

"What?" Sal had been bouncing on his heels a little, a habit he'd had since he was a kid, and we called him "rubber legs." When I mentioned The Orchid Hour, his legs straightened like steel girders, and he laughed. "What a riot. A Mustache Pete like Joe calling the shots at The Orchid Hour? No, no, no. He's got nothing to do with that."

"Zia, c'mon, let's go," shouted my brother, who'd followed me part of the way.

I wasn't ready for this conversation to be over. I certainly hadn't gotten the better of my cousin yet.

"You don't need to get riled up, Zia," said Sal, more seriously. "He's just somebody who felt bad about your father-in-law and wanted to do something. Even Joe Masseria is a person, hard to believe, I know."

Massimo grabbed my arm, no longer willing to wait, and marched me to the car.

He said in my ear, "I know you are tight with Sal, but consorting with him in front of everyone after we all see he's a top lieutenant for Joe the Boss? You want to make the Lucanias look as bad as humanly possible?"

"I wasn't 'consorting.' I was mad at him. I wanted to punch him, to be honest."

"Really? Because I could hear Sal laughing from across the cemetery. That's quite a punch."

So, my rash action hadn't done anything but make the wrong impression on everyone. I didn't realize just how wrong until a few minutes later when I was about to get into the back seat next to Michael. Roberto Pellegrino, in the front seat of the funeral director's car, gave me a long stare as they rumbled by.

My thoughts were such a pained jumble on the drive back. Bianca and Massimo kept up some chatter with Michael. One of their sons liked the same comic strips as Michael, so they knew enough to ask him questions about that.

We were nearing Manhattan when Michael fell asleep, his head in my lap. It was only then that Massimo returned to the topic of Joe the Boss.

"I don't get it, I just don't," he said. "They arrest Nettuno, everybody says, '*Bam*, we got the killer.' Except to murder De Luca like that, he'd have had to clear it with Masseria first, or it was Masseria's idea. And it wasn't, that's for sure. It's one thing to throw cops off your trail, but he wouldn't put on an act in front of Father Dominic, his family priest."

"Are Joe the Boss and Nettuno connected? From what you say, they must be."

"Nettuno is far, far down the ladder with the family. Like, at the bottom. But no one makes a move in Little Italy without Joe getting some cut. It used to be Guiseppe Morello. Now, it's Joe."

I tensed. "And you're sure he didn't order it and just come to the funeral?"

"No, no. Impossible. If Joe did, he wouldn't say the murder was a bad thing to the widow and hold his hand over his heart. He'd never lower himself, no matter what. Masseria is a Neapolitan, and so was your father-in-law. He wouldn't want an ordinary Neapolitan – a businessman everybody liked, and who was paying collection without any argument – to be shot in his own store. Nettuno must be out of his mind. I heard from someone he's sick. That's the only explanation. He's sick in the head."

I felt a rush of emotion. Was this the moment to tell people in my family what I thought, what I *knew*, about how Luigi De Luca died?

No, I'd gone through enough turmoil today and put everyone else through enough of it too. Lieutenant Hudgins said he'd call me or come to see me tomorrow, Monday. That's when everyone would learn what I'd learned.

CHAPTER SIXTEEN

FRANK

After Frank left Zia in Beth Israel Hospital, he started making telephone calls immediately. She clearly had not known that there were fifteen newspapers in the city. It took until the end of the following day to finish the calls. Frank got through to every single daily newspaper covering crime and spoke to each reporter on the Miles Watkins case. The answer to the question, "Did you approach Mrs. Audenzia De Luca and offer her money to tell her story?" was *no* every time.

In the case of the *Daily News*, Frank also talked to the city editor. Maybe it wasn't the reporter assigned to Watkins' shooting who went to Little Italy to get her story but a second writer. Frank wanted to cover all the bases.

"We don't pay people for stories," the city editor snarled. "We don't need to stoop to that."

"How about your competitors?" Frank pressed. "Who *would* do it?"

"Pay for the librarian's side? We got all there is worth printing. Don't think the deputy mayor was shtupping her. The dead son makes people feel sad. And his murder's not a hot story anymore. Plenty of other crimes to cover that are juicier."

When Frank put down the phone, it was six o'clock Friday. He headed home for the weekend feeling unsettled. By now, he should have identified the reporter who wanted to offer Zia money. Not only did he have no leads on that, but also the city editor, in all his crudity, had made a convincing case that no real journalist would offer a "big bankroll" for Zia's story.

So who went to De Luca's Cheese Shop in search of Zia? He had to have some idea of that before speaking to her. He'd promised her a call by early Monday. By that time, something had better have taken shape in his brain.

All day Saturday, Frank felt restless. There were a dozen half-completed chores in the small house he'd shared with Berenice before her health broke down. When she got better, he didn't want her to return to a home falling down. Yet he found himself without focus. He couldn't seem to finish anything, not the collapsed bookshelf nor the sink that didn't drain right.

He could not get his mind off Miles Watkins and Luigi De Luca. She could not be correct when she said the two murders were connected. Why would someone go after Watkins and then turn toward her? If no genuine newspaper reporter had shown up trying to pay her for her story, who was that man she'd heard upstairs arguing with her father-in-law?

Sunday was one of those bright, sunny days in New York that promised summer around the corner. It made for a comparatively easy drive upstate. Turning onto the drive to Highland Retreat, Frank noticed that the forsythia bushes no longer blazed brilliant yellow but were turning green. It depressed him, as sometimes happened when he had no choice but to observe the change of seasons.

There was no question that Frank felt more irritable than usual when the nurse opened the door to the fourth-floor special ward for family visiting day. Someone propped up Berenice in bed the same as always, silent and staring. Actually, she looked worse. It took him a while to figure out what it was.

"Nurse, did someone new wash and set Mrs. Hudgins' hair?" he asked.

"I don't believe so," she said.

"The part in her hair is all over the place. My wife always, *always* took good care of her hair. For the fees you charge here, can't she look presentable on a Sunday?"

"I think her hair looks the same as it always does, but I will pass on your comments to the rest of the staff, Mr. Hudgins," the nurse said, her cheeks reddening, before she stalked off.

Lord, that was a blunder, Frank thought. He needed the nurses to be on his side, to be motivated to take care of Berenice. After sitting with his wife for a while, he got up to stretch his legs and brainstorm a graceful apology to the nurse.

Peering out the window, Frank took note of all the people walking the grounds, enjoying the view of the Hudson River. Too crowded for his taste.

One blond man who stood near the entrance to the grounds, his eye on the front door, made Frank's wandering gaze stop. He squinted. That looked an awful lot like Johnny Devlin, but how could it be?

The man below turned to get a better look at the figure of a young woman walking by. That sidestep double take was a move Frank had witnessed for years.

"What the hell," he whispered.

It *was* Captain John Devlin.

Minutes later, Frank was downstairs. Devlin waved when he spotted him and grinned.

"You planning on telling me that you just happened to be in the neighborhood?" Frank said.

Devlin's smile froze. "We need to talk," he said.

The two men walked in silence to a spot overlooking the sparkling Hudson River. Sailboats drifted by. On a little piece of land jutting out a hundred yards to the south, a family of picnickers had spread a blanket. But they couldn't relax because their dog kept barking at large birds swimming just out of reach in the water.

Frank said, "What's so important it couldn't wait for Monday morning?"

"You know I've got family upstate. I like it up here. I've never seen Highland Retreat – just heard about it. 'Sposed to be a place with fees that would break the bank."

"Why is that your problem?"

Johnny narrowed his eyes, "Because you're becoming *my* problem, Frank. Why are you calling every newspaper in New York City asking whether they sent a reporter to offer money to Audenzia De Luca?"

So *that* was what had brought the police captain to the Hudson Valley.

"I got an interesting tip," Frank said with a shrug.

"Yeah? Well, it got interesting all right. Your little phone calls got back to somebody and caused the kind of interest you don't want – and I don't either. You're going to drop it. Now. You're off the Watkins investigation."

Frank was struck speechless by this reaction. Devlin turned away to stare at the river.

"You're my oldest friend, Frank," the captain said in a low voice. "I'm looking after you, and that's God's truth."

Frank regained his voice and spat, "Bullshit."

"Whoa. Watch it, buddy."

Frank said, "Do you know who killed Miles Watkins?"

"No."

"I don't believe you. Why else are you steering me away?"

"Believe what you want. You always do, you like to put your head in the sand and not deal with reality. I don't get that break. Watkins was becoming a threat to people who don't play games."

"How could he be a threat to anybody?"

Captain John Devlin stayed silent for a long time. The picnickers' dog grew even more frantic. His barking was hysterical. But the birds were geese – vicious when they chose to be. The dog could lose his snout if he didn't watch out. Frank waited for the captain to answer, impatience mingling with dread. He both wanted to know what Devlin was circling telling him and he didn't.

"You know that this year, it became the law – the *law* – that the New York police were not supposed to use their resources to enforce the Volstead Act, the federal law that prohibits the sale of alcohol," Captain Devlin said.

"Everybody knows that. What has that got to do with Watkins? You tell me what's really going on – and *then* we can talk about me dropping the investigation."

"Booze can serve a lot of purposes, Frank. It's not just about getting ossified. Drinking can bring different people together. Important, necessary people. There's something new called The Orchid Hour. It can't be touched. This was the wrong time to go to Washington, D.C. about illegal alcohol."

Frank shoved his hands in his pockets, struggling to figure out what Devlin was trying to tell him. Was this all about protecting bootleggers?

"The Orchid Hour," he repeated. "What the hell is that?"

"Christ, I just explained it to you – it's something we can't touch," said Devlin. He threw his arm out in a wide circle, taking in the river, the emerald-green lawn, and the stately brick building. "This is quite a nice hospital. Is Berenice getting better?"

Frank didn't feel like talking about his wife. But Johnny had been the best man at the wedding. It wasn't out of line for him to ask after her.

"With this chronic condition, it's pretty tough," Frank said. "There hasn't been much change in the last year."

"I'd hate to see her have to leave Highland Retreat."

Frank caught his breath, "Why would she leave?"

"It's time to get off your high horse. C'mon, there's no chance that you are paying for this place on your salary. It's being covered with your share of the A Fund."

Frank shook his head in disbelief that Devlin said it. Within six months of Prohibition becoming law, the bribes started rolling in. Police officers were paid to stand down with discreet shares of the A Fund, and since practically no one on the force thought alcohol should be illegal, they were happy to take the payoffs while concentrating on solving *real* crimes.

Johnny said, "It seems I need to spell it out. If you don't pull out of the Watkins investigation and everything to do with Audenzia De Luca, that spigot gets turned off. You're on salary alone. Understood?"

Captain John Devlin held the gaze to make sure.

"You son of a bitch," Frank said. "You miserable son of a bitch."

Devlin slapped his oldest friend on the back. "I've got to hit the road, buddy. You take care." He strode toward the parking lot, calling over his shoulder, "And give my love to Berenice."

CHAPTER SEVENTEEN

ZIA

On Monday morning, I walked Michael to school, a duty I was glad to take over from Mama. It was the only thing to be glad about. I wasn't wanted in the store. My brother Massimo was right. Boy, was he ever.

"You need a break, Zia," Roberto Pellegrino told me in the flat. "Take it easy for a while. We got the store covered. You concentrate on Mama and Michael."

"You are going to need me downstairs," I said.

"But you were kept in a hospital overnight from shock, Zia. It'd be wrong to put you to work right away in the same spot where we lost Luigi. I'm not saying forever. Just a week. Or maybe a month. We're just thinking about you."

"I *always* helped Papa with the accounts," I insisted. "I have a complete system set up. I won't be on the floor, but I need to work on the books."

"We can handle the books." Roberto took my hands in his, clasping them tight as he smiled down at me. "This is what your mother-in-law wants, too," he said, the shadow of a warning in his tone.

I needed to hear from Lieutenant Hudgins. After taking Michael to school, I hurried back to the apartment, my stomach fluttering with tension. I learned that no one had telephoned while I was gone.

However, two of Mama's friends were paying a call. I made coffee for them and served it. Her friends had brought dishes for lunch, which we did not need. The refrigerator and cabinets were bursting with food. However, to be polite, I prepared their offerings to be served. I also washed the breakfast dishes, cleaned the kitchen counters, swept the floor, and gathered clothes from the bedrooms for laundering.

I don't hate household chores. It's usually Mama's domain, but housework was the least I could do under the circumstances. It felt strange to be neither at the public library nor the cheese shop. As I scrubbed and grated and brewed and swept, I couldn't help but ask myself why Roberto did not consider me too weak for this work, but I had to be spared from labor at De Luca's Cheese.

After the clock ticked past noon, I could no longer wait and excused myself from Mama's lunch. It was risky to make this call in the kitchen, but that's where the telephone was.

"Lieutenant Hudgins, please," I said when someone answered at Police Headquarters, speaking just loud enough to be heard on the other end of the line.

"What's the nature of the call?"

"This is Mrs. De Luca. He'll know what it's about."

I waited so long that I thought they'd forgotten about me. Finally, someone picked up the telephone, a different voice from the one before.

"Lieutenant Hudgins is unavailable, Mrs. De Luca."

I relayed the message that I needed to hear from him, gave the number again, and hung up.

The next few hours felt increasingly unbearable. The phone rang a few times, but it was friends or family wanting to check on Mama and me. I hurried them off the line, trying not to be rude. And still, Lieutenant Hudgins failed to call.

154

I retrieved Michael from school. By the time we got back, I found we'd welcomed more of Mama's solicitous friends, bearing dishes of course. I brewed coffee and returned to cleaning. And though I hated to face how late it was in the day, I had no choice but to start preparing dinner.

All sorts of uncomfortable thoughts kept bubbling up inside me. What was my place here? The *ordine della famiglia* meant that I must not act in my interest but for the good of the family. There was no question about how to do that when Papa was alive. I lived here with their grandson. But what about now? I didn't feel the same loyalty to the Pellegrinos – and I suspected they were not that crazy about me, either. I couldn't imagine moving in with Massimo and Bianca in the Bronx, though.

I'd just put food on the table when the telephone rang. Telling myself it was another family friend, I answered the call calmly with, "De Luca residence."

After a few seconds of silence, a man grunted, "Zia De Luca?"

"Yes. Who's calling?"

"I got your… message that you left." The words sounded slurred, but I recognized Lieutenant Hudgins. Relief flooded through me.

"Do you have news?"

To my horror, he started laughing. "News? Yeah, I have news, but nothing for you. Can't do it. Orders. Can't."

"Are you – have you been drinking?" I asked incredulously.

"Sure have." He stopped laughing. "It's the only thing to do now." The lieutenant sounded so despondent that it was possible I just heard his voice break.

My fingers tightened on the long phone cord. Nothing in his character that I'd seen so far made me think he could lose control of himself. The worst was I sensed it had something to do with the investigation that involved me. What in God's name had he learned to reduce him to such a state?

"I need to talk to you immediately," I said. "Where are you?"

"We can't talk again, Mrs. De Luca. No way. Not on the phone. Not in person. Jesus, not in person."

"Why not?"

"Because of *Berenice*," he said, turning belligerent. "I can't put her in some city hell hole. You wouldn't want that kind of hospital for her, would you?"

"No, of course not," I said, trying to soothe him while having no idea what he was talking about.

"Good."

"But I think we should talk tonight," I said. "We can meet somewhere that no one will see us."

There was a long silence.

"What the hell," he muttered. "What the hell. Come to Tompkins Square Park, southwest corner."

"I'll be there as soon as I can," I said. "Wait for me."

Mama looked aghast when I said I had to go out. "I need to see a friend," I said. "Everything is fine. I won't be long."

"I heard you say on the telephone, 'Have you been drinking?'"

"No, no," I said with a forced smile. "I asked her if she had any coffee left for me. That's all." I snatched a sweater from the hook on the wall and ran for the door. "Save me a plate of dinner. And don't worry."

Tompkins Square Park wasn't far, but it wasn't around the corner either. It would be dark within the hour, and I feared after that, it would be a challenging task to find a drunk, unstable man. Walking as fast as I could short of running, a stitch was pulling in my side when I reached 7th Street and Avenue A.

I didn't spot Lieutenant Hudgins standing on the corner. I couldn't figure out why he'd chosen this particular park. It was the radicals' favorite stomping ground, notorious for being the place of protests, marches, and calling strikes. For generations, police had beaten people in Tompkins Square if they fought for their rights, often hitting them with batons while on horseback. I had to wonder if there was a message in this locale for me.

But the man I'd spoken to on the phone sounded broken, incapable of either a bad joke or an implicit threat. I finally found Lieutenant Hudgins slumped on a park bench twenty feet from the corner, staring at the ground. He wasn't wearing his blue uniform or even a hat.

"Lieutenant," I said, loud enough to break his morose stare.

He looked up. "Mrs. De Luca."

"You're not in uniform," I said, feeling awkward.

"Put myself on plain-clothes detail today," he said, trying to smile but failing. I could smell the whiskey from six feet away.

"I can see you are… upset, but you said last week that you would let me know by Monday morning what you've learned about the newspaper reporter who came to the store."

He nodded. "That I did."

"So, what happened?"

He took a deep breath, as if preparing to execute a feat of strength. "I called every newspaper, Mrs. De Luca. You know what? None of them sent a reporter to offer you money for your story."

"What?" I asked. "I don't believe it. Are you trying to say you think I made it up?"

"No, I'm not."

Lord, this was hard. I wanted to shake him.

"Then what's the explanation?"

"Someone wanted to talk to you about Miles Watkins, but not coming from any newspaper. Someone dangerous."

I froze where I stood. "Why? Why would anyone do that?"

He shook his head, looking down again.

"Please don't say you don't know," I said, losing grip on my frustration. "You *do* know. And you're not supposed to tell me. Because you've been threatened, right?"

"Not me," he said. "I don't give a damn what happens to me."

He must be referring to "Berenice." Someone had threatened her, said she'd be put in a hospital. She had to be his wife or girlfriend. Who would do that to a police lieutenant without fear of reprisal? Whatever pressure they put on him, it worked. He didn't want to pursue this any further. But if there was one thing I was sure of, it was that I would keep pursuing this. I had heard the voice of the "journalist," and I knew I would recognize it again. That was my ace in the hole.

To take next steps, I had to get more information out of Lieutenant Hudgins. The trouble was, how? I could tell he wanted to help, to do his job, but someone blocked him.

I sat next to him on the cold bench. "Isn't it important that the truth comes out?" I asked, not with anger but in a reasonable tone. "Nettuno is a terrible man, but if he didn't shoot my father-in-law, shouldn't that be known?"

"Ha!" He twisted away from me on the bench. "I don't think it matters to Nettuno."

"Why not?"

"Because three hours ago, someone stuck a knife in him, not once or twice but seven times. He's dead."

More violence? The nightmare kept deepening.

"How could a man be murdered in jail?"

He said wearily, "It happens all the time in The Tombs."

I said slowly, trying to keep my voice steady, "So when you say that someone dangerous came to the shop, it's with the knowledge of not just the shootings. You're also thinking of Nettuno getting stabbed seven times. These three deaths – Mr. Watkins, my father-in-law, and Nettuno – are connected."

"Yeah, I think they could be connected. To prove that, there would have to be an investigation with a lot of manpower and a lot of resources. But that can't happen."

A young couple strolled by, beaming at each other. The woman broke the gaze of her beloved for a second to look down on me sitting with Lieutenant Hudgins. She smiled as if to say, "Isn't it wonderful to be in love? Don't you feel it too?" Mercifully, the two of them kept going.

I turned to Lieutenant Hudgins and said, "If you *were* able to investigate, what would you do?"

I was silently thrilled to see him consider my question for a while. His drunkenness might have receded just the right amount. I could draw out of him some police knowledge.

He said, "I'd sweat that secretary at City Hall. She knows a lot more than she's told so far."

The chances of me being able to "sweat" a deputy mayor's secretary were so remote as to be non-existent.

"Anything else?"

"I'd put an undercover officer in The Orchid Hour, either a regular customer or, even better, on the staff."

The cast-iron streetlamps came alive just as he said that. They must be on a timer. The golden globes illuminated the sidewalks, scraggly bushes, and low trees. I didn't care about being able to see the park. The switch from darkness to light was my awareness bursting that The Orchid Hour played a part.

I suspected that Lieutenant Hudgins assumed, in his alcohol-fueled state, that I already knew that The Orchid Hour was involved. I didn't want to spook him, so I said, as casually as possible, "And who is behind that nightclub?"

"Arnold Rothstein and a bunch of gangsters." He looked past me at a large bush. "Yeah, you thought I wouldn't be able to find out anything on my own, but I'm not the moron you think I am!" He wasn't talking to me, I realized, or to the bush, but to someone who had underestimated him.

"I've heard of Arnold Rothstein," I said, keeping it conversational. Which was true. Newspapers wrote about Rothstein, and I remember Roberto mentioning him. He found Rothstein remarkable, but not for deeds that would win anyone praise from the New York City mayor. Unfortunately, I was hazy on just why he was newsworthy. I didn't want the lieutenant to realize how little I knew.

"Why do you think Arnold Rothstein is backing The Orchid Hour?" I asked.

"Well, he's The Brain, right?" The lieutenant's voice was full of loathing. "The man who fixed the World Series. That's why they call him The Fixer too. He only goes for sure things. There's something about this club that means big money for the group. It can't be just another speakeasy opening."

"And this 'group' is behind the murders?" I asked, my heart racing. My cousin Sal was one of the gangsters who owned the club. Could Salvatore, my blood, bonded to me from childhood, the man who gave me a special birthday present and visited me in the hospital, be capable of such deception and violence? I ached to ask about Sal's role. But I'd introduced Lieutenant Hudgins to my cousin on Mulberry Street – I'd not used his street name of Charles, although I had said "Lucania," and there hadn't been any recognition at the time. I don't think he knew about Sal's specific involvement in The Orchid Hour or anything about my cousin.

"Could be one of them behind the murders, could be all of them," Lieutenant Hudgins said. "That's what the undercover would try to find out. Who has so much to lose with The Orchid Hour that he'd shoot Deputy Mayor Miles Watkins or hire someone else to do it? That's the question. And how could Watkins have stopped them from doing anything? What the hell did he know?"

"And you think an 'undercover' policeman could find out?"

"That's what they do. Take on a new identity, try to blend in, get the criminals to trust them, and—" Lieutenant Hudgins broke off and hit his thigh with a closed fist, "That's it!"

"What?"

"They think *you* know something, that Watkins might have taken you into his confidence about something that could lead to The Orchid Hour. That guy posing as a journalist was planning to give you money to coax it all out of you."

"But I don't know anything."

"They don't know that. Yeah, someone was trying to cover the bases."

Unable to hide my anger, I said, "How does shooting my father-in-law instead of me 'cover the bases'?"

"I don't have any idea, Mrs. De Luca." He staggered to his feet, took out a handkerchief, and wiped his face.

Sounding less drunk, he said, "Listen, even though I've been ordered off the investigation, if you could call it that, I'm not going to turn away for good. I have to lie low for a few weeks, maybe a month. They must think I got scared off. We can't meet, you and me. I have to find out what happened. I won't know how to live with this if I don't. You *will* hear from me again. But you can't do or say anything to anybody until that time. These people are ruthless. They tried to get at you once."

"What about the threat to you?" I asked.

He was quiet for a moment. I wondered what he'd been talking about earlier when he'd said "hell-hole hospital" for Berenice.

"If evidence comes in that no one can deny or hide away, then the investigation will be damned hard to kill," Lieutenant Hudgins said. "It won't be a matter of making me shut up. The crime will be too big."

"Lieutenant Hudgins," I said, "I'm sure you will get that evidence."

I knew what I had to do. And I knew who would help me, even though he wouldn't know why he was doing it – even though it might wreck his plans. But it didn't matter.

Salvatore could not turn me down.

CHAPTER EIGHTEEN

ZIA

The St. John the Baptist
The Atlantic Ocean, 1906
"Audenzia, come down, now."

I could tell by the weariness in my mother's voice that she had already called to me several times. We weren't more than fifteen feet from each other, but it was hard for me to hear her in the steerage compartment. All of us, at least one hundred people, were crammed into one long, dim chamber below deck. It made for some bad smells and a lot of noise.

The beds ran along the long walls, stacked two or three in height with enough room in between for someone to sit up, provided they weren't too tall. I was lying on a top bed, on my side, cradling my picture book to capture the light filtering down through a crack in the ceiling. It helped take my mind off being hungry.

Hearing my mother, I put my book down and swung off the mattress, hurtling past my brothers, Massimo and Giovanni, playing checkers on their homemade board on the middle bed. I was often alone because Giovanni, thrilled with the attention, was our oldest brother's willing servant and no longer my faithful playmate. I did not hold it against him; I knew he'd be back.

I landed with a bounce on the swaying ship floor. "How can you read?" groaned Aurora Lucania, my mother, stricken with waves of seasickness. Without waiting for my reply, she held up the chunk of gray soap she'd used to scrub our clothes in a tin bucket. No matter what, my mother upheld her standards of respectable appearance. We must be clean, inside and out.

"I'm finished for now," she said. "Take it to your aunt. But you must be careful."

"Yes, Mother."

A hand closed around my wrist. "You keep up your reading, angel," said my father, pulling me to him and kissing me on the forehead. But his voice rasped. A week on this boat had weakened him, as it had all of us.

I kissed my beloved father and set off for my relations, moving warily among the passengers. I'd been told so many times to keep clear of anyone but family. At least two-thirds of those in steerage were rough men from the countryside, not from the city like us. At eight, I could read better than most of them. My mother called our fellow passengers "the peasants" – but in a low voice, so they couldn't hear. Most Sicilians who made the voyage to America left behind their wives, daughters, mothers, and sisters. They sent money home, and sometimes, they arranged for their families to join them later. Sometimes, they didn't.

The boat surged just as I walked around a large group of the peasants. As I stumbled, I collided with the thick leg of one of the men. I looked up to see who would get my apology.

Oh, not him. Not him.

The man we knew as Storrino scowled as he shook me off his leg like I was a dog. He hated children. Storrino was older than most of the other men without families, and fatter. He had a scarred, mangled left cheek. Massimo speculated that he had been burned in a fire set by his own family.

Storrino's mouth moved as he chewed. A bright pink paper flashed between the fingers of his right hand before he shoved it into the pocket of his long, black coat.

"I am sorry, sir," I whispered.

The look in his eyes shifted from anger to something peculiar, like he was the one in the wrong and defied *me*.

I backed away, my heart pounding as hard as the ship's pistons.

Although he was my father's cousin, I addressed Antonio Lucania as my uncle, his wife as my aunt, and their children as my cousins. I wish I could say that once I reached them, my worries ended. But as I approached, I could tell from how my aunt and cousins cowered and flinched, that my Uncle Antonio was angry about something, and his rage was a thing to be avoided at all costs.

Our lives were humble, my father being a cobbler in the city who did not own his own business. It was even worse for them. My uncle Antonio labored in the sulfur mines, and I'd heard whispers that he couldn't earn enough to feed his children.

My aunt pleaded, "Don't take this out on him," her arms encircling her son Bartolomeo.

I didn't witness any blows. But Uncle Antonio's neck turned red, and a vein bulged like a long rope surging under the skin.

I caught the eye of my cousin Concetta and slipped her the soap, yet I didn't return to my parents. I'd counted only four heads among my cousins. There was a fifth child in the family, and he was the one I liked the best.

I had a shrewd idea of where to find Sal.

I made my way to the door leading to the narrow steps connecting to the higher levels of the ship and stood behind it. A couple of minutes later, I heard feet stomping down the steps, and the door swung open. It was one of the ship workers, his arms full of boxes. Before it clicked shut again, I slithered through and hurried up to the top.

We weren't forbidden to walk on the ship's deck, but steerage passengers were only supposed to take the air at set times. We mustn't crowd the first- and second-class passengers, entitled to a better voyage. It didn't take long for Sal or me to figure out that they didn't enforce the rules when it came to children. It wasn't fondness for the young. There just weren't enough of them to keep track of us.

I burst through the little door opening to the deck and had to cover my eyes. The sun was so bright. I took a deep breath. I always relished the salty tang of the ocean.

As did Sal, whom I found in his usual place, an opening between two large crates, standing on the side of the boat. He was pressed against the railing, his black hair whipping in the wind.

Salvatore Lucania was one year older than me and at least three inches taller, with a pair of large brown eyes, wide cheekbones, and a pointed chin. I tugged on his tattered sleeve.

"Don't you know what happens to little girls who go where they're not supposed to?" he said mockingly.

I laughed and pushed him to the side so I could squeeze in and get the same view, though I had to stand on my tiptoes to peer over the railing.

Faced with the rolling ocean, I said, "I can't believe this is going to end."

"Just seven days till New York City," he said. "Maybe eight."

The new home that awaited us had never seemed real, not when my parents informed us we would join all the other Sicilians pouring out of the country, and not even now. Papa gave my brothers and me a list of commonly used English words, and I immediately practiced saying them. It was all the "s" sounds that unnerved me. I sounded like a snake when I practiced, and I kept picturing myself walking down the streets of Americans speaking this way – it would be like a pit of vipers.

I peered up at my cousin. "You scared?"

"Nah."

It's important to know this about Sal – from as far back as I can remember, I had never seen him scared of anything or anyone.

"How long you been up here?" I asked.

"Hours."

So, he'd missed the midday meal. I had lined up for it with my parents and brothers but only nibbled at the brown-bread crust tossed onto my plate. It was worse than stale. I would have welcomed stale. It was damp and moldy. All the food – brown bread, potatoes, and herring – was rotten in one way or another. Years later, I learned that this was common on the ships to America. The captain made money by paying even less than what was apportioned for passenger food and pocketing the rest.

What kept me from starving to death was my mother. She had baked a large batch of mustasole, hard cookies for ocean voyages. Each morning, she handed me my cookie of the day, reminding me that if I gobbled it immediately, there would not be another until the following day. And so I forced myself to wait until late afternoon before eating my mustasole, chewing as slowly as possible, as if I could swallow one crumb at a time.

167

I took a closer look at Sal. Maybe it was my imagination, but his cheekbones looked higher than before we set sail, his chin more pointed. My aunt hadn't baked cookies for her family. I don't know how I knew that, but I did. Yet he'd prefer being up here than below, where they served food. I knew he loved the sun and the air, but also I guessed it had something to do with the angry coil pulsing in his father's neck. I'd overheard my father saying Sal brought out the worst in his father, something I didn't understand.

With care, I fished out of my left pocket the white handkerchief bordered with tiny gold crosses that enfolded my mustasole of the day.

"Let's share," I said to my cousin, holding up the cookie.

Hunger flickered in his dark eyes, but Sal shook his head. "That's from your mother," he said. "She'd want you to eat it, not me."

"We're all family," I said.

Sal had made up his mind, though. He wouldn't touch it. I shoved the cookie into my pocket since I couldn't eat it in front of him, even though my stomach quaked with hunger.

"They sell food on the deck – I've seen it," he told me after a minute. "People can buy fruit and candy – these little candies come folded up in pink wrappers. It ain't cheap. They don't care if you're a kid. No cash, no food."

But I've just seen a pink wrapper.

I told Sal about Storrino eating something in a secretive way and spotting the wrapper in his fingers.

My cousin said, "If I had the money for candy, I wouldn't be in steerage. I'd be in second class."

I started to laugh. I thought it was a joke – Sal in second class, alone, without family? But there was a bitter look to him. He hated steerage.

And why shouldn't he?

Anger washed over me like a wave crashing over the side of the boat. A monster like Storrino gobbled candy while the two of us starved. I hated the feeling of helplessness, of utter weakness this inspired.

"I have an idea," I said to Sal.

It didn't take much to persuade my cousin. In fact, he worked out a much cleverer way for us to succeed than I could.

That night, when the ship workers set up the table with supper for steerage passengers, Sal and I were ready. We waited until we saw Storrino find a place in line and scrambled to go right after him. He wore his long black coat from earlier in the day, thankfully. But his arms hung down straight, his hands either inside or near his pockets. He took no notice of us, and he spoke to no one. Storrino was undistracted.

Sal tugged my arm and nodded, his lips pursed.

It was time.

My heart sped a little faster. It wasn't fear but excitement, like the moment before a pageant began in school.

When we reached the table where the wretched food was being scooped onto plates, I again bumped into Storrino, but this time on purpose.

I heard him grunt and felt his vast bulk stiffen, but instead of recoiling, I forced a smile and said, "Mr. Storrino, I can't believe this! I am so clumsy. What can I do?"

"Nothing," Storrino said.

"Can I get a plate for you – hold it for you?" I babbled. "Can I help?"

"You can go away," he said, growling like a bear.

Sal leaped to my side, "I apologize for my foolish cousin. Come with me, Zia."

Storrino scowled. I was relieved to be able to fall back with Sal, out of the range of Storrino's hideous gaze, but my cousin refused to meet my eyes. Had he failed?

"What happened?" I whispered.

"Hush," Sal hissed, pulling me back farther until we had reached our own families' circle. Disappointed, I shuffled with them in line. Giovanni grabbed my braid, and I tried to force a smile.

Once I'd reached the front, I held out my plate for food, as did everyone else. The chunk of herring reeked.

I felt someone's breath on my hair.

I turned to behold a Sal who was transformed. His eyes danced as he rubbed his palms together. "Tomorrow morning," he said.

It was always difficult to sleep aboard that ship – the snoring and coughing mingled with the talking that never died down – but that night, lying next to my mother, I doubt I closed my eyes for more than a couple of hours. Sal had done it!

Morning came, and finally, after spinning stories to parents who were too exhausted or seasick to challenge them, Sal and I slipped away for the deck.

It wasn't until we were back at the side of the boat, side by side where no one else could see, that Sal held out the two candies he'd extracted from Storrino's pocket, both wrapped in that bright pink paper.

It was wrong. It was a sin – and I was a girl who, up to that minute, had never missed Mass, who followed the rules at home, school, and church. Yet nothing tasted as good as that candy on the deck of *The St. John the Baptist*.

Afterward, I put the pink paper in my handkerchief. It was so pretty; I didn't want to part with it.

We slipped back down and joined our families. I ate my cookie a few hours later, just after another disgusting luncheon was served.

How lovely to crawl up to the highest bed and curl up with a book without hunger pains.

"Audenzia, come down."

Just like the day before, my mother's voice rang out. This time, her tone was edged with something else. Not weariness. I knew my mother so well, every slight change in her expression or voice. How could she ever sound strange to me?

When I swung down, I was confronted with not my mother but a large group of people – my father, my aunt and uncle, Sal, Storrino, and a ship steward.

My throat closed in panic. Even if I'd wanted to, I couldn't have said a word.

"Yeah, that's her," growled Storrino. "The two of them," he pointed at Sal, "did it. They stole from me."

"My daughter would never, ever steal," said my father. "You're wrong."

Hearing his faith in my goodness was the worst thing in the world.

"I had them in my pocket before dinner," Storrino said. "They were dancing around me, real strange. That night, the candies were gone."

My aunt said, "Anyone could have done it. How could you accuse these two children?"

Uncle Antonio said nothing, but his face was flushed as he visibly struggled to control his temper.

I stole a look at Sal, but he didn't meet my gaze. He shook his head, not embarrassed or anything, but as if he were baffled. *How could anyone think this of me?* That's what he seemed to be conveying. I must do the same. I tried to look baffled instead of how I felt – terrified.

"Search them," said Storrino. "C'mon!"

"I don't have time for this," groaned the steward. Hope jolted through me like lightning. If we kept denying the theft, what could anyone do?

"Go ahead and search me," said Sal. "I didn't do anything."

The steward edged away, needing to return to his other many duties.

I exhaled in relief – until two adult hands grabbed me by the shoulders and pulled me close. I stared up into the face of my mother. As well as I knew her, she knew me.

Mama plunged her hand into the front pocket of my dress and pulled out the handkerchief. Seconds later, the pink wrapper I fancied was displayed for everyone to see. It no longer gleamed and beckoned. In the dim steerage hold, it looked cheap and ugly.

Whenever I think about what happened next, it's like silence fell over us like a thick blanket. But that could only have lasted for a few seconds. Then there were screams, demands, threats, and frenzied apologies.

I barely felt my mother shake me or heard Storrino curse. For me, there was only the heartbreak in my father's eyes, like a hot knife tearing my soul, before he begged the steward to be allowed to pay Storrino to make amends.

"Sal made Zia do this," said my mother. "He's older. He's responsible."

My aunt had already pushed Sal behind her to protect him from her husband. He was grabbing for Sal like a man possessed.

"No," I said. It was the first time I spoke. "It was my idea. Mine!"

Uncle Antonio didn't hear me, he was dragging Sal away, my aunt weeping noisily. My two brothers stood by, confused and upset. Giovanni kept saying, "I don't understand."

I pulled away from Mama to go after Sal, but she caught me by my dress. Seconds later, Papa had me too.

"I'm sorry, Sal!" I shouted. "I'm sorry."

"Sal, Sal, please forgive me!"

CHAPTER NINETEEN

ZIA

I woke up even more determined to take on the challenge than I'd felt in Tompkins Square Park. First, I needed to smooth things over on Mulberry Street. I had upset my mother-in-law and son when I'd rushed out of the apartment and disappeared for close to two hours. After I returned, my dinner was cold; they were worried. I succeeded in persuading them both that I was okay. I think they could hear the new-found strength in me. It reassured them.

My period of confusion was over. I knew what I needed to do.

The first hurdle was locating my cousin Sal. He moved around a lot. I feared the phone number I had for him was useless, and sure enough, the number had been disconnected when I tried it.

Massimo was the only person I could think of who would know where to find Sal. He'd gotten wine for my birthday party through our cousin a couple of weeks ago. I wanted to put my plan into motion with all speed, but unfortunately, I had to wait for my brother to get home from work. And then I knew it was best to let him have his dinner with Bianca and the kids before disturbing him. I'd have to wait to call.

Mama had another visitor that afternoon. Her church friend, Loretta, came by to offer comfort and support. Her concern had

173

wandered from the spiritual to the earthly before she'd been in our apartment for an hour. I was taking in their coffee cups when a question confirmed something I'd suspected for the last couple of days.

"Luigi always took care of everything so beautifully, did he make sure you will be taken care of going forward?" asked Loretta.

"Oh, yes, he went to see a lawyer after Armando died in the war. The store comes to me. Thank the Lord I have my brother Roberto to run it. I know I'll be fine."

Why was it so unthinkable that I manage the shop? I persuaded Papa to buy the refrigerator and to focus on selling the highest-quality food we could find. I came up with the bookkeeping system that kept us on track with bills.

Hearing this made me want to reach Massimo on the telephone even more. He reacted as I predicted.

"Why do you want to talk to Sal?" my brother demanded. "You should keep your distance, Zia. We all should."

"I have a question for him. It's absolutely nothing to do with Joe the Boss or anything along those lines."

Which was true. Joe Masseria had nothing to do with The Orchid Hour. Sal had been pretty convincing on that point at the cemetery.

After more argument, Massimo finally gave me the phone number. I tried it right away. No answer. I waited a half hour and tried again. Still no answer. After six more attempts, I decided to give up for the evening. Who knew what Sal was up to? He kept extremely late hours. He'd only go to bed before one in the morning if he were deathly ill.

I put Michael to bed, and after some reading, I fell asleep. A dream woke me with a start. I threw on my robe and tiptoed to the kitchen. There was enough light from the street streaming in the windows to be able to read the clock above the stove. It was two-thirty.

I dialed Sal's number, which by this point, I'd memorized.

"Yeah?" he answered curtly on the third ring.

"Sal, it's Zia," I whispered.

"What's wrong – why're you calling this hour?" he asked, now his usual self.

"Nothing's wrong. I just need to ask you something."

"Sure. Ask."

"No, let's meet. Can you do it tomorrow?"

"I got a lot going tomorrow." There was a pause. "How about I stop by the store around four?"

"I'm not working at the store these days," I said. "That's part of the reason I need to talk to you. Where else can we meet?"

Sal said, "How about we meet outside my old school, PS 110, at four o'clock, and we figure it out?"

I agreed and was soon back in bed, but for a long time, I was too agitated to fall back asleep. Sal was the key to everything. If he didn't give me what I wanted tomorrow, that would be it. I didn't know how I'd be able to learn anything crucial about The Orchid Hour for Lieutenant Hudgins.

Just as it surprised me that Lieutenant Hudgins picked Tompkins Square Park to meet, I was taken aback that Sal had selected PS 110 on Delancey Street. He'd been so miserable there.

By four in the afternoon, I was at the meeting place, halfway down the chain-link fence that stretched along the side of the school. Between the Delancey corner and here, broken glass littered the sidewalk.

The school was four stories high, its steps crumbling, its sooty brick walls covered with graffiti. Arching nearby was the massive Williamsburg Bridge, the uglier cousin to the Brooklyn Bridge. A lot packed with overflowing trash cans hugged the side of the East River. I'd bet every cent in my purse that the lot was crawling with rats.

I had been waiting about ten minutes when Sal showed up. He was the liveliest thing on Delancey Street, bouncing up the sidewalk to meet me. To my amazement, he was whistling.

"Doesn't the place look great this time of year?" Salvatore asked, brushing aside a shard of broken glass with his freshly polished shoe.

I had to laugh. "Why do you want to go anywhere near this school? You *hated* it."

"Worst two years of my life," he agreed. "I find it real useful to return, to think about my teachers. I talk to them in my head all the time. I have some good come-backs after they call me a dirty, stupid dago."

He ran his hand along the chain-link fence, and I could almost hear those conversations myself.

"So how can I help you?" he asked.

I had come up with a plan of how to lead up to my request, but when he said that, my instincts told me a straightforward approach was best.

"You can get me a job," I said.

Sal already knew I'd been fired from the library. I explained my present status at the cheese shop – politely banished by the Pellegrinos.

"But isn't the store going to go to your son?" Sal asked.

"It belongs to my mother-in-law now. I always thought she'd want it to go to her only grandchild. And I still think it will pass to Michael rather than to her brother and his children. But I don't have a role in the family in the meantime except to cook and clean upstairs."

"You've always wanted to do more than that, and you should," Sal said. "But *cucina*, I'm sorry. I'm just not sure I know the kind of people with businesses that'd have a place for you. I don't set foot in libraries, you know."

"Sal, I'd like a job at The Orchid Hour."

My cousin laughed for a few seconds before looking closer. "You're not kidding. Zia? Oh, c'mon, that's ridiculous. It's a nightclub. You go to bed by ten, right? We're gonna *open* at eleven."

"I can stay up late. And I was a waitress the summer before I got married, remember? At the De Paulo Coffee Shop on Grand. I could be a waitress at The Orchid Hour."

"Only men will wait tables at our place. They're being hired as we speak, along with the barkeeps."

"You're not going to have any women anywhere in the nightclub? That sounds odd."

"There'll be cigarette girls, coat check girls. The word here is *girls*. Zia, I'm sorry, but none of these tomatoes'll be older than twenty."

Sal was shooting down all my ideas. But I had no intention of giving up this easily. "You know I helped with the orders at the cheese shop. I did a lot there. Don't nightclubs have food? I learned a lot from Papa. I know all the best suppliers."

My cousin just shook his head.

Sal said, "Zia, I can't get you in there. It wouldn't be right. We're trying to make this a world-class joint, but at the end of the day, it's a fancy speakeasy. Get it? We're gonna serve alcohol, and selling alcohol is a violation of the Volstead Act. There is a possibility – not a huge possibility, but it exists – that we get raided. Think about that for a minute. When the police bust in, the workers get arrested and hauled off in a paddy wagon. I couldn't stand it if that was you. And

I'll tell you something else, your brother'd kill me. He wouldn't just get mad. He would *kill* me."

"Forget about Massimo. I can handle him. This is me, Zia, asking you, Salvatore, for help. You said if I ever needed anything, you'd do it. You promised. Remember?" Our experience on the ship and years of friendship afterward quivered between us.

Sal's discomfort turned to anguish. "I know, but I never in a hundred years expected you to…" He looked me up and down. "I don't want you to feel bad about yourself, not after everything you been through. This is the bottom line, Zia. You're a nice librarian wearing terrible shoes. The Orchid Hour ain't hiring nice librarians wearing terrible shoes. I can't *make* them find a place for you. Once they see you, it's just gonna be out of the question."

I found this encouraging. Although he was still resistant, Sal described something that sounded like an interview for a job.

"I can look like someone who belongs there," I said. "I might not be twenty years old, but I'm not *old*."

Sal studied the wall of the school he hated more than any other building in the world, but at this moment, it was something he'd rather look at than me.

I blurted, "I'm not an idiot, though I realize nobody cares about a woman's brain."

"Hey, hold on, nobody knows how smart you are better than me," said Sal earnestly. I knew my cousin had a high opinion of me. No one might have had a higher one now that Papa was dead. And I was trading on that regard to do something that, if revealed, could make things bad for Sal, even put him in danger.

Did he deserve it?

There was no getting around the fact that my cousin was deeply involved in a business that was so important in some unfathomable way it was getting people killed. And I was the only one seeking justice for the dead.

I put my hand on Sal's arm. "Why don't we meet tomorrow evening? I'll make some changes to how I look. If, after you see me, you honestly think I'm just too much of a frumpy little widow, I won't push it."

"Yeah, I have to emphasize it's not *me* you have to persuade, Zia. There's a fellow who is doing all the hiring. He's the one in charge of how the club looks and sounds, even how it smells. I'm one of the guys putting in money, but he's running it. His name is David da Costa. He's an actor. You probably heard of him. He's in a Rudolph Valentino movie."

I took that in. "An actor? That's not usual, is it, to hire an actor to run a club?"

"Tell that to Texas Guinan! But David's nothing like her. He's got real class. He's the nephew of one of our major investors. He talked David into doing this – he had to send a trio of guys to Europe to bring David back to New York. We're paying him, yeah, but there are other things he could be doing. He wants to run The Orchid Hour. My point is, he's the last word, backed up by his uncle."

I barely heard the parts about Europe or style aside from the fleeting thought that being in a Valentino movie didn't sound all that classy to me. I latched onto one word. "This David's a *nephew*? You see how it goes, Sal? I'm your cousin. You should get a place in the nightclub for a family member too."

"Hmmmm." Sal looked distinctly unconvinced.

"Where will we meet tomorrow?" I asked. "Let's make it near The Orchid Hour. I need to get a sense of the neighborhood. I don't even know where it will be, so you'll have to choose again."

We agreed to meet at Café Dante on MacDougal Street at six, which I knew was in the South Village. That surprised me. I assumed The Orchid Hour would be in or near Times Square, not downtown. Weren't they calling Broadway the new entertainment capital of the world?

"If nothing else, this will give me an excuse to buy new shoes," I said as we parted.

Sal tried to smile. He still looked as if he'd been tricked into a dental procedure.

I stopped by a newsstand on the way home to buy some magazines. My first choice was *Ladies' Home Journal*. I'd been reading it for years. But I knew I needed fashion inspiration from haughtier authorities. I picked *Vogue* and *Harper's Bazaar*. At the last minute, I also grabbed *Photoplay*. If I had to impress an actor at this interview, I should know about the movie business.

After dinner, I spread the magazines out on my bedspread. It took only a minute for me to face the inescapable: I'd have to get my hair cut. I couldn't show up in Café Dante tomorrow with my hair in a bun. That was the moment I came closest to pulling back from my plan. A woman cutting her hair short was a big step anywhere in America, but on Mulberry Street, it could bring the walls down around me.

How could I take the plunge? I flipped the magazine pages nervously. These women sporting bobs were supposed to be the latest in feminine appeal. But to me, they looked hard and heedless – and most significantly, completely carefree. I was a mother with responsibilities. Was I about to make a massive fool of myself?

I put the women's magazines aside for *Photoplay*. Its tone was curious – here, I found photographs and illustrations of performers of unearthly beauty, yet some of them claimed to yearn for the comforts of home and family. One actress posed next to a roaring fireplace and a pillow-heaped couch in a loose pink silk gown slipping off her exquisite shoulders, her tiny feet clad in something that looked like half bedroom slipper, half geisha shoe. I freely admit to owning "terrible" footwear, but how could anyone walk down a New York City street in these?

"*Women Dress to Charm Men – Why Not Be Frank About It?*" asked the alluring Nita Naldi in the form of a headline. She'd also appeared with Valentino in the bullfighter drama *Blood and Sand* that had come out last year. Nita was indeed being frank in a sleeveless black chiffon velvet gown that hugged her body. "*Clothes should not cover – they should veil, hint, whisper secrets.*" *Hint?* Is that what she was doing?

Valentino himself penned an article in the same magazine. It was subtitled "*An Open Letter From Valentino to the American Public*" as if he were a national politician addressing weighty issues. The point seemed to be to justify how few films he was making. The studio wouldn't allow the director and writer of Valentino's choice to have the final say, so he had balked. He was also grumbling about his pay.

"*My salary of $1,250 a week may seem a great deal of money, but it is actually less than the salary of any other prominent star on the screen,*" he wrote. "*Mary Miles Minter makes $8,000; Norma Talmadge and William Farnum both make $10,000; Thomas Meigan $5,000, to mention but a few.*"

I had to roll my eyes. Valentino had come to America from a southern Italian town when he was young, just like the rest of us. He worked as a hotel taxi dancer and was paid to tango with women lacking partners, until he captured fame as the "Latin Lover." Women were mad for his Spanish bullfighters, Arabian sheiks, and Russian bandits. He never portrayed an Italian, of course, and he avoided

Italian immigrant communities in the U.S. He lived with his moody Russian wife in a Beverly Hills villa and whined over only making $1,250 a week when it was a struggle for some people to clear $1,000 in a whole year.

I turned the page to see the headline "*Does Rudolph Valentino Have a Successor?*" running across the top. On each page was a large photograph of a man in a three-quarter profile. The actor on the left had hair slicked back like Valentino and the same furious intensity. The actor on the right was unlike either the man he faced or Valentino. He had wavy dark hair and high cheekbones, his dark eyes fringed with long dark lashes. There was a hint of a smile above his cleft chin. He looked serene.

I read the short photo caption: "*David da Costa, one of the supporting actors in* Blood and Sand, *put his aristocratic Spanish heritage to excellent use in that film. Can we hope to see him smolder in other tales of love and death?*"

So, this was the man I would have to impress tomorrow – if Sal decided I was good enough. It was like making an appointment to see one of Botticelli's dark angels.

At that moment, Michael, curious, jumped on my bed to look at the magazines. "She's pretty!" he said, pointing at a photo of a smiling actress with a strawberry-blonde bob.

"You like the way she looks?" I asked, genuinely curious.

"Sure. *You* should have your hair like that," he said, before taking out his box of marbles.

My wavering ended. Why not cut my hair at least? I'd been submissive to what the family wanted for so long. The truth was, I was getting sick of it.

CHAPTER TWENTY

ZIA

The following day, after taking Michael to school, I went to the bank and withdrew the large sum of thirty dollars. My destination was Macy's Department Store. I rarely ventured north of 14th Street, but today would be different.

When I reached the ladies' floor, I stood on the perimeter of racks and racks of dresses, deeply unsure of myself. I knew I couldn't wear one of my hand-sewn black dresses this evening, and I didn't have time for something to be measured and made for me at a familiar boutique. I had to plunge into the world of department stores and ready-to-wear.

"Could you use some help, ma'am?" asked a smiling saleswoman about my age.

"Yes, I think so," I said. "Thank you."

"Is it for day or night?"

"Is what?" I asked.

"Your frock. What you came here to purchase."

"Night," I said. It would be nice to know what I was doing here.

The saleswoman led me to a section of evening gowns shimmering with silver sequins or long panels of bright rhinestones. I backed away as if she were trying to hurl me into Mount Aetna.

"I can't," I said. "Too much. I'm very sorry. I do need an evening dress, but those are out of the question."

That's when I came within seconds of fleeing. My feet itched to make a mad dash for Macy's wooden escalator and forget this whole crazy idea.

But the saleswoman brightened. She said, "Ma'am, I have an idea of a dress that would look wonderful on you. It's nothing like these. Let me show you."

She steered me to a rack twenty feet away and an iridescent, deep blue frock, edged with delicate gold stitching. I did like the color. I slipped on the dress in the fitting room. The waist hung inches lower than I was used to, and the material was so light, I barely felt dressed. Yet, looking in the mirror, I had to admit the dress was lovely. "This is 'Luxor,' one of the brand-new colors," the saleswoman said. "Egyptomania."

"Luxor," I repeated, puzzled. "Isn't that the name of the actual city in the Valley of the Kings? But that's in a desert. Where would you possibly find this blue?"

"Oh, this is fashion!" said the saleswoman with a laugh. "Who knows? What's important is it flatters you. And you're lucky. You have the slender figure for the new lines."

Putting myself in the saleswoman's hands, I bought another dress, this one in a subtle violet and white pattern, as well as some very stylish shoes – one-inch heels and single strap – and silk stockings. Both dresses stretched to a point halfway between my knees and ankles. It was shorter than I was used to, but I saw plenty of other dresses that were even shorter.

Back in the apartment, I managed to hide my purchases from Mama. I picked up Michael from school but explained to them both that I had to meet a friend from the library, someone who could help me find a new job.

I *was* following Rachel Rodman's lead with my next stop, although she would not be accompanying me. I knew she was a regular at Marie's Beauty Salon on Prince Street, so that's where I went for my hair.

The last thing I thought before settling into one of their suspended chairs was how much Armando loved running his hands through my long hair. Bobs hadn't come into style when he left to fight in the war. Women had just started experimenting with shorter cuts. Once, after passing a woman on the street, Armando shook his head and said, "Why would any girl want to look like a boy?"

At the beauty parlor, they seemed accustomed to women walking in with hair to their waist who wanted a bob. I had to still my nervous hands when I felt the scissors slicing close to my throat. I had the crazy impulse to grab the scissors and protect myself. But I was *paying* for this. I kept my eyes down, too nervous to watch.

"All done," the beautician announced. I looked up and glimpsed myself in her mirror. I looked nothing like the seductresses of *Photoplay.* No, I didn't resemble a boy. But I'd become a *gamine*, a waif.

A giggle erupted. I clapped my hand over my mouth, but it came through my fingers.

The beautician smiled as if she'd witnessed this reaction before. "You're free," she said, patting me on the shoulder.

Was I free?

I changed into my new dress, shoes, and stockings in the salon's lavatory. I'd bought some coral lipstick at the pharmacy and applied it. This was as good as it was going to get.

When I arrived at Dante's, my cousin was already sitting at a table, his long legs stretched out in the aisle with ankles crossed. I was over-dressed for a café. A waitress peered across the room at me. A man sitting at a table by the door gaped. But only one person needed to see me like this if I were to get over the first hurdle.

As I approached, Sal was exhaling his cigarette smoke in giant circles, something he'd enjoyed doing since he was thirteen.

Mid puff, he broke into sputtering coughs. "Madre di Dio, Zia," he croaked.

He looked at my hair, shoes, and everything in between, his eyes wide with shock.

"Are you ready to introduce me to David da Costa?" I asked casually, taking a seat.

He laughed for a long time, so loud that heads swiveled around from all directions.

"Yeah, sure, I'll take you to David," he said. "But I gotta admit, I'm curious why you want a job there this bad. You chopped your hair! I mean, this ain't cheap stuff you bought either."

I was prepared for him to bear down on my reasons. He probably hadn't done it yesterday because he wasn't taking me seriously. "I need to make my own money," I said. "I want Michael to go to college, whether he gets the store someday or not. And I assume the pay will be good at your nightclub."

"Yeah, it'll be good, but I'm still not sure how you'd fit in," Sal said. "I'm gonna keep my word and make an introduction. That's all I can do."

"Thank you, Sal. So, when do you want to do it? Do you have time tomorrow?"

"Tomorrow, hell. Let's go now." Sal tossed some coins on the table to cover his coffee. "The nightclub opens next Friday."

"Now?" I asked, alarmed. "You know David da Costa's at The Orchid Hour?"

"He's always there." He looked at me quizzically, "Thought you wanted a job. It's a five-minute walk from here. Let's go."

Back out on MacDougal, Sal turned left, and I followed. "You're putting a fancy nightclub in the South Village?" I asked in disbelief. MacDougal had a few restaurants and coffeehouses, some Italian, not all. There was a sign for a cobbler, another for a stationer's store.

"Everyone calls this part of it Greenwich Village now, Zia. Not South Village. You gotta keep up."

An essential part of my plan needed to be set up before I met David da Costa. We were minutes from doing that. I had no choice but to bring it up now.

"Sal, I want to talk to you about my name," I said.

"Yeah?"

"There was that *Daily News* story about me. I was Mrs. Audenzia De Luca. I don't want them to know that was me. I don't want anything about Mr. Watkins' death or Papa's death to come into this. I can't talk about any of that with a stranger. Plus, they might not want me around if they knew."

Sal said, "I can see that."

I was talking to someone who'd changed his first name, so he had no problem. Relieved, I continued, "So introduce me as Audenzia Lucania, my maiden name – and your name too. It's perfect. Forget about the library. That's not exactly work experience that will count. Plus, I can't be connected to the Seward branch. Just say I used to work at the coffee shop."

"A coffee shop on Minetta isn't going to impress anybody. But what the hell. You look great."

Sal turned off MacDougal onto a narrow side street I'd never noticed before, though I'd walked up and down MacDougal many, many times. Somehow, I'd always missed it.

Sal and I were the only people visible. This street, just one block long, wasn't paved the way most others were in New York City. I had to pick my way across uneven cobblestones in the fading light of early evening. There weren't any sidewalks. Old two-story brick townhouses ran along each side of the street, with no gaps between them. Their square outlines and black window boxes were from a type of architecture popular at least a century ago. The townhouses hadn't been built at the same time. Some were dark red brick, and others were light gray or white. Their heights varied. Gleaming dark-green ivy crawled up a few walls. I noticed each house possessed a wooden door, but a small one. Not like a front door at all.

"Is this a back *alley*?" I asked, incredulous.

"Shhhhhh." Sal put a finger to his lips as if I might disturb someone. The noise of New York had fallen away on this strange cobblestone lane. How was that possible amidst a city of seven million people? I felt as if I were no longer in the year 1923.

"Sal, once you open, you think people will be able to find this place?" I asked skeptically.

My cousin smiled and didn't answer.

We'd just passed a house that jutted out, covered with thick ivy. Beyond its far corner was a new, long brick building. The door had been left ajar, a sign fixed to it with elegant black lettering. A rich golden light poured out, creating a long triangle that reflected on the cobblestones. It was a business, the only one on the lane. I drew closer. The cream sign read, "*Stelis & Sons Floral Design*."

Sal made a flourish, "After you, Miss Lucania."

I caught my breath as we stepped inside the brightly lit room. It *was* a florist, and the fragrances of a dozen flowers enveloped us. Roses, lilies, and gardenias led the assault on my senses, but I smelled peonies too and sweet lavender. It made me dizzy, a little sick. Intense warring smells sometimes overpowered me. But it was more than that. An old story nagged at my memory, something about a woman who found doom because she followed the scent of a flower.

I ground my fingernails into my palms to stay focused. Looking down, I noticed a tiled floor with alternating black and white diamonds. It gleamed as if it were brand new.

Remembering the nightclub's name, I scanned the shelves and square wooden tables in the shop. No sign of any orchids. How baffling.

"All of this was a carriage house – one big stable for some rich families off Washington Square," Sal said. "We got it for a low price, but you wouldn't believe the work that's gone into it."

Someone moved behind the cut blossoms and long floral branches and delicate fronds. A slender, hatless man wearing an elegant grey suit was laying wax paper on a counter to wrap flowers. This was a real florist, taking orders and everything.

"Good evening, sir," said the young man, barely looking up.

"Good evening, Edgar," said Sal. "We need to go through."

I heard a rattling buzz from behind the florist's counter and a click to his left. Sal moved toward the click and a large mahogany door. Smiling, Sal beckoned for me to join him. We'd walk through together.

As I approached the door, I heard the murmur of voices on the other side. There really was a person in there I'd shortly have to impress. I pushed a strand of hair out of my face and nodded to Sal. I was ready for the man who smolders.

"Whoa, what about your ring?" Sal said, staring at my left hand.

I'd forgotten entirely about my wedding ring. I pulled it off and slipped it into my handbag. I would need to be a *lot* more careful.

Sal pushed open the door, which had done an excellent job suppressing most of the noise. Someone was hammering, two people were talking, another was carrying boxes to the back of the space – and the room went back quite a ways. I could see this had been an enormous stable once upon a time. But I wondered if that just meant there was more space to deal with, more than they could handle. This nightclub that everyone was obsessed with was a real mess.

In the middle of it all, a man was having some sort of tantrum. It took me a while to recognize him as David da Costa from the article in *Photoplay*. The person theatrically waving his fist in the air and stomping his foot didn't look anything like a sought-after film star. The angelic serenity of that photo was nowhere in evidence. He hadn't shaved in days, and his wavy dark hair stood on end. And his *clothes*. He wore baggy trousers with a rope for a belt, a Yale school sweater, and a beige scarf wrapped around his neck, though it was a warm spring evening.

The man on the receiving end of David da Costa's adult fit was a calm, middle-aged Black man sitting on a long wooden box.

"Joe, you can't tell me that you have no drummer with less than two weeks to go – you can't say those words," said da Costa. "You're a bandleader, which means you're supposed to solve talent problems, not dump them in *my* lap!"

I expected my cousin to be horrified by this outburst, but Sal seemed unbothered. He strolled over to the actor as I hung back.

"David, I thought I'd swing by to see how you're doing and to introduce you to someone," Sal said.

"Charles, I'm not doing well," said David, adjusting his scarf. "It's all a complete disaster. I can't shake this cold. I've tried lemon and tea, and I've tried brandy. This is the worst time for me to be sick. I'm a wreck."

I couldn't believe what I was hearing. A grown man who looked to be in his late twenties feeling sorry for himself – and making everyone else miserable – because he had a head cold? When Armando or my brothers were down with the sniffles, they'd never carried on like this.

"Maybe it'll cheer you up to meet my cousin, Miss Zia Lucania," said Sal, beckoning for me. "She's heard a little about our venture here. In fact, she's interested in a job, if you have something?"

This was the moment for me to make a good impression. It was what the clothes and haircut had all been for. But I'd been struck dumb. I took two steps forward and stopped.

For the first time, David da Costa noticed my presence. His eyes flicked over my face and figure.

"So, can you play drums?" he asked.

A few people laughed, including the bandleader and Sal. I should have joined in with a joke and tried to impress him with my wit. But words failed me.

David said, "I'm sorry, Miss Lucania, you've caught me mid-crisis. Music is crucial to what we're trying to accomplish here. I'm sure you like jazz, don't you?"

"Yes," I said. "It's not my favorite music, but I realize it's very popular."

"Oh, you do, do you?" said David, cocking his head. "That's awfully big of you. And what's *your* favorite music?"

"The opera."

David blinked twice and adjusted his scarf again. "Indeed, indeed," he murmured. And then, louder, he said, "Charles, I appreciate you coming by, and your opera-loving cousin is delightful, I'm sure, but I've filled all the positions for girls. There's nothing for her to do. I wish it were otherwise."

Sal said, "I was thinking that she could—"

"No, that's fine, Sal," I interrupted. Neither of us was going to plead with David da Costa. I had wanted to do this so much. I thought I could get the answers here no one else could and help Lieutenant Hudgins, but it was obvious my plan wouldn't work. I realized this was about more than helping the police. I burned to know the truth. By finding out who had committed the crimes, I could best protect myself and my son, better than any policeman would, surely.

But I'd failed. Right now, I just wanted to leave the place with dignity.

Somebody new approached da Costa. They began a conversation about chair costs. My "interview" was at an end. Sal caught my eye and gave a tiny shrug. I smiled at him. This certainly wasn't his fault. He *had* warned me.

It was time to find our way out. As I peered around the chaotic room, an older man moved past us, walking very carefully, looking down at the floor as if he needed to avoid landmines. He was carrying a flowerpot, and inside, sprouted a live flower, a white one, very delicate and drooping. An orchid. It looked like a slipper. I remembered reading about this in the book I'd pored over in the library. It matched the illustration.

I said, "I thought that kind of orchid was extinct."

"*What did you say?*"

I thought David da Costa had moved on to other matters and was unaware that I was still there, much less listening to me. But he hurried back and asked me to repeat myself.

The older man carrying the flower stood still.

"Isn't this a Lady Slipper orchid?" I asked. "I thought they were extinct. That's what I said."

"No one else knows or cares about that fact in this abysmal city," he said. "What else do you know about orchids?"

"I assumed that if the nightclub were going to have actual orchids in it, they'd be cut flowers in vases, not live ones in pots," I said. "Displaying them that way is an interesting choice, but it could be challenging."

"How so?" asked David da Costa. His tone was casual, but I sensed that everything depended on my answer. I thought back to what I'd read at the library. It would be rude to say that orchid collecting, due to the expense, was a frivolous pursuit for only the wealthiest Americans. I'd have to talk about botany, God help me.

"They have difficult growing conditions," I said, trying to sound authoritative. "They can't get too much light or too much heat, but if they don't get enough of either, that's fatal too. I suppose one would have to know precisely what the orchids need to flourish."

David da Costa bit his lip, peering at me as if he were a little afraid.

"Hold out your hands," he commanded.

Bewildered, I did so. To me, the place where the wedding ring used to be looked different, with dents in the skin of my fourth finger. David da Costa stared for a long time while Sal stood by, trying not to fidget.

"She has the right hands," David announced. "She can be an assistant to Heinrich and serve as liaison between him and the club. He needs help but can't abide Edgar or anyone else I've suggested."

"Heinrich, the man who came with you from Berlin?" asked Sal.

"Yes, he's spending the week at the greenhouse in Summit, New Jersey, to be near the orchids we will be bringing in for the opening week. He'll be back Saturday." David da Costa turned to me, "Can you start on Saturday and assist us?"

"What about her salary?" Sal asked.

"We can work out all the details later, I just have to talk to Arnold," David said dismissively. He clasped his hands together, "The question is, Miss Audenzia Lucania, will you help us?"

With him so close, I could finally see the resemblance to the man in the photo, the high cheekbones and cleft chin. But he lacked serenity. It seemed impossible that he could ever be a Botticelli angel. I wondered if he had any control over himself. It looked like I was about to find out.

"Yes," I said.

David smiled and seconds later veered away, swallowed up by questions of chairs, drummers, paint, and other matters as I stood there, stunned. Sal chuckled and said, "Zia, you did it."

"Yes," I said, not quite believing it. And then, thinking of Mama and Michael, I said, "We should go, where's the main exit?"

"This is the way out, too," said Sal, pulling me back through the florist's shop. It seemed a bizarre way to enter and exit the club but no more bizarre than other things I'd witnessed tonight.

Back on the cobblestone lane, the gas lamps were flickering. They were far older than the ones in Tompkins Square Park. I felt even more deeply as if I had stumbled into some other time.

"He's something else, right?" said Sal, laughing.

"He's certainly not what I expected," I said.

"David's the nephew of our biggest investor."

We'd almost reached the end of the lane when I said, sounding as matter-of-fact as possible, "And who's that investor?"

"You heard David mention Arnold back there? Well, that's him. Mr. Arnold Rothstein."

CHAPTER TWENTY-ONE

ZIA

Now that I had managed to get myself a job at The Orchid Hour, Sal said I needed to understand the world I was entering. He offered to set aside a night to take me around the city to get a look at other establishments serving alcohol. "They're not the competition, not really, but they're making money, so I try to keep an eye on them," he explained.

It wouldn't be easy to explain to Mama why I was going out that night. I didn't know how to explain my new job. I'd have to lie. I didn't plan to work at the nightclub for more than a week, two at the most. Surely, that would be long enough to learn something useful for Lieutenant Hudgins.

But even a week of late nights would be tough to get away with on Mulberry Street. Just getting my hair cut had delivered a severe blow to my mother-in-law. She looked on the verge of tears at the sight of me until Michael rejoiced, "I told you I wanted to see you like this, and you did it! You look beautiful."

After making yet another excuse the following night, I met Sal wearing my other new dress from Macy's. He was right that I needed to have a better grasp of nightclubs. But while spending this time with him, I hoped to draw out of him more about the origin of The Orchid Hour itself. The lieutenant had said something about it needing protection – and that protection extended to needing to have people killed. So far, all I knew was that it was run by a high-strung actor off a hidden alley in Greenwich Village with a jazz band and some flowers. Why would anyone need to die for that?

Sal seemed preoccupied as he led me to East 14th Street. If his first school in America had harsh memories, I wondered what this street meant to him. Once, he was "Sal from 14th Street." I heard so many different things at the time. It could be the worst he did was become king of the street craps games, get into fights, and shoplift. I never wanted to believe the other persistent story that he delivered illegal goods as a runner for gangsters.

Sal knew every store on East 14th, and today, he led me into the kind I'd never go near in a hundred years. The cigar store had a floor layered with dirt. A repellent man with a greasy mustache sat behind the counter. To my dismay, he nodded at Sal. They knew each other.

"Havana," Sal said.

I heard a faint alarm. The back door opened. Standing there was a tough guy, even uglier than the one behind the counter. He grinned, revealing blackened teeth, at the sight of us.

"Hey, Mister Lucania," he said with a sycophantic ooze.

I realized Sal wasn't looking at either of these cretins but at me. He was waiting.

"Are you ready, Zia?" he said.

Whatever test of nerve my cousin had in mind, I had no intention of shrinking from it.

"Lead the way, Salvatore," I said.

We stepped into a small, dim, windowless saloon fashioned out of what once might have been a storeroom. A barkeep served a half dozen sorry-looking men. There was nothing joyful about them. These men desperately needed a drink, which was the sole reason for being here. When the Temperance Movement gained momentum across the country, it was to save the souls of men such as these and spare their families. Apparently, they didn't want to be saved – and to hell with the families.

Sal held up two fingers to the barkeep and pointed at the only table with chairs in this grim room.

"Now that's where I draw the line," I said. "I won't sit on one of those chairs in a new dress."

"Fair enough," Sal said, leading me to the bar. We would stand.

At the bar, he turned to scrutinize me. "So, Nettuno got himself carved up in the Tombs."

I wondered why Sal was mentioning that. Was he brooding over my coming to work at The Orchid Hour and connecting that desire to the string of deaths?

"Yeah, I heard he died a few days ago," I said. "No one's sorry to see him go."

"That means there won't be a trial," he said.

I couldn't tell from his tone whether he thought that was good or bad. At first, my mother-in-law was disappointed that Nettuno's death in the Tombs thwarted justice. But the trial of her husband's accused murderer would have put her through a terrible ordeal. She accepted that justice *had* been served, but we'd never know by whom or for which specific reason.

I wondered if Sal shared Lieutenant Hudgins' opinion that Joe the Boss might have ordered Nettuno's death because he thought

197

the low-level thug had acted independently. Did anyone besides me believe Nettuno hadn't murdered Luigi De Luca at all?

The barkeep set two glasses in front of us, both filled with a brownish liquid. I had no desire to drink it, but I couldn't risk failing Sal's test. I reached for the glass nearest me. Sal seized my wrist and lowered it to the bar before the glass touched my lips.

"Okay, okay," my cousin said. "I won't let you drink that. It could kill you. I'm not kidding." He looked around the room with contempt. "They call this rotgut. It does just what the name says too. People will go through hell to get a drink. If they don't have much money, they'll find a place like this, and maybe the booze they pay for will ease their pain, or maybe, it will cause a new kind of pain. There're thousands of joints just like this one in the city."

"Thousands?" I said skeptically.

"I'm telling you, people are drinking just as much as they did before Prohibition passed. Maybe more."

"Why did you bring me here, Sal?"

He scowled. "Because I didn't sleep too well last night, Zia. I don't know if it's a good idea, you working at The Orchid Hour."

I was beginning to understand. "So, you brought me here to frighten me? Oh, please. You're not my father."

"No, but I remember your father. He and both your brothers and – after – Armando, built a fortress around you. They worked hard to protect you from everything bad… and dangerous. They sure wouldn't want this for you."

"I'm going to be taking care of orchids for an actor who manages a nightclub. It's hardly making my living on the street."

He shook his head. This wasn't persuasive. I'd have to try something different, or I feared the job was about to evaporate.

I blurted, "Sal, maybe I don't want to live in a fortress anymore."

My cousin thought for a moment before saying, "I can see that."

It seemed Sal could buy this as my motivation – and in truth, I was yearning for freedom, and I was willing to chop off my hair and buy colorful dresses to move with the times. What I was struggling with was how good it felt to change my appearance and get a new job. I had to keep reminding myself I was doing this for a serious reason. A dead serious reason if I wasn't careful.

He shoved his untouched glass away, "Okay, let's get out of here. I know a place that's more your style."

We climbed into Sal's maroon car and headed west but remained south of 14th Street. I thought he might be taking me back to The Orchid Hour, but we drove farther west instead. I rarely ventured into this part of Manhattan – a warren of narrow streets that twisted and turned. There were coffeehouses, newspaper offices, and other places favored by young artists and radicals tucked among the narrow townhouses. The West Village was known as the bohemian part of town.

Sal led me down a quiet, nondescript street called Barrow, but we stopped before we reached the corner. I saw a sign that said "*Bedford Street*" on that corner. We slipped into a courtyard between townhouses. A battered-looking door was at the very back of the courtyard, nearly hidden among the ladders and rakes. Sal knocked three times, and a minute later, the door groaned open. After stepping in, I looked back. The door had been disguised as a bookshelf.

We'd found our way into another speakeasy. Now, I understood why opening one off MacDougal Alley wasn't crazy.

This place was a notch above the East 14th Street joint, but it lacked glamor or even real comfort. I spotted sawdust on the floor.

We were standing in an ordinary tavern with a barkeep, serving some sixty people who crowded the bar or clustered in booths and at free-standing tables. Yet, it was certainly popular. There was a steady hum of conversation.

"Welcome to Chumley's," Sal said as we took the only empty places at the bar. "You can order a drink here. It won't make you sick, but it won't taste all that good either."

"How enticing," I said. "Don't worry. I rarely touch alcohol. I'm here to see the competition, not get soused."

"We're putting out something different at The Orchid Hour," Sal said. "Some of the people in this room might be interested. We'd like them to be."

"You would?"

I heard a woman laugh. I turned on my stool to see. Wearing a chic bell-shaped hat called a cloche, a slender woman of perhaps thirty held up a finger to make a point. She sat at a table of six people in their twenties or thirties. Half of them were women.

I said in a low voice to Sal, "I didn't think women would be allowed."

"You're wrong. Women are welcome at speakeasies, especially these kinds of women. You're looking at writers, editors, poets, playwrights. The men are the same. Chumley's a writer. He bought the building – it used to be a blacksmith's shop – and turned it into a speak."

"That explains the sawdust," I joked. But I couldn't take my eyes off the table with women and men drinking together. To make a living as a writer or a poet and come here to enjoy yourself – not as a flapper giggling over fooling Daddy, but a grown woman, making her own choice – that was a life I'd never have thought possible.

"Writers – men, women, whatever – are one of the three types of people we want to attract at The Orchid Hour," Sal said. "If they like a place, it's a big deal."

"What are the other two?"

I thought Sal was about to tell me, but he just smiled and sipped the beer the barkeep slid in front of him. He would rather drink second-rate beer than divulge the secrets of The Orchid Hour. But I was going to keep chipping away.

"What does David da Costa drink?" I asked.

"Champagne, but only once in a while. He's not much of a drinker. He used to be. When he made *Blood and Sand* in California, he was drinking and doing other things. He got messed up. Mr. Rothstein had to bring him back east and dry him out."

"I thought someone had to send three men to Europe to drag him out of there. He seems to need a lot of rescuing."

"Yeah. But David wasn't drinking in Paris or Berlin. He was – God knows what he was doing. He goes on about the music and movies and orchids of Europe, and I don't know what the hell he's talking about half the time."

"I assume he met Heinrich there, the man I'm going to assist?"

"Yeah, he says Heinrich is the authority on orchids, and he made Mr. Rothstein pay to bring him over, along with a bunch of his other discoveries. A doctor had to treat Heinrich once he got to New York. He was weak. I think he's better now. David saved his life."

Sal had just told me a whole lot about David da Costa. It didn't add up to a person that made sense, though.

A new group of young people, men and women, rumbled through the Barrow Street door, laughing over their entrée by way of the secret "bookshelf" door and bright-eyed with excitement. They called out to friends they knew at the bar or a table and flung themselves into the drinking and the fun.

"This isn't what I thought a successful speakeasy would be like," I admitted. "I suppose I expected something like Delmonico's."

Sal chuckled. "Delmonico's shut down a month ago."

"You must be joking."

I couldn't believe the best-known restaurant in New York had closed, especially when plenty of rich people roamed the city with appetites. Sal explained that many of the city's ritzy restaurants and evening revues no longer attracted paying customers because there wasn't any alcohol served. The owners who obeyed the law went bankrupt.

Sal said, "Delmonico's had to close, Maxim's was already history. Everything's changed in New York, and I mean everything. What's funny is almost no one realizes it." He smiled to himself again and said, "C'mon, let's go uptown."

Our next stop was West 42nd Street and Broadway, the locale of the Knickerbocker Hotel, one of the grandest buildings in New York. Or so I thought. I saw few guests in the lobby. Was this another famous institution destroyed by Prohibition?

Sal steered me to a pair of doors deep inside the Knickerbocker. "This is the King Cole Room," he said. While it wasn't easy to find, the room wasn't exactly hidden. There was no password or secret bell or disguised entrance. The man at the door recognized Sal immediately. Sal's hand darted into his right pocket and extracted a tight roll of bills that he slid into the man's hand.

"We'll have a table for you in a minute, Mister Lucania," he said with an obsequious smile.

Inside was a larger crowd than at Chumley's but not by that much. Maybe seventy people. Nicely dressed couples swayed and dipped on a small dance floor. Others chattering at their tables. Through the white cloud of cigarette smoke, I spotted wine and liquor glasses in people's hands.

"They're breaking the law, but this place isn't hidden, anybody could walk in at any time," I said. "I don't understand."

Sal looked around to ensure no one was listening and said, "The police look the other way – if you pay 'em enough."

I knew the New York police had a reputation for having their hands out for bribes, so I wasn't too surprised. I said, "Well, why didn't Delmonico's stay open and pay off the police? Why doesn't everybody do it?"

Sal was considering his reply when he suddenly beckoned a couple over, saying, "Hey, here you are, perfect timing." The man was perhaps thirty with a round face, wearing a proper suit and tie as if he worked at an office in midtown. He and Sal shook hands like good friends. The woman was a little younger, sporting a fashionable bob and pretty clothes.

"Zia, I'd like to introduce you to Frankie and Lauretta Costello," he said.

"I've heard a lot about you, it's so nice to meet Charles' cousin at last," gushed Lauretta as her husband smiled at us both.

I appreciated their friendliness, but I'd never heard of the Costellos, and I had no idea I'd be meeting people during my tour of the Manhattan night. Although they didn't look like it, the fact that the Costellos called him Charles meant they were part of his shadow life. And I feared this meant I'd have no more opportunities to question him about The Orchid Hour.

"Table for four," Sal said to the maître d, completely unruffled that our party had doubled. A couple of minutes later, he led us to a spot two tables back from the dance floor.

"I like your dress very much," Lauretta said.

"Zia went on a shopping spree," Sal said.

"Well, this is the end of the spree, you know," I said.

"Hmmm, you're gonna need more than two dresses, sorry to say," said my cousin. He broke into a smile. "I know somebody who might be able to help out."

A waiter took orders before I could find out who he had in mind, and Sal quizzed him on the various champagne vintages as I listened, amused. We'd traveled less than thirty blocks from East 14th Street but were a universe away.

Something odd caught my attention across the nightclub. I didn't realize what it was in my first moments in this dark, smoky room, but now, I saw a series of large paintings covering the wall behind the bar. The paintings must have been eight feet tall. In rich, vibrant colors, they seemed to tell a children's story with clouds, trees, and a man on a throne, jesters cavorting. The man had a strange grimace, not quite a smile.

Frankie Costello, noticing my interest, said, "The paintings are supposed to tell the story of Old King Cole. That's where this joint got its name."

"Oh, of course. The nursery rhyme." I paused, remembering the words, "*Old King Cole was a merry old soul, and a merry old soul was he. He called for his pipe, and he called for his bowl, and he called for his fiddlers three*. So these fellows dancing around are fiddlers." I peered closer. "But I must say, the king doesn't look like a merry old soul."

"There's a reason for that," Costello said. "John Jacob Astor IV, the American millionaire, he owned the Knickerbocker Hotel, and he paid the artist a ton of money to paint Old King Cole, but he had a special request – the king's face had to be Astor's face."

I sighed. "Yes, that's what a rich American millionaire *would* do."

Costello smiled and said, "Now I understand why you're the one person in his family that Charles gets along with."

At that moment, a woman appeared on the small stage next to the band, a spotlight following her. She didn't need a spotlight to be blinding. She wore a gown stitched with silver sequins *and* ermine furs *and* multiple strings of pearls. Her hair was arranged in short white-blonde curls, and her lipstick was fire-engine red.

"Hello, suckers," she shouted. "Better a square foot of New York than all the rest of the world, am I right?"

The entire room cheered. I smiled and tapped my fingers. I didn't share the sentiment, but I didn't want to attract attention for being a spoilsport.

"That's Texas Guinan," Sal told me after the raucous crowd quieted. "She was an actress in the movies, Westerns mostly. She came to New York last year, looking for stage parts and couldn't get any. So next thing you know, she's the main attraction at the Gold Room over on Fortieth Street. The manager at King Cole poached her."

The blonde "main attraction" was sashaying across the floor, pointing at this person, waving at another. I even saw a couple of playful slaps. "Her brain is as good as new," she shouted at one table. Insults were a part of her repertoire – and everyone relished them.

As she made her way to our table, I shifted in my chair. I didn't want to be the subject of public ridicule. No matter how "fun" insults were supposed to be here at the King Cole Club, volunteering for one was unthinkable for a Lucania. I peered over at Sal. He was chatting with Lauretta, but he had an eye on Texas Guinan. It could be my imagination, but he looked wary. He didn't want to be one of her targets either.

But that did not stop her.

"Lookee heeeere, it's my own Charlie Boy," she shouted at Sal. "He's Mister Manhattan – here, there, and everywhere. Don't you have no home to go to, lover?"

My cousin smiled tightly. Texas Guinan looked the rest of us over and moved on, to my relief. The waiter brought drinks – four glasses of champagne, fizzing perfectly at the top.

"Drink 'em down, then we're outta here," Sal said.

"But I want to dance," protested Lauretta.

Her husband shot her a reproving glance and said, "Of course, Charles, you know we're ready to leave whenever you are."

Lauretta, realizing her mistake, chimed in nervously with, "I'm so sorry. Yes, we can go now."

My cousin gave a little benevolent wave as if to tell her to calm down, and he focused on his drink. The entire exchange left me feeling uncomfortable. Why did my cousin, a gambler and investor in nightclubs, have this kind of sway over other people?

I sipped my champagne. It was delicious. With effort, I pushed the glass away. I needed to hold onto my focus.

Outside the Knickerbocker, Sal's spirits lifted. He said, "I think we gotta make a Larry Fay stop, but we have another one first." We walked a block west into the heart of the theatre district, its sidewalks jammed, bathed in the thousands of dazzling electrical lights turning night into day. The names of the venues blasted into the night – the Selwyn Theatre, the Stuyvesant Theatre, the Hudson Theatre, and the Lyceum Theatre. Each had a big show going.

Our destination was not an entire block away – the soaring New Amsterdam Theatre on 42nd Street, the largest on Broadway and home of the Ziegfeld productions. "I'll be back soon," Sal announced and darted around the side of the theatre on his own.

The theatre's marquee said in tall lights, "*'Neath the South Sea Moon*," and in far taller lights, "*Ziegfeld Follies of 1922.*" The colossal poster showed a parade of blondes. The night's performance must have just ended. People poured out of the big golden doors, propped open to the street.

The Costellos drew me off to the side so we wouldn't be pushed and pulled by the crowd. Lauretta and I fell into an easy conversation about music and movies. She adored Eddie Cantor and Charlie Chaplin.

"It should be real interesting working for David da Costa," said Lauretta. "A thousand girls in New York would kill to be in your place. He's a real movie star – so good-looking!" She stepped closer to me so her husband couldn't hear and said, "But you know he's kind of *meshugge*."

When she realized I didn't know the word, she said, "Oh, sorry, that's Yiddish for crazy."

Before we could dig into it further, though, I was dumbstruck by what I saw crossing the street: my cousin Sal emerging from the side of the New Amsterdam Theatre with his arm tight around a woman wearing a midnight-blue dress and matching round-toed shoes in the new fashion. She had glossy black hair cut in a bob, huge brown eyes, and full lips. She was close to Sal's height, and even with the drop waist of her dress, you could see she had long legs.

Sal's expression left me reeling. He was smiling, no, he was *glowing*, gazing at his companion with what could only be described as adoration.

My cousin was in love.

CHAPTER TWENTY-TWO

ZIA

"Audenzia, I'd like you to meet Julia Morel," Sal said with the same degree of pride as if I were meeting Norma Talmadge.

She put out her hand to shake mine, saying formally, "It's a great pleasure to make your acquaintance." A tall woman, she had a small, delicate hand. Her Southern accent intrigued me. "I like the name Audenzia."

"You can call me Zia if you like," I said.

"I like," she said.

It was time for the next stop, the El Fey Club. It was only four blocks north, but we had to drive. Sal walked Julia and me to his car while the Costellos took theirs. "We won't put Zia in the back by herself," Julia declared and insisted we both sit in the back while Sal drove.

"You know Charles was once a chauffeur, don't you, Zia?" she said, smiling. "He's an excellent driver. I'd much rather have him drive than Vito. But you've probably never met Vito."

"I *have* met Vito," I said, "and I'd much rather have my cousin drive too."

"Stop picking on him!" protested Sal. "Vito Genovese isn't so bad."

208

Julia and I exchanged a glance and burst into laughter. Sal, watching us in the mirror, grinned.

I said shyly, "So, you're one of the Ziegfeld girls?"

"She's the most *beautiful* one," Sal insisted.

"Well, Florenz Ziegfeld Junior wouldn't agree," she said dismissively. I was impressed with how little regard she had for Broadway's great impresario. "He's very attached to his blondes. I almost didn't pass my audition, even after I learned the dance steps in a minute. I broke into French while talking to him, and that, along with my name, made Mr. Ziegfeld think I *was* French. His first wife was French."

"And you're not?" I asked.

"She's as Sicilian as you and me," said Sal, angling the car into a parking spot.

Now, I understood. Julia had done what Mrs. Tuckle advised me to do. I said, "You changed your name then?"

She shook her head. "No, Morel is my name."

Sal parked the car, and once more, I joined the crowd of New Yorkers on a street brightly lit, even though it was close to eleven o'clock. I was heading into a fourth illegal drinking establishment. My feet hurt a little, and my eyes blurred. It seemed as if every billboard and every nook and cranny in Times Square was electrified. Among the grand, ornate theatres that dazzled all were the little hotdog booths, the chop-suey joints, and the juice stands. Thanks to the blazing lights, they were part of the "Great White Way" too. It all made me long for the dim slumbering peace of my room on Mulberry Street.

But I had assured my cousin I'd have no problem staying up late. I must push on.

Sal gave me some background on Larry Fay, the owner of the nightclub we were on our way to visit. He was "one tough Irishman from Hell's Kitchen" who made his living driving a cab after the war ended. One night, when Prohibition was kicking in, Fay picked up a man in his taxi who talked him into a four-hundred-mile trip to Montreal to take possession of whiskey crates. Fay found out a lot during that long drive. With his own money, he got in on the action. He turned ten dollars of Canadian booze into eighty dollars of whiskey imported to America. The desperate fledgling speakeasies of New York were willing to pay sky-high prices for genuine alcohol, stuff that wasn't rotgut. Two years later, Fay was one of the city's leading bootleggers and owned a fleet of taxis with special flashing lights and musical horns.

"But what he really wants is to run his own nightclub," said Sal. "He wants to hobnob with the snobs. Trouble is, Larry doesn't have any class."

The El Fey Club resided on the second floor of a nondescript building on West 46th Street, right above a restaurant. At the top of the narrow stairs and next to a closed door stood two men, one small and stooped over with a wizened face and the other so large and muscular, it looked like Hercules had catapulted himself from Greece to Times Square.

Once again, my cousin Sal murmured a word or two while pulling out a fat roll of bills. After Sal had greased the wizened one's palm, Hercules stepped aside, the door eased open, and the five of us were welcomed inside.

The El Fey Club was larger than the King Cole Room but not better. Tables were crowded in front of a scuffed dance floor and, rising above that, an ordinary stage. On one side of this stage, a small orchestra played a song I didn't know.

There were no paintings of kings and troubadours here, no special charm. Waiters frantically delivered bottles of champagne and glasses of whiskey, gin, and rum. People sitting at tables or the bar gulped their drinks like they'd been given an antidote to a poison that would kick in by midnight. They might have been wearing silk shirts, Oxford shoes, or pearl necklaces, but this crowd was as desperate for a drink as the patrons on East 14th.

The mood in the room lifted when a dapper man in his thirties with a pair of dark, sparkling eyes and a pointed chin leaped onto the stage holding a microphone and said, "Welcome, one and all. On behalf of the El Fey Club, I'm delighted to see you – and boy, do we have some treats for you tonight."

He had a slight accent, one I couldn't place. Lauretta whispered, "He's Swedish."

The man continued, "Our vocalist, Johnny Vincent, will perform the new hit song of the season, accompanied by The El Fey Club Orchestra. Give a cheer for *Yes, We Have No Bananas*."

The orchestra launched into a jaunty tune I'd heard a few times before. To me, it sounded so old-fashioned, like the corniest musical theatre. But the slender young man on stage, Johnny Vincent, poured everything he had into the lines like, *"We've string beans, and onions, cabbageses, and scallions."*

Each time it came to the two-line chorus, everyone at the El Fey Club joined in, chanting loudly:

"But yes, we have no bananas,
We have no bananas today."

At the song's end, everyone, even Sal and Frankie Costello, shared a laugh. The Swedish master of ceremonies popped back onstage and said, "Thanks a million, folks. Tonight's show will begin soon, bringing you the most beautiful girls in New York, most of them bona fide Ziegfeld girls, but first, I must tell you that also a Ziegfeld girl is out in the house tonight. We're honored to welcome Miss Julia Morel."

211

He pointed at Julia, and all heads swiveled to see the beauty in question. I was impressed with her response. I would have crawled under the table, but Julia smiled and inclined her head, perfectly calm.

The master of ceremonies said, "And, ladies and gentlemen, in honor of Miss Morel, let's enjoy the Ziegfeld song of the season, *'Neath the South Sea Moon*."

The singer launched into:

"*We all love to wander,*
It's nature to roam,
That's something that's born in us all…"

While the singer warbled, I kept my eye on my cousin. Sal was having trouble coping with the attention focused on his girlfriend. He had the strangest look – pride and protective jealousy warring for the upper hand. Julia moved closer to him and whispered something reassuring in his ear. Within seconds, his mask was back on – Sal, the carefree gambler and man about town.

After *'Neath the South Sea Moon*, the regular show of the night began. Six skimpily dressed young women danced across the stage and began to high-kick, exposing their entire legs. I couldn't help feeling embarrassed. This was the sort of "entertainment" my parents and in-laws most disapproved of. I had to remind myself that I was twenty-seven and had been married. I could handle this.

The Swedish master of ceremonies made his way over to our table. "Don't be mad at me, Julia!" he said pleadingly. She gave him her hand to kiss.

"If you behave yourself, I'll introduce you," she said. "You've met my friend, Mister Lucania. This is his cousin, Audenzia, and Frankie and Lauretta Costello. Everyone, this is Nils Thor Granlund, though we like to call him N.T.G. Press agent, talent scout, and now, it seems, an employee of Mr. Larry Fay."

"Not an employee, please," begged Granlund. "Just helping him out, like I do lots of people. He doesn't know how to put anything together, how to recruit performers. That's my specialty. If you ever wanted to come aboard, Julia…?"

"Oh, darling, you know that's not going to happen," she said, but with a warm smile. I had to admire her ability to manage men. "After a night of dancing at the New Amsterdam, I couldn't keep it going here."

"The dancers never mingle with customers – I made them put a private lounge upstairs for the girls to rest in, so it's not so bad for them after the Ziegfeld show," he said.

"I have something that keeps me occupied after the Ziegfeld show," she said, and without even looking, she reached over to caress Sal's cufflink. The look my cousin gave her left no one in the dark on the nature of their relationship.

At that moment, the owner, Larry Fay, appeared at our table. He was the opposite of the charming, fast-talking N.T.G. Incredibly tall with a long face marked by a few scars, he wore a ghastly green suit I fear he thought was smart. It was like welcoming a tree to our table. While the Swedish talent manager focused on Julia, Fay talked only to Sal and Frankie.

"Heard you fellas made a stop at King Cole. Whatcha think of Texas Guinan?" Fay sounded wistful. Maybe he wanted to poach her.

"She's got a patter going," Sal said.

"Not the kind of thing you got cooked up for MacDougal Alley?" he asked.

Sal folded his arms. "Nope," he said, a trace defiantly.

So Larry Fay knows about The Orchid Hour.

The cab-driver-turned-bootlegger smiled, revealing teeth and gums that were best concealed. "There's room for more," he said and lumbered on.

Julia said, "N.T.G., must you?"

Nils shrugged. "Guys like Larry took over Times Square by the third month of Prohibition. If you want to stay in show business, you deal with them. And he's not so bad. Just a tougher breed of businessman. No contracts, nothing in writing, but he always keeps his word. I'm just happy I don't have to have anything to do with Owney..."

At the sound of that name, people looked at one another. A chill settled over our table.

Sal asked, "What's Owney Madden got himself up to after Sing Sing? If he's not working with Larry, how's he keepin' busy?"

"I wouldn't know," Nils said, looking away. "My job is the entertainment. Those who deal with the liquor end of it, I don't get involved. Ever. Now excuse me – Julia, you're looking so exquisitely lovely tonight – but I have calamities to prevent."

The Swede hurried off, and attention should have returned to the dancers on stage. With Julia and Lauretta, it did. But Sal and Frankie muttered to each other in Italian. I thought "Costello" was an Irish name, but if I didn't know it already, this drove the point home. Frankie was Italian. With the orchestra blaring, I could only make out a few words here and there: "Harlem spot" and "Jack Johnson."

When the dancers took a break, I hoped to eavesdrop more effectively, as Sal and Frankie were still in deep conversation. However, this is when Julia decided to talk, just the two of us. She switched chairs with Sal so we could sit beside each other. We were closer physically than at any time tonight, closer than in the car. I wondered if beauty came down to symmetry. Her eyes, her nose, and her mouth were all perfect.

"Charles is like your personal Charon, isn't he?" she asked. "He's taking Persephone around for the night."

This was more interesting than I'd expected, though she had it all tangled.

"To the Greeks, Charon was the ferryman to the underworld," I explained. "He guided them across the River Styx for a coin, so if you consider these sorts of places the underworld, that fits nicely. But it was Hades himself who personally brought Persephone down, not Charon."

"Oh, is that it? How did Hades do it? I don't imagine he had an elevator."

I laughed, but something stirred, a memory explaining why I'd felt overwhelmed when I stepped inside the florist shop off MacDougal. According to the legend, Persephone spotted a beautiful flower in a meadow, and when she reached out to pluck it, the earth opened and Hades in his chariot appeared, seizing her.

I told Julia the story, which she took in with interest. "I liked to read the myths when I was in school, it made me feel as if I could understand Sicily better," she said. "But I've forgotten some details."

"You left Sicily when you were very young?"

For the first time tonight, Julia looked unsure of herself. I felt as if she were sizing me up, deciding something.

"I was born in New Orleans," she finally said. "My mother left Sicily and came to America when she was expecting me. She married Jacques Morel when I was a year old. He's the only father I ever knew. And he was a good father too."

215

I must admit to being shocked. Sure, young people fooled around without being married in Italy or America, but if the girl got pregnant, the guy had to marry her. Her family would kill him otherwise. How could a pregnant girl end up with nobody to marry her *and* find her way to America? But it was brave of Julia to reveal these intimate details. She had put trust in me to confide like this. I had to respond right and not by questioning her more about her parents.

"Well, the story of Persephone has always had special meaning in Sicily," I said. "She's the only wife Hades ever had. Zeus had lots of wives and mistresses. Hades just wanted her."

"What are you talking about Hades for?" asked Sal. The girls had ceased their routine, mercifully, but the orchestra played on.

"Just discussing the underworld," I said. "Doesn't everybody?"

"You're a little bit like Hades, you know," Julia teased.

"Oh, yeah? Well, this devil would like to dance." Sal held out his hand, and soon, they were on the dance floor, but slowly swaying, hardly bothering to keep with the beat. He gently tipped her chin for a kiss, and in response, she nestled close, kissing him deeply as she ran her right hand through his hair. I'd never even met any of my cousin's girlfriends before. Now, Sal was putting on an exhibition in front of me and everyone else in a public place. But these two were a force of nature. You'd have better luck stopping Niagara Falls than keeping them apart.

After about ten more minutes of this, Sal and Julia were back at the table. Sal announced it was time to leave, with Julia clinging to his arm, practically fainting. I was grateful for their carnal agenda. It was well past midnight, and I was finally going home.

If anything, the El Fey Club was picking up steam. We had to flatten ourselves against the side of the not-so-clean stairwell as we went down because a line of people was coming up. I followed Sal and Julia, the Costellos behind me.

Halfway down, we passed a man with a party of people coming up who reacted strangely. He was about forty, wearing a tweed suit, with prematurely gray hair – practically snow white – peeking out beneath his hat. His eyes flicked sideways at the sight of Sal, and he nodded. Then he spotted Frankie Costello behind me and nodded to him the same way.

On the street, Sal pulled Frankie aside and spoke to him again in Italian. They must do this when they were out with their women. But while Lauretta and Julia might not understand the language, I did. I eased closer, my heart pounding. I knew that this was what I'd been waiting for.

"I thought he was a silent partner and never came in person to any of the clubs," said Frankie.

Sal responded, "That group must all think the coast is clear, after what Rothstein said."

"What did Rothstein do? What happened?"

Sal said, "I don't know who it was, and I don't know how it was done or who he used, but the stone has been removed from our shoe."

CHAPTER TWENTY-THREE

LOUIS

Louis had told Yael that she didn't have to dress any particular way for where they were going. There was no reason for them to try to look like a couple anymore. He didn't need her for that purpose.

But when he picked her up in Brownsville, Louis was surprised by the outfit she had chosen – trousers, a baggy shirt, and a vest along with her favorite cap. He'd never seen Yael, or any female, in trousers before. Sitting beside him in the Model-T, Yael looked like a skinny boy. He didn't know how he felt about that. He worried that it might make it tougher for him later if things went badly at Lindy's and he had to take certain action.

The messenger that Arnold Rothstein sent found him at home this time. "You're expected at eight o'clock tonight," he said.

Louis had been waiting to hear from Mr. Rothstein. It had been almost two weeks since the death of Luigi De Luca, and nothing. Silence. He didn't know if that was a good or a bad sign. The murder in Little Italy had made it to the newspapers, and then, just a day later, the same newspapers reported the arrest of Victor Nettuno. They all included the fact that the victim was the father-in-law of Audenzia De Luca.

Sometimes, he wondered if Mr. Rothstein had lost interest in the affair. But at the same time, he knew that was hope, not reality. The Fixer, the Great Brain, the Judge, whatever name you used for Mr. Rothstein, nothing slipped his mind.

Yael was unusually quiet on the drive into Manhattan. Maybe she had suspicions.

"Who're they talking about these days at Rose's?" Louis prompted. "It's not still Albert Anastasia, right?"

"Nah, he's in prison for two more years. People are wonderin' about Owney Madden. He's out of Sing Sing."

"Oh, yeah, I heard he got released."

"Did you know he killed five people by the time he was twenty years old?"

Louis said, "Doesn't surprise me. Those Irish gangs are the most vicious of 'em all. Us Jews? Nope. The Italians? Nope. Look, everyone gets worked up, you know. Stuff you gotta do, you gotta do. But that gang he was in, the Gophers, they fought like maniacs at the drop of a hat. Over a square foot of turf on the West Side, which is the biggest pile of dung in the entire city. Why do you think they call it Hell's Kitchen west of Tenth Avenue? The Irish got pushed there a while ago and decided to act like it's a place to be proud of. I don't get it."

"You know they call Owney the Duke of the West Side."

"Aw, that's like saying someone is Grand Poobah of the Shithouse."

Yael burst out laughing, that snorting giggle of hers that he was relieved to hear because it meant she was over her brooding. But his stomach seized up at the sound of it too. Nobody else laughed like that.

Thankfully, she turned to telling the old story of Owney Madden getting shot on West 52nd Street by a guy in a rival Irish gang.

Madden survived, which was a sort of Hell's Kitchen miracle. Yael said he was plugged eleven times. Lou had heard it was eight. Bullets just kept multiplying.

With difficulty, Lou found a parking spot on a block west of Lindy's. He usually saw Rothstein before dark, before curtain time for the Broadway shows drew the droves into midtown.

"Stay in the car, don't get out for any reason," he told Yael.

She nodded. She hadn't asked why he'd brought her to Manhattan or the plan. That wasn't good. He half-expected her to be gone when he got back to the car. But that wouldn't be a serious setback. He knew where she lived and where she worked.

Lindy's was packed. Peering at Rothstein's usual booth, Lou saw it was empty.

Leo Lindemann refused to give Lou any message when he asked about Mr. Rothstein. He jerked his chin at a waiter, the oldest one, who stopped what he was doing and said, "If you're Louis, Mr. Rothstein wants you to come at ten o'clock."

What was he supposed to do for two hours? It wasn't enough time to return to Brooklyn. By the time he got to his neighborhood, he'd just have to turn around after an hour at most. He had no choice but to occupy himself in Manhattan. With Yael.

"Come on, let's go for a walk, get something to eat," he told her back at the car.

"Go for a walk," Yael repeated, her eyes widening.

"We got two hours before the meeting, the time was changed."

"Okay, Lou. Whatever you say."

She seemed to relax once they reached Times Square. How could anything bad happen to her in the most brightly lit blocks in the entire world?

So many other people were walking on these sidewalks, they didn't attract any attention, even with Yael looking like a street urchin. Everyone was staring up – taking in the names of the theatres and their shows – *A Night of Love* and *A Royal Fandango* and *'Neath the South Sea* and *Anything Might Happen*.

Louis thought the plays sounded dumb. If he made real money, this wasn't the life he wanted for himself. A lot of guys he knew craved the high-roller style: Broadway shows, bottles of champagne, and showgirls. But Louis dreamed of something else. One night, when driving on Park Avenue north of 57th Street, he'd passed a fine brick apartment building, its lobby suffused with lamplight and fringed with potted plants. The floor gleamed like finely spun gold. In the middle of the lobby stood a smiling doorman greeting a couple who'd just emerged from the elevator, holding their child by each hand. Louis had stared at the tableaux, fixing it in his memory.

"Lou, you said we could get something to eat?"

"Yeah, sure."

She pointed across 42nd Street at an opening between two theatres, a crevice really, which had its own little electrified sign, "*Hotdogs, Five Cents.*"

"You know those ain't kosher, right, Yael?"

She grinned, "*Opposite* of kosher."

When Louis gave the go-ahead, to his astonishment Yael ran across 42nd Street, even though it was clogged with cars. Horns honked. The crosswalk was far away, so he had no choice but to jaywalk too. More horns.

He couldn't yell at her once he caught up. She was so ecstatic to be ordering a hotdog. He bought two for each of them, along with orange sodas.

They hadn't reached the next corner before she'd wolfed hers down. "Thanks, Lou. Those were as good as Nathan's on Coney Island. You ever eat Nathan's?"

"Sure. You like Coney Island, Yael?"

"Nothin' better. They open the park next week, Memorial Day." She took a few more steps and tugged on his sleeve, "Am I gonna get to go to Coney Island, Lou? What do *you* think?"

He looked down. Her eyes looked funny. Maybe it was the lights reflecting in her pupils.

"Why not?" he said irritably, pulling his sleeve away. "You wanna go, go. Ride the roller-coaster all day. What do I care?"

They walked side by side in silence for a couple of minutes. A sign caught Lou's attention. It didn't seem possible. He squinted. Yes, that's what it said: "*Hubert's Museum and Flea Circus.*"

"Talk about Coney Island!" he said. "What's this doin' here?"

When she saw it, Yael jumped up and down. "I never been to a flea circus, Lou. Can we go in? Can we?"

Trying to act nonchalant, Louis bought tickets. The truth was, he was eager too. "*Seeing Is Believing!*" said a sign behind the ticket-seller's head.

And did they ever see. A man with a tiny misshapen head greeted Louis and Yael with great politeness. Around the corner, standing under a spotlight, was a woman with a beard over one foot long.

The star of the evening was Prince Randian, the Human Caterpillar. A man without arms or legs, he rolled around on the floor and lit a cigarette using only his lips.

But it was the flea circus that left the two of them speechless. On a long table, spotlights shining down, the keepers of the fleas demonstrated their marvel for ticketholders crowded around. The tiny insects, delicate wires attached, jumped into hoops, kicked balls, pulled a miniature stagecoach, and even shot out of a cannon.

Louis and Yael reacted as one, laughing and gasping and cheering on the fleas each time they pulled off a miraculous feat. At the show's end, they clapped until their hands were raw.

"I'll never forget this, Lou," she whispered on 42nd Street. "Never. First hotdogs and then the museum. A real pinhead, the human caterpillar, and the circus. Those fleas. No matter what happens, all I gotta say is... Geez."

A lump formed in the back of his throat. *Damn.*

"Must be time to get back to Lindy's," he said. "Let's hit it."

On their walk to the car, Louis was so frustrated with the situation, he almost brought it up again, what Yael had done, even though there was no point. What was done was done. He shouldn't need to justify himself.

That afternoon, while he'd talked to Luigi De Luca about interviewing his daughter-in-law, Yael had stood quietly in the opposite corner, hidden behind one of the shop's sale exhibits. She had begged to be allowed to hear his pitch, and he didn't see any harm, as long as she was unobserved. After his argument with the cheese shop owner, the guy had stormed through a door that looked like it led to a cellar. There had been nothing for Louis to do but leave himself, cursing his failure.

"De Luca better not make the call to the newspaper," Louis fretted. "That might get back to The Fixer, he won't like that I bungled it."

They got back into the car, but Louis, before turning the ignition, slammed the steering wheel with both hands. What a mess he had made!

"Lou, hold on," Yael said. "I dropped something in the store. Lemme go back."

"Aw, forget it," he said. "I wanna get the hell out of Little Italy."

She pushed open the door. "It will only take a couple of minutes."

And that was the unbelievable part. She *was* back in a few minutes – ten at the most – a funny little smile on her face. With a sigh, he started up the car. As he pulled out of the spot, he heard a woman scream. People were running... toward De Luca's Cheese.

"Yael," he said, studying the rear-view mirror, "What did you just do?"

"No witnesses, no indictment, Lou. That's what you told me."

He'd gone into shock until they got to the other side of the Williamsburg Bridge. Then he was the one doing the screaming. How could she be so stupid? De Luca hadn't witnessed Louis doing anything that bad, just impersonating a newspaper reporter. But now, he could be pulled into a genuine murder, the kind they hanged people for.

"But I'm not gonna get caught," she said. "No one noticed me on the street, I swear to God. And nobody knows me in that neighbor-hood even if they did."

Even after he'd ranted and raved for so long that his throat hurt, Yael didn't see that she'd done anything bad. He demanded her gun – a cheap little .38 special she said she'd stolen from the back seat of a car last month – and threw it down the storm drain. After that, he tossed her out of his car too and told her he'd kill her if she ever blabbed.

"I did it for you, Lou," she said, puzzled, like she had gotten him his favorite candy bar from the lowest shelf at Rose's and he'd thrown it back in her face.

It was a miracle that the police arrested Nettuno, and the man got killed in jail soon afterward. But a miracle might have an expiration date.

Off Times Square, Louis ordered Yael to stay in the car, and once again, Louis made his way to Lindy's. At five minutes to ten, Arnold Rothstein was in his usual booth. Walking toward him, Louis put every ounce of effort into looking like he did last time they met – curious, amenable, eager to please. He must not show guilt.

Rothstein was sipping a glass of milk as Louis sat down. Patting his lips with a napkin, he said, "It's important to act when an opportunity is just right. Not let the moment pass. Wouldn't you say, Louis?"

He wasn't sure he liked the sound of that. But Louis nodded.

"We've got a deeply stupid president right now in Warren Harding. He's easy to take advantage of. His oldest friends are stealing the country blind right under his nose. We're doing important business with a few of those friends. Of course, stupidity isn't always enough. The mayor of New York is stupid, and we've done fairly well with him in office, but there is so much more that we could be doing. The trouble is, Mayor Wyland sometimes listens to the wrong people. It's just a matter of finding the right man for that job. Someone who will listen *only* to us. This is one of our chief priorities."

Rothstein finished his milk and took a closer look at Louis.

"We are going to be able to set up business very nicely now the way is clear. You played your part in that, Louis. I won't forget that."

"I'm only too happy to help, sir."

"I know that. There's just one loose end."

Louis did his best not to react too strongly. "You mean Mrs. De Luca?" he asked after a couple of seconds. "You know there was a murder in the De Lucas' store a few days after we talked? Some Italian gangster the old man owed money to shot him. There were cops everywhere. I've been lying low."

"So you never talked to anyone at the store, Louis?"

He'd planned to say no. How would Rothstein know differently? The man was dead minutes after Louis left. No one witnessed the argument except Yael. But some danger quivered in the air. In a split second, he changed his mind about what to say.

"I never got to the girl. The same day that he died, I went in, and I said what we agreed. De Luca didn't go for it. He said forget it. I couldn't talk to his daughter-in-law. I left. What else could I do?"

Rothstein sat back in the booth, "Thank you, Louis. You were honest. I appreciate honesty. I know that someone saying he was a reporter from a newspaper went into De Luca's Cheese and tried to pay for her story the day of his murder."

It was a test. And Louis passed... just.

Arnold Rothstein was so hard to fool about anything. When the greedy White Sox baseball team went looking for gamblers to pay them to throw the World Series in 1919, everyone knew Rothstein was the only one with a fortune large enough to pay off the players *and* make carefully placed bets. Some other crooks jumped in and tried to double-cross Rothstein, but that was simply impossible. When the "Black Sox" scandal broke, everyone suspected Rothstein was at the heart of it, but he was never arrested. Thanks to his ties to the politicians of Tammany Hall, the Fixer was untouchable.

"Do you want me to try to talk to her again, Mr. Rothstein?"

"Not as a newspaper reporter, no. It wouldn't be believable that you'd offer to pay for her story. Too much time has passed. No one is following up on Watkins' death with much enthusiasm. It's just so strange, Louis, her father-in-law getting shot the same day you talked to him."

"I didn't like it when I heard about it," Louis said truthfully.

"The police arrested someone. I've since heard that the man, Victor Nettuno, had syphilis. That affects the brain."

"Oh, wow."

"He was murdered at The Tombs by the order of Joe Masseria. That's what I've been told. Joe doesn't want anyone to think his collectors can act independently, no matter whether they're sick or not. And this female has been quiet, from all accounts. Still, there's something about this whole business…" He drummed his fingers on the delicatessen table. "I want you to wait two weeks, make sure all the police heat is off, and then follow Mrs. De Luca around for a couple of days, like you did with Watkins. See where she goes, if she goes anywhere. Report everything to me."

"Sure. I can do that."

"Very good. You know, Louis, I have you in mind for something else. You have any dealings in the garment district? No? Well, let me tell you how it could work. You should have something to eat while we discuss it. Allow me to buy you a slice of cheesecake. It's top-notch at Lindy's."

Louis had heard the expression "walking on air" but it had no meaning for him until tonight. After the conversation with Rothstein, he felt like he was floating back to the car. He saw the silhouette of Yael in her cap a half-block away and couldn't wait to reach her.

"Everything's swell!" he told her after jumping in the car. "You're goin' to Coney Island next month, Yael. I'll take you myself."

They laughed together, hers edged with hysteria. No denying it had been a rough night. He drove down to 42nd Street and turned west to plunge through the heart of Times Square. Why not? Get a last blast of electric light.

"Lookee there, Lou," she said, pointing at a crowded sidewalk on 42nd while they waited at the intersection. "It's Charlie Lucania and Frankie Costello with a bunch of broads."

He glanced over. "Yeah, Lucania's something, isn't he? He's got a girl on each arm, one brunette and one redhead."

"At Rose's, they say those two are the up-and-comers to watch, Lou."

"Yeah? Well, you happen to be sitting next to another up-and-comer, Yael. I got a whole new thing going with The Fixer. I'm gonna be *rich*."

The red light turned green, and Louis hit the gas. "I just got to take care of one more small job first."

CHAPTER TWENTY-FOUR

ZIA

Hearing a tantalizing snatch of conversation – *the stone has been removed from our shoe* – convinced me that if I spent time in The Orchid Hour, near the action, I'd soon pick up enough information for Lieutenant Hudgins.

I had something already, but not much. Rothstein was involved, but the lieutenant already knew that master gambler Arnold Rothstein was the principal investor in The Orchid Hour. It was common sense that he'd have a part to play in actions concerning the nightclub. Who killed Mr. Watkins, my father-in-law, or even Nettuno – that was a blank. I had no names.

The afternoon following my descent into the underworld, as Julia Morel had put it so memorably, I was expected to start work at The Orchid Hour. When I woke, my head hurt, and my stomach shuddered. I had consumed only a little alcohol, but there had been absolutely no food served anywhere. No one had offered me a glass of water. I guess anything besides booze was pointless.

I forced down a slice of bread with my coffee and told my mother-in-law, who was signaling a great deal of quiet distress over the lateness of my return home, that I had an appointment at Café Dante for a waitressing job.

"Why do you need to work way over there?" she asked. "We have friends much closer to home who might need help."

Café Dante's location – and the fact that Mama and the Pellegrinos didn't know its owners – were the reasons I had chosen it as my "employer." I would need to have a cover at home for going undercover at The Orchid Hour. How would I keep it all straight?

I murmured something vaguely placating to Mama and then got ready to go to MacDougal Alley. I sponge-cleaned my violet print dress from the night before. I didn't want to appear in the same blue dress that I'd worn when I met David da Costa.

The exertions of the night before took a toll on me, for I found that when I turned from MacDougal Street onto the cobblestone alley, my stomach was still turning over.

Edgar recognized me and released the lock on the door so I could enter. I heard a particular voice the minute I slipped inside.

"No, no, not the orchid pink, the *rose pink* for that stripe. My God, have you no sense? Did we hire senseless people to paint the walls of the most important room of the season?"

David da Costa was in high dudgeon again, lecturing a crestfallen painter standing by the wall, holding a brush. This time, at least the actor wasn't dressed like an eccentric on an absinthe binge. He wore regular trousers and a shirt, though he had fewer buttons fastened at the top than most men I knew.

A woman laughed. I hadn't noticed her at first. She was sprawled full length on top of a wooden packing box, her head propped up with one hand. "Is that the same orchid pink shade that Cecil B. De Mille had that limousine painted for Gloria Swanson?" she asked.

"Lord, I hope not," said David da Costa. "C.B. has the worst – the *worst* – taste of any man alive."

He changed his stance, spreading his feet wide and pounding his thigh as if he held a whip. In a deep, pompous voice, he shouted, "If a man clogs the wheel of the Pharoah, he shall be ground into dust!"

The young woman squealed her appreciative laughter and sat up. A second later, she called out, "Who's this?" while pointing at me. She was wearing the same Yale sweater that David da Costa had on the other day.

"Oh, thank goodness you're here," said David, hurrying over. "Miss Lucania, I will have someone run you up to Riverside Drive. Heinrich is back in town, and he can show you everything."

"Riverside Drive?" I asked, taken aback. That was uptown, miles from MacDougal.

"We found an apartment on Riverside and 73rd that has the light Heinrich needs," he said as if that explained everything. "Alexander can take you. I'll find him."

After he'd careened in a new direction, the young woman said, "So David hired *you* for the flowers?" She was undeniably pretty, with tousled blonde hair, light blue eyes, and a mouth like a bow. "What did he say your name was?"

"Miss Lucania," I said.

"*Miss* Lucania?" she said sarcastically. "Well, I am *Miss* Westwood." Her eyes flicked up and down my figure. "You don't fancy being sent up to Riverside, huh? I suppose you were planning on begging David to tell you all his stories about being in *Blood and Sand*."

"That's not too likely, since I haven't seen *Blood and Sand*," I said.

"Oh, my." She turned, cupping her mouth with braceleted hands, "Woo, hoo, David, you've hired the one woman in America who's never seen *Blood and Sand*."

I was mortified – the last thing I wanted to do was insult my employer – but David da Costa said, "That's the best news I've heard all day." He smiled in my direction, a flash of perfect white teeth.

After introducing me to Alexander, a ruddy-faced older man, he said, "Miss Lucania, you'll need to tell the doorman you want to go to apartment seven-G. And tell Heinrich I'll need two orchids and the new Byrdcliffe panels tonight. We'll have to figure out how to transport them later."

"Yes, Mr. da Costa," I said.

"Oh, please, call me David. Can you do that?"

I nodded. He stood, waiting, not agitated or mocking me or anything. Just waiting. I wanted to comply but couldn't. I wasn't ready to call this man by his first name.

Someone shouted for him from another corner of the club, and he whirled around. I took that as my cue to leave with Alexander.

It didn't take as long as I expected to reach Riverside. Alexander drove so far west that he was practically in the Hudson River before turning north and rumbling at a fast click to 73rd Street. It meant that when we arrived at the building, I hadn't had enough time to overcome my dislike of Miss Westwood. I didn't want to be close to the club to swoon over David da Costa but to gather information. She'd made it clear she was David da Costa's girlfriend and was acting absurdly territorial. He mocked Cecil B. De Mille's taste but what about his own?

I tried to put the woman out of my mind and concentrate on this grand white-stone apartment building. It reminded me a little of the Seward Branch library, which meant it had been designed by Stanford White or someone like him fifteen or twenty years ago.

When I told the doorman seven-G, as instructed, he said, "You must be Miss Lucania. You are expected."

How nice. Could it be that efficiency was intruding on the chaos associated with The Orchid Hour?

The seventh floor was also the top one, and I stepped out from the elevator onto a carpeted hallway. Apartment G was at the end. My nervousness bubbled up yet again. The first time I talked to David da Costa, he said no one had met Heinrich's standards. How would I accomplish this feat when all I knew about orchids, I had learned from a single book that I didn't even finish?

I knocked three times. For several seconds, I heard only silence, then a series of faint thumps on the other side. One... two... three.

"Miss Lucania?" said a voice with an unmistakable German accent.

"Yes, Mr. Zimmer, it's Audenzia Lucania."

A lock clicked and a second one below it. The door opened wide. Heinrich was on crutches, his left leg gone below the knee. Then I observed that while his face was lined, he had a younger man's lively gaze and a thatch of thick brown hair. It was impossible to guess his age. He could have been anywhere between thirty and fifty.

Leading me out of the tidy foyer, Heinrich made his way into a large room with floor-to-ceiling windows serving up a magnificent view of the Hudson River and the forests of New Jersey rising above the bank's far side. But for me, the room was all about orchids. At least thirty plants emerged from red clay pots, carefully arranged on two long, tall benches.

"I take it this is the best light for them?" I asked, recalling what David da Costa had said and trying to sound knowledgeable.

"For orchids? Yes, Miss Lucania, this is good. They need eight hours a day of indirect sunlight and best placed near a window facing the west."

His English was excellent. I noticed that Germans who immigrated to America prioritized working on their English. But Heinrich had only been in the city a few months at most, as far as I knew.

Heinrich continued, "Also, David understands that I could only live on the perimeter of a modern city. I couldn't be trapped in the center of New York, and neither could my orchids."

I had no idea how to respond, so I asked, "Would you like to walk me through my duties?" I opened my handbag to fetch my notebook and pencil.

"First, I think we should have tea, Miss Lucania. I hope you wouldn't mind preparing it? The kitchen and pantry are to the right. The kettle, tea leaves, and all that goes with it should be self-evident."

As I made my way to the kitchen, I wondered if this meant I hadn't won the position quite yet. Would he decide after tea? I sighed. What did Julia call it? An audition – I was forever auditioning for this part.

At least my tea preparation would be spot on. Everything was easy to find, as he said. I measured the Orange Pekoe tea leaves while the kettle warmed and organized sugar and cream. As I put the porcelain cups and spoons on a silver tray, I noticed a variety of tins, boxes, and sacks on the shelves, indicating that Heinrich took all of his meals in the apartment. It looked like he slept here too. Perhaps there was a bedroom off the corridor stretching to the left of the main room. For a woman, this place of work lacked propriety. But then, everything about The Orchid Hour lacked propriety.

I set up the tea at a table about six feet from the orchid benches. Heinrich propped his crutches and swung into a chair with an efficiency of movement. "Thank you, this is delicious," he said after his first sip. "So, you know the story of the Lady's Slipper?"

"I'd read that it was extinct."

"Yes, the Victorians went orchid mad. They over-harvested the Lady's Slipper, Miss Lucania. Too much competition. It was declared extinct in England more than five years ago. But while I was in Berlin, my contacts informed me that a similar subspecies grows in the wild in America. They were correct. And there are about ten nurseries surrounding New York that grow the orchids as well."

I glanced over at the benches covered with orchid plants. I saw delicate flowers of different sizes, white, pink, and yellow. Some plants had no flowers at all, just light green leaves.

He cleared his throat and said, "Allow me to tell you something about myself. I'm from an old Prussian family, with all the unfortunate aspects that implies. My father permitted me to study botany at university, and I was most fortunate to be hired by the Berlin-Dahlem Botanical Garden. Do you know their history begins in 1573 in the kitchen garden of the royal palace? Now, Berlin is second only to Kew in all of Europe. The orchids were my responsibility… before it was decided to release me because of financial problems."

He paused, biting his lip. The last sentence was laced with bitterness. If only I could tell Heinrich about the library and emphasize that I understood how he felt.

As I sympathized silently, he gathered himself and pushed on. "I met David just after the Botanical Garden dismissed me. He was staying with a family friend, the Countess Stein. He's an amazing student of the orchid. When we met, he knew next to nothing. Now, I think he could run his own greenhouse."

This bit of the story confused me. "Mr. da Costa didn't travel to Berlin for the orchids?"

"Oh, no. He was drawn to Berlin because of Decla Film."

My blank face prompted him to say, as if it were obvious, "The German studio that made *The Cabinet of Dr. Caligari*. It revolutionized film as art."

"I see."

"David is interested in German Expressionism, Miss Lucania. I thought everyone knew that that type of film is his passion. When we left Berlin, it was with ten orchids and a renegade copy of *Nosferatu*." He laughed dryly.

And I was left with a new piece to the puzzle of David da Costa, but one that didn't fit anywhere.

"So, your responsibility will be to care for the plants every afternoon," Heinrich continued. "They thrive on consistency. I must make short trips outside New York City to our greenhouse in New Jersey and to meet with people who sell orchids. I also have appointments at the New York Botanical Garden in the Bronx."

I poured Heinrich another cup of tea, my hands steady while my thoughts were not. How was I to learn the dangerous secrets of The Orchid Hour while taking care of plants all afternoon on Riverside Drive?

He said, "Also, while staying in New York, I have doctor appointments. The physicians here have been cooperative, more than I expected. I did not think they would be agreeable to treating a German war veteran."

How could I not have realized this? He'd lost his leg in the war. For all I knew, this man I'd just served tea could have fought opposite Armando and Giovanni on the battlefield.

I put down the teacup I'd been studying and reluctantly met his gaze. The lines on his face seemed to have deepened. "My history troubles you, Miss Lucania, I can see that," he said. "This position might not be the right one for you."

"The war is over," I said in a faltering voice, unlikely to convince anyone.

"In America, it seems easy for everyone to forget the war ever happened. Not so for those of us on the other side of the Atlantic. What does it say in *The Waste Land*? '*He who was living is now dead. We who were living are now dying* ...'"

"'*With a little patience,*'" I finished. Heinrich blinked rapidly, surprised.

"A friend of mine here in New York was fond of *The Waste Land*," I explained, my heart pounding. "And I must tell you, *he* thought of the war quite often."

I had barely thought of Mr. Watkins today. But he deserved justice, and I was the only one who cared. With renewed determination, I said, "I would very much like to perform these duties, Mr. Zimmer."

He nodded. "Very good. Very good. Take out that paper and pencil. I will instruct you on the orchids. We shall call each other by our Christian names, yes? I am Heinrich. I may call you Audenzia?"

"Yes, Heinrich."

For the next two hours, I made notes on the incredibly detailed regimen laid out by Heinrich for his orchids. Periodically, he would say, "Audenzia, I know *this* will surprise you," and then rattle off some point of instruction. It never seemed odder than anything else he was saying, but I nodded as if to agree. He assumed I knew a lot about orchids already and kept urging me to radically change these assumptions. He grew quite emotional when it came to watering orchids and how many plants had died over the years because of people's blunders.

What struck me throughout his lecture was how the plants themselves seemed indifferent to all the fuss over their welfare and the emotional turmoil they'd caused to blundering human beings. Orchids were sweet, slight creations with an air of whimsy. Yes, the petals of some orchids resembled a slipper. Others looked like a tiger's paw. Or a child's ball. The orchids were saying, "We're having fun with this business of being many thousands of years old."

One thing that disappointed me was the orchids' scent. It was subtle. For some reason, I thought the flowers would be quite fragrant. I had a lot to learn.

Heinrich gave me the decorative panels: four long wooden boards with orchids painted right on them. Byrdcliffe was, he explained, an "artists' colony" in upstate New York where David da Costa had stayed a couple of years ago. While there, the actor met artists skilled at painting on wood. He commissioned these after taking the position at The Orchid Hour. Someday, David wanted to return to Byrdcliffe to try painting himself. I was having difficulty keeping up with my boss's shifting enthusiasms.

As Heinrich prepared the live orchids for transport, I detected the first crack in the alliance between David da Costa and Heinrich Zimmer. "I do not know if these will fulfill David's wishes," he muttered as he gently placed two with green and white petals in a box.

"They are beautiful," I said. "Is there another purpose to serve?"

"Never mind, never mind," he said. "Time will tell."

Even after listening to Heinrich for hours, I didn't understand why they were going to so much trouble and paying through the nose to station orchids in pots throughout the nightclub. But I had asked the question too directly. My problem is I'm not too good at ferreting information out of people that they didn't want to share readily.

Alexander responded to the call for a driver to convey me, the Byrdcliffe panels, and the orchids to the nightclub. He carried the panels in while I concentrated on the orchids.

The smell of fresh paint met me the second I walked through the door. They had accomplished so much in the last four hours. The club's unusual color scheme struck me – cream, black, pale silver, and the two different pink shades, one of them the hotly debated orchid pink mentioned earlier.

What also intrigued me was the seating placed in the middle of the room – a round table and two chairs. They were of lacquered wood, painted black, with seating upholstery of pale silver and a pink stripe running along the table's rim. On the chair, the silver was muted, like the color of winter frost, while on the walls, the silver gleamed. I have to say, this furniture was extraordinary. I'd seen nothing remotely like it at any speakeasy I'd visited with Sal – or any place in New York City. There were workmen around but no sign of either David da Costa or his dreadful girlfriend. I didn't want to leave the orchids just anywhere. I had learned enough to know that he could consider the orchids' welfare more important than most human beings.

At the back of the club, to the left of the stage, I noticed a window for the first time, up high. The blinds were down on the other side of the window glass, but there was a light on, probably a lamp, and I could make out the silhouette of a head. Maybe this was David da Costa's office.

A door even farther to the left might lead to the room behind the window. It wasn't easy, but I managed it while holding the flower box and walked up the short flight of stairs. As I ascended, I recognized two men's voices: David da Costa's and my cousin Sal's.

It was a small office occupied by four people. I knew three of them – Sal in a chair, David behind a desk, and his girlfriend in the back corner. The fourth was a man of about thirty, with his shirt sleeves pushed above his elbows. He didn't look happy – none of them did.

"Thank you, Audenzia," said David. He hit the second syllable of my name with more emphasis than most people. "I'm afraid you come upon us in the middle of a crisis. The man I hired to run the kitchen has decamped for another job, and his replacement, Edward, tells me that I have been taken for a ride. The small kitchen here and the staff could never pull off this menu." He picked up a long, folded piece of paper.

"Most nightclubs don't even bother to serve food," said Sal.

"I *know*," said David, anguished. "It was one way we would present ourselves as different and better."

His girlfriend giggled. She wore a black cloche hat, its fringe hanging down to her shoulders, and when she laughed, it trembled. "You never eat – how could you know anything about food?" she said. "Mustn't be chunky on camera."

"Shut up, Sally," he snapped.

"Could I see the menu?" I asked. He handed it to me. It was a lengthy one with dishes right out of Delmonico.

"What's your opinion?" David da Costa asked.

"Even if you had a vast kitchen and an army of chefs, I don't see beef tenderloin and gravy being served on the table I just saw downstairs," I said. "You'd never get the gravy stains out of that upholstery. It's not the right kind of food for this place."

Edward, the new chef, said ruefully, "She's right about that."

Sal said, "She sure is."

I was getting ready to return the menu when my eyes stopped on the line for appetizers. I spotted "*chilled shrimp.*"

Looking at Edward, I suggested, "You could cook up some shrimp and chill them and serve the dishes straight out of the refrigerator with lemon slices?"

"Sure."

I told David, "There's a range of appetizers you could serve while calling them small dishes. That would be one way to go. So people would have something to eat. To serve only drinks, well, that's fine for a blind pig, but not this sort of establishment."

Sal covered his mouth with a hand to stifle his laugh.

"Yes, yes, that's what they're doing in Paris," said David da Costa, jumping out of his chair. "I forgot! People eat only first-course food at parties. It's the new thing. *Canapes*."

"If your dishes had high-quality ingredients, like the best mozzarella, you'd still make a strong impression with your menu," I said.

"And *you* know where to get the best mozzarella?" demanded David's girlfriend, pointing at me with a nail painted dark red, something I'd heard women were having done but never seen before.

"As a matter of fact, I do," I said.

I could feel Sal's gaze burning the side of my face. When I shot him a look, he shook his head, half impressed and half aghast.

David asked Edward if he could create a streamlined menu based on small dishes and canapes. The answer was an enthusiastic yes.

"Could you help, Audenzia?" David pleaded. "We open in five days. I know it's a lot to ask on top of the orchid care, but we all need to jump in on everything."

I assured him I'd be able to handle both areas. To me, this was a lucky break. Now, I had a way into the club, at least for a week or so.

I naturally gave Edward the name of De Luca's Cheese for the mozzarella. And I promised to come up with a list of other places to source high-quality ingredients once he'd created a new menu. He said he should have that ready by the following afternoon.

The meeting broke up, and I got ready to leave the club to go home. But there was one more conversation left to have.

Sally Westwood stood next to the door connecting the club to the florist. Now that I could see her full length, not huddled in the corner of the dark office, I realized what she wore: a dress that shot straight down, a dropped waist, shimmering in blue, green, and gold, with a dramatic black fringe. This was, I realized after scanning magazines and chatting with the Macy's saleswoman, the total "Egyptomania" look.

"You came to the rescue today, Miss Lucania," said Sally Westwood, with sardonic emphasis on my name. "David thought you had the right temperament for the orchids, but who knew you'd suit working with the food?"

"The right temperament," I repeated. I knew immediately that was a mistake.

"Yes, he called Heinrich this morning to tell him you were on your way. David said, 'She seems intelligent, and she also seems to be quite a cold woman. Just the sort we need.'"

CHAPTER TWENTY-FIVE

ZIA

It should not have bothered me that David da Costa thought me cold. When I was at school, I gloried in being seen as aloof. I hated the stereotype of the histrionic Mediterranean female, laughing or crying at the drop of a hat and, worse, flirting with any man around. I once overheard my mother saying with pride, "I never have to worry about Audenzia that way."

Armando was such a kind and thoughtful man that I felt comfortable with him right away. I was a happy bride, and I'd like to think I made him a devoted wife.

To me, "cold" meant unfeeling, which I objected to. I adored my son, and if I didn't care about my family or my friends, what was I doing trying to gather information at this nightclub?

But the biggest question was – why even care what David da Costa thought of my character? He'd hired me and now seemed to want to give me a lot to do. That's what counted.

The next several days were such a frantic blur that I often forgot the comment about my being cold. I rushed back and forth between the Riverside Drive apartment and the nightclub with scarcely time to catch my breath. But I had to make time to shop for clothes with Julia Morel. As Sal said, two dresses were not enough.

Those hours with Julia were both enjoyable... and disturbing. First, she had a wealth of contacts at boutiques throughout Manhattan, even though she'd only been living here a year. Some of these shops had dresses that fit me with a few quick stitches or were as ready-to-wear as the ones I'd bought at Macy's. And they cost less. As she explained, an actress or dancer had to look chic while all too often having very little money of her own. There were tricks to pulling that off. Julia was skilled with a needle and insisted on hemming one of my new skirts after we bought it downtown.

In her Gramercy Park flat, after she'd finished the hemming, she said, "If things continue to go well at the nightclub, do you plan to move out of your mother-in-law's home?" After discussing it first with Sal, I'd told Julia about being a widow with a child, fired from the library, and caught up in a police investigation. She agreed to keep my secret.

"I can't move in with my brother, he drives me nuts, and he lives in the Bronx, so if Michael and I don't live on Mulberry Street, we have no other place to go."

She looked at me with a puzzled frown, although, being Julia, she still looked beautiful.

Trying to make light of my situation, I said, "Who knows? I could meet a Sicilian widower who needs a new wife."

Julia said, shaking her head, "Zia, with all the gifts you have, all your intelligence, this is the best future you can come up with for yourself?"

I assured Julia I was joking. But she wouldn't let this go.

"Why not get your own flat for you and your son?" she asked. "Sal told me your wages would be good. I'm sure you could find something big enough."

I was about to tell her that a woman couldn't live on her own, even a widow, unless she had absolutely no choice, when I remembered that Julia lived in this flat by herself.

"You do believe in following those rules don't you, Zia? The rules of *ordine della famiglia*?"

She spat out the Italian phrase as if it were poison.

"You don't believe in them?" I asked.

"No, I don't. I'll tell you why. My mother was attacked in Sicily by a man she barely knew. The *ordine della famiglia* says that after that happens, the woman is supposed to marry the man – the man who raped her. She refused. A couple of months later, she knew by the signs every woman gets that she would have a baby. She had to run away and go through a lot of hardship to avoid marrying that man – she had to go all the way to New Orleans. And even here, in America, there were people in the Sicilian community who looked down on her because she had violated *ordine della famiglia* in coming here alone."

The story of Julia's mother horrified me. It took great courage to do what she did. I could not imagine marrying a man who had raped me, but fleeing to another country?

"Were things better for your mother after she got married?" I asked.

"She loved my stepfather, so she was happy in that way, but she was an outcast among the Sicilians. My stepfather was a Creole, Zia. Do you know what that means?"

I shook my head.

"He's of mixed race. The Creoles are the most wonderful people in New Orleans, but the Sicilians look down on them because they're not white. What they don't accept is that to the American Protestants, Italians aren't white either. We're barely human!"

She laughed, but it wasn't a happy laugh. Her eyes glistened. While she had talent, beauty, and intelligence – all the things that are supposed to matter most in a woman – Julia felt she had little status in the eyes of others. And it hurt her, as it would anyone.

After a few minutes, she said, "Forgive me for burdening you like this. You're like Charles, a good listener."

I realized after she said it that she was right. Sal *was* a good listener.

"He's going to the top," she said proudly. "And he doesn't believe in *ordine della famiglia*. Charles is modern. And he's not prejudiced."

To the top of what? I wondered. Although a part of me resisted probing, I was desperate to learn more about my cousin's business.

"He's got a nice setup with The Orchid Hour," I said neutrally.

"He and Costello have tapped into the best routes for carrying premium liquor – not just the Bahamas but Canada too," she said. "It took a lot of hard work, but now, it's all paying off."

My heart sank, but I could not say I was surprised. I'd been getting the message for a while that Sal was a major bootlegger. No one in New York City was giving up drinking alcohol, creating a gaping need, one to be filled illegally.

"I just wish he'd focus on that and forget about some of the other stuff," she said.

"What other stuff?"

"Nothing, nothing," Julia said quickly.

That gave me a bad feeling indeed. What was worse than being a bootlegger? Did Sal commit the same kind of crimes as Joe Masseria – extortion, counterfeiting, and the rest? Or, even worse, was he responsible for violence? But I couldn't believe my cousin had gunned down Mr. Watkins. And I *knew* he was not the one who shot my father-in-law.

Now that I knew my cousin and Frankie Costello arranged the liquor supplies for The Orchid Hour, some things made more sense. But not, crucially, the need for murder. Other speakeasies and nightclubs operated with impunity. What made The Orchid Hour different?

It wasn't just Sal and Frankie who were busy supplying the nightclub on MacDougal Alley. After reviewing the final menu with Edward, I met two more of Sal's friends one evening. They were both young, in their early twenties, but that was where the similarity stopped. One was short and thin and wore clothes I suspect were intended to make him blend in as much as possible. The other was Sal's height with dark hair slicked back and wearing something I'd never seen before on a man – a purple shirt.

"Zia, I'd like you to meet Meyer Lansky and Guiseppe Dotto," said Sal.

"Pleased to meet you, but you can call me Joe Adonis," said Guiseppe with a big smile.

"Oh, no, she can't," said Sal, annoyed.

The smaller man said, "Have we met, Zia?"

"Jesus, not you too, Meyer!" shouted Sal.

"I feel as if we've met somewhere," said Meyer, not flirtatiously but in all seriousness. "I know your face."

Later, when we were alone, Sal told me that Meyer had grown up on the Lower East Side, near the Seward Park Library, and he might have been a patron and seen me there. "Of all my friends, he's the only one I'd call the bookish type," Sal said. "I think that's why Mr. Rothstein likes him so much."

"I don't remember seeing Meyer there, but a lot of people come in and out," I said.

Sal said, "You know, we should tell everyone your real name. I think it's gonna come out. Neither of us is gonna look too good when it does."

"I would prefer you didn't," I said. "At least wait another week, okay?"

Sal reluctantly agreed.

I wondered what David da Costa would think of my being a widow and mother with a past. I'm sure he wouldn't care. To David, I was a capable employee, nothing else. That's why I was surprised when he insisted I be there on what he called "opening night," the official unveiling of The Orchid Hour.

"I'm not sure it will be possible," I said. I couldn't tell him why, that The Orchid Hour *opening* at eleven o'clock caused problems with my mother-in-law. I had been gone every day at my supposed job at Café Dante and home by six. I could say I had to work a night shift, but the café closed at eleven.

"Don't you want to see your hard work brought to fruition, Audenzia?" he asked. "The orchids will be in place, we'll have delicious food at every table. And there are so many other wonderful things! I've a musical surprise, you know. I want you to listen the first night."

He was like a little boy, begging me to admire his marble collection.

"All right," I relented. "I will be there, but I can't stay for hours and hours."

He smiled and said, "I'm so happy about this – and may I make another request? You should wear that same blue dress as the first night you came in. Will you?"

I nodded, surprised he would remember what I wore.

He did not move on, though I knew that a hundred matters required his attention. Sal said David got little sleep. His dark hair looked hopelessly tousled as if he didn't have a minute to run a comb through it. He was pale with purple shadows under his eyes. Yet energy poured out of him.

"It's quite something, how far the club has come in a week," I said.

"Oh, a lot can happen in a week," he laughed.

The day that The Orchid Hour opened to customers, little things went wrong: the shrimp was delivered hours late; a few band members had complaints about the musical program choices; the barkeep, Basil, picked a fight with David da Costa at eight o'clock over the chosen brand of gin for a gin gimlet.

For me, the biggest revelation before the club opened came early in the afternoon, when Heinrich finally revealed to me on Riverside Drive the plan for how a particular type of orchid would enhance the experience of The Orchid Hour.

"We have to focus on the *Brassavolas*," Heinrich said solemnly of a row of orchids with small white petals. The first night and each night afterward, at least three of the five orchids displayed on their stands must be *Brassavolas*.

I couldn't understand why. We had other orchids that were lovelier or more striking.

"It's their fragrance," Heinrich said, taking note of my puzzlement.

But I smelled nothing coming from the *Brassavolas,* and I said so. It was then that Heinrich filled me in on their strategy. This particular type of *Brassavola* grew in Guyana and Colombia, hunted, secured, and brought to North America at great expense. The reason? The flower gave off a delicious fragrance, but only at night.

"You know that insects pollinate most orchids, but it's special with orchids. Each variety evolves to attract a particular insect," Heinrich said. "The connection between them, the attraction, is exclusive. It could be a bee, a wasp, a gnat, or a butterfly. The orchid puts out a fragrance that is irresistible to that insect. It's not always agreeable to us. Flies are attracted to flesh, and certain orchids smell like dead animals for the purpose of drawing in a specific fly. It's horrible! This type of *Brassavola* is the opposite. It gives off a fragrance that this particular moth cannot resist, and it's one that we humans happen to love too. The moth in question only flutters at night, so that's when the orchid releases its scent. They call it 'The Lady of the Night.'"

Heinrich had inhaled the fragrance of the *Brassavolas* at midnight on Riverside, and he said it was as enchanting as he'd hoped for. But would it happen in the nightclub? He didn't know, and I could see he was nervous.

I conveyed them to MacDougal and saw to it that the *Brassavola* orchids were placed on their chosen stands. I leaned down and inhaled, one by one. Nothing. Was it too early? Or would they decline to cooperate at any hour tonight?

I changed into my blue dress in the ladies' room at ten-thirty. The door opened behind me, and I flinched. I didn't want to encounter Sally Westwood. She hadn't been around the last three days. It was too much to hope for that she'd skip the club opening.

But it was Julia who rushed in, laughing. "Isn't this thrilling? I ran out of the theater the minute the curtain call finished, and Charles was waiting at the curb with the engine running to bring me down."

She had a bag of cosmetics and insisted I put on lipstick and rouge. When we emerged, Sal swept Julia up in a kiss as she fended him off and scolded him for mussing her face.

My attention drifted to the other side of the club. David da Costa stood in the doorway to the steps leading to his office. He wore a tuxedo the likes of which I'd never seen. His tight waistcoat fit perfectly, and the coat swung down almost to his knees. Who knew trousers could even crease like that? Topping it all off, a white bowtie.

As he moved across the club floor, I watched each step. It was impossible not to. David was like a different person. Instead of throwing his arms in the air, stomping his foot, or shouting over some disappointment, he exuded elegant calm. He'd become the man I saw in *Photoplay*.

David da Costa's an actor, I reminded myself. This is what they do.

He might be exuding confidence, but a part of me feared that no one would show up at eleven. We'd put ourselves through this for nothing. You couldn't advertise an illegal establishment. I didn't know how the word had gone out about The Orchid Hour. When I asked Sal about that, he said, "David knows how to stir the pot."

Did he ever.

The first people showed up at eleven on the dot, and there was a steady stream afterward. I could read on their faces how awed they were by the decor of the club – the color scheme, furniture, art, and light fixtures. All the details that David had fretted over night and day. As I was in and out of the kitchen, I knew very well that everyone shown to a table ordered a small dish of food as well as drinks. The music, mostly jazz, seemed to meet with the crowd's approval. The dance floor was packed.

One of the highlights was David da Costa and Julia Morel dancing the Argentine tango. As they were trained dancers, their tango's precise yet animalistic grace was something to see. They looked as if they were passionately in love, barely able to control themselves. I knew that it was part of the act. But how *convincing* they were. The tango ended with David nearly flinging his partner to the floor as he quivered with seeming desire. Applause filled the club; I glanced at my cousin. Sal had the same look as when N.T.G. singled out Julia at the El Fey

Club. He was proud, but he exuded a certain possessive wariness. Maybe he did disdain *ordine della famiglia* as Julia assured me, but there was only so much you could expect of him.

My cousin's true nature was driven home even more when he grabbed me and insisted I stop running around. "You been working for over twelve hours, Zia. Enough. Enough. We're gonna have our own moment of celebration."

Sal guided me to a table for two, set with glasses of champagne and small plates of lobster.

"We shouldn't eat the kitchen's best dishes," I said, horrified.

"Why the hell not? Do you know how much I put into this club?"

David glided by, talking to two women and three men who resembled the patrons I saw at Chumley's. He glanced at us and smiled, not at all upset that Sal and I were eating lobster and drinking the finest champagne.

"He pulled it off," said Sal, nodding in approval. "Mr. Rothstein said that David is somebody who knows New Yorkers, knows what they are looking for before *they* even know it. Mr. Rothstein was right."

I finished my champagne, the fizziest I'd ever tasted.

"I wonder where his girlfriend is," I said.

"She went back to Los Angeles to shoot a movie," Sal said. "Why do you ask? What do you care, Zia?"

"I don't," I said. "Just making conversation."

It was after midnight when I celebrated with Sal, past time for me to leave, but I lingered at The Orchid Hour for two reasons. One was curiosity about the famous Arnold Rothstein, the chief investor in the club. I knew he held the key to understanding the ugly side of this beautiful place. Perhaps Sal would introduce me to him. I'd have to be ready for that and make the most of the opportunity.

The second reason was my curiosity over David da Costa's "musical surprise." The orchestra was quite good, but nothing they had played so far surprised me.

Just as I was getting ready to give up on both hearing the musical treat and meeting Arnold Rothstein, David stood on the stage and called for everyone's attention.

"We are privileged tonight to welcome a performance from a trio who were celebrated on the stage of the Troika of Rue Fontaine in Paris this year. They will now share with you a song from their lost homeland."

Three bearded men silently took their places in chairs set out for them, each carrying an instrument resembling a guitar but not like one I'd ever seen. When the music started, I knew I had never heard anything like it either. Their music was mournful but stirring. It soared and ached and cried out for something, if only I knew what.

Someone near me whispered, awestruck, "I think they're Russian gypsies."

I didn't know if they were from Russia or the planet Mars. I only knew that their music touched my soul as no other music had except opera. Their last chord was so powerful that I had to close my eyes.

When I opened them, I looked at the musicians and David da Costa at their side. The host of The Orchid Hour wasn't focused on the musicians or his important guests.

He was staring right at me.

I don't know how long we held each other's gaze. It could have been three seconds or half a minute. I was the one who broke off, backing away toward the kitchen.

I should have left the club. But I couldn't. I told myself that Edward needed me in the kitchen. And, of course, I had to monitor the orchids.

It was time to find out if the *Brassavola* magic was real. I leaned down, breathless with suspense, to inhale. My senses came alive. The scent of the *Brassavola* was like a gardenia but with a trace of something I could only compare to a rich soap, one created for pampering, and best of all, a dash of lemon. I adored lemon, the fruit of Sicily.

My head spun with the delight of the orchid, our Lady of the Night.

"Zia, enough with the orchids," said Joe Adonis, suddenly beside me. "You can't keep saying no. One dance. *One!*"

I gave into his pleadings and danced the foxtrot. Joe grinned down at me the entire time. It was the same flirtatious smirk he turned on every female in the club. Nothing to take seriously. But I would be lying if I said this wasn't fun. I never went dancing when I was in school. My parents forbade it. I was married by the time I turned eighteen. Pregnancy swiftly followed. Who would have thought I'd sail across a dance floor now, in my late twenties?

Through it all, even while dancing with Joe Adonis, I kept turning over in my mind that instant when I opened my eyes to find David da Costa staring at me. Why did he do it?

When the orchestra stopped playing and David formally bade the room good night, my high spirits faded. I was terrified to look at the time. How could I explain this to Mama? Would she believe I'd lost track of time while talking to a friend from Café Dante? As weak as this story was, I had nothing else.

The worst part was I'd learned absolutely nothing tonight about The Orchid Hour worth taking to Lieutenant Hudgins. This entire undercover business was becoming ridiculous. Instead of discovering what needed to be protected here, why people were dead, I got sucked into the pleasures of the nightclub, just like anybody else.

Sal tapped David da Costa's elbow and pointed toward the door to the office. I noticed that not only was Joe Adonis waiting there but Frankie Costello and Meyer Lansky too. I hadn't realized the last two were in the club.

The five men trooped upstairs. Julia sat at a table, looking sleepy, waiting for Sal. I should have gone to talk to her.

Instead, I made my way to the door to David's office. My plan was to creep up the stairs, listen to whatever was being said for a couple of minutes, and knock on the door. I'd inquire about the orchids – where should they be put now that the guests had left?

I opened the door as quietly as possible and tiptoed up the steps. The door to the office was shut. I had to pray that no one decided to come down before I was ready to announce myself. Huddled on the second-to-the-top step, I could hear their conversation.

"The numbers look good for the night, we don't need to go over this in detail now, do we, Charles?" said David. "We can study them with a clear head tomorrow when Arnold is here."

"There's just one more thing," said Sal. "It's about Audenzia."

"Your cousin?" asked another of the men.

"Yeah, she's my cousin," said Sal. "But I consider her a sister. And that's what I want to explain. There are rules to this thing of ours. We don't normally talk about them. But in the case of Zia, I gotta do it because I need to make sure this one rule is understood."

He paused and said firmly, "No one can touch her, just like no one can touch a man's wife or daughter. If you do, that's it. I'm sorry, but I'd have to shoot you."

CHAPTER TWENTY-SIX

ZIA

I did not go to The Orchid Hour for over a week. I still worked, but I performed my duties on Riverside Drive. I either cared for the orchids with Heinrich or made telephone calls to Edward about supplying the kitchen. Edward asked twice whether I'd be coming to the club. Each time, I made an excuse.

I knew that what I really should do was resign. I hadn't learned anything significant to pass on to Lieutenant Hudgins. What I *had* heard – the threat issued by Sal – made me want to hide in a hole in the ground.

Sal's warning to the men of The Orchid Hour to never touch me or face being shot was humiliating and outrageous. Julia told me that Sal didn't take seriously the *ordine della famiglia*. That wasn't what it sounded like when Sal issued his threat in David da Costa's office. Where else would these "rules" have come from?

Sal and I shared a special bond, but I didn't need my cousin to stand guard over my virtue at the age of twenty-seven. I was more than capable of taking care of myself. Frustratingly, as I'd heard his threat in a spot of eavesdropping, I couldn't bring it up.

As much as I resisted thinking about Sal's threat, I wondered what had prompted him to make it at all. Could it be his witnessing that one foxtrot with Joe Adonis? I suppose that *might* have been enough to kindle the protective instincts of a Sicilian man, even one who claimed to scorn the morals of the "Mustache Pete." I never gave a second thought to a dime-store Romeo like Joe Adonis. Didn't Sal know me well enough to realize that?

But it was otherwise for my boss, David da Costa. All I did was inquire about David's missing girlfriend, and Sal was on to me.

I couldn't pretend I didn't find the man attractive. He was being compared to Rudolph Valentino, and dressed in a tuxedo and dancing the tango, it looked like Valentino might get a run for his money.

David da Costa was, aside from being handsome, sophisticated, talented, and well-traveled, in possession of a pretty girlfriend, whether she was out of town or not. I had little to offer. I wasn't beautiful or sophisticated. When it came to my character, hadn't David already said I was cold? It was ludicrous to think he'd be attracted to me.

But then why had he looked at me like that after the Russian trio played their haunting music? It wasn't casual. It was as if he were trying to tell me something.

It turned out that Heinrich knew the Russians in question. They'd come across the Atlantic on the same steamship. "David da Costa's collection of refugees" was the way Heinrich put it with a dry laugh.

In Paris, he explained, the Russians were a sensation, playing the kind of music that was unknown to New Yorkers.

"The White Russians have flooded Paris," Heinrich said. "The enemies of the Bolsheviks lost everything when they fled their home-land. They had to sell their jewelry and work as seamstresses or cab drivers or whatever they could get. When they have earned a few coins, though, they go to the cabarets on the Rue la Fontaine and drink too much and listen to this music. They weep, oh, the Russians weep."

The music spread from being an obsession with Russian emigres to finding popularity with French audiences. From there, it was only a matter of time before Americans with the means to travel to Paris, like David da Costa, discovered them.

Heinrich said, "This could be the farthest these kinds of Russians have come since the war – all the way to New York City. Though I've heard they took refuge in China too."

That was the thing about Heinrich. He was so interesting. As I watered and nurtured the orchids, he told me stories of not just Berlin but Paris and other great cities. He was delighted with the charts I created to track the light and water the orchids received. "You are so organized, are you sure you're not German?" he teased.

In my heart, I knew I should resign my position – how much longer could I fool Mama and the others with this "job" at Café Dante? If I wasn't going to pick up information for Lieutenant Hudgins, it was pointless. But when I thought of forsaking my job to return to the apartment on Mulberry Street day and night, my heart sank. I didn't know what kind of future was right for me. My thoughts kept wandering to Julia's little apartment in Gramercy Park and the freedom she enjoyed.

One day, Edward telephoned Riverside Drive and said there was a questionable food order. We might have to make a fuss with this supplier. But he needed me to see it too.

I was not ready to be in David da Costa's presence just yet. Greater than my fascination with David, my dedication to my work, and even my desire to find out the truth about the murders was my horror of making a fool of myself. I realized this was childish.

"I'll come down to MacDougal later this afternoon," I said.

There was no sign of David when I arrived. Edward and I were in the middle of scrutinizing the substandard food when I heard footsteps outside the kitchen. Peering into the nightclub, I saw a middle-aged man dressed in a tweed suit walking across the floor. He was headed for David da Costa's office. A larger man walked right behind him.

"That's Arnold Rothstein," whispered Edward. "And his bodyguard."

I felt a chill. This was the man at the root of the violence. I toyed with the idea of appearing at David's office with some excuse. But what were the chances of anything important being said in front of me? Next to nothing.

In the kitchen, Edward told me that The Orchid Hour was going to stay closed the following evening – "Go dark," as he put it – and he wondered if the two of us could take the opportunity to visit an establishment named Club Deluxe in Harlem. In addition to serving alcohol and presenting jazz music, the club had a good kitchen, he heard. It would be wise to check out the competition.

I agreed to go with Edward the following night, provided we didn't stay late. We'd meet on MacDougal and travel uptown together. And with that, I made ready to leave The Orchid Hour. I'd be expected on Mulberry Street soon.

I couldn't help glancing over my shoulder as I left the club. The light was on in David da Costa's office. He must be meeting with Rothstein. My breathing quickened.

This is foolish, I scolded myself. *Put him out of your mind, or you're going to be sorry.*

The following day, after working on Riverside Drive with Heinrich, I changed into one of the new dresses I'd purchased with Julia. I was going to a club and should try to look nice. I wasn't nervous about the evening as I didn't have to worry about seeing David da

Costa – there'd be no reason for him to come to the club when it wasn't going to open.

Therefore, I was stunned to find waiting for me not Edward but three other people – David da Costa, Sal, and Julia.

"What are you all doing here?" I asked.

David smiled and said, "Guess what? I'm standing in for Edward. He telephoned me at home to tell me is ill – a fever. We were going to meet today about a couple of things, so he called me to cancel. He asked me to let you know that he couldn't go to Club Deluxe. But I thought instead of conveying the message, I'd go in his place. I'm also quite curious about it."

Sal said, "I'd like to see Club Deluxe too but not because of the kitchen. I got other reasons."

"As do I," said Julia.

This seemed odd. It crossed my mind that Sal had heard that David wanted to go with me to the Harlem club, and he intended to serve as chaperone. That would be embarrassing. But David and Sal were acting casual and comfortable with the situation. Julia was the only one who looked troubled. Something was bothering her.

As we left, the men fell into discussion over who would drive and how many cars. I didn't care how we got there, I wanted to find out what was wrong with Julia.

"Did the Ziegfeld show go dark as well?" I asked.

She shook her head, "I told them I was sick. One of the other girls will cover for me during my numbers."

"Julia, I can't believe you'd do that just to come with Sal to a club uptown."

"Tomorrow is the last night of the run anyway. They change the cast every year. Time to put together the Ziegfeld revue of 1923. I'm sure it will seem just as embalmed as the Ziegfeld revue of 1922." She shook her head, her little square earrings vibrating. "The truth is, an old friend of mine is playing saxophone at Club Deluxe, and... it's really important to me to see him."

I smiled. "You're such a woman of the world. To have an old friend who plays the saxophone. Who else can say that?"

"What you don't know is my stepfather owned a club in the Upper French Quarter – I grew up among musicians," she said. "I danced there from the time I was thirteen. They called our street the Tango Belt because that's what everyone wanted to see. But there were other kinds of dances too. And jazz. A *lot* of jazz. It started in New Orleans, you know. People up north act like they invented it."

We climbed into a large automobile that was possibly owned by David da Costa. I do know it was driven by Alexander. Three people could fit in the back seat. Somehow, Sal ended up in the front. David sat at the window behind Alexander, Julia behind Sal, and I perched in the middle.

I'd never been so physically close to David before. He had a clean scent, like peppermint. I think it was his shaving lotion. Crossing my arms, I tried to think of something else. But after we'd driven just a couple of blocks, David turned in his seat to talk to me.

"I hope you don't mind my asking, Audenzia, but do many women in Sicily have red hair?"

"She's a *normanne*," said Sal, obviously listening from the front.

"What's that?"

"You know the Normans conquered Sicily, right?" asked Sal. "It was nine hundred years ago, but the red hair lives on."

I didn't care for being talked about as if I were a breed of dog and spoke up. "My mother's mother had red hair," I said. "She used to say it skips a generation."

I unfolded my arms and asked David, "What about *you?* Aren't you descended from Spaniards?"

"Well, in a manner of speaking," he said, rubbing his chin.

"So, the article in *Photoplay* had it right?" I asked. "You're related to Spanish nobility?"

David burst out laughing, "Oh, Audenzia, this is a wonderful new side to you. You read *Photoplay* magazine!"

I felt my cheeks flush and couldn't answer.

"I'm sorry to tease you," he said, his tone kind. "I'm no relation to any nobility. I'm a Sephardic Jew. My people left Spain a long, long time ago rather than be forced to convert to Christianity. The Spanish Inquisition could be persistent, don't you know. Da Costa is my name. I know, you probably think I changed it so I could play the 'Latin Lover' onscreen. Everybody assumes that. But no, it's real. A lot of us have Spanish or Portuguese names."

Julia said, "*Photoplay* is shameless."

"It's the studio press agents who come up with this nonsense in the first place," David said. "You have to feel sorry for Theda Bara. A nice Jewish girl from Cincinnati, Ohio. The studio turned her into the '*Arabian woman of mystery, born in the shadow of the Sphinx.*' She had to hide her real parents in a hotel."

The rest of us laughed, but David sighed and looked out the window. "What a ridiculous way to make a living," he said.

"It's quite a living, though," Sal pointed out.

"Money isn't everything," David said.

Sal said nothing but caught my eye before turning to look out the window himself. I was pretty sure I knew what he was thinking.

Easy for David da Costa to say money wasn't important when he'd always had enough of it. David was spoiled, no question. Why was I so interested in him? Perhaps it was because his life was unlike mine.

"My agent keeps hounding me to take another film contract," David said. "He says, 'They're going to give Ramon Novarro all the parts you're perfect for.' Fine. Give them to Ramon."

Julia said, "I heard they're planning to film *Ben Hur*. Don't you want to be considered for that?"

"Cast of thousands? I don't think so," David said. "Though it would be nice to play a Jew for once!" He laughed a little and said, "Before the club opened, I went to see Somerset Maugham's *Rain* onstage. I wish I could be considered for things like that."

Club Deluxe was at a 142nd Street and Lenox Avenue. There was a theatre on the first floor. We trooped up to the second floor, as with the El Fey Club. Sal led the way, and at the door, he said, eagerly, "Is Jack here tonight?" His face fell when the man at the door said no.

"Who's Jack?" I asked Julia.

"Don't you know? Jack Johnson owns this place."

This made a little more sense. My cousin loved boxing. He idolized Jack Dempsey, the "Manassa Mauler." Naturally, Sal would grab any chance to talk to a champion, even one whose glory days were over.

Johnson's Club Deluxe looked more like a dance hall than a club. There was a band playing onstage and a huge floor with only five couples dancing. The tables were one-third full. Well, it was on the early side. I took a careful look at the menu. No, they didn't offer the same kinds of dishes that we'd created at The Orchid Hour. It was more traditional food here. At my suggestion, we all ordered something different to get a feel for what the chef could do, along with a bottle of champagne.

After we sat down, Julia barely paid attention to the menu, the champagne, or anything else. Her focus was fixed on the band. There were two saxophonists, both Black men. Julia's friend was the younger man. He acknowledged her with a single short wave.

She had a frown on her face as she listened to the music. It sounded fine to me, but every once in a while, she winced. Something wasn't right.

"How long has your friend lived in New York?" I asked.

"Not long," she said. "Sam got his start at my father's club, but then he hooked up with Louis Armstrong and the Creole Jazz Band. No hard feelings. We couldn't have been happier for him. He traveled up to Chicago with Satchmo. But he had to leave that band, so he made his way to New York City to pick up work."

David said, "This place seems fine, but it'd be a real shame for anyone to have to leave Louis Armstrong's band."

She nodded, and then to my alarm, her face crumpled.

Sal put his arm around her comfortingly. "It's okay, baby," he said.

"No, it's not okay, not at all," she said.

Julia stood up and said fiercely, "*You* should know that better than anyone else," and ran out of the room. A few seconds later, Sal went after her.

The band launched into another song, for which I was grateful. I was alone with David da Costa. I didn't know which movies were about to be made or what was succeeding on Broadway. The music gave me some cover. I glanced over at him periodically, and each time, he smiled. We'd just have to wait for the couple's quarrel to blow over.

After another two songs, Julia and Sal hadn't returned. "I think I should go find Julia and see if she needs my help," I said.

"I wouldn't," David said. "I think those two need to work it out."

"I don't know why she's so upset," I said.

David took a cigarette out of its case and lit it. "I'm afraid I do." He inhaled thoughtfully, glancing over at the stage where Sam was playing his music. "He looks a little... sleepy."

"I have no idea what you're trying to tell me."

"He might be high," David said, his voice a whisper. "He's on morphine, or maybe heroin."

"Oh." I sat back in my chair. "That's terrible."

"Indeed it is." David took another drag of his cigarette. "I should know. I had my own go-round with morphine in California. It was hard to kick, but I did it."

Sal had told me about this, but it was one thing to learn gossip about a stranger and another to hear about the experience from David's lips. In the flickering candlelight at our table, he looked melancholy.

"It haunts you still," I said.

"Yes," he said, extinguishing his cigarette. "More than anyone can know. Except I feel as if you'd understand, Audenzia, even though it's unthinkable you'd ever be so weak yourself. That doesn't make much sense, does it?"

"Sorry to interrupt, folks," said a voice with a distinct English accent. Or was it Irish?

I looked up. A man in his twenties stood next to our table wearing a fine black jacket but a cheap striped shirt underneath. He was handsome, black hair swept back with Brilliantine and wary blue eyes. There was something about him that reminded me of Sal's friend, Vito Genovese.

"I'm the new owner," he said, holding out his hand to David. "Owney Madden."

David rose and shook Madden's hand with his usual elegance. "It's a pleasure to meet you. I'm David da Costa."

"Yeah, I know. You're fronting the club downtown for Arnold Rothstein and his favorite boys."

I could see the man was trying to provoke him. If it were Sal, he would have laughed or come back with a smart crack. But David struggled with what to say.

Madden chuckled and patted his arm. "No offense, pal. Just wanted to tell you I've heard good stuff about The Orchid Hour. It's makin' me look at this place different. We're gonna pour some money into this joint too. Close it down, fancy it up, and reopen with a new name."

"How nice," said David coolly.

"What do you think of 'The Cotton Club'?"

Without waiting for us to answer, Madden ambled away. David sat down again. It took us a few minutes to recover from this visit. Our food arrived, but neither of us had much appetite. I drank my champagne as David smoked another cigarette.

He said, "You know what great success The Orchid Hour had on its fourth night, a coup that everyone says has been bringing in the curious ever since? Jack Pickford made an appearance with his second wife."

"Mary Pickford's brother?"

He nodded. "Jack's first wife, Olive Thomas, died in the same Paris hotel I stayed in last year. Olive was an ex-Ziegfeld girl. I met her in California, and she was… rather nice. Olive drank poison in the hotel bathroom. The police say it was an accident, but the rumor mill has it she killed herself because she couldn't get any heroin for Jack to take that night."

I shuddered. "That is truly…"

"Depraved? Oh yes. And probably untrue. I've always thought Jack Pickford was just a drunk. But his downing a gin gimlet at my club can make everybody want to visit. I do have to wonder what I'm doing with The Orchid Hour."

This was it, I'd get no better opportunity. I hated to ask questions as he was confiding to me in a spirit of trust, but I forced my way through it.

"What *are* you doing there?" I asked. "What's the purpose of the club?"

"Besides making Arnold and Charles and the others a whole lot of money?"

I nodded.

"They want it to be a sort of meeting place for deals, very important deals. Not for thugs like that," he pointed his cigarette in the direction that Owney Madden had gone, "but for politicians and men in finance. They want people to feel the need to come to The Orchid Hour not just for the booze but because it's the place to be in New York for writers, actors, and beautiful people. The best people. And they must feel safe from police or federal enforcement agents or anyone like that while they are there, whether it's for an hour or till closing time. I know that my uncle considered that crucial. He plans to hand-pick the next mayor of New York City, and that's just for starters."

As I sat there in the nightclub next to David da Costa, host of The Orchid Hour, I heard Mr. Watkins' voice in the back of his car that rainy night – *There could be a reckoning – there will be a reckoning. It's in my hands.*

"Arnold has always helped me when I needed it," David said. "And he's paid for everything I thought was essential for the club. We're not even related by blood. His wife, Carolyn, is my mother's sister. She was in show business too."

David continued, "What I find interesting is Arnold's dedication to guiding younger men in their enterprises, not only me. Some are legal ventures, some aren't. I've lost count of his protégées."

Like my cousin Sal, I thought. He always said "Mr. Rothstein" with such respect.

"He doesn't have any children of his own?" I asked.

David shook his head.

He said slowly, "I guess I thought that having this purpose for The Orchid Hour would elevate it. It'd be more than just a place with bootlegger booze. They'd be conducting important business. But sometimes, I'm not so sure… What do you think, Audenzia?"

Finally, finally, I was getting an idea of why Mr. Watkins had to be removed. I was tempted to open up to David. I wanted to tell him about the murders. But it was such a risky step. And Sal could reappear any minute.

I said, trying for a shrug, "All the politicians are crooked, does it make much of a difference who's officially running things?"

He smiled. "Fair enough. Audenzia, would you care to dance?"

I had to laugh. "Oh, no. No. I saw you do the tango, remember? I could not even try – remember, I don't have any special dance training."

"My God, do you think I care? I don't want 'dance training.'" He looked at me with all seriousness. "I want you."

My laughter died. I couldn't believe he'd come out and said it. David stood and held out his hand. I wanted to refuse – and I couldn't. I rose and took his outstretched hand.

On the dance floor, he placed his left hand on the small of my back and interlaced the fingers of his right hand with mine. We began to move to the music, though I was barely aware of the song.

I'd never known a lighter touch. I was on the verge of trembling and trying not to.

His fingers tightened just a bit. I felt his lips brush my hair, and my trembling became impossible to control. He must have felt it, for his hands became steadying. We danced through to the end of the song. He didn't let go of me, and when the next song began, we danced to that one too.

"David? Zia?"

My cousin was standing a few feet away, calling out to us.

I turned toward Sal. He stood with a hand on each hip, his dark eyes blazing, "Julia's not feeling well. I need to take her home. I think we *all* need to go home. Now."

CHAPTER TWENTY-SEVEN

LOUIS

Louis sipped a coffee on Mulberry Street and wondered where his luck had gone.

Aside from Yael shooting Luigi De Luca – and admittedly, that was a big aside – everything had gone smoothly for him since Mr. Rothstein had asked him to follow Miles G. Watkins.

The thing of it was, The Target, as he still preferred to think of him, had been a deputy mayor. And Louis had handled him. Now, he'd been asked to follow a nobody, an Italian woman smaller than him, an ex-librarian, for Pete's sake. And he hadn't caught a glimpse of her in six days.

Louis followed Rothstein's instructions and didn't go near the cheese shop for two weeks. Then, one bright, warm morning in June, he rolled out of bed and decided: This is the day to track Audenzia De Luca. He took the subway to Little Italy. Even though he was sure that no one had spotted him and Yael in his Model-T that day, he didn't want to take the slightest chance.

He was confident that he'd be able to spot her easily. That night in the rain, when Watkins walked her to his car from the library, wasn't the only time he'd seen her. Though he hadn't shared this part with Mr.

Rothstein, Louis had swung by De Luca's Cheese the day before the shooting. He slipped in the door in the early afternoon. Not only were there a dozen people milling around the shop, but a guy had buttonholed the shop owner, Luigi De Luca, asking to talk to his daughter-in-law.

A real reporter had beat him to it.

De Luca was polite about it, but he said the woman in question was not there, and he didn't know when she'd be back. The whole time, a slender young woman wearing a black blouse and a long checked skirt, her dark-red hair in a neat bun, worked behind the counter. Two minutes after the reporter left, De Luca made a beeline for her, and they talked quietly. Yeah, that was Audenzia De Luca for sure. And she didn't look happy.

Louis retreated from the shop, forming a new plan. There was no chance of success following in this reporter's footsteps. Louis would give it a day and return near shop closing, when there wouldn't be so many people around. That was an error, he realized now. By the time Louis got to him, Luigi De Luca was angry about it all, and he lost his temper with Louis.

Now, walking toward Mulberry, Louis didn't give much thought to De Luca's demise. He sucked in the smell of pastries floating through the air. It wouldn't be a hardship, spending a few days in Little Italy. He'd keep an eye on Audenzia De Luca in the cheese shop, make sure she didn't go anywhere unexpected or talk to anyone suspicious.

But she never showed up.

He peeked in the cheese shop once, twice, a half dozen times over four hours. A middle-aged couple was working the store with what appeared to be their son and daughter. Thinking that Audenzia might be taking time off, Louis returned the next day. Again, she never set foot in the cheese shop.

Rothstein had told him the De Lucas lived in an apartment two floors up from the store, pretty typical for the neighborhood. So Louis stationed himself opposite the ground-floor door to the building on Mulberry. There was only one way in or out. The trouble was, there was no doorman, just a door for which the tenants had the key, and there were a *lot* of tenants. People were packed in like sardines in Little Italy. He watched them come and go for hours and never spotted a petite woman in her twenties with auburn hair in a bun.

There was another problem, too. Louis had thought it'd be easy to keep an eye on the store and larger building in a crowded neighborhood like this. He wouldn't stick out. But as it turned out, he *did*. Yes, there were a whole lot of people around, but each seemed to have a specific place and purpose. Louis became increasingly aware of store workers and apartment dwellers staring at him. He feared that someone would try to talk Italian to him. Then the jig would be up.

The fourth day of this assignment and the second of watching the apartment door, it rained fitfully. Louis tried to take shelter under the awning of a fruit and vegetable stand across from De Luca's Cheese, until a man asked him something in Italian.

Louis stalked away, shaking his head.

It was then that his feelings toward Audenzia De Luca shifted. At first, he hadn't cared about her one way or another. She might not be most men's idea of a juicy squeeze, but Louis understood where Watkins had been coming from. Louis thought she seemed quiet and compliant. She'd be a nice source of support compared to those brassy, demanding types, like the two broads Louis saw being squired by Charles Lucania on 42nd Street.

But as he walked around Little Italy in the rain that day, Louis burned with resentment. She was making life difficult for him. Plus, there was one thing that'd been nagging at Louis all along. How did Arnold Rothstein know that Louis talked to De Luca at all? Was it possible that even though he was positive there was no one else in the shop during those minutes he argued with De Luca, Audenzia somehow found out?

Louis went back to the cheese shop after the rain had stopped, feeling not just annoyed and suspicious but a little desperate. How could he go back to Arnold Rothstein with nothing? She couldn't have disappeared. She must be holed up in the apartment above the shop. That was the only explanation. But he had to have that confirmed.

Peeking inside, Louis saw the middle-aged couple weren't there and the two young people were waiting on customers. Not a lot of customers. This may be his chance. Taking a breath, he pushed open the door and strolled inside.

"Hey, how are you?" Louis said in his friendliest tone to the kid at the counter. He looked maybe eighteen. Louis was twenty-five, but everybody thought he was younger.

"I'm fine, can I help you?" the kid responded, a little distracted.

"My name is Robert, and I'm from the public library. Mrs. De Luca had her friends there. Like me. I just wanted to say hello to her. Let everyone know she's okay. She's not working at the store today?"

"She doesn't work here anymore," the kid said.

Okay, now we're getting somewhere, Louis exulted.

"That's nice, she's spending time with her family," he said, trying to sound approving.

In response, the kid said, "Nah. She's got another job. She's a waitress at Café Dante."

Louis thanked him and left as quickly as he could. It wasn't what he'd expected – she'd gone from librarian to family shop counter worker to café waitress? – but the most important thing was he had an answer.

Or did he?

A half-hour later, Louis peered into Café Dante through the large glass window facing MacDougal Street. He could see a couple of waitresses taking orders, carrying little trays. Neither was Audenzia De Luca. He killed some time in Greenwich Village, returning to the café after nightfall. The shift changed, and new waitresses appeared. But no luck.

Louis went home that night seized by an uncomfortable mix of frustrated and hopeful. He'd been *told* she worked there. Audenzia would have to show up the next day. She'd have to.

The following morning, he drove to the café neighborhood, found a parking spot on MacDougal, and hurried to Café Dante. His stomach didn't feel great – his morning coffee in Brooklyn hadn't gone down well.

The sourness in his stomach turned into a burning pit of anger after he got to Café Dante, and yet again, no sign of Audenzia De Luca. Enough was enough. This assignment was turning into a nightmare.

Louis entered the café and asked the nearest waitress, "Is Audenzia De Luca coming in today?"

"Who?"

"Audenzia De Luca."

"Nobody works here by that name."

Louis stumbled out of the café. Had that cheese shop kid *lied* to him? It sure hadn't seemed like anything funny was going on. What would be the damned point?

He had no choice but to return to Little Italy. Louis tore open the door to his Model-T and started up the engine. Right now, he sure could use a joke or story from Yael. He'd decided to keep her out of his Rothstein assignments from now on, but she'd have been good company on this one, especially now.

Louis drove south on Bleeker for a couple of blocks. At a stop sign, he waited for a big truck to lumber along. The midday sun beat down on the people standing on the curb, waiting to cross. One was a woman wearing a fashionably short skirt with her hair cut in a bob. The sun picked up her hair color – dark red.

Louis, squinting, shot forward in the front seat so far, the steering wheel pressed into his chest. Was it possible? Yes, yes, that was *her*. That was her face and her build.

When the way cleared, she crossed the street. Louis followed, driving slowly. Someone honked behind him. He waved at him to go around. He had to stay behind her, as he had no idea where she was going. It would be better to follow on foot. But the sidewalks were crowded, and she walked fast. In the time it took him to park the car, he could lose her.

What the hell was her destination? Louis wondered. She turned onto MacDougal, and he silently rejoiced. She *did* work at the café, that broad at Dante's didn't know her. But to his amazement, Audenzia walked right by it. She didn't give the place a second glance.

And here he'd thought she was a submissive little librarian. Quite the minx!

She needs to be taught her place, thought Louis.

She kept walking on MacDougal, turning left when she reached West 4th Street. For the next few blocks, he maintained a safe distance, careful not to overtake her, focused on that dark red bob moving steadily west. Louis was sure she had no idea she was being followed.

She paused on the corner where West 4th met Christopher Street. And then she did the one thing that he really, really did not want Audenzia De Luca to do.

She descended.

"Not the subway – no, no, *no!*" he shouted at the steering wheel.

Louis frantically swung into a space on the street – not a legal parking space, but the hell with it – and jumped out of his car. He sprinted for the Christopher Street station for the IRT, scrambling down the steps so fast he tripped and nearly fell.

She had already started down the second set of steps in the station when he landed on the platform next to the ticket booth on the first level. He could make out that auburn bob heading down and pivoting left – she was going for the Brooklyn-bound trains.

He could hear the loud grinding hiss of an approaching subway car.

Cursing, he fished out a nickel for the fare and paid. Shoving people out of his way, Louis hurtled toward the Brooklyn platform.

Ding, ding.

He was three steps from the bottom when the subway doors slammed shut. There was another, shriller bell, and the subway heaved forward with a mechanical shudder. Louis watched the train chug into the tunnel, the round red light fixed to the last car growing smaller and fainter until it disappeared.

She was out of his reach.

CHAPTER TWENTY-EIGHT

FRANK

Frank Hudgins was not happy to be expecting Audenzia De Luca at his house in Brooklyn. Audenzia had called him at Police Headquarters and said she had something to tell him. She suggested coming to the precinct or meeting at Tompkins Square Park again.

"No," he'd said sharply. The last thing he needed was for word to get back to Captain Devlin that they'd met.

"If you have to talk to me, we'll do it in Brooklyn Heights. I'll give you my home address. Come at two o'clock tomorrow."

He'd regretted it within seconds of hanging up the phone. It had been almost a month since the murder of Luigi De Luca, and he hadn't come any closer to knowing who had shot him – or who had shot Miles G. Watkins in front of the library.

But he had found out that Watkins made a genuine plan to go to Washington, D.C. on that Friday, and who Watkins was planning to meet.

Frank had been outside Captain John Devlin's office, the door slightly ajar, when he heard Devlin's side of the conversation:

"He says Watkins was supposed to be in his office that Friday evening... The State, War, and Navy Building? Where's that? Forget

277

it, doesn't matter… I mean, if the man's waited this long, he can't have real suspicions… That's good to hear… Of course, I'll keep an eye on it here. You don't have to worry about that, sir. I've got things in place."

Frank had pulled away from Captain Devlin's door and busied himself fifteen feet away at the counter with the daily newspapers piled on it. All these stories by reporters taking pot-shots at the police. If only they knew what really went on in this building, Frank thought grimly.

Devlin had emerged and within ten minutes, was off the floor. Frank had eased into the police captain's office and hurried to his desk to see what was on the writing pad next to the phone. Johnny always liked to make notes or scribble when he was on a nerve-wracking call, Frank knew that about him.

Next to the telephone, on the top page of the pad was:

"*John Hoover*"

"*State, War, and Navy Building*"

Frank had hurried out of the office, the name and place burned in his brain. He did not need to write anything down. But neither did he know what to do with this.

A police lieutenant from New York City couldn't reach out to some official in Washington, D.C. Who knew what bells would go off? More than ever, Frank was sure that this was the kind of mess he needed to stay out of. Johnny had sounded deferential on the phone. This was all coming from way, way up the chain.

Why did Audenzia De Luca have to make trouble?

Frank was asking himself this for the fiftieth time when there was a knock on his front door. He cursed. Not least among his resentments was that she'd last seen him when he was at his worst – drunk and feeling sorry for himself in Tompkins Square Park.

All that went out of his head when he opened the door. He almost didn't recognize her. She'd cut her hair. She had on lipstick, her skirt barely made it to the middle of her calves, and she even wore long earrings.

Audenzia De Luca looked like a damned flapper.

As she stepped inside his house, she acknowledged the shock of her transformation. She said matter-of-factly, "I had to change how I look to be an undercover employee at The Orchid Hour."

Frank said, "I didn't hear that. My God, I didn't hear that. You're joking. Please tell me you're joking."

"No, I'm not joking. Why would I do that? You said if you could put into place a real investigation, it would include an undercover officer at The Orchid Hour."

"You're not a police officer and have no idea what you're doing!" Frank picked up a book and threw it at the wall. His lack of self-control jolted him into more civilized behavior.

"Mrs. De Luca, this was not something *you* should have done. You could get yourself killed. This all goes way, way up. It's a very dangerous matter."

"How do you know it goes way, way up?" she asked, frowning.

"Because it's obvious," he said quickly. "Now, tell me what you know, and then I am going to insist – *insist* – that you quit whatever you're doing, whatever job you have. I will take it from here."

She repeated as if she'd memorized it what the host of The Orchid Hour had told her the purpose of the club was three days earlier. He had to wonder why this David da Costa had told her. Actors had no sense of discretion.

Frank absorbed her revelation. So, Rothstein and his partners wanted to create an enticing environment for criminal enterprises to form, one that was well insulated from the law. He was thinking big.

"My belief is that Mr. Watkins was going to do something that would make it impossible for The Orchid Hour to open," she said. "Something to do with how the club gets its alcohol. My guess is there was a lot of money at stake."

Hudgins nodded slowly. "Watkins was responsible for two areas that connected to nightclubs: Prohibition and the U.S. Coast Guard. He might have rubbed shoulders with some disgruntled people deep in the system. The better grade of alcohol – the real whiskeys – come via the Bahamas or down from Canada. There are a lot of junctures in either pipeline where things can go wrong."

Audenzia said, "Maybe he was going to expose someone, pressure the government to enforce the Prohibition law. Is it true that some police take bribes to let the speakeasies operate?"

Frank felt his face burn. "It's possible," he muttered.

Audenzia's expression changed. She'd picked up on Frank's discomfort. She looked around the front room they were standing in for the first time. The floor hadn't been swept in weeks, and the kitchen's dirty dishes stank so bad, the odor reached them. Frank saw the place through her eyes and felt humiliated on top of everything.

She didn't comment on the mess. Instead, she made her way toward the fireplace mantle. A wedding photo was mounted there.

"Your wife is lovely, Lieutenant Hudgins," she said.

"Thank you," Frank said.

"She's not well?" Audenzia said softly.

"No, she isn't."

"I'm very, very sorry," she said. There was no prying into the details. In that minute, all the flapper gear receded, and he saw again the dignified, discreet woman he'd met at Police Headquarters. And brave. My God, he thought, she had five times his bravery. She'd spent weeks in a den of criminals.

With that, Frank Hudgins made his decision.

"Mrs. De Luca, there is something else I can do that could bring everything to a head. And I will do it. I will make the first phone call today. But in return, you have to quit working at The Orchid Hour. Do you hear me?"

"Do you promise to make this call?"

"I promise."

"What will happen then?" she pressed.

"An investigation, a *real* investigation. At the very least, The Orchid Hour will be shut down."

"Then yes, I will leave."

There was something funny about how she said that, almost like she didn't want to quit.

"You're in danger," he insisted. "I can't emphasize enough that these are ruthless people."

"I know that." She held out her hand. "Good luck, Lieutenant Hudgins."

Frank paced the room after she left. What was he going to tell this Washington official? He didn't have enough evidence to pick up Rothstein for questioning. It was hearsay and all pretty vague. But maybe this man had some of the other pieces.

He glanced at the wedding photo that Audenzia had admired less than an hour ago. If John Aloysius Devlin had the slightest clue that Frank was making moves, he'd follow through on his threat to cut off the money that he needed to pay Highland Retreat. But he could not have Audenzia De Luca's murder on his conscience, which could very well happen if she didn't get the hell out of that nightclub.

His palm sweaty, Frank picked up the receiver and started dialing. It wasn't easy to go from the State, War, and Navy Building switchboard to the right department for John Hoover. It turned out this man worked in the Justice Department within the Bureau of Investigation. Three times, Frank was put on hold. Twice, he was told to give a message to someone who would convey it to Hoover. Frank refused to give his name at every turn, just that he was "a New York City government worker with important information." The long-distance charge for this call was going to be astronomical.

Finally, just as Frank prepared to give up, a new voice came on the telephone line. He was a young man with a slight Southern accent.

"Hello, this is J. Edgar Hoover. What information do you have for me?"

"I'm calling about Deputy Mayor Miles G. Watkins."

A humorless laugh, "You are calling *me* about Watkins? That is a switch. I have gotten nothing but the run-around from everyone in New York City on the status of his murder investigation."

"The police investigation is not active, no matter what they tell you, but I may have information for you."

After a five-second pause, Hoover said, "Are you in law enforcement? What's your name?"

"Sorry, I can't tell you that."

"But I cannot proceed like this."

Frank said, "Then you don't want this information?"

"I always want information. Go ahead."

"There's reason to believe that Deputy Mayor Watkins was eliminated because he was attempting to see that Prohibition laws were enforced."

"Do you have any idea who killed him? Watkins told me he was trying to push for enforcement. But there aren't the resources to do it. The police couldn't handle the load. That's what they keep insisting. They told Watkins that, they tell me that. Incompetents. I need to know who was involved in this on the federal level."

Then the man became agitated, "I have questions, many questions about my fellow employees in the Justice Department. Gaston Means is on the payroll of the American government. He reports directly to the Attorney General of the United States, and do you know Gaston Means is a bootlegger and a swindler, maybe a murderer? I have my eye on him, you may depend on it. Miles had a file to give me on the U.S. Attorney General's office, information he'd collected on bribery. Of course, no one has that file. What do *you* have?"

Frank repeated what Audenzia had told him – what she said David da Costa had told her.

"Planning to pick the next mayor of New York? Why should I care about that? That city is rotten to the core. It is irredeemable." Hoover made an impatient noise. "Fine. But I will need to meet with you and interview you and get the names of your sources."

"I might have to conceal some names."

Hoover groaned, "All right. You and I will set up a meeting. You will have to tell me who *you* are. I can protect you. Until we meet, you need to use strict precautions. Where are you calling from?"

"Not from… er, my place of work."

"I would hope you're more intelligent than that. And you have no reason to believe they have their eye on you as a leak? No surveillance? No possibility they're wiretapping your phone where you're calling from right now?"

"No."

"Good. Can you come to Washington, D.C. next week?"

After Frank set the meeting, he should have felt relieved, even triumphant. But he did not. A cold, nauseous dread overwhelmed him. The staff of the Attorney General of the United States? He knew the name of the A.G. under President Harding – Harry M.

283

Daugherty. *That's* who this Hoover was going after? His ultimate boss?

"You're in over your head, Frank," he muttered aloud.

He wasn't sure about the voice on the other end of the telephone. An arrogant, unpleasant young functionary from the Justice Department. Not his favorite kind of person. And he'd be putting his life in this man's hands. The last person to do that, to plan a trip to Washington, D.C., was Miles G. Watkins.

And there was something else.

No surveillance? No possibility they're wiretapping your phone where you're calling from right now?

Frank didn't believe that John Devlin would put a wiretap on his telephone at home. He knew that Johnny was enthusiastic about the potential of wiretapping. He'd brought in specialists to train police on it last year. But to do that here? He'd only put a wiretap on Frank if the matter were serious.

Very serious.

What did Johnny mean when he said, *"You don't have to worry about that, sir. I've got things in place."*

Frank thought back to what he'd heard in that training session about wiretapping. How could you know you were tapped? Wasn't it a clicking sound on the other end?

And hadn't he heard some clicks just now during the call to Washington?

Frank stared at the telephone sitting on a table in his front room as if it had become an instrument of torture. At that instant, it rang.

After five rings, Frank picked up the receiver. "Who is this?" he asked, his mouth dry.

"Mr. Hudgins? This is Samuel Schmidt from Highland Retreat. I'm calling about your wife. There's been a change."

CHAPTER TWENTY-NINE

ZIA

I left Brooklyn Heights that afternoon, determined to quit my job at The Orchid Hour. I no longer had a choice. Lieutenant Hudgins had made that clear. For all I knew, the police would be storming the door next week. The entire trip on the subway, transferring twice, I practiced what I'd say at Riverside Drive.

When I stepped into the apartment on the seventh floor, though, I found Heinrich in a state.

"I have to talk to David, and it has to be a serious discussion," he said, pivoting across the floor on his crutches. "This is wrong. I can't go along with it anymore."

I froze where I stood. Had Heinrich also learned of the darker criminal purpose of The Orchid Hour?

"What is it?" I asked.

"The orchids are suffering from being in that nightclub," he said, anguished. "The fragrance only lasted the first week."

Heinrich told me that the *Brassavola* orchids we'd placed on their stands no longer gave off their nocturnal alluring scent and it was worse than that. They were fading, even losing their petals.

"It's too warm in the nightclub. I told David that. At night, orchids should not be in a room warmer than sixty-five degrees Fahrenheit. And the room must be well-ventilated! They require fresh air. Instead, they're being immersed in cigarette smoke. I've done the research – I've talked to people at the New York Botanical Gardens. Orchids can suffer in this atmosphere."

"There is a cloud of cigarette smoke in every part of that club," I said. "I've seen it."

"Do you know that David thought the orchids would *thrive* in the club? It's all because he heard that the scent is strongest at night with this orchid. He wanted to put everyone under the spell of the *Brassavola*."

"Now I see how he came up with the name of the nightclub," I said.

Heinrich nodded. "I've tried to talk sense into David, but when he gets a thought into his head, he won't give up… what a situation. Well, I am his partner in the orchid part of this enterprise. Don't you think I should talk to him?"

"I think the place could do with more honesty," I said.

"Thank you, Audenzia. Thank you. I do rely on you."

Heinrich hated the telephone, but I set him up with the phone at the tea table for his conversation. I told him I'd brew tea for us both while he talked to David. I didn't want to be standing there while the telephone conversation happened.

Quitting my job was going to be hard on Heinrich. I didn't know what effect it would have on David. But I had to leave, not only because my purpose had been accomplished by passing on information to Lieutenant Hudgins, but because I wasn't sure I could control my feelings for David da Costa. We had no future. Even he would have to agree on that. So, what was I doing?

Just listening to Heinrich's voice in the other room, knowing that David was on the other end, sent me into a tizzy. I could hear the band playing at the Club Deluxe again and feel his lips in my hair. I hated being a helpless, yearning girl.

"Audenzia?" called Heinrich from the other room.

"Yes, tea is ready."

"It's not the tea. David needs to speak to you."

I wanted to refuse, but such rudeness would further upset Heinrich. I'd speak to David da Costa, but for just a moment.

"Audenzia?" Even the way he said my name, emphasizing the second syllable, made my insides feel wobbly.

"I'm sorry about the orchids," I said stiffly. "Heinrich has identified something. We need to deal with it."

"Are you going to come to the club later?" he asked.

"No. I can't."

There was silence for a bit. "I wish you would come." He sounded tentative. "I think we need to talk. Don't you? Audenzia?" I didn't hear any of his usual dash. It would have been easy to push him away if I had. I wanted to see his face at that moment. There was nothing else that mattered.

"I'll come tomorrow," I said.

I was in terrible turmoil. I feared seeing David da Costa again. It wasn't just the sight of him. It was the sound of his voice, his laugh, his smell. The touch of his hands. I knew I was approaching a tipping point when any shred of reluctance would surrender to the longing.

I forced David out of my mind as I finished my work for Heinrich and headed home to dinner with my son and mother-in-law. Fortunately, it was Friday night. Michael didn't have to go to school the following day so we could sleep later.

That's why I was confused to feel a hand shaking me so early Saturday morning, just an hour after sunrise.

"Wake up, Zia," said a voice belonging to someone who really should not be in this room.

"Massimo?" I bolted up.

"Put on your clothes, we gotta talk to you," said my brother roughly. He was both angry and embarrassed. I glanced over at Michael's bed. It was empty. "Your boy is with Bianca, don't worry about him."

I scrambled into a blouse and skirt. Mama and her brother, Roberto, and his wife, Ileana, sat in the living room.

"We know you don't work at Café Dante," said Roberto. "It's time for some answers."

He told me that a young man, a stranger claiming to be from the library, had come to the store the day before looking for me. Paolo had told him I was working at Café Dante.

"When I heard that, I got worried," said Ileana. "So, Roberto went over there to warn you in case this man wasn't who he said. You'd never mentioned a man working with you at the library. And then Roberto was told no one had ever heard of Audenzia De Luca."

Massimo broke in, saying, "They called me. It was the right thing to do."

"No, it wasn't," I said. "You don't need to be here."

"But where do you go every day?" asked Mama pleadingly. "Why do you sometimes come back so late at night?"

Roberto put his arm around his sister to bolster her. Amid my anger and embarrassment, I felt ashamed to have worried her.

"I will tell you," I said. "You'll understand why I did this and why I couldn't tell you. It's complicated, though."

Massimo demanded, "Are you mixed up in something with Sal?"

"Sal helped me get this job," I said. "But he doesn't know why I really wanted it. If you'll let me explain—"

"He's been arrested," Massimo said. "It happened yesterday. Sal's in jail. His mother told me last night."

I gasped, which made Roberto turn away in disgust.

"What for?" I asked. "Something to do with alcohol?" My mind was whirring. Was The Orchid Hour collapsing? Perhaps there'd been a raid last night. Had David been arrested too?

"No, Zia, it's much worse than that," said Massimo, his voice rising. "He was arrested for *narcotics*. He was using a storeroom at 164 Mulberry, a spot just a block from here, for heroin. Somebody tipped off the police. He's a damned dope dealer. You got that? He's not just some gambler who happens to know Joe the Boss. He's a bootlegger and a dope dealer, a thief, a pimp, and God only knows what else."

"In Italy, Mussolini is cracking down on the mafia," announced Roberto, his arms around Mama. Ileana was ashen. "If only someone would do that here."

"It's the narcotics they got him on," said Massimo. "That's what the police are grilling him about. So, now that you know what kind of man our precious cousin is, you're gonna tell me exactly what kind of job he got you. I must know the mess you're in."

"I take care of orchids," I whispered.

"*What?*" said my brother.

"I work for a nightclub on MacDougal Alley called The Orchid Hour. They serve alcohol there, but I have nothing to do with that. During the day, I take care of the flowers for the club at an apartment on Riverside Drive, and I help with the ordering of the food."

"Oh, sweet Mother of God, the mozzarella orders," said Roberto. "That was you?"

I nodded.

"All right, it's not as bad as I feared," said my brother. "So, you call up whoever you do this work for and tell them you're not coming in again."

"No, I must tell them in person. Today's the last day."

Massimo argued with me for a long time, but I refused to budge. Then he said he would drive me to The Orchid Hour, go in with me, or at least wait in the car outside.

"That won't work – I have to see someone first," I said. "Then I'm going to the club."

My brother stepped toward me, his face beet red. "Enough of this crap. You'll do what I tell you to do. I am the head of our family, Zia. You've caused everyone enough worry. You will settle down and go back to the way things were before you took this job."

"I am twenty-seven years old, and I don't have to 'settle down,' obey your orders, or anyone's orders," I threw back at him.

I heard Mama gasp, and it had no effect. "I'm going to do this my way. If you try to stop me, if any of you do, you will be sorry." I ran into my bedroom, snatched the blue dress, new shoes, and a few other things, put them in a bag, and marched for the front door.

Roberto said, "Zia, if you don't come back in the next few hours, I don't think you should come back at all."

"You can't keep me from my son," I said.

"Don't be so sure about that," Roberto said. "You are associating with criminals, Zia. When you do that, you don't have rights."

I almost broke down and followed the family's orders. But it was more than my desire for David or my loyalty to Heinrich that prevented it. It was Julia. She must be in agony after Sal's arrest. I had to go to her.

Massimo followed me out the door. I could see he was torn between anger with me and fury over Roberto's threats. "I'll keep Michael for the weekend," he said. "You quit this job and then get to The Bronx. We all – we all need to cool down. But listen, it could get real ugly with the Neapolitanos if you don't shape up. *Real* ugly. You gotta think about your son."

Tears blinded me as I raced down the steps and left our building. What would happen if Michael's grandmother, great-uncle, and great-aunt all stood against me? Would I be able to hold onto my son? If we left Mulberry Street, what would it do to him to be ripped from the family he'd known all his life? I was so upset that I dropped my bag of clothes. A shoe and a few small things came tumbling out. Two women on the sidewalk offered to help.

As I sorted the bag and thanked them, I noticed a man standing ten feet behind me on the sidewalk. He was watching me with close interest but hadn't offered to help. He was dark-haired and young, maybe as young as twenty, with big brown eyes.

The man looked away as I stared at him. Perhaps he felt funny offering to help a woman he didn't know, especially one in emotional disarray.

I took a bus to Gramercy Park, trying to think how I would find the words to comfort Julia. She might not even be home and this breach with Massimo and my in-laws was for nothing. When I arrived at her apartment, though, she buzzed me in from the lobby.

"You know?" she said when I opened the door. Her eyes were red, but she had her "face" on and was dressed as if she were going somewhere.

I nodded, looking around her apartment. The walls were bare, and her belongings were stacked or thrown into piles. Two suitcases stood near the door.

"Where are you going, Julia?"

"Back to Chicago, for starters. I have more friends there than New York. I may end up going back to New Orleans. I don't know yet."

I couldn't believe she would abandon my cousin.

"But Sal – Charles – he may need you. There'll be a trial or something. And you can go to that. Or maybe he will make bail—"

"It's because he may make bail that I'm leaving tonight. I have a ticket for the seven o'clock bus. I'll be in Chicago tomorrow. I'm not going to see Charles again. Ever. It's over."

"Oh." It took me a minute but understanding dawned. "You'll never be able to forgive him for the narcotics."

"It's more than that, Zia." She stared at me as if she were waiting for something. I sensed fear in her as she waited.

"You were the informant," I whispered. "You told the police about the dope in the storeroom on Mulberry."

She winced. "If you can guess, so can Sal. Your minds work in similar ways."

"Julia, did you have to go to the police? He could be in prison for years. His life…"

"I did it to *save* his life, Zia. Or at least his soul. You're probably the only other person on this planet who knows how ambitious he is. He hides it well. I don't care about most of the crimes he commits – what choice has he really had in this city? Everything has been stacked against him. I don't even care that his name is on the deed to two brothels south of Times Square. But not narcotics. Not after I've seen it destroy people. Sam – and other friends of mine. My stepfather for a while, and those were terrible days. I told Charles he had a choice – me or the dope. He chose the dope."

Julia's eyes filled with tears. I hugged her, struggling to find the words equal to this tragedy. She had betrayed Sal. But what he did betrayed his family. And what of the victims out there, those whose bodies and minds were ravaged by narcotics?

"Part of me thinks, fine, he goes to prison for a few years, maybe that will be enough," Julia said. "He can come out and start over. Oh, God, have I done the right thing?"

"I don't know," I said. Everything she said was true, but he was... my cousin Salvatore.

"I can't do this, I have to pull myself together," Julia said. "There's so much left to do. I'm shipping some of this to New Orleans, some to Chicago. But also, I have to go to the New Amsterdam Theatre. There are things to collect. I must pay some bills and—"

"I'll help you," I said. "I can stay with you today."

"Thank you." She gripped me by the arms. "Thank you."

I knew this would mean I couldn't return to Mulberry Street this afternoon. Later, after I settled everything at The Orchid Hour, I'd telephone Massimo. As much as he'd want to strangle me, I was still his sister. He'd have to come to get me, no matter what the hour. And Michael was safe with him.

We sorted through her belongings and packed the things to ship to Chicago. We'd carry them out first. Out on the street was a familiar car. My heart jumped into my throat. It was Sal's car. He was already out of jail! What kind of fight would I have to break up?

But a second later, I saw it was Vito Genovese. Sal must have gotten through to him to make sure Julia was okay.

"What's goin' on?" Vito asked, getting out of the car and eyeing the boxes in our arms.

"We should tell him to beat it," I whispered to Julia.

"No, he can be useful for once," she said. She took a letter out of her handbag. It had "*Charles Lucania*" written on it. "Give this to Charles," she told Vito.

He snatched it out of her hand and got back into the car.

"I was going to give it to his lawyer," she said with a sigh.

"You're not telling Sal it was you that went to the police in the letter?" I asked.

"No. As much as I feel I did the right thing, I'm not ready to do… that." She hugged herself as I wondered if she was afraid of Sal.

"I wrote him a letter saying never to come near me again," she said.

After walking a block in silence, she said, "I wish he'd sent Meyer Lansky to check on me, not Vito. I always preferred Meyer. It would have been nice to say goodbye."

"I only talked to him once."

"He's one of Charles' oldest friends. They met in the schoolyard. Meyer was small and got beaten every day. Charles said he would protect him from the beatings, but he'd have to pay him for protection. Meyer refused. Said he'd rather take the beatings than have to pay. Charles likes people who stand up for themselves."

The tears gathered in Julia's eyes again. Her multitude of tasks dried them. With the mailings and errands and a trip to the theater, Julia barely had time for a half-hour in her Gramercy Place apartment before she had to make her way to the bus station.

Julia put on a suit for traveling and brushed her beautiful black hair before picking out a hat. "I'll miss this place," she admitted. "Listen, Zia, I'm paid up for the month. You can stay here if you want."

"Me?"

She handed me the key. "I think you should see what it feels like to have your own apartment."

As I stared at the key in my palm, she said, "I know I got part of the Persephone myth wrong. But I remembered something else. Persephone was warned she'd never be able to leave the underworld if she ate pomegranate seeds. But she did anyway. When her mother found her, it was too late. She could spend half the year above, but for the other half, she had to be with Hades. I always wondered why. Why did she eat those seeds?"

I didn't know what to say to that. What was she trying to tell me?

Julia insisted on taking a taxi alone to the bus. "I will write to you," she said. "I'm very grateful for everything you've done. You're a true, true friend. And there's one more thing." She bit her lip. "Look after Charles. I can't forgive him, but maybe you can. He will need family, and I'm pretty sure you're the only family who gives a damn about him."

After our final goodbyes, I felt drained. I decided to rest on the small couch in the apartment. It had come to Julia furnished. There was a couch, a bed, some chairs, and a table. What *would* it feel like to live on my own here? It was so quiet. I liked the way the sun, low in the sky, streamed into the back window through the tree branches, thick with leaves.

Sitting on that couch, I thought about the first place I lived in when we came to New York City. It was a third-floor flat in the tenements: two rooms, no windows, no bathroom. We had to share a bathroom with over fifty other people. Neighbors screamed and fought and loved on the other side of thin walls. There was sickness running through the buildings. I remember an entire family went down with tuberculosis, one by one. It was so cold that first winter, we thought we would die. It seemed so long ago, yet the sounds, the smells, and the feeling of being cold and hungry were with me still.

I suddenly realized I was starving. Fortunately, Julia had left a little food behind. I sliced a piece of bread and finished off her cheese. There was a half-full bottle of red wine in the bottom cupboard – Sal had undoubtedly brought it. I filled a glass with wine and drank it.

"Thanks, Salvatore," I said. It sounded funny in the empty apartment.

After washing up, I changed for the evening, putting on my blue dress one more time. I left my things in the apartment. I didn't want to carry a bag around all night. I could come back tomorrow and fetch it. I had the key.

When I left, there was no sign of Vito, thank goodness. Since it was one of those warm early summer evenings in New York, the kind everyone savors, I decided to walk to the club. It wasn't all that far, but I'd need to go slowly to avoid looking a mess when I arrived at MacDougal Alley.

The sun had just set and the lamps had come on, reflecting on the smooth cobblestones of MacDougal Alley, when I made it. I knew the nightclub would be opening within a couple of hours.

My left heel became stuck between the cobblestones a few feet from the florist's door. I bent down to pull it out. After freeing myself, I stood there one last minute, preparing.

Something like a soft footstep landed in the alley behind me. I turned, and a shadow darted to the side, out of my vision, behind a wall.

Why would anyone hide? Was it a guest to The Orchid Hour who realized he'd come too early? I waited, but the shadow stayed out of sight.

As I lingered in the centuries-old alley, curious to see if the person would re-emerge, I suddenly thought of what Roberto said this morning. A man claiming to be my friend from the library showed up at the cheese store and wanted to talk to me. Who could that have been? I had no such friend there. Lieutenant Hudgins' pleas for me to quit my job and protect myself made more sense in light of this. Well, tonight would be my last night at The Orchid Hour.

I said hello to Edgar, and moving past the flowers, I pushed open the door to the club. There was the usual low murmur one would hear in the hours before official guests arrived. The band was setting up, the bartender was preparing, and the kitchen staff was chopping and boiling.

"Audenzia."

David, wearing his tuxedo, approached me slowly, his eyes full of concern and relief. I was relieved too. Though my heart leaped at seeing him, I was in control. I would not disintegrate.

He said, "You didn't go to the Riverside Drive apartment today or call. Heinrich was worried. I've been, well, I've been going out of my mind."

"I'm sorry. Something happened in the family today." I looked around to make sure no one else could hear. "My cousin has been arrested."

"Charles? Arrested?"

"Yes, nothing to do with the nightclub. I am sorry to say it has to do with narcotics."

"I see. I'm sorry too." He studied me for a minute. "You're going to leave the club, aren't you? This is it."

I nodded. "Yes, it is. I'd like to hear the Russian musicians one more time. Are they playing tonight?"

"They are." A tentative smile played on his face. "So, we can talk later, Audenzia? You do not need to leave early tonight?"

"No," I said. "I'm not leaving early."

I almost told him what I was thinking. "*I ate the pomegranate seeds. They warned me, and I knew it was dangerous. But I did it anyway. And now my life can never be the same.*"

That night, I fully appreciated how good David was at doing this. Greeting the guests, talking to them a bit, and finding a table. He never doled out insults, like Texas Guinan. The Orchid Hour didn't offer a bevy of gorgeous showgirls. The decor was beautiful, the music accomplished, and the food delicious. Of course, the drinks, the forbidden drinks that everything else revolved around, were excellent. And then there were the orchids with their mysterious allure. I was sure Heinrich would find a way to keep them beautiful.

But none of that was what made The Orchid Hour magical. It was him. David da Costa. He was handsome and charming, of course. But the secret to the appeal of this place was that everything you saw, heard, smelled, and tasted reflected him – his interests. What excited him. In coming into The Orchid Hour, we were all drawn to David, like a hummingbird dancing atop a flower, trying to get the nectar.

And who were these fashionable guests that everyone pursued so intently? I had thought a rich crowd would be draped in furs and diamonds, a more extreme version of what I saw at the Knickerbocker or the El Fey Club. But this group was something different. I still saw the Egyptomania look. On this summer night, other women wore what looked like tennis skirts just barely covering their knees, but with pearls flung around their necks, bright lipstick, their faces shining. A few men wore short trousers like they just came off a golf course. They were all grown-up children, playing games and savoring their toys. Right now, their favorite toy was The Orchid Hour.

David and I stood side by side while the Russian trio played, sharing our deep pleasure in their sad, sad music. They *were* a remarkable discovery. After the Russians bowed and left the stage, the jazz band started up again. I heard a whisper go around the club and grow into a shout: "The Charleston! The Charleston!"

The band leader glanced over at David, and he nodded. Seconds later, the musicians launched into a celebratory song, punctuated with jaunty horns. Couples charged onto the floor and danced facing each other without touching, with matching arm sways, dips, and back kicks. I'd never seen this dance, but they all had the steps down.

"What's happening?" I asked.

"It's a song from the Broadway show *Running Wild*," David said, smiling.

It wasn't just couples dancing. I saw three men – and two women – dancing the same steps all by themselves. They looked around as they did it, gleeful and defiant. I doubt it would have been as joyful to dance alone in a room where no one could see. Everyone must witness each dancing without a partner and be a little shocked. That was the fun.

After The Charleston was over, the club guests cheered. The band shifted to a more subdued song, for which everyone seemed grateful. No one could keep up that manic pitch for long.

I heard a shout of laughter at a table next to the dance floor. Five men were sitting together, none paying attention to the dancing. One of them I recognized: the man with the white hair I'd seen going down the stairs at the El Fey Club, who had recognized Sal and Frankie Costello.

"Do you know who he is?" said David. He'd noticed I was staring at that particular table.

I shook my head.

"He's Jimmy Hines, the district leader for Tammany Hall, the group that, from what I understand, runs the city. I am not sure who his guests are. I think I heard a Boston accent. One man mentioned Montreal. My uncle will be pretty pleased."

I'd heard enough. I reached for David's hand. "Can we talk now? Alone? I must tell you something."

"Yes."

I didn't let go of his hand as we skirted the dance floor and made it to the back of the nightclub. David opened the door, and we hurried up the steps to his office.

We burst into the room at the same time. I waited for David to turn on the lamp, but he didn't. The light of the nightclub streamed in through the Venetian blinds – they were tilted halfway open.

David pulled me close to him, seizing both hands. He said, "When you came in with Charles, I heard, 'cousin,' and I turned around and I saw this… this magical creature staring at me with such *eyes*. To me, you were one of the sea nymphs from the myths. Do you know those stories?"

"The Nereids," I whispered. "That's what they call them in Sicily. They protect people from the rocks. David – David – that's what I need to talk to you about. I must protect *you*."

He cupped my face with his hand and said tenderly, "Protect me from what?"

"I've been lying to you this whole time. You don't even know my real name."

David blinked and dropped his hand. "What are you talking about? You're Charles' cousin."

"Yes, I am, but Lucania is my maiden name. My married name is De Luca."

At the word "married," he flinched.

I pushed myself forward. "My husband died in the war. I have a son. You see? You had no idea. I worked for years at a public library, and a friend I had there, Mr. Watkins, he was shot in front of the library because he was the deputy mayor, and he wanted to cause trouble for people who have illegal nightclubs, places like this one. And then my father-in-law was killed too because the police and the newspapers were bothering me. They all thought it was Nettuno, but I knew it wasn't."

"Stop, Audenzia, stop," he pleaded. "I – I don't understand."

"The police know. They are going to finally do something. I don't know when. That's why I have to leave. But you must come with me. You love this place, it's all about you, but you have to do it. I couldn't stand it if anything bad happened to you, David. I couldn't."

David grabbed me by both arms. "Why?" he demanded. "Because you care about me?"

"Of course I care about you, you *idiot*."

He gathered me in his arms. The last thing I saw were his eyes swimming with desire before he kissed me, his lips pressing hard. If I thought after our dance at Club Deluxe that he would kiss me gently, I was wrong. My lips opened, and I threw my arms around his neck. He pulled me in so close I thought I would melt into him. All of my half-formed fantasies were becoming real in a way that leaped well beyond my imagination. I would do anything – anything – to be with David da Costa tonight. I could sense a shock of recognition running through his body. He felt the same.

"What do you want me to do?" he gasped. "Tell me what to do. I'll help you find out anything you want. I'll go to the police with you tomorrow. But… but… there's Charles. Your cousin, I must tell you that he threatened me, he threatened everyone that if—"

"I know what he threatened. I'm aware. But he can't do anything to us."

David said, "No, he can't. He can't stop us. No one can now."

CHAPTER THIRTY

FRANK

"I can't promise a full recovery, but your wife is much better," said the director of Highland Retreat. "The doctor thinks it is possible, with the right treatment, that Mrs. Hudgins could come out of this. She might be able to go home within the month."

"I have to see her," said Frank. "She spoke today. She *spoke*."

"I wish that were possible," said Samuel Schmidt. "Those few words, and her movements, took a lot out of her. She was asleep by six o'clock. It would be unwise to wake her now, at eight o'clock. That's why I advised you to come here in the morning."

Frank shook his head, laughing. There was more than a bit of hysteria to his laugh. "You have to understand that I couldn't wait until tomorrow."

Schmidt's professional smile approached genuine human warmth. "Yes, I understand. And I know it would be difficult for you to drive back to the city now. There's an inn nearby, in the town of Highland, with which we have a relationship. They leave vacancies for us. You could take a room there and return first thing in the morning."

"Couldn't I see her tonight? I'll stand six feet away. I won't try to wake her."

Schmidt's smile dimmed. "Come now, the patients on the entire floor are being prepared for the night. Their routine cannot be disturbed. We have rules. You are someone who enforces the law. You must see this is right. Now, allow me to phone the inn."

Frank checked into the inn just three miles away and ordered a late supper in a main-floor room that was once a tavern but now served as only a restaurant. He found himself genuinely hungry and able to enjoy his chicken parmesan and bread rolls.

You are someone who enforces the law.

Not when Berenice's recovery was at stake. Before he'd finished eating his chicken, Frank had changed his mind about going to Washington, D.C. That plan was off.

He felt a wave of relief wash over him immediately. Frank hadn't liked the sound of J. Edgar Hoover on the phone. The whole thing was nuts. He was in no position to help this kid bring down the Justice Department. Since Hoover never got his name, he couldn't track Frank down once he didn't show. He knew that Audenzia De Luca would be upset, but he'd have to make her see sense.

After a surprisingly restful sleep, Frank was up at dawn, more excited than he'd been in a long time.

In his car, driving down the road that threaded the west side of the Hudson River, 9-W, Frank struggled with the terror that Berenice had regressed overnight. That was such a dire possibility that his hands clamped the steering wheel in a death grip.

But his fears were groundless. Berenice was awake and responsive again. She was doing even better, according to the nurses. He paced the lobby impatiently until a nurse came to bring him in.

Berenice was a beautiful woman – on Frank's wedding day, he thought he would shatter with happiness – but he had never felt more love for her than now, sitting by her bedside, her face chalky and gaunt, her hair limp, her arms desiccated.

"Frank," she said hoarsely, peering up at him, tentative and slightly confused.

"I'm here, honey," he said tenderly. "You are not going to get rid of me."

The nurse stayed with them for a half hour, checking Berenice's reactions and shining a light in her eyes. Throughout it, his wife gazed either at Frank or beyond him, at the windows showing off the spectacular Hudson. He was prouder than ever of getting her admitted to this hospital and making sure she was in a bed with a view. When they'd wheeled her in the front door over a year ago, she was already too far gone to realize where she was.

When the nurse left, Berenice was visibly tired but beckoned Frank to come closer.

"Where is this, Frank?" she asked. "I thought I heard the name, but it can't be right."

"Highland Retreat," he said with a smile.

"No. No."

She peered at the windows as if a tornado were about to burst the glass and kill them all. "Highland is where the rich people recover – or dry out," Berenice said. "Nobody we know has ever stayed here. There's just no way on earth we can afford it."

That's right. She'd grown up twenty miles north of here. She would have been familiar with Highland Retreat. Early on, Frank had thought about that, but he assumed it was a mark in the hospital's favor. It never occurred to him she nurtured a bad opinion of Highland.

Frank said, "Sure, it's expensive, but I've made the payments."

She stared at him in silence for at least a minute. "On a police salary?" she said in that raspy new voice.

"Yeah. Well, maybe I had to cut a few corners at home."

"Frank, what did you have to do to pay for this?"

He couldn't believe it, but she was angry. This must be an effect of coming out of a long illness. She wasn't thinking straight. "Don't worry about it, Berenice. Please. You focus on…"

"How many bribes did you take?"

"Shhhhh," he hissed, looking around the room. "What are you doing, Berenice? You've got to calm down."

"I want out of here. Today. Tomorrow by the latest."

"They are taking excellent care of you here. There are the treatments you need to recover."

"I'd rather be dead than stay here."

Frank sat back in his chair and closed his eyes. Was this a nightmare? Had he dreamed everything – including the call from Schmidt?

"Listen to me, Frank." She didn't sound angry anymore. He opened his eyes. "It's not right. What you do as a policeman. It needs to end. I believed this before, you know I did. Now, I can't live with it. I don't want to be here. I'll call my father or my sisters if you won't get me out of here. There's a small hospital in Kingston. Catholic, yes, but it's better than here."

Frank said heavily, "You want Kingston, you'll get Kingston. I thought being near the river would help you…" He couldn't continue. It was too painful. After a few minutes of silence, he sensed she was ready to say something. Maybe the anger would be spent. She'd say she missed him and she loved him. He longed to hear those words.

Berenice said, "So I don't need to call my father, Frank?"

305

"No, you don't. I'll pull you out. Hell, maybe I'll quit the police force and stay up here."

The words flew out before he could stop them. He was about to correct himself when he saw something new on Berenice's face. She was smiling. Her lips were curling into a smile.

"Could you do that, Frank?"

Frank nodded. Everything was falling into place. "Yeah. I just need to go back and finish a few last things. There could be an out-of-town trip next week. But I'll sell the house in Brooklyn. We'll start with that."

She groped for his hand. "Thank you. Yes."

The nurse returned, saying she needed to do some things for Berenice. Just after lunch, the doctor arrived to talk with Frank. The next steps wouldn't be easy, but he thought they were manageable, even in Kingston.

After an afternoon conversation with Berenice, Frank decided to return to New York City that day. Initially, he thought he should stay at the inn all weekend, but there was a lot to do in the city now that they had formed a new plan. He had to get ready for the trip to Washington, D.C. His new life with Berenice had to start clean. He was going to tell Hoover everything. Let the chips fall where they may.

He stayed by his wife's bedside until after six and then drove to the inn to check out of his room. To prepare for the long drive, he ordered another big dinner with coffee.

Frank wasn't happy to see the sun had set entirely when he emerged from the inn. He wouldn't be home until midnight at the earliest. Still, he felt alert. And it was only the first twenty-five miles or so of country road leading to Newburgh that lacked street lighting, and he would need to rely on headlights. The closer you got to New York City, the more electrical lights appeared to guide you.

As he started the trip, he thought that one of the things that always struck him about the Hudson Valley was how everything shut down after sunset. It was the opposite of New York City. Driving south on 9-W, he was the only one on the road.

When another car appeared behind him, he appreciated the company at first. Another after-dark traveler. But those headlights got brighter – and brighter. They filled up Frank's front seat.

Why was the car driving so damn close? Frank didn't want someone riding his tail like this. Especially not when the road veered so close to the Hudson, and he was about to make that tricky curve.

CHAPTER THIRTY-ONE

ZIA

Half asleep from our afternoon nap following another spell of love-making, I asked David why he thought I was a cold woman.

"You – cold? Are you out of your mind?" He moved his arm so that my head rested in the crook of his arm, "Why would I ever think that, my darling?"

"You telephoned Heinrich and said so. Now, you did say it was a good thing. At least, that's what Sally said you said."

In one of our snatches of conversation in the last twelve hours, David told me he'd ended his rocky romance with Sally Westwood just before The Orchid Hour opened, and she returned to Los Angeles. I wasn't trying to prod for further details about their relationship. I was curious about the matter of being "cold."

"I can't believe she told you that! Well, maybe I can. She must have picked up on my interest in you. But the thing is, I meant it as a compliment. Heinrich likes to say that orchids seduce you and become an obsession. A person needs a certain temperament to be around them. Intelligent and confident. I never thought you were truly *cold.*"

I ran my finger up his shoulder, "Hmmm, not sure I believe you."

"Well, let me convince you." David kissed me and began to caress me.

"We can't – we can't," I murmured. "We are going to die without food."

After insisting he didn't need food, David asked if I wanted to leave the apartment to find a restaurant. "I'll take you anywhere you want to go!"

I swung out of bed, telling him it was possible some bread was left in Julia's cupboard. I put on David's shirt, inhaling his smell with a shiver of pleasure, for my expedition to the kitchen.

I couldn't remember feeling this content. It was not because I expected David da Costa to devote the rest of his life to me. A voice said that he was a man of ever-changing enthusiasm. I was one of those enthusiasms – today. Who knew for how long? But I was happy to have had this night, to feel things I hadn't felt in years. To desire and to be so deeply desired.

I'd scrounged not only a quarter loaf of bread but also a can of pears when I heard something clicking in the main room. Or was the noise coming from the hallway outside? I went around the corner to see what it could be.

The door swung open, and my cousin Sal charged into the room.

We stared at each other for a few seconds. His eyes shifted to the shirt I wore. He felt in his jacket for something and strode toward the bedroom.

David called out, "Audenzia?" at the same second that I screamed, "*David!*"

Sal got to the bedroom first, and his hand was out of his jacket. He held a gun. I leaped on him to get the gun away, but he shook me off.

"Don't – Sal, don't hurt him," I shouted. "You can't."

"Yes, I can," Sal hissed. "And he knows why."

David sat on the bed, the sheet wrapped around his middle, and said, "Charles, I can't believe you'd do this." He looked more shocked than frightened.

I threw myself in front of David and shouted, "You shoot him, you'll have to shoot me, Sal. Because otherwise, I promise you, I will kill you."

My cousin opened his mouth and shut it, the whites of his eyes glittering. I'd never seen this kind of rage pouring out of him – never.

"God, Zia, how could you do this?" he said thickly.

"I haven't done anything wrong," I insisted. "I'm not married, David's not married. Why do you think you have to shoot him? What kind of insane rules are you following?"

Slowly, slowly, Sal lowered his gun. "Get dressed, both of you," he said. "There are some questions you need to answer, Zia. I've been looking for you. I hoped I wouldn't find *him* with you, even though he's been missing too."

"What kind of questions?"

"Just get dressed. I must take you – and now, I gotta take him too."

David and I dressed silently, with Sal on the other side of the door. "It will be okay," David whispered, "I'll talk to Arnold."

My stomach clenched. David didn't know everything I knew about Arnold Rothstein.

Once we emerged in the other room, I asked, "What are you doing here? Massimo said you got arrested. You got bail already?"

"I worked something out with the cops," Sal said. "I don't wanna talk about it." He looked terrible. I realized he wasn't just enraged with David and me. It was paining him to be in Julia's apartment.

Sal had his car running outside, with Vito in the driver's seat. During a second when Sal couldn't see it, he treated me to a lewd smirk as I walked up to the car. I longed to slap him, even more so since he'd spotted me here with Julia and must have given Sal the idea that I might be at the apartment today.

"MacDougal," Sal muttered to Vito.

"You're taking us to the club?" David asked.

"If I were you, I would say as little as humanly possible," said Sal. "If you weren't Mr. Rothstein's nephew, you'd be dead already, and Vito here would be figuring out how to dispose of your body."

David blanched. I realized that while he'd greeted a garden variety of gangsters to The Orchid Hour, he didn't know what they were capable of. I did. And I had a clue as to how to act. First thing was, don't show fear. I grabbed David's hand and squeezed it. Catching his gaze, I sent him a silent message to toughen up.

Sal alone walked us into The Orchid Hour. I knew we would be meeting Mr. Rothstein. His bodyguard was no surprise. But I didn't expect to see Frankie Costello, Meyer Lansky, and Joe Adonis.

And neither did Sal. This wasn't good, not good at all. "What are you guys doing here?" my cousin asked.

"I asked them to stop by," said Arnold Rothstein. "But why is my nephew here?"

"He was with Zia."

"David, you can go home now," said Rothstein firmly, as if he were sending a child to bed.

"I'm leaving when Audenzia leaves," David declared, looking at me. My heart leaped with pride.

"Oh, my," sighed Arnold Rothstein. "I'm afraid this is becoming quite… complicated." He turned to me, "You are Audenzia De Luca, aren't you? Although you took the name Audenzia Lucania when you came looking for a job."

"That was my idea," Sal said. "Look, Zia wanted a job. Her name had been in the papers because of the library shooting. She used her maiden name. It's my name too."

So, despite being angrier with me than he'd ever been in his life, Sal was going to try to help me. It was good to know. Aside from David, he was the only one in the room I could look to in hope of getting out of this situation. The others sitting there – Frankie, Meyer, and Joe – all stared at me coldly. Any politeness – or in Joe's case, flirtatiousness – had vanished.

"It's not that she wanted a job," said Mr. Rothstein. "It's *why* she wanted a job. I have it on good authority that someone talked to the police about things we don't want to be discussed. It's impossible for me to think you could have had any inkling of it, Charles, but I think your cousin here might have been sent to The Orchid Hour by the police."

Sal exploded, "No! That's impossible. She needed money – for her kid's college, for herself. Zia is not a rat."

David looked surprised by what Rothstein had said – more surprised than he should have, considering what I'd told him in this club only last night. Then I remembered – David was an actor, and a good one.

My lover wasn't the only one who could put on a performance. I knew what I was going to have to do.

"Salvatore," I said, deliberately using his birth name and not his street name, "I didn't tell you the real reason I wanted to get a job here."

Sal's mouth fell open. "Zia," he breathed.

I turned to the others, "I don't know if any of you will understand this fully, but there are rules to be followed. One of them is vengeance. I am entitled to vengeance. Yes, I knew the deputy mayor, Miles Watkins, not well, but I knew him. And I was interviewed by the police, sure, but that was their doing. They didn't send me here. I swear on the soul of my son that no cop told me to get a job here and go back and share the information."

I paused and looked at each of the men in turn. "I came to this club to get vengeance for a man who was like a father to me. I came to get vengeance for Luigi De Luca."

"Why would you come to The Orchid Hour because he got shot?" asked Frankie Costello.

"Yeah, Zia, that makes no sense," said Sal.

"I wanted to find out who killed him," I said. "When one of the cops questioned me, he told me that the murders of Mr. Watkins and Luigi De Luca had to do with The Orchid Hour."

"But Nettuno killed him, you know that," said Sal.

"No," I said. "I was there, downstairs, when Papa was shot. I didn't see, but I heard. It was not Nettuno."

Arnold Rothstein tilted his head as if he were thinking about a particular equation. He spoke quietly to his bodyguard, who nodded and left.

"Mrs. De Luca, why do you think any of us would have wanted your father-in-law dead?" Rothstein asked.

"I don't know," I said. "I have never been able to figure it out. That's the reason I came here."

"Well, there is a possibility," Rothstein said. "Something to explore. I asked a person following Mrs. De Luca to meet us here today in case she tried to deny everything. Which she isn't doing, not exactly. But he may prove useful. I suspect he is the key to what happened to her father-in-law."

"You asked someone to follow Audenzia?" asked David angrily.

"Yes, and imagine my surprise when my man reported that he tracked her to the door of this very club yesterday," said Arnold Rothstein. "Today, David, I learn that she's one of your dolls. Although, if I had known that, I think it would have become even *more* important to follow her and discover her true motivations."

I hated the way he talked to David. I hoped he would snap back at his uncle, but while he looked upset, he said nothing else.

Rothstein said, "We may have a bit of a wait until this person shows up. Is there anything to eat here?"

To my dismay, David obediently got up and went into the kitchen. And soon, we had a spread of food to choose from – mozzarella, cold shrimp, crackers, and stuffed mushrooms. I didn't touch it, nor did David. But everyone else dove in with enthusiasm. The mood in the room relaxed, and the men started chatting. Babe Ruth had played well the day before.

It occurred to me that it had been David's intention to defuse the murderous tension by offering a meal. I glanced over at him when no one else was looking. He nodded very slightly.

Arnold Rothstein took Sal aside for a one-on-one conversation. At first, I thought they were discussing my fate. But Rothstein was counseling Sal on how to deal with his recent arrest. I listened closely while trying to hide my interest.

"I look bad," said Sal anguished. "I had to give some names to get out of going to jail. Nobody important to Joe the Boss or anybody else of weight, but I'm gonna suffer from this."

"I have an idea of something you can do," said Rothstein. "An important fight is coming up at Madison Square Garden in a couple of months, correct?"

"Yeah, Jack Dempsey versus Luis Angel Firpo. They're calling it the fight of the year."

"I think you should buy a block of good tickets, way ahead of time, and then give them to certain people. Big shots like Flo Ziegfeld, for starters. We should talk to Jimmy Hines about who should get a ticket at Tammany Hall. I have a list of judges. The tickets will be gifts from you. Along with entertainment. We will do something special at The Orchid Hour."

"How much is it gonna cost me?" Sal asked.

Rothstein thought for a minute. "I'd say twenty-five thousand."

That was a fortune, the kind of money that someone might hope to earn over a decade, maybe a career. How could Sal possibly come up with it?

"That's a great idea," said Sal with enthusiasm. "Thank you, Mr. Rothstein."

So arrived the moment that I understood the cousin I loved had gone to a place I couldn't follow.

"I'm more concerned about someone knowing enough about our Mulberry Street enterprise to go to the police," said Arnold Rothstein.

"Our" Mulberry Street enterprise? I had to struggle to hide my surprise and my fury. I had wrongly thought this was Sal's solo racket. So this was what Rothstein wanted his protegee to do? Sell narcotics?

"You don't have to worry," said Sal. "The person has… has left town. Won't be a problem any longer."

I tensed. Sal had figured out it was Julia who had betrayed him. Whatever was said next would be critically important. Her life could depend on it. But Arnold Rothstein turned away from Sal.

"What have you got there, David?" he asked.

David stood beside the table with all the food spread across it, but he wasn't holding a dish. He was gripping a flowerpot. "I was checking on the orchids," he murmured. "Something's wrong."

Meyer Lansky looked up from his stuffed mushrooms. "I gotta tell you, that one looks like it's dying," he said.

"Yes," said David. "It is."

The orchid had lost all its green and white petals. As Heinrich had warned, a nightclub was no place for an orchid to thrive.

I heard the door to the florist open, and three men walked in. One was Rothstein's bodyguard, the second was a smartly dressed younger man, and the third was a man who was still younger. Not much more than a boy dressed for a day outside, having fun. He looked around the club, wide-eyed – clearly, he'd never been here.

I recognized him. He was the same young man I'd seen on Mulberry Street yesterday morning after I dropped my bag. He must have been waiting outside my building in the morning and followed me all day and into the night. Everywhere I went, he'd tracked me, up to casting a shadow on MacDougal Alley.

"Louis, thank you," said Arnold Rothstein. "I'm sorry for the short notice."

"He was on his way to Coney Island, I got him on Saratoga Drive," said the sharply attired fellow who brought Louis in. Rothstein nodded and asked him to go out and get the evening newspapers.

"Oh, it's no problem, Mister Rothstein," said Louis. "I'm always ready to help. Whenever you need me, I'm available."

I knew that voice too.

"My God," I said, rising to my feet. "It's him."

"Zia, what is it?" asked Sal.

I pointed at Louis, who was looking back at me, all innocence. But I knew I wasn't wrong. "*He's* the one who was in the store. He talked to my father-in-law upstairs, and then he left. He was pretending to be a newspaper reporter. Five minutes later, someone came in and shot Papa dead."

Arnold Rothstein frowned. "This is not good to hear, Louis. Not good at all."

"I didn't shoot Luigi De Luca," said Louis calmly. "I told you the truth, sir."

"Then how can you explain this?"

"I'll have to go to my car," he said. Joe Adonis laughed while Frankie Costello rolled his eyes. "I don't expect to go alone."

Sal, Frankie, and Joe walked out of the room with Louis. Five minutes later, they returned with another person. To my astonishment, I saw it was a girl, but unlike any girl I'd ever seen. She was a feral teenager, wearing a long raggedy skirt and her hair pulled up into a cap. She must have weighed one hundred pounds at most. The girl didn't look at anyone else but Louis, who had her by the arm. I didn't think they were related, nor did they look like sweethearts. I couldn't figure out what connected them, besides being short and skinny.

"Tell them the truth, Yael," Louis said.

She nodded rapidly. "Okay. 'Bout what?"

"About what you did in the cheese shop on Mulberry Street while I was in the car."

She clutched her hands. "I shot that guy, I didn't tell Lou I was gonna do it. He had no idea. I was in the shop when he tried to talk to him. That guy was nasty to Lou. I heard. Wouldn't give Lou a chance. We got into the car, I said I had to go back, that I forgot something.

That older guy said he was gonna get Lou in trouble. I didn't want that. No witnesses – that's what Lou always says."

I stumbled and fell into a chair, reeling. I could see the surprise on everyone else's faces. For me, it went beyond shock that this girl could be Papa's murderer. How could anyone be so matter-of-fact about taking a human life? And it was all to protect this young man who'd followed me, who himself looked bizarrely unconcerned by it all.

Arnold Rothstein said, "You doing that caused a great deal of trouble for the people in this room. You realize that, don't you?"

"Yes, sir, I know, and I'm sorry," she said as if she'd been caught stealing a candy bar.

For the first time, Arnold Rothstein seemed to be at a loss. Frowning, he said, "Charles, do you think—?"

With a swift movement, Yael reached into her pocket, pulled out a small handgun, and stuck it to the side of her head.

"Sorry, Lou," she said, and fired.

"*No!*" I screamed. "*No, no, no.*" David pulled me toward him and turned so that he was shielding me from seeing, but I'd already seen. I could feel David's heart hammering. He was as distressed as I was. After a minute, I found the strength to push him away in order to see.

Sal and Meyer were bent over the girl, murmuring to each other. Louis stood silently a few feet back, staring at her as the others felt for her pulse or mopped up the blood. I thought I saw a vein quiver in his cheek. That was Louis' only sign of distress.

"She's gone," Meyer said after a time.

"Well, Mrs. De Luca, are you satisfied?" asked Arnold Rothstein.

The tears spilled from my eyes, although I wanted more than anything to be able to stop them. "I didn't want that," I insisted.

"You said you wanted vengeance. I'd say you have achieved it."

"What are we going to do about this, Arnold?" David asked.

"The girl committed suicide, it's regrettable," said Rothstein.

Meyer said, "I recognized her. Yael Shapiro was her name. She doesn't have any parents. She's got nobody. She worked at Midnight Rose's in Brownsville."

Louis said, "That's true, sir. She didn't have anybody."

"Except *you*," said Meyer, accusation in his voice.

Louis was silent for a bit. Would he finally show some guilt or responsibility – any feeling at all?

"I hope this isn't gonna mean we can't do business together in the future, Mr. Rothstein," he said.

Rothstein and Sal and all the other men exchanged glances. "I'll be in touch with you tomorrow," said Rothstein. "You can go now, Louis."

The young man nodded respectfully and made his way toward the door.

"Wait a minute," Sal called out.

The young man halted and half-turned.

"What's your name?" my cousin asked.

"Louis Buchalter." He took one final look around the room, tipped his hat to Arnold Rothstein, and left. The smartly dressed man passed him on the way, carrying newspapers. He handed the bundle to Rothstein.

David whispered, "Audenzia, are you all right?"

I swallowed and nodded. "I still have more questions," I told Arnold Rothstein, forcing myself to stop shaking.

"I thought you might," said Rothstein. "But first, you may want to take a breath and read the newspapers." He opened a tabloid, folded it to perhaps the third page, and began reading.

319

There was some special purpose to this. With growing dread, I read the headline to the page he wanted me to read.

"*NYPD Lieutenant Killed in Upstate Fireball Car Crash.*"

I took a step closer, my heart pounding, until I could make out the dead man's name. It was Lieutenant Frank Hudgins. Did Arnold Rothstein know that I had spoken with him – and that the lieutenant would do something? He told me in Brooklyn he would make a call that very day.

Had they killed Frank Hudgins?

Something stirred deep inside me, a grief I was determined not to show. I would have to put it alongside my sorrow for the others who were lost. As I stood there, I knew I would never be able to mourn them as they deserved to be mourned.

Arnold Rothstein folded the paper and put it on the table next to the mozzarella. "You may have questions about the death of Deputy Mayor Miles G. Watkins. No one in this room killed him, Mrs. De Luca. If he was murdered, it was also initiated by people not in this room. People who can never, ever be challenged or brought to any sort of accounting. Do you finally understand?"

"Yes," I said.

I did understand what kind of power was wielded by the men of New York, those who've held onto money and influence for years. I have always despised them, just as they despise me and people like me: Immigrants, Catholics, Jews. As Julia said, "What chance have we ever had?" Intelligence, talent, resourcefulness. It didn't matter if we had those qualities. We weren't fully human. What I didn't understand until today was that Sal and Rothstein and the others in the group seized the opportunity offered by Prohibition to create a rival power. They sought to have their own place, one that not only provided what everyone craved – high-quality alcohol – but was also finer, more beautiful, and more exciting than any other place like it in the city. The Orchid Hour would draw in whomever they needed. The group wanted to make deals in safety, but in order to feel safe, they took steps. The chain of death began with Miles G. Watkins. Today, it claimed the life of this girl. I knew that there would be more deaths. It was inevitable.

"I want to leave The Orchid Hour now," I said.

Rothstein sighed and said, "I'm not sure I can allow this, not yet. We have to get some things straight."

"I'm going with her," said David.

"You work *here*, David," Rothstein said. For the first time, his voice rose. "I got you everything you wanted. And it worked. The Orchid Hour is a success. It's what I want and what you want."

I walked across the club, my shoes clicking on the floor. I didn't look behind me to see if David followed.

"Mrs. De Luca, stop," said Rothstein.

My cousin Sal said, "Just a minute. You don't give her orders. Zia?"

I halted and turned. "Yes?"

We stared at each other for a minute.

"If Zia wants to leave, she leaves," said Sal. "She's family. That's the way it has to be. If anybody has a problem, speak up." He didn't show anger; it wasn't a threat. But there was a command in the way he said it, a command no one else had. The rest of the men in the room eyed him with respect, even, in the end, Arnold Rothstein.

"Goodbye, Charles," I said. It was time to use the name he'd chosen for himself.

"Goodbye, *cucina*."

I made my way across the floor of the nightclub. My knees felt weak. I feared for a second I'd collapse before making it those last final yards. But an arm encircled my waist, propelling me forward.

"Let's go," said David da Costa.

I put my hand on his arm and pushed away, disentangling myself. David could decide to leave with me, and maybe I wanted him to leave with me, but I needed to make it out on my own.

I pushed open the door to the florist, stepped inside, and hesitated. I turned around and beckoned to him. David came forward.

"I don't know if this is right for you," I said. "You created something spectacular here."

"Not after today," he said, shuddering, as he looked back at the motionless body of Yael. "There's nothing that can make up for what happened."

I took his hand. "David, in a week, you may be sorry and wish you still had this."

"A lot can happen in a week, don't you know that?" he said and smiled.

Together, we walked through the flower-filled space to MacDougal Alley and the streets of New York City beyond.

CHAPTER THIRTY-TWO

ZIA, 1963

That night it had grown freezing cold on the bench facing the East River. But even with the wind whipping my face, I wasn't ready to go home. My thoughts were captured by the year 1923, and it was hard to break free.

I never set foot in The Orchid Hour again. What may seem surprising is that neither did David da Costa. We were together as a couple for far longer than a week. Unable to bear my in-laws any longer, I took Michael with me for a summer away from the crowds of New York City – and David came too. I rented a small cabin for my son and me in the Hudson Valley in Woodstock. David's cabin, where he set up his easel and tried to paint, was a five-minute walk up the hilly path. We struggled to recover from what had happened in the city. Watching the deer, wild turkeys, and rabbits wander by our cabins helped. Michael happily found swimming holes to dive into and trees to climb and even learned to ride a bicycle. I cooked meals over a fire pit, and later, the three of us would lie on our backs and look at an impossibly bright canopy of stars in the velvet sky.

Sometimes, I think it might have been better for me if David *had* stayed behind at The Orchid Hour because I fell deeply in love with him. We talked about marriage. When the trees turned gold, red, and yellow and fell from the trees, it changed, though. One afternoon, he told me about an opportunity, a part in a serious play on Broadway. What else could I do but encourage him? I found a job in the city that I liked through Heinrich. He had secured an important position at the New York Botanical Garden, and I thrived in the administrative office. But the gardens – and the little house I found for Michael and me – were in the Bronx. The life I made there didn't blend well with that of David, an actor on Broadway. When the play's run ended, David followed his long-time dream of joining the film community in Berlin. Our talk of marriage faltered, though he continued to visit me in New York. I lived in an agony of uncertainty for a couple of years. It all ended when I once more read about David in *Photoplay*, this time as the new lover of the hedonistic beauty Louise Brooks.

Hurt and lonely, I found someone else and married, quickly and disastrously. We divorced after eighteen months of continuous arguing. And then I met Vincent. I wondered how Julia would have reacted to hearing that I'd married a Sicilian widower – and found happiness with this kind and thoughtful man. I soon grew to love his two daughters as my own, and Vincent was very good to Michael. Massimo approved of my new life, which I tried not to let bother me.

Ghosts from my past flitted in and out. Julia corresponded with me for over five years – from Chicago and then Los Angeles, where she had found success as a choreographer. The reason I never learned her reaction to my marrying Vincent is simple. Her letters stopped. I suspect she thought it wise to create distance between herself and every single soul in New York City because of what happened with Sal.

Did The Orchid Hour serve the purpose that Sal and Arnold Rothstein had envisioned? They found someone to replace David and manage it, and the nightclub went along until it was eclipsed the following year by the glamorous success of Owney Madden's The Cotton Club. I never asked my cousin any questions about his business affairs after the day he insisted I be freed from The Orchid Hour. It was as if we'd formed a new pact. But I could draw my own conclusions. By 1926, New York City had a new mayor, "Jimmy" Walker, a friend to every speakeasy. The police remained at bay, except for sporadic padlocking of the nightclubs, though they sprang up in new locations after every closure. Sal's good fortune grew and grew, even after the murder of Arnold Rothstein, never solved, in 1928. Sal lived in luxury at the Waldorf Astoria Towers on Park Avenue, accompanied by a rotation of showgirls, all pale imitations of Julia. To distance himself further from his hostile father, Sal changed his last name to "Luciano," and after he survived a rival's knife attack that would have killed anybody else, he became known to the city – and eventually, the world – as "Lucky Luciano."

Did Sal, like Icarus, fly too close to the sun? Perhaps. He became a target of embarrassed district attorneys, and eventually, the law brought him down. Sal went to prison in 1936. Everybody said he would die behind bars – everybody who didn't know him. He ran his empire from prison, using Frankie Costello, Meyer Lansky, and Vito Genovese as his main representatives and go-betweens. No one could deny his influence. The U.S. government had to turn to my cousin for help during World War II. He cleared the New York City docks of enemy informants and served as a liaison between the American Army and Sicilian bigshots during the Allied invasion.

As a reward, Sal was freed from prison but with a condition: He must go back to Italy. In 1946, they removed him from Sing Sing but took him to Ellis Island in a dreadful reversal of our families' ocean journey. He never stopped trying to get back to New York City. During those years, I wrote regular letters, trying to keep him up to date on all the family news, and he faithfully wrote back in that elegant handwriting which was the one useful skill he gained at PS 110.

I got a moving letter from Sal, filled with sympathy, after Vincent died four years ago. It was such a terrible time. The cancer was relentless, and he suffered no matter what the doctors did. Two days before the end, Vincent said, "Zia, you are the love of my life." I kissed my husband and assured him of my love and devotion. But I couldn't lie to such a fine man and use those exact words. I had had three husbands, and yet David da Costa, that spoiled, inspired, passionate actor, was the love of my life.

Sal's death was not only a blow but a devastating shock. I hadn't known anything was seriously wrong with him when I got the news of his fatal heart attack last winter. He had a grand funeral in Naples – the coach carrying his coffin was pulled through the streets by *eight* black horses – but at his insistence, Sal was buried at St John Cemetery in Queens. I stood by his grave, with Massimo on one side and my son Michael on the other, just as I'd done in 1923 for Luigi De Luca. Sal had finally made it back to New York. But his grand marble crypt didn't say "Luciano." It said "Lucania."

I still live in the Upper East Side apartment where Vincent and I spent most of our marriage. Michael and my stepdaughters never stop coaxing me to give up the place. My new home could be in Westchester County, where my son and his family live, or out on Long Island with the girls and their growing broods. "You shouldn't be alone," they keep saying. "The city is a mess, it's running out of money, and it's dangerous."

I love them all, but I can't leave the city, even though this fuss at the Valachi hearings is about to splash my name in the papers again. It's not as if I am one of those people who praise the wonders of the "Big Apple." So why not leave?

As I sat there, staring at the dark outline of Roosevelt Island and, beyond it, Queens, I realized I just wasn't willing to give the city that satisfaction.

"They're not going to chase me out, Sal," I said to the river. "Not yet."

I'm sure it was nothing but my imagination, but I thought I heard my cousin laugh in the wind.

With that, I stood up and turned around, ready to face the dazzling, cruel lights of New York City. And whatever may be yet to come.

AUTHOR'S NOTE

My idea for this historical novel grew from my fascination with Jazz Age New York, a place and time filled with both the exquisite and the ugly. It's almost as if one can't exist without the other. F. Scott Fitzgerald, who wrote *The Great Gatsby* in 1924, knew more than most people about New York's power of illusion and craving for wealth and beauty and how orchids can embody that. He wrote in that novel: "*Daisy was young, and her artificial world was redolent of orchids and pleasant, cheerful snobbery and orchestras which set the rhythm of the year, summing up the sadness and suggestiveness of life in new tunes.*"

The characters of Audenzia De Luca, Frank Hudgins, David da Costa, Miles G. Watkins, Massimo Lucania, Yael Shapiro, Heinrich Zimmer, John Devlin, the public library employees, and the members of the De Luca and Pellegrino families are fictional. But I placed them in the milieu of real people: Salvatore Lucania (better known as Charles "Lucky" Luciano), Arnold Rothstein, Louis Buchalter, Frank Costello, Meyer Lansky, Vito Genovese, Larry Fay, Nils T. Granlund, Owney Madden, Joe Masseria, James Joseph Hines, and Texas Guinan. J. Edgar Hoover is obviously a real person. Less well known than his directorship of the FBI is his early struggle against corruption within the Justice Department and the administration of Warren G. Harding, now considered one of the most corrupt presidencies in American history.

The Orchid Hour as a nightclub has never existed, though MacDougal Alley is a genuine little-known treasure of Greenwich Village. Chumley's in the West Village was one of the only speakeasies open in the 1920s that could still be visited up to the twenty-first century. Unfortunately, the Covid-19 pandemic seems to have finally shuttered it. The Seward Park branch of the New York Public Library on East Broadway is open to the public. When I visited in November 2022, the library's main floor reading tables were full of patrons. Little Italy in lower Manhattan is far smaller than during its turn-of-the-century peak that covered thirty blocks, but you can find some restaurants and cafés that were there during the same period as my novel. One is Ferrara Bakery & Café on Grand, which opened in 1892 and is still in family ownership, with that family's third, fourth, and fifth generations to be found inside.

Prohibition was barely enforced in New York City. While it seems a number beyond belief, the figure of 32,000 is often cited as how many speakeasies existed in the city between 1920 and 1933. Although the Jazz Age image is one of carefree fun, New York and the rest of the country went through wrenching changes over this timespan. I read many books on the period and the personalities in order to write *The Orchid Hour*. If you are interested in learning more about the 1920s, whether it's Prohibition and organized crime, America in the wake of World War I, the eugenics movement, or the explosion of New York culture, I particularly recommend the following books:

Prohibition New York City by David Rosen

American Midnight: The Great War, a Violent Peace, and Democracy's Forgotten Crisis by Adam Hochschild

The Case Against Lucky Luciano by Ellen Paulsen

Rothstein by David Pietrusza

The Guarded Gate: Bigotry, Eugenics, and the Law That Kept Two Generations of Jews, Italians and Other Americans Out of America by Daniel Okrent

Five Families by Selwyn Raab

Dry Manhattan: Prohibition in New York City by Michael A. Lerner

Low Life: Lures and Snares of Old New York by Lucy Sante

Top Hoodlum: Frank Costello, Prime Minister of the Mafia by Anthony M. DeStefano

Blondes, Brunettes and Bullets by Nils T. Granlund

Damon Runyon: A Life by Jimmy Breslin

The Black Hand by Stephan Talty

I also recommend the Ken Burns documentaries *Prohibition* and *Jazz*; the brilliant podcasts *Bad Blood: The Story of Eugenics* and *1922: The Birth of Now*, produced by the BBC; the episodes devoted to Rudolph Valentino, Olive Thomas, and other 1920s performers in the Hollywood podcast *You Must Remember This*; and the NYC history podcast *The Bowery Boys*.

I'd like to thank the New York Botanical Garden, one of the city's gems, for inspiration and help, and in particular Marc Hachadourian, Director of Glasshouse Horticulture and Senior Curator of Orchids, for his generous sharing of knowledge about orchid growing in the early 20th century. The museums that proved enormously helpful to me were the Tenement Museum on the Lower East Side and the Museum of the City of New York. This novel could not have been written without the encouragement and insight of my friend and fellow novelist Emilya Naymark. I also want to give special thanks to Michele Koop and Harriet Sharrard for their careful reads and to Elizabeth

Keri Mahon and Lisa DePaulo for their help. I am grateful to my sister, Amy Bilyeau, and my cousins. Friends who offered advice and encouragement: Kris Waldherr, Mariah Fredericks, Donna Bulseco, Evelyn Nunlee, Elaine Beigelman, Laura Joh Rowland, Sophie Perinot, Erica Obey, Dawn Ius, Libbie Grant, Christie LeBlanc, Stephanie Jones, Dulcy Israel, Daniela Thome, Adam Rathe, Elaine Powell, Triss Stein, Shizuka Otake, Susan Elia MacNeal, Amy Bruno, Sue Trowbridge, and Jenn Kitses. I wrote a portion of this novel while living as an artist-in-residence at Byrdcliffe in Woodstock and would like to thank the Byrdcliffe Guild, in particular Catherine McNeal and Henry Ford.

I'm grateful to Aubrie Artiano, Head of Publishing at Lume Books, and to the talented team I worked with: Miranda Summers, Tanuja Shelar, Imogen Streater, and Eve Lynch. Their creativity and enthusiasm made it possible for me to bring this book into the world.

Finally, I owe everything to my husband and children for their patience with me as I fretted and dreamed my way through this historical novel.